The Girl Who Chased Spaceships

Daniel Basil Lyle

LylePublishing

Sulphur, Oklahoma

The Girl Who Chased Spaceships

ISBN 978-0-9794101-9-2

Published by LylePublishing
505 W. 12th Street, Sulphur, OK 73086
(www.LylePublishing.com)

Printed by CreateSpace, an Amazon.com company. Available from Amazon.com and other retail outlets. Also available as an ebook on Kindle and other devices.

LCED08042019

DISCLAIMER and FORWARD

Although this book draws heavily from some of the author's own experiences, all characters are fictitious. Any resemblance to real persons, living or dead, is purely coincidental. Although the historical Virginia and Galileo Galilei are depicted in this book, their words and behavior are fictionalized. This book is a sequel to *"The Girl Who Flew Too High,"* beginning where that book left off.

Chapter 1

<u>**INTO THE WILD**</u>

What fun to "get back to Nature"
When you've got camping gear and supplies
And powerful guns to shoot deer and beers
All the weapons and benefits of modern science
Bending the harsh realities of cruel existence
Into a happy stroll along peaceful streams
But when you're alone, lost, and defenseless
It's actually not the fantasized mild dream
But a terrible nightmare of starvation
Sickness, injury, and even death
But hey, it teaches lessons
If you can survive!

The Minstrel's Lark, 1:6-9

"Hey, get off of me!" Billy yelled from beneath Suzy.

"I'm not on you, it's that big lizard!" Suzy gasped, squirming in the tight, dark space.

In the dim blue light of the compartment, she saw a *bird-like beak* pressed against her cheek complete with a mouthful of sharp teeth!

"Get the top open! Get the top open!" Billy fearfully cried-out. He was struggling to stand on top of the squirming animal and push up against the snapped-closed panel above.

"Stop kicking!" Suzy yelled at him as she tried to get oriented around the *thrashing* legs, arms, and thick tail of the man-sized lizard.

1

"Breeeeeppppp!" the reptile growled, seemingly as afraid as them.

Abruptly the gentle "thrumming"—that they'd first felt as they'd walked up to look into the buried compartment in which they were now trapped—became a TEETH-JARRING VIBRATION! Then their prison began violently *lurching* back-and forth!

The thought flashed through Suzy's head that she and Billy should have obeyed her folks and worn their helmets when they'd gone out biking in the park, instead of riding "dare-devil" style. She was getting bashed around quite unpleasantly!

"Auuuggghhh!" Billy shouted-out beside Suzy. "Make it stop, Suzy! Make it stop!"

And—just as fast as it began—it *stopped*.

The compartment-panel above *popped* outward and the person-sized lizard squashed in next to them *sprang* upward and out. Then everything was still.

Soft sunlight streamed into the compartment. Outside, Suzy heard birds singing and crickets chirping. Everything was calm.

Trembling in shock at what had just happened Suzy slowly stood up inside the small compartment. Tentatively she stuck her head above the opened top.

Blond pigtails to each side of her head flopped around as she looked in all directions.

"Wow, what *was* that?" Billy gasped. He wobbly stood up beside her, though his head didn't quite reach to the opening. He didn't have to worry about pigtails getting in the way. His black hair was styled in a short, military buzz-cut. "Was it an earthquake? I almost peed my pants!"

All she saw above the rim was long, waving grass. And the weeds seemed much higher than they'd been just a couple minutes before. What was that crazy big lizard thinking about, anyway? *Why* did it come up behind them and knock them all down into the buried compartment? They weren't a threat or anything. They were just curious about what the lizard was trying to dig up out there in the woods!

"Uh...I don't know, Billy," she carefully replied. She was trying to stay calm, soothe him with her "adult" words, though she was still shaken up herself. "But whatever it was, I think we better get outta here."

Yes, it was time for her to be the "reasonable" ten-year-old "grown up" sister. Of course was *her* that had impulsively led her six-year-old brother off the well-established Park trail into the woods in the first place. But she *had* to pursue that strange big lizard. If it were really an extinct dinosaur, it would be the discovery of the century!

She'd be famous!

But then again, it couldn't be true. It was impossible to discover a *living* dinosaur in her own little town of Sulphur, Oklahoma. Maybe you might find a few fossilized bones if you dug into the rocks of the nearby low hills. But that was all. Or was it?

"But Suzy," Billy whined, apparently starting to regain his normal bravado, "we just found this opening that's stuck down here in the ground. Don't you want to know what the dinosaur dug up? Maybe it's the entrance to a *pirate treasure ship* buried here. Maybe if we figure out how to go deeper there'll be gold and diamonds!"

Suzy snorted derisively as she grabbed onto the lip of the opening and hoisted herself out. She reached down to grab her protesting brother's shorter arm and pull him up also, whether he liked it or not.

"First of all, whatever that animal is, it can't be a dinosaur," she said, slowly hauling him up after her. For a little kid he was heavy. Suzy grudgingly noted he had a lot of solid muscle in his small frame. She looked around quickly, but didn't see the big lizard lurking anywhere nearby. "Dinosaurs died out millions of years ago. It must just be some sort of mutant bird or something. There are ostriches over at the zoo, aren't there? It sort of looked like an ostrich, right? Maybe it was just some weird species that escaped from the Arbuckle Wilderness Park. They've got all sorts of animals running loose out there, right?"

"They ain't got *no* ostriches like that!" he firmly contradicted her. "It had big sharp teeth plus a long reptile tail! Plus it had arms instead of wings. And double-plus, ostriches 'honk,' right? That guy said 'BREEP'!"

"Well, whatever," she snorted derisively. "And pirate ships don't get buried down in the ground—they sink into the ocean, dummy!"

With her help, he finally scrambled up to flop down beside her in the thick grass. She sank down onto her back as well, trembling.

They were both in shock at what had just happened to them, lying there panting, looking up at the sky. Suzy was sure she had messed her clothes all up. Mom was going to be mad at them! She glanced down at her grey, opened light jacket. A pink shirt was visible beneath it. At her neck, a green T-shirt peeked out. For having gone down into some sort of cave her clothes looked remarkably clean. Even her purple pants looked ok. Her white tennis shoes, though, were muddied-up. But that was to be expected out mountain biking in the off-trail area.

Billy, however, was covered with dirt. But that wasn't surprising. He *attracted* dirt! His opened grey jacket was muddy. His light green T-shirt with its stenciled-on Brontosaurus dinosaur was filthy. His dark green pants were smeared with dirt. His brown shoes had gobs of caked-on dirt.

"I'm not dumb," he pouted, brushing dirt off his jeans and shirt as he wobbly stood up and looked around. "Hey! Where are our bikes?"

"Oh, Billy!" she laughed, hopping up and taking a couple unsteady steps over to where they'd just laid down their red and blue mountain bikes on the ground, "They're right over...here?"

But they were not.

They had vanished, without a trace. There wasn't even smushed-down grass where they'd been.

What? Had someone snuck up and stolen them? But they were way off in the wilderness area of the Park. There wasn't anyone else around except for her and Billy!

"Uh...Suzy?" Billy gulped, now not focused on the missing bikes but looking all about him in confusion...

—as the big lizard suddenly *darted* past them, diving *back* down into the compartment from which they'd just emerged...

"Hey, watch it!" Bill yelled, spun-around by the animal...

"BREEP!" it blurted, seemingly mocking them from back inside the buried chamber.

—when the ground suddenly LURCHED beneath their feet, *knocking* them both down again into the thick grass!

"Just stay still, Billy," Suzy said, reaching over to grab his hand as the earth continued to shake beneath them.

Suzy was really scared. It *was* an earthquake that hit them while they were in that strange buried compartment. And now they must be experiencing an aftershock. This was dangerous. They'd best get home quickly—bikes or no bikes!

The rocking and rolling of the ground continued for another couple minutes, then slowly stopped.

A strange blue haze hung in the air as Suzy got back up to her feet. It was slowly fading away. Suzy was dismayed at the wide grass-stains that now marred her clean pink blouse and purple jeans.

But Billy was over to the side, staring down at something.

"Come on, Billy," she dazedly said, feeling dizzy. "We'd better get started back right now and..."

"Look at this!" he said in a low voice, pointing.

Walking over, she looked down at where the opened compartment they'd just climbed out of should be...

—which was now a *wide, deep* trench! It was at least twenty feet across, twenty feet deep, and a hundred feet long. It looked like a big rectangular *building* of some sort had been buried down there!

And as the blue haze completely dissipated, rocks and dirt cascaded down into the opened, deep gash in the ground.

Whatever had been in there had just departed, taking that big lizard along with it!

Jesus, this was all getting really freaky.

"We're going home, Billy, right now!" she insisted, thoroughly frightened. "This is too scary."

She grabbed his hand and forcefully led him away from the ominously empty trench.

"But...?" he protested, jerking away from her and walking sullenly a few steps to the side. "We gotta find our bikes!"

"No 'buts'!" she sternly ordered him. "We're going straight home and tell Mom and Dad what happened. They can come out here—maybe with the police—and figure things out. This is too weird for us! And the police can look for whoever took our bikes."

"Huh..." Billy snorted again. "Well, *I'm* not scared!"

"Well I'm not either!" she snapped back at him.

"You said you were."

"That was just to get you moving!"

"I'm comin', I'm comin'."

A dreamy look came over Billy's face as she again grabbed his hand and dragged him resolutely along behind her.

"I bet it *was* a nuclear missile down there—that launched up into the sky!" he grinned as he yet again jerked free from her grasp to now skip happily along at her side. "That's why the ground shook so much, I bet-cha! And the big lizard was afraid and ducked into it to hide. Stupid lizard. He's probably up in orbit around Earth right now, lookin' down at us. Hi, lizard!" he grinned, looking up at the blue sky and waving his hand.

"Maybe..." she uncharacteristically agreed with her little brother. "But it's getting too late to worry about all that right now. The sun's going down. As it is we're barely going to get back home before it gets dark. Mom and Dad are going to be worried to death about us."

"Yep, that's right," Billy agreed. He was now not as "bubbly" as a moment before, considering the consequences of their little misadventure.

Whatever had happened to them in their Saturday evening bike ride out into the *Chickasaw National Recreation Area*—known as "The Park" to the locals—was very unusual. The most excitement that the small town of Sulphur, Oklahoma usually experienced from The Park was people visiting with their boats and campers, dining at the many fast food places on the town's main drag. Suzy had never heard anything about nuclear missile sites being hidden out in the woods. But then again, she was only ten years old. She didn't know everything, just mostly everything—certainly more than her sassy little six-year-old brother!

But she was beginning to regret taking off into the woods chasing after that strange, big "lizard".

Their bikes were gone, probably stolen while they were trapped in that small underground compartment, making the trip back a lot longer on foot. But she resolutely trudged along in the direction of town, with Billy trailing behind her, traversing the rough ground of the "off road" wilderness area.

"Suzy...?" Billy said as he, uncharacteristically, came closer to her and impulsively grabbed onto her hand.

"What?" she said—lost in her thoughts.

"Do things look...kinda strange?" he gulped.

Only then did she look up from the ground where she'd been concentrating on not stepping into holes or running into boulders or tripping over fallen branches.

Indeed, things *did* look...different!

But she was loath to admit he was right.

"What do you mean?" she cautiously asked as she stumbled along with him over the uneven ground.

"Those big funny trees—I never noticed them before out here in the Park," he said, pointing.

Indeed, also used to the small trees in the Park, what Suzy now saw was shocking: *very tall* white-barked trees with *crowns of leaves* up high! And, come to think of it, the shrubs around her also looked radically different. Now the low growth seemed mostly *ferns with large fronds.* And each of the fronds was split into many "fingers"! It was creepy, like the plants were reaching out to grab you. And the early-spring flowers looked different as well—no longer the small white, purple, and orange flowers she was used to, but *many-fingered* red clumps.

Jesus, the whole landscape looked different!

Plus, there was a lot of pooled-up water around. It made the air smell very musty. And a *mist* was rising up from all that standing water, making the normally clear air of the Park very hard to see through. The Park was usually rather dry, with artisan underground wells feeding defined creeks. What they were now walking through seemed more like a *swamp!*

And there were a lot more "animal sounds" than normal: different "clicks" and "squeals" and "barks" she'd never noticed before.

It was really spooky.

She wanted to get out of the Park and back to their home now more than ever!

"Do you think maybe it rained when we were trapped down in that compartment thing?" Billy gulped, splashing through low water beside Suzy.

She swatted at some strange-looking big flying bugs. They were also new to the Park!

"We were only in that buried bunker thing a minute or two," Suzy softly replied, careful where she put her feet. She knew that there were copperheads and even water moccasins out in the Park. You hardly ever saw one of them if you kept to the official, beaten-down trails. But now that they were off the trails without their bikes, walking along on foot, there was a real danger that they might step on a poisonous snake and get bit!

Suzy knew that Billy would love to see some wild snakes. He helped their Dad take care of a collection of harmless pet snakes, lizards, and tortoises. Both their Dad and Billy really loved them, particularly the snakes, taking them out and letting them crawl up on their shoulders before nestling comfortably around their necks. Suzy could take them or leave them. She was more like her mother in that regard—who considered snakes to be beautiful, simple animals deserving protection in Nature but hardly pets!

"Well, at least that looks like Bromide Hill up ahead," Billy cheerfully said, pointing again, breaking Suzy's chain of thought.

Indeed, not too far from them was the raised ridge of low hills where, from the top, you could look out over an abrupt cliff down at the town of Sulphur, Oklahoma. Whenever they biked up to its top on the paved road that was on this side of it, they liked to go to the lookout point and peer down at the streets of the town. They could easily see their own house from up there!

"But...where's Veterans Lake?" Suzy frowned as they kept walking along through the strangely unfamiliar territory.

From the thickening mists sounded strange "*caws*" and "*cluckings*" that were oddly different from the bird-calls she was used to hearing.

Veterans Lake was a small, artificial lake where people liked to go boating and fishing. It took about an hour for Suzy and Billy to bike around it on a cement walking/riding path. It was a nice ride, with winding slopes that went up and down. It was fun. She and Billy did the circuit about once a month, enjoying how the vegetation and water changed with the seasons.

But now...the *entire lake* was missing!

"Wow, maybe that earthquake sucked it dry?" Billie gulped, his eyes stretched wide.

But it wasn't exactly that "dry" either.

Where Veterans Lake should have been was yet another swampy expanse loaded with more of those strange "umbrella" trees.

Suzy sure didn't want to try to go slogging through that lower, muddy, scary area. No, they'd better stick to the higher ground. Going up and over Bromide Hill sounded just fine. They'd hit the paved road and could take that around the peak. Or they could just walk down the back-and-forth twisting hiking path that went straight down the cliff from the peak to the Park's main entrance area.

Yep, they had a "plan of action." It was a relief to find a known landmark. From the foot of Bromide Hill it was only a few minutes to get back to their home.

But Suzy glumly realized they weren't zooming along on their sturdy mountain bikes. Instead they were slowly climbing upward on foot—and she was held back by a little six-year-old boy.

So it took a good thirty minutes more of trudging just to reach the peak itself.

And there wasn't any paved road. Like so many other things, it had just *vanished*...as if it were never there in the first place.

Things were definitely getting very, very strange.

And it was getting gloomy, the sun having disappeared over the horizon. Soon it would be pitch black. Their little misadventure was getting worse and worse. They couldn't go climbing down a cliff in the dark. They could topple over the abrupt edge of the path, tumble down, and die! But if they stayed on the peak they'd have to stay in the Park overnight!

Oh, wow...this was getting to be too much for Suzy to process.

She felt like sitting down on the wet ground, burying her head in her arms, and crying.

But no, she wasn't a little baby! She could figure it out! Once they got their bearings they could decide what to do.

"We're almost there," she encouraged her brother as they both "puffed" and "panted" their way to the top. "And from here we're almost home where..." she confidently stated as she arrived at and looked over the top of the peak.

Billy stood trembling beside her as they together gazed down from the high point over what should have been the many streets and houses of Sulphur, Oklahoma.

—where she again saw *nothing!*

It was just more of the high trees, swamps, and grasslands spread below them on out into the gathering misty gloom...as far as they could see.

Suzy shakily pulled out her slim cellphone from her top shirt pocket, frantically clicking on the numbers for her Dad and Mom.

Nothing!

"I'll call 911," Billy said, pulling his out as well.

Nothing...

"Suzy?" Billy gasped, now reaching out and gripping her hand tightly. "I'm scared now."

Off in the distance Suzy heard peculiar "honks" and screeches...

—and deep, booming, *roars!*

It seemed to Suzy that were new *predators* out there in the gathering mists, preparing to go hunting in the night.

The sun was almost down. Everything was getting dark. And they were all by themselves in a spooky, totally unexpected wilderness.

She had to make a decision, quickly!

"We'll climb a bit down the cliff and hide in the Cave," she firmly nodded, leading him to the edge.

Under some overlapping mammoth boulders, there was an alcove that she and other town kids would regularly go to and "hide" when they were playing in the Park. Since it was higher up, the tourists mostly didn't know about it. She always thought it was her and Billy's own personal "cave"—though her Mom had told her about "hiding" in it herself when she herself was just a kid growing up next to the Park. So lots of people knew about it.

But now it was the safest place that Suzy could think of hiding.

They carefully started down the cliff toward the alcove, grabbing onto protrusions and hugging the cliff face.

"S-Suzy," Billy gulped as they reached a small ledge, "w-where did the t-town go?"

She knew that the little boy was starting to comprehend their peril, about to break down and start crying. It wasn't like him to stammer.

"Don't worry," she firmly ordered him. "We'll just sleep in the cave for the night. We'll be safe. Then tomorrow when the sun comes up we'll find out where the town went."

Her words sounded confident—after all, she was his older sister. She had to be brave! But inside, her heart was sinking. It wasn't just a weird lizard bedeviling them anymore.

Veterans Lake, the paved road, and an entire town couldn't just vanish. It was *impossible*.

But they had.

She desperately missed her bike, a hot meal at home, her room, and her nice warm soft bed.

And most of all, she missed her Mom and Dad.

As she and Billy huddled together in the cold "cave" Suzy promised herself she was never again going off of the established trails in the Park. Going "into the wild" wasn't near as romantic or heroic as she'd thought. Instead, it was just plain *terrifying*.

Dave King and his wife Sally found their kids' bikes the next day, having followed the distinctive tracks off the trail into the wilderness.

When the kids didn't returned home by the evening meal, Sally, their mother, got very worried. And when they hadn't returned by the time the sun went down, she was frantic—going out to the "work shed" to get her husband Dave. Together they jumped in their car and went into the Park, looking in all the obvious places. But they found nothing.

Then they went back home, got out their own mountain bikes, and—though it was by then the middle of the night—went back out onto the trails which were inaccessible by car. With flashlights they searched straight through the night along the routes the kids liked to ride, but again found nothing.

Then, as the morning sun began to peek out above the low hills—cold and exhausted—Sally spotted a double-track of bikes leading off into the woods. It didn't take them long to follow the tracks to an isolated part of the Park where few people ventured.

There, lying neatly on the ground, side-by-side, were two small mountain bikes, one red and one blue. It was their kids' bikes.

And right beside them was...

"Is that...?" Sally gasped, looking at the length and width of the partially collapsed-in trench.

"It can't be," Dave groaned. "You said you left the Obelisk behind in that dying twin Universe!"

Sally shook her head in apparent bewilderment. Her red-brown hair was cut short on her head. She was now in her thirties, but still athletic. Though birthing and raising two kids across more than a decade of time had put extra pounds on her previously slim body she was still in good physical shape. Her *big green eyes*, though, were the same as they'd been when she was in her twenties: bright, wide, and flashing with excitement at anything new or novel.

Dave did not feel any excitement, only waves of regret and fear. He knew he should have insisted they tell their two kids all about their own past misadventures through time and space. But they'd decided to put it all behind them, hoping to give Suzy and Billy a normal upbringing—and themselves a fresh start.

Versus the incredible upheavals and bizarre world's they'd fought their way through previously, they wanted nothing more than to settle down to a perfectly ordinary, dull, small-town life. In fact, Sally had complained to him on several occasions that their life was too *boring*.

But he insisted to her that boring was *good*. Any hint of their previous misadventures had to be eliminated. They should totally forget their incredible history and hide it from everyone, especially their two kids.

That now seemed to Dave a colossal mistake.

If the kids had somehow been swept up into it all, they were clueless and helpless.

And that was all because of Dave's prior decisions.

"When I was keeping the Demon trapped—as our friends severed the connection to our own Universe—the Obelisk was still down in the main hanger of the Harvester," Sally frowned, addressing Dave's previous question. "If it somehow survived the explosion of the Demon's spaceship, it's still back there in that corrupted Universe. But, then again...I suppose that whatever transported me back into Sally's earlier mind could have also retrieved the Obelisk."

"That's assuming what was buried here was even the Obelisk from that timeline," Dave gulped, shivering at the implications.

"You're right, Dave," Sally nodded. "We've no idea where it came from or how it got here."

Dave was already agonizing at the implications of the empty trench when he saw *animal tracks.*

Now an icy pit opened up in his stomach. He recognized those animal tracks. There was no doubt in his mind what made them.

They hadn't escaped their past after all. The pleasant life they'd built for themselves over the past decade in the small town of Sulphur, Oklahoma was just a temporary illusion.

Sally bent down over the distinctive animal tracks and fingered them thoughtfully.

They were deep imprints of a man-sized, three-toed creature. And a winding pattern behind and beside the tracks suggested a swinging, reptilian tail.

"It's Breep!" she gasped, reaching up and tightly grasping Dave's hand.

She'd originally saved the newly hatched small dinosaur from flying pterodactyls, bringing it with her from 125 million years in the past into the present.

"The kids must have seen him and followed him out here," Dave grated through clenched teeth.

"And then Breep somehow got them into the Obelisk—which could have taken them...*anywhere* in space and time!" Sally shuddered. "This can't be some cosmic accident. This was done deliberately. Who would steal our children from us, and *why?*"

"I've got a pretty good idea about that," Dave grimly replied. "I hope I'm wrong—but I'm afraid it's your evil 'twin' whose timeline I destroyed when I helped Galileo survive and flourish in the other Dimension's past."

"But we *don't know* what the repercussions were of your changing the past to the *present* parallel Dimension," Sally gulped. "Look Dave, we can't jump to conclusions. The *other* Sally was probably just erased...right?"

Dave was shaking his head in confusion and despair, still looking down at Breep's undeniably fresh dinosaur tracks.

"Whatever happened on the other side of the dimensional divide, you know what this means for us," Dave grimly replied, running a trembling hand through his now fashionably graying hair.

She sighed deeply.

"Yes, it means starting up that which we swore to never use again. But it doesn't matter," Sally said, slowly standing up straight beside him. She continued staring down at Breep's tracks in the freshly disturbed dirt. "Even if it means we must restart the Dark Energy revolution and risk provoking Judgment Day—we have to do *whatever's* necessary to find our kids!"

She reached down to grab onto Suzy's small blue bike. Then she picked it up and deliberately dropped it down into the deep trench.

Dave saw she obviously wanted it hidden, not moved from the place they'd discovered it. It was their one and only "crumb" to find the trail leading to their kids.

"We will," Dave promised, picking up Billy's bike and doing the same. "We *will!*"

Dave saw that Sally's Turtle Tattoo on her wrist was *glowing*. The sight filled him with a deep dread.

He wished he still had his Anaconda Tattoo but that wasn't yet part of his previous incarnation.

Sally's tattoo hadn't "lit up" since they'd started their new life here more than a decade ago.

There was no doubt. Whatever was guiding them before was doing so once again.

Perversely, Dave felt reassured—that they had a chance of finding the kids. But it also caused a *chill* to go down his spine.

Whatever the effect of their present actions might be, their once-peaceful life with Suzy and Billy in the small town of Sulphur, Oklahoma was finished.

It was *all happening again...*

They'd left too many "threads" hanging loose in Time and Space.

And those "loose threads" were coming back to strangle them.

Chapter 2

A WAKING DREAM

Sometimes dreams turn into nightmares

While at other times sleep is soothing

But be it horrible or wonderful

Letting the mind run loose is strange

For who knows what will pop up

When the Rules no longer apply

And all your thoughts are dangerous

When anything you can conceive

Can suddenly come to life?

Beware rampant imaginations...

The Minstrel's Lark, 2:32-34

Billy was standing at the mouth of the cave, silently looking out, his back turned to Suzy.

"B-Billy?" Suzy blinked at him, waking up and painfully stretching out her arms.

It had been a rough night. They were sleeping on hard rock. There was hardly any protection from the cold wind that whistled through their shelter. They'd been huddled together, with only their thin jackets to keep them warm. And all through the night there were very strange sounds outside. Rather than being safe inside an actual enclosed cave they'd just been lying under some jumbled overlapping large boulders. Any predator out there could have easily crawled in and gobbled them up!

And to make things even worse, overnight there'd been a storm. Cold water dripped in all around them. Flashes of lightning lit up the rocks like Halloween strobe beams. And the thunder was deafening.

But, somehow, Suzy had managed to fall asleep. Awakening, for a moment she thought she'd just had a weird dream.

But their fantastic misadventure was all too real.

"Come take a look," Billy said without turning around.

His voice was higher than usual, both uncharacteristically restrained and over-the-top hysterical.

Suzy got to her knees and then to her feet, having to duck down not to knock her head into the boulder "ceiling" above her.

At the entrance she was able to stand up straight up next to her little brother.   Looking outward and down she saw a wondrous but very scary vista...

The sun was just coming up. Thick mists drifted up from a swamp that seemed to stretch out as far as she could see in all directions. Clumps of tall trees stuck their high branches and bunched leaves up out of the roiling fog.

And "chomping" happily upon the elevated leaves of the trees were the elongated necks and heads of what looked convincingly like *giant dinosaurs.*

They were happily "snorting" and "honking" at each other.

"What...are...those?" Suzy gasped, not believing her own eyes.

"Well..." Billy hesitantly answered, sounding like he was in shock. "According to my dinosaur book at home, those are '*Sauroposeidons*'...way big, huh Suzy? Bones of them were discovered right here in Oklahoma...yep, right here."

Suzy turned her head to look down at her little brother. He was being amazingly calm about all this. But his bulging, stretched-wide eyes betrayed his extreme agitation.

Though she was seeing them from a distance, it was obvious that the long-necked beasts were colossal. As best as Suzy could judge from over a hundred feet up on the cliff face, the biggest one in the herd was somewhere around a hundred feet in length and sixty feet high. Through the clearing mists, Suzy saw at least a dozen of them, including babies that were "only" as tall as a human.

"So...how long ago did you say they lived here in Oklahoma?" Suzy asked. She was feeling light-headed both from the height of their "cave" on the cliff-face and having missed two meals in a row.

"Well...they're from the Middle Cretaceous," Billy hysterically chirped, still staring out across the vast swamp.

"Ok...and just how long ago was that, again?" Suzy asked, not up on her dinosaur epochs.

"Oh—about 110 million years ago," he softly replied.

Billy sure knew his dinosaurs. He really loved them. But Suzy knew he might not love them as much when they could easily step on and *squash* him!

"And how much does one of those things weigh, do you think?" Suzy asked, weakly sitting down and dangling her legs over the sloped edge of the narrow ledge.

Billy sat down next to her, still staring out at the misty swamps stretched-out below.

"A grown one—probably, oh, sixty tons," Billy nodded again. "That's like, oh, a big dump-truck."

A huge *SCREECH-SQUACK* sounded from beside them, startling them! Suzy grabbed Billy, just stopping him from toppling forward off the edge of the cliff.

They both shrank back into their "cave"—while carefully peeking out around the edge of a large boulder.

Above them to the side sat three *giant bat-like lizards*...staring hungrily down with bright red eyes!

They each had long pointed beaks, a sharp horn on the top of each of their heads, and folded leathery wings.

"And those guys are *Pterodactyls*," Billy grinned rather giddily at Suzy. "I don't think they'll attack us. Their long beaks are mainly for stabbing fish. There's probably lots of fish down in the swamp out there, I guess..."

As his voice trailed off his lips began quivering.

He looked like he was about to start crying.

Suzy grabbed him and moved him back into the partial shelter underneath the giant boulders. She felt him trembling uncontrollably in her arms.

"W-what's goin' on, S-Suzy?" he sobbed, now breaking into tears. "D-did w-we really go back in T-Time? W-was that thing we g-got stuck inside of a time m-machine?"

"I don't know...maybe...but we can't stay here, Billy," she soothed him, trying to focus his attention on their immediate situation. "We've got to find clean water to drink and something to eat. I think it's important that we don't panic. We've got to stay alive until Dad and Mom can find us."

"You...you think...they c-can...f-find us?" Billy blubbered in Suzy's arms.

"You know that Mom and Dad are the smartest people in town," she insisted. "And Dad's always inventing stuff out in his workshop. If we've really gone back in time he'll make his *own* time-machine! So we've just got to concentrate on staying alive until we can be rescued, that's all. Got it?"

She felt his trembling lessen.

"Ok," he replied in a weak voice. "Well, I guess...it is sort of fun...to be back with real live dinosaurs...for a while."

He "hiccupped" as he started to get himself back under control.

"Hey! That's right!" she tried to confidently soothe him. "It's like a field trip, huh? We just gotta use our survival skills for a while. It's like being off with Mom and Dad on one of our family wilderness vacations, except that they're testing us."

"T-testing us?"

"Yep—on how well we survive left to ourselves."

He pushed away from her, rubbing his red eyes. Then he looked at her defiantly.

"This isn't any test," he frowned. "Dad and Mom wouldn't do this to us!"

"Uh..." she grimaced. "Ok, you're right. But we know a lot about camping, right? Remember all those trips they took us on? It was just like this...except without giant dinosaurs. That's all..."

"Yep, that's true," he hesitantly replied. He crept back to the entrance and looked down with renewed purpose. "This is just like then—'cept we got no tent, no food, no water, and no tools."

"But we've got our brains, right?"

He thought about that a moment as if not so sure. Then he visibly perked up.

"Well, I think we can climb down the cliff over to the right. The zig-zag path is gone, of course. But the cliff face over there doesn't look too steep. Plus there are lots of rocks pushing out we can grab onto and..."

Suzy sighed gratefully, letting his voice drift off and away from her. She just needed to keep him focused on the next step. He'd always been a "doer" even when he was a baby. She was the "thinker" who would worry a problem to death before actually starting to tackle it. But he just dived right in.

But now she was *very* worried indeed.

Wherever they'd managed to wind up—despite her confident-sounding claim to Billy—Suzy was afraid that the odds of Mom and Dad finding them were slim.

"But where should we head for?" she interrupted his "verbal mental musings," trying to keep him focused.

He squinted out across the high vista.

"There!" he pointed with his small hand.

"What? What do you see?" she eagerly asked as she too crawled back to the entrance and looked out over the misty plains.

"Smoke!" he gleefully chortled. "There are more of us humans out there!"

Ready to respond with quick criticism, Suzy instead kept quiet. She didn't want to put a damper on his enthusiasm.

Yes, there was a thin pencil of smoke snaking up through the mists way off in the distance. The smoke was a distinctive brown-black versus the bellowing white fogs. But it could be coming from any random fire. Suzy thought it probably was from a lightning strike during the night.

If they'd really gone back in time, it would be over a *hundred million years* before anything resembling humans ever walked upon the face of the planet.

That is, beside them.

Suzy suddenly felt lonelier than she had ever before felt in her entire short life. Before, even when riding her bike alone out in the Park, she'd always known that a whole town filled with people was nearby. Now, however, the *entire world* out there might be empty of fellow humans!

She had a new appreciation for her irritating, nasty little brother. He was a pest, but he was *her* pest.

"Then that's where we're going," she nodded to him. "Good work spotting that smoke-column, Billy. You grab my hand and I'll lower you to those rocks below us."

"Ok, Suzy," he now-happily replied. "But first there's our fish-stabber 'friends'."

He jumped up straight and flapped his arms at the three vulture-like, waiting Pterodactyls.

"Go on, *git!*" he yelled at them. "You ain't eating us today! If we fall down the cliff and get killed on the rocks below then you can come peck out our eyeballs. But not until then! Go on, *fly away!*"

With another loud SCREECH the three five-foot tall creatures leapt off the higher boulders and sailed away into the mists.

"Impressive, Billy," Suzy encouraged him, grateful to have those watching beasts scared away. "Well done!"

"Thanks, Sis," he grinned, carefully getting on his knees, turning to face the cave, and tentatively reaching his legs down for the first foothold.

After he'd safely moved down a few feet, she carefully wriggled her own body over the edge of the rock face.

Though she was focused on each step of the dangerous descent down the 140-foot cliff, her mind was racing.

Even if they'd somehow been thrown back in time by the strange compartment they'd fallen into, something still didn't *feel* right.

Indeed, the Turtle Tattoo on her left wrist was *itching* terribly. And glancing at her arm where the tattoo was covered up by her shirt and light jacket, she was startled to see a *light* glowing from beneath the cloth and fabric.

It redoubled her unease and suspicion that they were being *watched*. It was like that old church song she and Billy had sung many times on Sundays: *"There's an all-seeing eye in the sky."* But the intensely blue sky above them held no such eye. Yet she was sure something was indeed watching their every move...

—but who or what, she had no idea.

And the "presence" didn't seem at all friendly. Indeed, it felt very, very bad—like something was *laughing* at her!

Maybe she should start praying. But Dad and Mom taught her
that God wanted her to *struggle* to figure out the best answers for
herself: that, indeed, in the "struggle" was the true virtue and reward.

Well, she was definitely due for some sort of great reward. She
and Billy were not giving up. They were determined to mount a heroic struggle. But she was terrified they'd "learn" incredible lessons,
much more than they ever wanted to know. And she didn't even have
to go to Church to hear them.

It was Sunday morning, so there was no problem with their missing
teaching or coaching duties at the local high school. But Dave and
Suzy had responsibilities at the local church where they were faithful
members.

Dave called the church office on their landline phone and left a
message that they'd not be there due to a family emergency. He
didn't go into details. He didn't know what to say. He couldn't tell
them that he feared his children were lost somewhere in space and
time!

Plus he left another phone message for his good friend George
Johnson to come down every couple days from Edmond and take care
of his reptile collection. It was a long ride, but George was happy to
do it occasionally when Dave and his family were traveling.

"I'll call the school and let them know that we're both ill with the
flu and can't come in tomorrow for our classes—and to put us down
for indefinite sick leave," Sally said, picking up her cellphone. But before she did that, Dave saw her click the numbers to Suzy and Billy's
cellphones for the umpteenth time.

Still no answers from either of them...

She was leaving carefully worded messages at both the school office and to back-up substitute teachers when Dave left her and walked
to their shed. There he yanked open its wide door.

In it—carefully protected and maintained—was his black *Polaris
Ranger*. It was their super-secret "weapon"! Superficially it was an
ordinary open-air, 4-wheel drive, off-road vehicle, "ORV." It sported
thick curved bars that protected the driver and passengers. It was a
special-issue format that had a small backseat, in which the kids usually sat. Custom fitted onto the front was a Plexiglas windshield. On

its rear end was a 4-foot-wide open box, capable of carrying a wide array of supplies and/or equipment.

It was a wonderful vehicle for family adventures into various wilderness areas. Sally and Dave used it often, taking their kids into all sorts of exotic and isolated places. It even had its own flat-bed carrier for towing along behind their black van—when they went to distant places like Yosemite Park, the Blue Ridge Mountains, or Death Valley.

But Dave never thought he'd need it here in his sleepy little home town.

It was all black and military-green. It was raised up upon thick-treaded wheels. It was a *mean*-looking machine, a modified twin of one that'd done such a great job for him and Victor in their prior adventures. And it had been covertly modified by Dave and Sally to do far more than just go "off-road" into a bumpy wilderness.

Dave began quickly loading into the box an array of equipment: a powerful, portable battery, plus digging tools, antennas, and some sophisticated radiation detectors.

"Damn it all!" he swore, looking around for a coil of rope and not finding it.

He angrily grabbed a shovel and *threw* it at the wall of the shed where it "clanged" before bouncing back and almost slicing off his foot!

He grimaced at the pain of his mashed foot, almost burst out cursing...but just managed to hold his tongue.

"Perhaps we should both get some sleep before we return to the Park," Sally gently suggested from behind him. "We're exhausted from being up all night. We need to get cleaned up, eat some food, and get a couple hours sleep. We're no use to the kids if we can't think straight."

Dave slumped down behind the Ranger, his back to the wall, and was suddenly overwhelmed by a violent bout of *sobbing*.

Sally quickly slid down next to him, wrapping him up in her warm arms.

"We'll find them, Dave, I know we will," she comforted him. "We'll bring them back and retrieve our peaceful, boring life here in Sulphur. It's just a glitch! We can't expect not to have a few things from our past catch up to us after all we went through."

"But...it's...it's...*my* fault," he blubbered uncontrollably. "I should have been more careful...*stricter* with them and..."

"*Both* of us encouraged them to go out by themselves in the Park. We wanted them to be independent and smart," she gently chided him. "And this isn't the time to place blame. This is the time to focus on getting them back!"

"I...know all of that," he gasped, struggling to get himself back under control. "But...there are *deadly enemies* of ours still lurking out there in space/time—that I should have warned the kids about! I know we both decided not to tell them, to let them have a regular up-bringing. But I should have insisted! I was afraid of needlessly frightening them, dampening their joy of life. But I was wrong! They're part of us and should have known what they might face at some point. Because of my selfish desire to have some idyllically happy, ordinary family life—Suzy and Billy are totally unprepared."

He felt the whole world spinning uncontrollably around him...

"Now just hold on there," Sally said, releasing him from her tender hug and standing up. "We may have overly protected them from the nightmares we endured. But we also made them sure-footed with good survival skills, especially on our 'Ranger Adventure' ORV trips. And even more important than particular techniques, we taught them to think on their feet. That's much better than just frightening them about lurking Demons, Monsters, and cruel Enemies. Maybe our past has finally caught up with us, Dave, but we're *not* defenseless—and neither are they!"

Dave nodded in agreement, slowly getting back up to his feet as well.

He wiped the back of his hand quickly across his face, resolutely suppressing his tears.

"Well...at least we covertly equipped the Ranger for just this sort of emergency," he sighed, slapping a hand down on its gleaming black metal. "I just hope it all works. After all, we never dared test it."

Inside the outwardly conventional engine, carefully hidden within black-painted steel boxes, was equipment *far* more powerful than a mere gasoline motor.

"And outfitting the Ranger was over my objections, remember?" Sally reminded him. "I was just like you, Dave. I wanted to hide here in our charming little hometown, no matter how boring it might seem at times, and just forget the past—avoiding chancing repeating the most dangerous parts of our misadventures! But it was *you* that insisted we have the Ranger ready to go if needed. So don't start beating yourself up, Dr. David Richard King. Whatever's got our kids, *they* should be afraid of us, *not* the reverse!"

"Right...ok," Dave sighed, weakly giving her a firm hug.

"Now let's go get us some food and a shower. You stink!" she grinned at him.

He would have replied the same to her—but now as an experienced husband he knew that would not be wise.

One did not always have to tell the whole truth.

He'd learned a thing or two in their decade-plus marriage.

Galileo knew he should be dead. Instead, he owed his life to Time Travelers from the future!

It was a sobering assessment.

Galileo had refused to deny his own scientific observations that the world circled the sun instead of the sun circling the Earth. So the Muslim clerics of his Dimension—who believed that the Holy Scriptures taught the Earth to be at the center of worldly existence—convinced the Emperor of the still-thriving Roman Empire to have Galileo executed. The people of Rome had indeed enjoyed seeing the "uppity" scientist burned to death in a cage. But it was actually a Time Traveler from the future who died, a "Dr. King," who changed himself to look like Galileo with a futuristic projection device. But then the burnt body vanished after being hit with a huge blast from a futuristic energy gun!

It was then that a second Time Traveler, an oriental woman, tried to kill him, the surviving disguised Galileo—only to be stopped by a *third* Time Traveler, an "Agent Anderson," who warned him to escape to England.

So, masked by another future projection-device to look like a Roman General, Galileo quickly departed mainland Europe to the relative safety of England. There, the minority *Shia* sect of Islam was in charge. They were happy to have Galileo unexpectedly appear in their midst, having supposedly "fooled" the Roman *Sunni* Muslim majority that controlled Rome into executing the wrong person! So even though the Shia also didn't agree with him about Earth circling the sun, they were still happy to see the "orthodox" Roman Sunni leaders humiliated.

But it was the scientists of Europe who rejoiced the most. They'd thought that their hero, Galileo, was dead—executed by a brutal state. Now he was alive, having seemingly tricked the "backward" Roman Empire in the bargain. It was an electrifying event, changing the dispirited academic community into a rejoicing, energized force!

But Galileo was not so happy.

He sat forlornly on a stool in a café located on the London Bridge, looking out over the river Thames. He didn't like London. It was congested, dirty, and stank. Everywhere he looked, there were rats scurrying about underfoot. But the wide river flowing beneath the bridge was loaded with beautiful sailing vessels bringing goods in and out of England. It was a place where free-thinkers could be appreciated rather than executed as heretics! And he was doubly grateful not to be in the looming Tower of London where prisoners were kept. He'd had quite enough of being a prisoner back in Rome. At least here he was free to travel and lecture as he wished.

And he had—apparently—succeeded in changing future history. The Time Traveler who'd died in his place had given him amazing pictures that actually observed a future point in time, which *changed* following Galileo's escape. In one picture there was a sad-looking couple in chains awaiting their own execution that then became a happy couple holding hands. And in the other, a young man playing a game with a ball and a stick became a student looking through a huge telescope.

So he'd succeeded. But he didn't *feel* like he'd succeeded. Something was still missing.

"Have some more ale, mate?" a fat café owner asked him, holding a jug unexpectedly above his glass.

"No, thank you," Galileo politely declined in highly accented English. Being a learned man, a Professor, he of course knew other languages. But he was not near as fluent in them as he'd like. He preferred his native Italian. Having to live in a land that did not speak Italian was strange to him, awkward.

"You don't like our ale?" a young-sounding female voice came from behind him as the fat innkeeper walked away.

It was obviously a waitress.

"Oh, I like it well enough—in fact, too much!" Galileo laughed cheerfully without bothering to look behind him. "I must, however, restrict my eating and drinking to not allow those pleasures to take control of me. If I ate and drank as I wished then I'd be as fat as your boss! But I like to be fit and healthy even though I'm yet an old man of seventy years."

"Not near as ancient as *me*," another female voice replied, this one old and quavering.

"What?" Galileo frowned, now twisting around in his chair to see...

"You!" he gasped, jerking back in his chair.

Looming above him with a sharp butcher knife threateningly pointed at him was *the woman who'd nearly killed him* after the execution of his "duplicate" in Rome!

She was an oriental woman dressed all in black, with straight black hair dangling down past her shoulders.

And her black, slanted eyes were as cold as ice.

"Shall we dance?" she menacingly said as—before he could react—she slipped a slender arm around his thick neck with the blade poised at his throat.

"What do you want?" he gasped, afraid to move.

"It's not what I want, but the Commissioner!" the woman whispered in his ear.

"Oh, you've caused me *so* much trouble, Professor Galileo," the older voice chimed in from behind him. "You took away my entire world. You stole everything from me! Well, Sanako here will pay you back for your lack of integrity in not dying when you should have. Your 'assassination' now by 'Roman Muslim Agents' will convince all the dissidents that they were wrong to claim you as their conquering hero—and everything will return to its natural order!"

Twisting his head, Galileo now saw sitting at a table right behind him a dried-up, scrawny, old woman. She had on a strange blue dress belted at her waist with a golden chain. She had deep wrinkles in the loose, hanging folds of her face. Her splotched head was totally bald.

But it was her *bright green eyes* that disturbed Galileo the most—making her look like a decrepit but still-dangerous cat, waiting to pounce!

"Who...are...you?" Galileo gasped, his breathing impaired by the other woman's strong encircling arm.

"Someone who wants to see you suffer as you made me suffer," the old hag cackled. "We could have just killed you while you sat there admiring the view of this stinking, ancient river. But where's the fun in that? And besides, the world has to know it wasn't a random street thug that dispatched your sorry, astronomical ass!"

The strangling assassin's hot breath blew unpleasantly into Galileo's ear.

"And I *am* going to finish the job that I started back in Rome," she muttered in his ear. "But the credit will be given to the Clerics who you thought you'd so cleverly tricked. I'm going to stand up and make a short, fanatical religious speech before *cutting* your head off! As the Commissioner correctly stated, everything you've done to thwart history will then be cancelled!"

Galileo was terrified, but couldn't call out for help. The arm around his neck was pressing ever tighter. He couldn't even speak!

All around him on the London Bridge many people were obliviously milling past. The proprietors of other business booths were shouting out their wares, haggling, and loudly talking. Even police were strolling past. But Galileo was totally helpless!

I'm going to be beheaded right here in the middle of the thriving city of London!

This was it. He was about to die.

"Kill Galileo and your Boss dies also," a cold, deep voice sounded.

Galileo saw *Agent Anderson* appear right beside the old hag, with a big black gun held to her side.

She glowered at him with naked hatred.

"Let the Professor go, Sanako—and step back!" Anderson insisted.

He had on a black waistcoat and wide-brimmed black hat. Also, he wore those same thin, dark eyeglasses that Galileo had previously found so distinctive.

Reluctantly, Sanako pulled her arm away...

—as the Agent grabbed him by the arm and instantly hauled him away into the concealing crowd.

"So...you've saved me...yet again," Galileo coughed, still struggling to breathe normally. "And how many more times will this happen until those time-monsters succeed?"

"I thought that they'd let you alone once their world was destroyed—hopefully because they'd been erased," the big man sighed as he hurried Galileo along the crowded bridge. "But I was wrong. They escaped and are bent on correcting their timeline. So, my dear Professor, we've got to get a bit more drastic."

"*More* drastic?" Galileo mildly replied. "What...does that mean?"

"Do you still have your inactivated White Cube?" Anderson asked him.

"Of course I do," Galileo replied, getting his voice back. "It's an artifact of the future! It saved my life! I prize it greatly whether it works or not."

"Well, I'm going to turn it back on," Anderson stated, looking behind them furtively to make sure they weren't being followed.

"Sounds...fascinating," Galileo now grinned widely, giddy with relief to still be alive with his head still positioned correctly on his neck. "And will I then have access to all its future knowledge?"

"Yes, you will," Anderson said. "And I'm going to *remain* here as your bodyguard while you jumpstart the Scientific Revolution, hundreds of years before it would have happened otherwise. Together we're not just going to change the Commissioner's future world— we're going to totally *obliterate* any trace of it! And when the last vestige of it dies, so will she."

Galileo felt oddly happy.

He knew he was "cheating" to use future knowledge to alter the present rather than doing the "hard work" of discovering it all piece-by-piece. But his was a passionate quest for Truth. The images that the late-departed "Dr. King" had shown him of alien worlds had only made him want even *more*.

So be it! I'm not going to die today! Instead, I'm going to thrive beyond my wildest dreams!

All of future science was in his hands.

Chapter 3

ON THE RESERVATION

You'd think you could just set aside space
And there sequester what you'd like to keep safe
As if the very act itself would guarantee success
At keeping pristine the things you don't want lost
But the very act of preservation loses key parts
Indeed what matters most in an artificial world
That wonderful feeling of enchanting originality
The opposite of a well-arranged presentation
Not captured in a picture, cage, or barnyard
But everything so wildly unpredictable,
Dangerous, spontaneous, and real...
Break down all the barriers!
The Minstrel's Lark, 3:17-20

"I'm thirsty," Billy moaned. "*Why* can't we drink any water?"

"I told you that before!" Suzy irritably snapped at him, dragging her complaining little brother along by his arm. "It'll make you sick."

"I'm *already* sick!" he yelled petulantly as they splashed through the low, swampy water.

"Watch where you're stepping," Suzy warned him, pulling him up on the above-water clumps of grass that she was trying to keep them on. "You don't want to get bit by a water moccasin."

"There's no water moccasins 125 million years ago!" he argued, trying to pull his arm away from Suzy's strong hand. "At least...I don't think so," he uncertainly finished, now hopping out of the low water. "But it sure would be fun to see a 'dinosaur snake.' Wow! That'd be really cool!"

"I think you like snakes a bit too much for..."

"Yep, I sure do! Just like Dad, huh?"

"Well, Dad's not here, Billy. You've got to be more careful. If you get hurt then Dad and Mom can't just take us in the Ranger to a hospital."

"That's true," he soberly nodded, "There's no hospitals for 125 million years in the future. If I got bit by a cottonmouth I might not be able to wait that long."

"We don't know for sure what's happened to us," Suzy snapped at him again, yanking him even harder along behind her. "Maybe we went back in time but maybe not. We've just got to keep going and keep alive."

"And to stay alive—I need to drink some *water!*" he yelled as loudly as he could, hurting Suzy's ears.

"Jesus, Billy! Do you want everything around to hear us?"

She looked around fearfully least his loud shout had drawn the attention of the giant dinosaurs grazing in the distance.

Fortunately the long-necked herbivores didn't seem to notice.

But it was hard to see what was going on around them. Even though it was midday, thick mists still swirled about. It was the thick humidity and jungle. It was stupefying, sapping her strength.

They'd been stomping through the muddy, greenish water now for several hours.

"Once we find a new safe place where we can make a fire then we can find something concave to boil this swamp water inside," Suzy insisted. "Then we can drink the water, but not before!"

Yes, she was also getting dangerously dehydrated. Lack of clean water was very serious. The temperature must be in the nineties or higher. Sweat drenched her from her head down to her toes. Her mouth was parched and her lips were cracked. She was dizzy—from drinking no water as well as eating no food—and knew her little brother had to be in as bad if not worse shape.

They had to find food and potable water soon or they'd be too weak to continue.

And at the excruciatingly slow pace they were going it would take all day to make it to that thin column of black smoke they'd spotted from Bromide Hill that morning.

"Look, Suzy!" Billy cried-out, pointing ahead. "There's a raised-up island up ahead. Can we stop there and make a fire? Please?"

Suzy squinted through the foggy atmosphere, indeed seeing what looked like a low hill rising up out of the mists.

"Yep...let's try to get there," Suzy agreed, slogging onward.

All around them Suzy heard strange "hissing" and *squawking*. From the top of Bromide Hill getting to that "smoke signal" hadn't looked that hard. But down in the swamp itself, it seemed more and more impossible.

Both she and Billy badly needed a break.

It seemed like an eternity, but they managed to get to the low hill, dragging their mud-encrusted shoes up out of the swamp onto somewhat-solid ground.

They both collapsed down, exhausted.

"I'm...thirsty...and hungry!" Billy groaned, lying on the ground beside Suzy.

"Well..." Suzy gasped, pushing herself up to a sitting position. "Then we need—some fruit, maybe. You go find us some nuts or berries. But don't eat anything until we test it together! There's a bunch of lower trees here, all jammed together. See if you can find something there for us to try to eat."

"And what'll you be doin'?" Billy asked, slowly getting back up to his feet.

He looked terrible.

He was covered with mud. His short black hair was plastered to his head. He was breathing heavily. His lips were cracked. And his face and arms were covered with bug bites.

It seemed that mosquitoes were indeed already present 125 million years in the past. Suzy had been swatting them away herself now for hours. They were awful. And they were huge, many of them up to an *inch* across! They were draining them dry of their blood. And that wasn't even mentioning the ever-present *cloud of flies* that seemed to travel with Suzy and Billy once that got down into the swamp. And these were *biting* flies that just didn't land on you, but *nibbled* at any exposed flesh.

Misery!

The Park wasn't anything like this—at least it *shouldn't* be anything like this. In all the years Suzy rode her mountain bike on the trails in the park, she'd never been bitten by flies or mosquitoes. And the land should be mostly dry, mainly watered by occasional rain in the springtime plus underground springs, not an unending swamp!

But, as if to add insult to injury, it was now starting to rain.

It was a miserable, slow drizzle. But it was pure water from the sky! Both Suzy and Billy gratefully opened their mouths to the heavens, letting their swollen tongues find a little relief.

Then she turned back to the task at hand.

"I'm going to try and find some dry twigs or leaves so we can get a fire going before we get totally soaked," Suzy emphatically replied. "And see if you can find a rounded rock or hollowed-out tree trunk we can use like a bowl to put a bunch of water into for boiling then carrying with us. Us mammals need a lot of water, not just a few sprinkles," she added.

"Ok, Suzy," he said as he pushed his way into a thick stand of shrubs, "Mammals are *us!*"

"And don't go too far away from me," she ordered him as he vanished into the mists and thick brush. "Stay within shouting distance. We don't want to get lost from each other!"

"Ok, ok!" he petulantly called back. "I'm not stupid, Suzy. I know we gotta stick together. Us Mammals are *herd* animals. Yep!"

"Good!" she called back. "Just look around. Don't go wandering off!"

"I *said* I'm not gonna get lost!" he angrily yelled back. "I'm not a little kid!"

Suzy mentally groaned to herself. He was only six years old.

Oh yes you are!—Suzy quietly thought to herself as she rummaged around in the immediate brush.

She wished they still had their bikes. They conscientiously carried a well-prepared "survival kit" with safety matches and water purification columns and plastic "tents" and other neat stuff in their small "saddle bags" located on the back of both of their bikes. Their Mom and Dad insisted that they always have it with it in case of an emergency.

Fat lot of good that did them when their bikes were gone!

But Suzy knew enough basic survival techniques to make a fire on her own by rubbing two sticks together over dry tender. The trouble with that scenario, however, was that she'd never had to do it before—plus there wasn't anything dry! The mists and rains in this miserable swamp were keeping everything good and moist, if not dripping wet.

"Auugghhh!" Suzy groaned, ripping open with her fingernails a fallen, rotting log.

Yes! Inside were dry flakes of rotted wood. In fact, if she could find the right sticks, she could try to start a fire right there in the heart of the log. She wouldn't even have to go hunting for dry wood. There was plenty right in front of her. Ok. So maybe she *could* make a fire and...

"*Suzy!*" she heard a yell from out in the thick woods.

She jumped to her feet from where she'd been kneeling and ran into the woods toward the sound.

"Billy! I'm here! Where are you?" she called-out, trying to push her way through the thick brush.

"Over here, Suzy! I've got something!"

Thorns and sharp leaves tore at her arms and legs.

"What is it?" she urgently yelled as she came up behind Billy, who was crouched down and bent forward.

He was grinning widely.

"Look!" he triumphantly proclaimed, lifting a white object up in the air.

It was a large egg. It was oblong and leathery-looking. And it was a full six inches in length.

"Breakfast!" he laughed. "There's a whole nest of these! All we got to do is roast them on a fire. We can have *omelets!* Yummy!"

"Uh...Billy?" she gulped.

"What? I found us some real good food to...*uh oh!*" he gulped, his smile fading as he slowly lowered the egg back into the nest in front of him.

Above them—poking out of the misty jungle—was a FOUR-FOOT-LONG DINOSAUR HEAD sporting *six-inch-long* teeth!

It must be the mother.

It seemed confused, cocking its head to the side—as if not knowing what to think of these new little creatures picking up its precious eggs.

"Slowly...back off Billy," she gulped again, putting a hand on his trembling, small shoulder.

"*Wraccccckkkkkkkkkkkkkk!*"—the mother suddenly bellowed at them, apparently concluding that they were a threat.

"*Run*, Billy, *run!*" Suzy yelled, snatching him away and dashing with him in tow through the thick underbrush and clinging vines.

"It's gaining on us!" Billy shouted from behind as Suzy heard more bellowing and crashing sounds as the mammoth beast chased them.

Suddenly a flat, opened meadow appeared there before her in the mists. Either the open space would let them run fast to get away or let the mother dinosaur behind them catch up!

Whatever, it was their only way forward.

Suzy tripped on a rock, sprawling, rolling over to see...

—a *whole pack* of those T-rex-like beasts converging on her and Billy!

As if in slow motion, Suzy admired their stomping approach: the adults at least 40 feet long, standing on two powerful back legs, their bodies supporting huge heads with carnivorously pointed teeth, each with a low "sail"-like structure running all the way down their necks, backs, and tails.

Billy *grabbed* her by her pigtails and *yanked* her forward!

"Ouch!" she yelled as she snapped out of her reverie and leapt up, dashing with Billy across the remaining opened area.

"*Wraannkkkkkkkk!*" a furious *screech* sounded right behind Suzy, deafening her...

—as they both *dived* behind some big thick tree trunks, and the pack of dinosaurs skidded to a stop at the barrier of tightly packed trees. The ferocious beasts continued to *roar* and *screech* at the escaped threats, frustrated!

"Those guys are...*Acrocanthosaurus* dinosaurs," Billy breathlessly panted in her ear as they both gasped for air from their frantic dash, peeking out around their protecting tree trunk. "They're, like, top predators...just like T-rex but about forty million years earlier. Their fossils were first found here in Oklahoma. Yep! And *there* they are... Those ridges on their backs maybe are like heater or cooler fans—for keeping them warm or cool? Gee, nobody knew. But now we can maybe figure it all out! We jist gotta look and see if they tend to put their sails into the sun or the shade and..."

Suzy was totally exhausted. Her body hurt all over. She felt slime and dirt jammed into every crevice of her body. They'd just barely escaped being eaten alive by a pack of rampaging top-predator dinosaurs. And her brother was lecturing her on the mechanics of the sails on their backs!

"Shut up, Billy," she growled at him, forcing her own body to stand up and wobble onward into the thick growth. She pulled him protesting behind her as she squirmed forward through the tight-packed large tree trunks.

"But Suzy...?"

"I like dinosaurs as much as you do," she said, grabbing him around his shoulders and pulling him close to her, "but *not* when they're out there trying to find a way to get to us and *eat* us!"

"Uh...right," he agreed, grabbing her around her waist and clinging closely.

She just had to keep on going. They couldn't stop. This place was way too dangerous!

Whatever it took, they had to make it to that smoke column before the daylight faded.

She was pretty sure that out in the swamp, unprotected, they wouldn't make it through another night.

Chapter 4

OFF THE RESERVATION

Conservatives don't stray far

While liberals run with the wind

Surely there's room for both

If moderates are thrown in

Sprinkled with a few fanatics

Thickened with ultra-conservatives

Society is a delicious mix

Don't you think?

The Minstrel's Lark, 4:7-10

They turned off the paved two-lane road on the other side of the Rock Creek camping area. The heavily loaded Ranger "crunched" its way along a gravelly single-lane road. The ORV wound its way leisurely deeper into the wilderness area of the Park.

Sally was on her cellphone, trying to get a signal. Dave saw her frown, while giving the slender phone a shake.

"What's wrong?" he asked.

That was really a dumb question, he chided himself. There's a lot wrong! That ancient artifact, the Obelisk, had somehow stolen his kids! But he knew he had to keep Sally focused on the immediate situation or she'd go wild.

"I'm getting some weird noise on my cellphone," she grimaced. "I keep trying to phone the kids, but it's like the local cellular tower is out or something. I can't even connect with our home landline."

"It might be electromagnetic interference. Who knows what sort of pulse the Obelisk put out when it phased away from here?"

"But that should have been a momentary pulse."

"Unless something was left behind?" he grimly suggested.

"Could be...but I need a signal!"

"I know you do, Sally. Keep at it," he kindly supported her effort as he slowly steered the Ranger along.

"I keep hoping that they rematerialized somewhere within range of a cell tower. The world's practically covered with them now, even in previously inaccessible regions. Or maybe..."

"We know where the bikes are," Dave calmly reassured her, cutting off her increasingly desperate musings. "Once we get there we can hopefully pick up their trail. They may have wound up somewhere totally out of reach of our regular cellphones, whether on this Earth or not. Perhaps you should just stop trying to phone them, Sally. Concentrate on what we can do immediately. Could you use the laptop to make sure our 'upgrades' to the Rover are ready for us to use if necessary?"

Reluctantly she put the slim cellphone away.

"Yes, you're right Dave. But we'll be out at the site in a couple minutes. I can go through the checklists there. Do you think we brought everything we'll need?" Sally started verbally worrying again as she sat nervously beside Dave. He concentrated on steered the 4-wheeler ORV down the narrow gravel road. "I packed all the medical supplies we had in the house, but..."

"We've got everything except the kitchen sink," Dave smiled lovingly at her. "Don't worry, Sally. We'll find them."

"I don't know. I've a real bad feeling about all of this," she frowned, clutching nervously at her seatbelt. "It's like all our old enemies who we thought we escaped have suddenly reemerged! If that's so, we're royally screwed, Dave. What can we do against...?"

"Please stop, Sally," he broke in. "Pointless speculation won't get us anywhere. Besides, it may not be as bad as we think. This could all be just a coincidence, an accident that..."

"We'll know soon enough," Suzy agreed, abruptly cutting *him* off. But she did seem glad for his comforting, logical-minded presence. She put a hand on his shoulder, squeezing before releasing her hold. Yep, he needed to keep it together. She was the "weak link" here—the one who couldn't stand a boring, ordinary routine. She was an explosion waiting to happen! *He* was the strong one who could keep it all together. Yep...

—that is if one forgot his crying spell back in the garage. But that just made him human, a concerned parent, right?

Suddenly he didn't feel like the "strong" one at all.

At the end of the winding gravel road was an old sign designating hiking paths that people could take. Actually, the paths weren't defined trails but just mushed-down areas for hiking and biking. That was where they would edge their ORV into the woods to get to where they'd discovered the abandoned bikes. But instead of doing so, Dave suddenly turned right, continuing to follow the graveled road.

"Dave, what are you...?"

"Just a hunch," he replied, not sure what was happening but feeling a strong urge to take the brief detour.

Dave saw the expanded, dead-end parking area ahead. He swung in close to the woods and parked the Ranger. Unhooking his seatbelt, he started to get out.

"Why are we stopping?" Sally said, her big green eyes narrowing. "Did you see something?"

The hair on the back of his neck was starting to stand up. He felt a chill creeping into his bones.

"Yes, I did," he answered. He calmly reached into the backseat and pulled out his deer hunting rifle. It was a Remington Sendero SFII, commonly known as a *Beanfield Sniper*. It was heavy, weighing in at over ten pounds with its large scope. It was pitch-black, with silver metal components. Dave used it mainly for long, accurate shots. But its high-velocity shells would take out any target, close or far.

Sally slipped out of her door, grabbing her Marlin 336C, *Timber Classic* rifle from the back seat. Versus Dave's bolt-action, her gun had a lever pump. For a slight woman it was easier to handle while still packing a large punch. Also—with its large magazine capacity—it held more rounds than a bolt action gun could even dream of having. It was all polished brown wood and grey metal. Since Sally was a dead shot—far better than Dave—she didn't even have a scope on it. It was a very deadly weapon at short range.

So they were ready for anything. At least, Dave hoped that was true.

"What did you see, Dave?" she whispered as they both stared off into the surrounding woods, trying to catch a glimpse of anything moving.

"Well...I actually didn't *see* anything," he quietly replied, scanning the deserted woods quickly. "But I definitely *felt* something...but not like when our friendly dinosaur Breep was around—more like a *black cloud* suddenly moving in front of the sun, making everything *icy*."

She nodded.

"Yes, I felt it too," she answered, standing alertly there beside him.

Except for their Ranger the wide parking area was totally empty. Since it was early spring, vacationing campers were absent. And this section of the Park was at the extreme edge of the Rock Creek Camping Area anyway, where few tourists went. The morning sun was warm and welcoming. A gentle breeze stirred the woods around them. It was actually a pleasant day to be out in the Park. But to Dave the dark woods looked ominous.

"Maybe we shouldn't be wasting our time stopping here?" Sally mused. "We're still a distance off from where we found the bikes. Like you said we've got to get our equipment there and set up?"

Dave now shook his head in firm denial. He deeply sighed, biting his lip.

He might as well admit what they were both thinking.

"This wasn't some cosmic accident," he replied, carefully starting down a tiny path into the woods, barely wide enough for one person to venture along. "After all these years of nothing happening, for Breep and the Obelisk both to suddenly appear—and our kids to simultaneously disappear—it's clear something's after us, Sally. I think our worst fears are realized. But if we can take the initiative—track the threat down and stop it—then maybe we can nip this whole thing in the bud and get back to our regular, ordinary life?"

"I hope you're right," she replied, falling into step behind him, "not about the threat, but our stopping it in its tracks."

Silently, they slid down a short, steep slope. They avoided slippery muddy stretches by stepping on large exposed tree roots.

Then they were at the edge of a shallow expanded area of Rock Creek, a little lagoon. It was totally secluded. The clear water flowed gently past. It wasn't much more than an isolated bubbling glade surrounded by green waving grass, low bushes, and gently swaying trees. The sun was bright. Everything was very placid and pleasant in this little oasis of isolation. On a log out in the water a couple of flat brown turtles were serenely sunning themselves.

Everything seemed perfectly fine.

"Well, maybe I was wrong," Dave began, starting to turn back...

—when Sally gasped and jerked her rifle up...

—Dave spinning around to face...

"You folks lost?"

Dave staggered back a step, splashing into the low water. Luckily he had boots on and regained his purchase quickly, hopping back up onto the bank.

Smiling benignly from behind them was a medium-sized, uniformed man. He wore dark green pants, a blue short-sleeved shirt, a flat straw hat, and carried a backpack slung over his shoulder. Out of the backpack stuck a walkie-talkie's long antennae. Holstered at his waist was a standard handgun. And on his shirt was the gold badge of an official *National Park Service Ranger*.

Sally lowered her rifle and with one slender arm reached over to give the man a quick hug.

"Hi, Losa!" Sally grinned at him.

Dave was relieved to see a friendly face instead of some lurking past enemy. It was *Losa Yanash*, a long-time Park Ranger and friend of theirs. He was a full-blood Chickasaw Native-American who had worked as a Ranger in the Chickasaw National Recreation Area, the "Park," for many years. In addition, he and his family attended the same local church as did Dave and Sally.

"Hi Sally. Hi Dave. Saw your ORV parked here. Thought I'd walk down and say 'hey'! I'm missing church 'cause I'm on duty today. How about you folks?"

"You about scared the pants off of me!" Dave grinned, avoiding the pointed question for the moment. "You sure do move quietly, Mr. Yanash."

Losa nodded in acknowledgment of his stalking skills.

His wide, sunburned face was friendly. The deep wrinkles at the corners of his eyes were crinkled up. His thick lips were parted slightly in a smile, revealing somewhat broken, uneven teeth. His longish black-grey hair hung proudly straight down to each side of his head. He was a bit overweight but not grossly so. He was the picture of a competent, friendly, huggable Park Ranger. But his piercing black eyes were still *questioning*.

"Well, I am an Indian who..."

"A 'black buffalo,' right?" Sally noted, stepping backward to slump down on a big tree stump, cradling her rifle in her lap. "You move real quiet for a lumbering bison."

"Ah, you've studied the Chickasaw language?"

"She's a student of everything, Losa," Dave interjected, still very much on-edge. His wife had never referred to Losa's Indian origins before. It betrayed her extreme agitation. Dave knew that she was on edge, violently so. It wouldn't take much to set her over the edge.

He held his rifle at-ready, though now pointed at the ground instead of the surrounding trees.

"Well, that's what my Momma named me," Losa replied. "Yes, hopefully I don't stomp around as much as our Park's little herd of bison, but they're a strong icon of times past. Just like me," he cheerfully concluded.

"So you had to work this Sunday morning?" Sally repeated, leaning against the bark of a tree trunk and wearily closing her eyes. Clearly, she was exhausted. Dave knew she'd not gotten even the quick two hours of rest she insisted that he have. She'd been packing their ORV all the time he'd slept. "Were you out patrolling here in the woods? Maybe you're what spooked us into checking out the glade."

"Spooked you?"

"Suzy and Billy are missing, Losa," Dave hurriedly explained, still peering about the seemingly placid, sunlit brook and glade. He'd tell the friendly Park Ranger the truth, just not all of it. "They didn't come home from their bike ride in the Park last evening. We went out searching for them and finally found their bikes, abandoned, about a mile from here out in the wilderness. We were taking our ORV out there to do a more thorough search when we thought we saw someone out here in the woods, perhaps stalking us. If the kids have been kidnapped by some perverts or criminals—you know we get some weird types out here sometimes along with the overwhelmingly number of decent general-public people—then…"

His words choked off. He couldn't continue. The thought of what might be happening to Suzy and Billy was again too much to bear…or even if they'd just escaped the Obelisk and were now wandering around off the beaten paths?

He was starting to panic. His mind ran rampant with all sorts of scenarios, terrible possibilities!

"Ah," Losa nodded, putting his right hand down on his holster and looking about quickly, his eyes narrowing. "I knew you guys know all the Park rules. So you having your ORV out here when off-road traffic is forbidden, plus carrying hunting rifles into a designated camping area, well…"

Clearly, Losa now realized the dire situation Dave and Sally were facing!

"Yes, Sir—no hunting in developed areas, or vehicles off the established roads. I know all of that. But this is truly an emergency, Losa…even more than you can imagine!"

"Then you should have immediately called 911, filed a police report. You know us Park personnel would be out searching for your kids with an all-hands-on-deck effort. Come on, my friend. What's *really* going on here, Dave?"

Dave looked down at Sally as she sat exhausted on the stump, now just staring blankly back at him.

In the still of the peaceful glade, Dave debated how much to tell the Park Ranger. Too much and—church friend or not—Yanash would arrest them for public intoxication! Too little, then trying to satisfy the remaining many questions would likewise paralyze their rescue effort.

"I…" Dave began…

—as behind him came two loud "*slaps*"!

"What the…" he began as he spun around, noting that the two dozing turtles were no longer sunning on their log, having *dove* into the water…

—as out of the shallow creek a BLACK, MANY-ARMED APPARITION arose!

Dave stood frozen in place, gaping dumbly at the arising apparition, the stuff of nightmares.

It flickered in-and-out of sharp focus, as if it were *phasing* from regular space into something else...and across its slickly black surfaces were scattered many crisply delineated *eyes!* And they weren't normal eyes. Instead, they were each composed of red-glowing, multiple spots.

And the spider-like other-worldly thing *kept* on rising to an impossible dozen feet high, *looming* above them.

And, as if in slow motion, Dave saw Losa snap-open the holster at his belt...

—as Dave felt his attention being sucked into those hypnotically glowing red spots...his own arm holding the rifle drooping limply...

BLAM! BLAM! BLAM!

Sally's rifle jerked beside Dave, the *concussions* driving the giant Spider backward...

—as it *flailed-out* with a long black arm, a razor-sharp *talon* whizzing just past Dave's ear to nick Losa's arm and slice through his backpack, sending him spinning to the rocky ground.

—as yet another spider-arm whizzed past, *flinging* Sally's rifle off into the surrounding woods!

"*Kill* it, *kill* it!" Sally screamed at Dave, nursing her violently jarred arm...

—as he finally got his mind in gear, dropped to a knee, aimed his Beanfield straight at the largest agglomeration of eyespots, and pulled the trigger.

"BANG" his heavy sniper gun barked...

—as with an outraged "shriek" the giant Spider lurched backward again, with a neat white hole in its "front" while the corresponding back of its "head" around the "exit wound" was blown completely off! A green slime dripped down across its thrashing limbs as Dave took careful aim again.

His second shot split the "skull" completely in two.

The creature dropped with a huge "splash" into the creek and lay motionless.

One of the pond turtles stuck its head up above the still-churning water before paddling frantically away in fear!

"What the *hell* was that?" Losa gasped, lying on his back on hard rocks, squirming in pain. Nursing a bleeding arm he spasmodically grabbed at his split backpack lying next to him...

—and managed to grab-out his shattered walkie-talkie unit.

Sally, panting rapidly, reached down a hand to pull him back up to his feet.

"You ok?" she said.

"Not in the least!" Losa shakily replied, pushing away her supporting arm. "And again—what the bloody hell *was* that?" he shouted.

"It's an old enemy of mine," she gasped, staring out at a spreading pool of *bubbling green slime* that surrounded the poking-up, motionless black limbs. "I had no idea it could follow me here to Sulphur. But somehow it did."

Dave stepped gingerly into the creek, hesitantly approaching the shattered creature, his rifle still aimed at its head-region...

—when it suddenly jerked to each side, *splitting* into two separate entities, *each* of which wobbled away down the creek bed and out of sight around a bend!

"You...*didn't*...kill it?" Losa gasped, vainly trying to get his shattered walkie-talkie to function.

No luck. The radio unit was damaged beyond repair.

"Maybe we still can," Dave heard Sally resolutely state. She reached down to snag-out Losa's holstered handgun. "It's clearly been hurt bad. Let's try to finish it off. Follow me around the bend in the creek!"

"But...I-I've got to m-make a r-report," Losa moaned, pulling a cellphone from his shirt pocket. Nothing came from its speaker but a shrill static. "Damn thing's not working!"

"Mine's not working either, Losa," Sally gasped in reply. "We think it's from electromagnetic disturbances. But we've got more immediate concerns. There's no time for me to hunt for my rifle in the trees or for us to retreat. I've got to borrow your handgun. We've got to track down and finish that thing while it's vulnerable!"

Sally jumped into the flowing water up to her knees and splashed down the middle of the creek in the direction that the Spider's two halves had just escaped.

Dave followed close behind her, keeping his sniper rifle poised to fire.

Behind them both, Dave could hear Losa floundering, struggling to keep up.

And splashing around the bend, right behind Sally, Dave saw— sticking perversely ten feet up out of the creek bed—embedded deeply down into the mud...a giant *glowing-red pillar!*

"Oh, my God," Dave gasped, grabbing Sally by her arm and pulling her back.

"What? But...?" she complained.

Floating all around the garishly glowing red object were dead fish and bloated, motionless turtles. And the sides of the Obelisk weren't straight lines. They looked like they'd been melted in place—the previously sharp edges smoothed-down by incredibly intense heat!

"But Suzy and Billy...?"

"They weren't ever in it!" Dave knew without a doubt. "This isn't the Obelisk that took them away! This is a *different* Obelisk—or from another timeline. It's *melted*, Sally, *look* at it! What do you think did that? What could nearly destroy the seemingly indestructible Obelisk?"

"Oh...yes...I understand," she gulped, nodding. "So I'm not the only thing that survived the breakup of the two Universes. But, that means..."

Her voice trailed off as she stared at it in awe and fear.

Dave now knew without a doubt that their checkered past was finally catching up to them. He pulled Sally backward as she reluctantly allowed him to do so...

—as Losa splashed up beside them to stand frozen in apparent shock at seeing the bizarrely glowing massive object embedded down into the creek bed. Then he cautiously continued forward.

Dave stuck his rifle in front of the Park Ranger's wide chest, gently nudging him backward.

"But I need to inspect..."

"It's radioactive, Losa. Don't go anywhere near it!"

"Radioactive?"

"Yes...also putting out powerful electromagnetic pulses. That explains why our cellphones aren't working. Forget about tracking that 'spider' monster. We've got to evacuate this area, fast!"

"*Damn* right!" the Park Ranger snapped, looking around fearfully at the surrounding woods. "That is, if we can get out of here alive! That *thing* is still out there! Hey, Sally—give me my damn gun back!"

Dave almost laughed. He'd never heard his church-going friend Losa swear before. The bizarre events were as jarring for him as for Dave and Sally.

She ignored his command, still holding the pistol in both hands, aimed into the looming, surrounding vegetation.

"You've got a patrol car here?" Dave asked, shaking his head to clear it. He knew he had to quickly sort through their immediate priorities.

"It's parked right next to your ORV. We can get out of here fast— make it back to headquarters and..."

"Mind if we take a short detour first?" Dave interjected. "I really can't risk getting stopped by another of you alert Park Rangers. Can you please run interference for us, Losa?"

"To check on your kids?"

"Yes."

"Well, we *should* go straight to the Park headquarters and get help...but under these circumstances, I'll cut you a break, Dave. I'll escort your ORV to wherever you found those bikes. It can't be more than a few minutes from here. But it's got to be fast! We're going to have to evacuate the entire Park and bring in the Feds! This is...this is...*monstrous!*"

Then, despite his defiant words, Losa suddenly crumpled. He almost slipped beneath the deeper water there in the middle of the creek.

Clearly he'd been hit harder by that talon or the resultant fall onto rocks than he'd let on.

Sally grabbed him with one arm around his ample waist, helping him stagger up out of the water.

She slipped his pistol back into its holster before scrambling out into the woods.

"Found my rifle!" she called back. "It's intact!"

"Great, let's get out of here," Dave answered as he saw her emerging from the thick brush.

Dave led them resolutely forward—even though his mind still felt paralyzed from grief and shock.

He'd had a decade of peaceful, ordinary family life in a comfortably small town. Now...what price would he have to pay for it? And what would the *world* have to pay for their sin of straying "off the reservation" to other Dimensions, Timelines, Universes, and Alternate Realities?

He had no doubt of the answer.

He'd brought Hell down to Earth.

Suzy was at the end of her rope. She was totally exhausted. She was hungrier than she'd ever been in her entire life. And the little rain water she'd managed to snag from the air in her mouth was long since sweated away.

And Billy was in even worse shape.

He could no longer walk on his own. She was carrying him in her arms, staggering along under his weight. His head drooped over. He was mumbling incoherently, his lips swollen and cracked.

But at least they'd escaped those nasty dinosaurs!

The supposedly extinct monsters couldn't get through that thick growth of very large trees. On the other side of the thicket it turned out was a vast stretch of grassland. It was like films she'd seen of the prairies before the Europeans came to America. It was a "tall grass prairie" where the grass grew as high as Suzy's chin! In spots it was even above her head.

But it wasn't just weeds. It was also flowers—yellow, purple, white, blue, and red! Every step she took she saw a different vista. And all sorts of animals scampered about her: ground birds, foxes, raccoons, squirrels, woodchucks, and weasels. Clearly, she was no longer back in the age of dinosaurs.

What the hell had happened? Had they switched in time again? Were they now in the age of the Native-Americans before the Europeans arrived?

She wished she could talk to Billy about this, but he swung between being delirious and unconscious. He was a smart kid for being a little runt. But now he was just dead weight.

She couldn't carry him much longer. She knew she was rapidly reaching the end of her endurance.

However, she could now see the beckoning smoke-column rising off in the distance. It still seemed incredibly far away. Before, however, she couldn't see it at all—and now it was noticeably nearer. But she knew she couldn't reach it before nightfall. They'd have to spend another night out in the open. It was a terrifying prospect.

She dropped to her knees, unable to go forward.

Billy rolled over onto his face, groaning.

"I...can't...carry...you...anymore," she raggedly gasped, collapsing down beside him. "We'll just have...to stay here."

"S-Suzy?" he weakly gasped, blearily opening his eyes.

"Yes...I'm here...Billy."

"T-thunder..."

"What?"

"I...hear...thunder."

She looked straight up through the high grass into the darkening but still clear sky. There were no clouds, none at all. She dearly wished that a storm was coming. At least then they'd get a little to drink by opening their mouths to the falling rain. But there was nothing. Billy was just imagining it raining.

"No rain or water, Billy," she mumbled around her swollen tongue. "Just try to rest...and then maybe..."

He jerked back and forth as if he was convulsing.

Alarmed, Suzy sat up and put a hand to his heaving chest.

"Thunder!" he barked out, levering himself over to his knees. "We...gotta...run away!"

Suzy sighed deeply. What a dope! They didn't have the energy to stand up, let alone run away from imagined lightning.

But then she heard something herself.

It was a deep, "thrumming" off in the distance that got *louder and louder* until it seemed like the earth around them was shaking!

Startled, she managed to jump to her wobbling feet and peek out over the top of the thick prairie grass.

She saw what looked like an approaching AVALANCHE OF FUR-
RY BROWN BOULDERS bouncing up and down! *Hundreds* of them
were bobbing up and down in the grass, maybe thousands—or even
millions!

What the hell is that?—she grimaced to herself, entranced!

Wait...those aren't boulders—they're the backs of buffalos!

It was a giant herd of bison! It was a *stampede*: headed straight
for her and Billy!

They were about to get trampled to death!

Suzy knew that the Park had a "herd" of bison composed of a couple dozen domesticated beasts. She liked to go to their enclosure and
watch them graze. And even though they looked like furry cows, she
was always impressed with their horns, big hoofs, and powerful bodies.

And whenever she got close to one of them—when one happened
to come over to the fence—she saw a *wild glare* in their eyes that
wasn't present in domesticated cattle. It was like they knew they were
being kept in a big cage and were just waiting their chance to break
free.

And now a *gazillion* of them were headed right for her!

"Get up, Billy! We've got to run!" she yelled at him, yanking him
to his feet and grabbing his hand.

"W-what...w-where to?" he gasped, confused.

She remembered that they'd passed some fallen logs about five
minutes ago.

"Back the way we came! Hurry!"

The first of the giant beasts came thundering past, narrowly missing them!

"Yikes!" Billy squealed in fear.

She took off with Billy in tow, scrambling and dashing as more
and more of the bison came thundering past! Big bulls towered over
Sally, churning up clouds of dust. They bellowed and howled in rage,
angry at whatever. And clumps of smaller females swept through,
causing Sally to dodge and weave to get out of their way. Even the
calves were huge, appearing and disappearing into the towering grass
like hurtling people-sized battering rams!

"Unnggghh!"

Sally was suddenly *lifted up into the air* by a sharp horn that snapped into the fabric of her blouse, slinging her forward! She fell heavily to the side of the stampeding animal, ignoring her now-torn pink blouse. She desperately peered through the heaving animal bodies and dust for Billy...*there* he was!

She leapt over to where he'd also fallen, grabbed him up in her arms, and with her last ounce of strength carried him over beneath the fallen-over trees they'd passed by earlier.

"Just keep your head down, Billy!"

"What?"

"Keep your head *down!*" she yelled in his ear as the main body of the giant herd descended around them and the air was filled with *dirt, hoofs, thundering, pounding,* and *hurtling bodies* leaping right over her head to clear the logs!

"You tore your shirt," Billy blandly observed. "Mom's going to be mad at you for..."

—and the tree trunk was suddenly *bashed to the side* and they were again fully exposed! She leapt to her feet but saw no escape. Everywhere around them was a *solid wall* of bellowing 1-ton bison!

"This is it, Billy," she moaned, closing her eyes as they both stood there waiting to get trampled to death...

—when something *grabbed* her and *hoisted* her up into the air above the stampeding herd.

Startled, she glimpsed through the solid wall of dirt and churning prairie grass Billy being snatched away also.

Closing her eyes tightly, she clung to whatever had saved her, trying desperately to not fall off the hot, sweaty, bouncing surface.

And then the noise and the dirt slowly abated.

She opened her eyes. She saw that she was laid-across the back of a running horse. And with a strong hand clutched tightly onto one of her pigtails was what looked like an Indian. He had on a headdress with lots of swaying feathers. He wore buckskins around his torso and hips. His legs were bare. His skin was reddish-brown. And as he guided his horse along with his knees and a hand in a whipping mane he was *yelling* out a chant!

The galloping, heaving horse slowed to a walk then stopped.

They were on a low hill, looking out across the vast prairie. The stampeding herd of bison was now retreating off into the distance. Suzy saw below her a camp of Tepees. Many ladies and kids down there were working frantically, likely preparing for butchering and cooking killed bison.

Yep, right in the middle of the encampment was a big bonfire. A cloud of thick black smoke roiled up into the blue sky.

It was certainly the source of the smoke column which they'd been trying to reach.

"Ah hah!" Suzy thought giddily to herself as she felt her body totally relax and slip into unconsciousness. "Gonna be a feast tonight."

Chapter 5

<u>WHY SPACESHIPS FLY</u>

You'd think it was a chemical reaction

Contained explosions providing thrust

Or maybe the limits of gravity

Or aerodynamic designs

Thwarting destructive reactions

But those, though correct, are wrong

Taken to the heart of the matter

It's simply rampant Imagination

Refusing to believe that

Humans have no wings

Propelling us into the sky...

The Minstrel's Lark, 5:27-31

Tommy was happier than he'd ever been in his entire life.

But something wasn't quite right.

His spaceship sat surrounded by waving purple tendrils. It seemed like the small shuttlecraft was adrift on a giant shag carpet, frozen on a sea of soft illusions. The little spaceship didn't look like much. It was a truck-sized vehicle with a clear canopy, one main door, and jury-rigged scorched panels covering its exterior. But Tommy knew the vehicle was inert and safe, maintained on a raised platform as an honored monument to his very own bravery.

It was humbling, but true. He *had* been very brave!

When he distally triggered the nuclear weapons stored in the giant Harvester—the resultant explosion cutting off the putrid, dying Universe from their own healthy Universe—he figured that was the end of everything. But safe in the sturdy little shuttlecraft, he and his cargo was thrown into *SUB-sub*-subspace...and ended up here!

53

—wherever "here" was?

At first he thought he was back on Mars. It certainly appeared to be the huge canyon slashed into the face of the red planet. *Valles Marineris* was a four-miles-deep, 2,500 miles-long canyon. But it was no longer a dead, red pit. No, it was the vibrant, intelligent habitat he'd discovered in the distant future before being transported to the struggling Harvester by the Obelisk. The huge canyon sported an earth-like atmosphere plus prolific plant-like growth that filled its floor from wall to wall.

In fact, the waving, chest-high tentacles were the visible part of a vast "syncytium" of a brain-like creature evolved in the distant past from robot androids like him. They'd saved him before and apparently had done so yet again. Somehow, SUB-*sub*-subspace was a conduit to anywhere. And as he and his shuttlecraft faded out of existence in normal space his fond memories of Mars plus the attraction of his devoted future "followers" apparently drew him back!

Wow.

And yet, as time passed, something increasingly felt *wrong*.

"It's a nice day today," he grinned, climbing up on the Monument and going through the open canopy into the pilot seat.

"IT IS ALWAYS A BEAUTIFUL DAY WHEN YOU ARE WITH US, PROPHET TOMMY," the sing-song, synchronized-reply reverberated off the high cliffs around him.

"How did your song go last night?" he politely asked.

The Syncytium was always composing new songs. Actually, they weren't just simple melodies. They were more like a series of full orchestras accompanying large choirs. The "notes" passed far above and below human hearing. And the emotions engendered were displayed as living art from billions of waving tendrils changing their colors. It was sort of like Tommy remembered American "Fourth of July" fireworks accompanied by rousing music—but amplified ten thousand fold.

"WE COMPLETED A NEW SECTION," the powerful collective voice answered. "WOULD YOU LIKE TO HEAR IT?"

"Sure."

And as Tommy closed his eyes, leaning back in the pilot chair of the inert spaceship, an amazing wall of vibrations caught him up in its grasp.

It was simultaneously thrilling, enraging, and disturbing. It brought synthetic tears to his artificial, android eyes.

When it was finished he just sat there, silent.

"DID YOU LIKE IT, PROPHET TOMMY?"

He sighed deeply, opening his eyes.

"It's very pretty."

Down in the ancient subterranean complex beneath the surface of Mars, he knew that many humans paused in their various pursuits as the stirring vibrations reached down even to them. For a few minutes they'd been—just like him—transfixed with awe at the composition.

First built by the Holy Mother Linda Powers of the *Church of Perpetual Health*, the ancient subterranean complex now housed over a million humans miraculously transported with Tommy from the dying Harvester. The Dinosapiens that he'd rescued from the Harvester were there as well. And, most beloved of all, present also were their two honored leaders: "Young" Sally and "Old" Sally. It was a society built on mutual respect, enlightened discovery, and joy—powered by Dark Energy generators. No one lacked for anything. All their aspirations were achievable.

Yes, it was the perfect society.

But still, Tommy had a nagging feeling that something was missing.

"ARE YOU STILL TROUBLED, PROPHET TOMMY?" the concerned, melodic voice of the Syncytium tried to gently soothe him. "SHOULD WE SING YOU ANOTHER SONG?"

"No...thanks... I just want to think about some stuff, is all."

"AS YOU WISH."

And that's the trouble, isn't it?—Tommy mused to himself. Outwardly he looked like a five-year-old, curly blond-haired, cute little boy. But inwardly he was a mature, deeply aware, intensely driven, deep philosopher. Here, his every wish was met. Be it for technological pursuit, intellectual development, or artistic achievement he could do *anything* he wanted.

But somehow it still wasn't enough.

I better go talk to Mommy, he decided. *She'll know what's going on. After all, she made me. And she's fully biological, with a brain driven by chaotic disruptions. She sees things I can't. She'll help me figure out what's going on.*

Happy now that he'd made a firm decision—had a clear plan of action—he climbed back down from the elevated monument and waded through the sea of tendrils back to the entrance to the subterranean complex. There, he descended along cheerfully bright tunnels to enter the nearest city. The underground town was populated by his Dinosapien friends. Entering into one of the amorphous-looking "caves" he walked up to Dennis.

Dennis was sitting on his haunches, poised before a 3D computer display screen. On it were different overlapped layers of complicated, multi-colored schematics. He was busily darting the sharp claws of his three-fingered hands in and out, changing lines and relationships.

Dennis was a nine-foot-tall, T-rex-looking intelligent dinosaur. He originated in an Earth Dimension where the asteroid that killed off the dinosaurs never impacted the planet. Thus the dinosaurs continued evolving, eventually developing intelligence. Dennis and his wife Joyce were dear friends of Tommy. They'd all been through a lot together. Also, they were close associates of their two revered leaders, the beloved Sally-humans.

"Hi, Dennis," Tommy cheerfully greeted his friend. "What are you doing?"

"Oh, I'm working on the life-support systems of a new Starship," he answered, swinging his long oblong head in Tommy's direction. "Our old Dinosapien crew is thinking of going exploring again. Once we materialize the necessary components with our Duplicator Unit, it won't be long until we'll have a whole new spaceship that's far better than our broken-down shuttlecraft. Since the colony here is now nicely up and running, we thought we could start exploring our neck of the Milky Way. You're of course welcome to come along with us, Tommy—that is, if the Syncytium can do without its wonderful 'Prophet'?"

Tommy frowned. Maybe this was the answer to his nagging dissatisfaction? There was little challenge here in the Colony. Sure, all his needs were met. And the Syncytium certainly seemed to value his presence. But other than being a "hero" for rescuing everyone from the dying, twin Universe—he wasn't really needed here. He had no defined duties or responsibilities. But to go out to the stars, do more exploring, and perhaps discover new living entities? Wow! That could really be fun!

But...he should run this by the two Sally-humans. They'd know best. After all, they were his collective Mommies!

"That sounds interesting," he replied, grinning up at the large Dinosapien. "I'll sure think about it. But right now I was looking for Young Sally. Do you know where she is? The last I heard she was overseeing new constructions with Original Dave down in New Sulphur. Could you maybe check for me and..."

Dennis had a strange expression on his normally implacable scaly face. The Dinosapien cocked his big head to the side. A large orange eye peered down quizzically at Tommy.

"Who?"

"Young Sally," Tommy replied. "But if she's busy somewhere, then Old Sally is fine also. I just wanted to ask them some questions that've been bothering me about..."

"Who?" Dennis repeated.

Tommy started to get irritated with his friend. Surely Dennis was just having fun with him. He sounded just like an owl back on Old Earth—"who, who, who!" Hah. But Tommy really didn't feel like joking. He'd been struggling with this nagging feeling of something missing for a while now. And, having finally crystalized the thought, he wanted to deal with it. When he got something into his little noggin, he got very compulsive about it—pursuing whatever it was to its logical conclusion.

"Dennis!" he snapped. "I just need to find either of the Sally-humans. I can ask the internal Net myself, of course, but that's boring. And the Net is also kind of dumb. But if you haven't seen either Sally for a while, that's no problem—I'll just ask someone else."

Dennis reached forward, shut off the 3D display, and turned to Tommy.

"Are you feeling ok, Tommy?"

"What? Sure. I feel perfectly fine!"

"Then why are you asking me about people I've never heard of before?"

"What? Dennis, everybody knows our wonderful Leaders—Young Sally and Old Sally. They're our long-time friends. Stop joking with me! It's not funny anymore!"

Dennis squinted down his large orange eyes, tilting his large head to the side.

"I'm going to go get Joyce, Tommy," he slowly replied. "Maybe you're having a breakdown of some sort. She's a lot better than me at dealing with mental problems. After all, I'm just a geologist. So wait right here and..."

"Central Net!" Tommy yelled out as loudly as his high, boyish voice could manage. "Where are either Young or Old Sally at this moment?"

Dennis hastily exited the room, "clomping" away on his large feet into an opened doorway.

"There are three thousand, two hundred, and fifty six females named 'Sally' in the Human Community," a monotonic "computer" voice answered from speakers set in the ceiling. "To which of these are you referring?"

"I'm referring to our two Mars Colony Leaders!"

"Please specify further details."

Tommy was growing very impatient with the clunky central computer. It should only take it a few seconds, at most, to locate the Community's revered two Leaders!

Trying to control his anger, Tommy took a deep breath before specifying his request. Clearly, something was wrong with the computer. But it'd only take a minute to get it back up to speed.

"As you know perfectly well, *Young Sally* originated from Dave's human Dimension. She saved George and Alice's Dinosapien civilization in their dinosaur Dimension, got killed when stopping the Demon by crashing the Harvester into Cheyenne Mountain, and got resurrected in the other Universe with Dennis to stop the Demon yet again. And *Old Sally* was also killed in the crash as she was the High Priestess fighting against the human Resistance down inside the Cheyenne Mountain Nuclear Bunker. And then she was resurrected also to help get the Harvester working in the Bad Universe. I saved both of them in the shuttlecraft along with the surviving Dinosapiens when the rotten Universe collapsed! Satisfied? That's their 'thumbnail' history. Then when we got sent back here to future-Mars by whatever Power that was looking over us, the two Sally humans became our Leaders and *still* are very much our Founders. So where are they? Do I need to go to New Sulphur to the courthouse? Are they holding an open session or having a Council meeting? I need to talk to one or both of them as soon as possible...please!" he politely concluded.

There was a long pause. That was quite strange to Tommy. Being a very sophisticated computer himself, he knew that the search or reboot—whatever—should only take a few milliseconds.

Then the answer came.

"There are no such humans in the colony that match your specifications," the unemotional, matter-of-fact voice calmly replied.

Tommy shook his head slowly in denial as he heard Dennis and Joyce "clomping" back into the room.

"Something's wrong with the Net," he petulantly complained. He went over to Joyce and with both his short arms grabbed onto one of her stout, scaly legs. He closed his eyes and laid his shaggy head onto her warm reptilian flank. "I need to talk to Sally and the Net doesn't remember her. I guess I better go to Computer Central and see what's wrong with it. Maybe I can..."

"Sally?" Joyce said, laying a tender paw down onto Tommy's trembling back. "Who's that, dear?"

Tommy stepped back, looked up at the genuinely puzzled expression on her reptilian face—then abruptly turned and ran out of the house.

"Tommy!" he heard Dennis' concerned shout behind him.

But he didn't turn back.

His unease was no longer just a vague feeling. His fear was very, *very* real! And it was chillingly specific.

His two Mothers were missing...as if they'd never existed!

He didn't know what was happening. But he sure as hell was going to find out!

Suzy woozily regained consciousness in a quiet, dark room. A warm, thick blanket covered her. It was drawn up to her neck. And a soft pillow was behind her neck.

She was home! All that terrible stuff about finding a living dinosaur out in the Park, falling into a spooky compartment, climbing out into a place where her town had vanished, struggling through a terrible swamp, going without drink or food, carrying her delirious brother in her arms, and then almost getting trampled to death in a buffalo stampede—it was all just a terrible nightmare.

Ah...so good to wake up in her own, comfy bed. But...she still felt very weak, exhausted, hungry and thirsty.

That stupid nightmare was hanging on!

She heard someone walking into her room and struggled to get her sticky eyelids to open.

It was hard to see. It was dark. Someone should flip the light switch on!

"M-Mom?" she managed to gasp through cracked lips.

"*Halito! Chin chukma?*"

"Uh...say what?"

Suzy managed to get her eyes open and blearily saw a kindly smiling, brown-faced lady with braided black hair who was bending over her bed.

"*Oka'...*" the lady said, lowering a small jug into Suzy's vision and putting it to her lips.

It was cool, clear water!

Suzy grabbed the jug and upended it, guzzling it. It was delicious. It was the best thing she'd ever drunk in her entire life. It swept over her dry, cracked lips, across her swollen tongue, and into her parched body. It was *so* good!

"T-thank you," Suzy gasped, handing it back.

Oh, rats...maybe she wasn't back home after all? And if she wasn't waking up in her comfy bed in Sulphur, Oklahoma—then where was she?

"*Impa' chibanna? Bala'?*" the woman now kindly asked, placing a wooden bowl filled with some sort of steaming food to Suzy's mouth. The lady made "eating" motions with her mouth while gesturing with her other hand in an inward-directed feeding motion.

Suzy weakly shoveled hot beans into her mouth with one of her hands. They tasted delicious. It was the best meal she'd ever eaten in her entire life! And it settled smoothly into her stomach, making everything spin lazily around her.

And right before she slipped back into an exhausted but peaceful slumber she heard "whooping" and "yelping" outside. Wow. It sounded like a *whole tribe of wild Indians* was out there...say *what?*

Sally was desperate to find her lost kids, especially now that she knew a *subspace Spider* from the rotten Universe had made it to Earth and was now prowling in the Park!

She and Dave were carefully driving over the bumpy terrain into the wilderness portion of the extensive Park. They avoided the stands of short trees, sticking to the "trail" areas. Of course the trails were just rough paths that horses or hikers could follow. Even mountain bikes would find them tough going.

And slowly following the ORV—bouncing at odd angles as it inched through the uneven off-road rough terrain—was the official, white Park Ranger vehicle. Losa had the red lights flashing on the signal bar which sat on the roof of the car. He'd sternly warned Dave that he'd only allow them to do a quick check of the place where they'd found the kids' bikes. That was all. If there was an identifiable immediate danger to the kids then they could proceed. Otherwise they'd immediately have to return, file an official report, and get a full-scale search going alongside an emergency Park evacuation.

The Ranger's walkie-talkie and their cellphones were still not working.

Clearly, Losa was in shock from the bizarre appearance of the radioactive Obelisk plus its monstrous stow away. Sally hoped their Park Ranger friend would stay reasonably cooperative until she and Dave could pinpoint the exit path forged by the other Obelisk.

Sally knew they couldn't tell Losa about *two* Obelisks. He'd think they were totally crazy talking about multiple alternate Dimensions and diverging timelines!

"There it is, Dave," Sally said, excitedly pointing ahead.

Sure enough, the lengthy, collapsed-in trench was still there. And lying peacefully inside—where Dave and Sally had carefully dropped them the night before—were the two small blue and red mountain bikes.

Dave sprang out and grabbed several small parabolic dish antennae out of the ORV's back compartment, running to position them on supporting tripods in a circle about the bikes. Then he ran back to grab long shielded cables to hard-wire the five dishes to the ORV and to each other. Meanwhile, Sally worked frantically at a connected laptop, powering up and synchronizing each of the dish antennae in turn.

"What are you doing?" Losa asked as he walked up to the ORV. He was holding his left arm with his right hand. Blood was dripping down the sleeve of his injured arm.

"Oh...I'm so sorry to keep you from getting medical attention, Losa...but..."

"Don't worry about me, Sally," he bravely ordered her. "I'll be ok for a bit. It's just a flesh wound. But tell me what you and Dave are doing. We can't stay here much longer. This is taking more time than we can possibly spare before..."

"—just a little bit longer, Losa, please? We'll have the answer we need in just a couple minutes. I promise!"

Sally was coming to the conclusion she'd have to tell him more for him to allow them to keep investigating. But she was unsure of how much to tell him. Losa had already seen the other-worldly hellish spider, plus the Obelisk. She wanted to be truthful with him, needing his help. But he was the authority here and could stop everything in its tracks.

"Tell him everything," Dave called out to her as he was struggling off to the side of the ORV, still aligning the array of small dishes. If the alignment was off by only a few millimeters, the interactive field wouldn't form. Sally knew she had to distract Losa, give Dave time to finish.

"We're setting up a *neutrino detection grid*," Sally flatly stated, herself fully engrossed in configuring a 3D graph on her laptop screen. She was confident she'd start receiving data the instant the system was aligned and functional. Meanwhile, engaging Losa in the details might give them the time they needed.

"Neutrinos? You mean like come out of the sun or nuclear reactors?"

"Yes, that's exactly right."

"I'm no scientist...but I've read that they hardly ever interact with normal matter—so you have to have a giant apparatus, preferably buried deep underground, in order to detect only a handful of them. How could you possibly detect neutrinos with anything you've got here in your ORV?"

Sally sighed, shaking her head in frustration.

She knew she couldn't tell Losa the real details of what she was doing. But she also knew that Yanash was a highly intelligent individual who was interested in technical subjects. He wouldn't be put off by superficialities. And he'd be much more likely to delay going off to sound the alarm over the alien artifacts crashed into the Park if Sally could manage to keep him fully engaged, for just a few more minutes.

Once Federal Agents swarmed the Park, Sally knew there'd be no hope of personally going after their kids. Suzy and Billy might then be irretrievable.

It was a prospect too awful for Sally to contemplate.

They *had* to find a path forward—and do so *now!*

"Yes, normally that's true, Losa," Sally continued. "In fact, over a trillion neutrinos are passing through our bodies every second. But instead of frying us, few if any react with the molecules of our bodies. You're correct."

"That's because they have very little mass and lack an electrical charge, right?"

"Well, Dave can explain it better than I," she answered, her fingers flying across the keyboard. "After all, he's the Ph.D. physicist. I'm just a mathematician. But in essence you're exactly right. Neutrinos are pervasive but very elusive tiny little beasts."

"So how can Dave and you detect them with just those few little dish antennae?"

Sally hesitated again, not wanting to admit anything more. Fortunately, Dave stepped in.

"Losa, it's another of my new inventions," he called over to the man. He was just finishing up precisely aligning laser beams from each of the antennae. A grid of red lines appeared, hanging in the air, visible because of the dust and dirt they'd kicked up arriving at the site. "It's highly experimental, but we think it'll work. And that's because these dishes are more than just receivers. They're also projecting a whole new type of radiation. See the blue glow?"

Losa squinted over at the five tinfoil-looking antennae dishes sitting atop their supporting tripods.

Now forming around the red grid lines was...

"Yes—I see a faint blue glow from each," Losa nodded, now fully engrossed in the experiment.

Sally was greatly relieved. At least this stage was working. Now that the dishes were aligned, they were projecting a faintly shimmering sphere which encompassed the area of the trench that contained the bikes.

"That's an aspect of something called 'Dark Energy'—for which Dave and I discovered a way to tap-into and control," Sally continued, further distracting Losa. "We have what we call a 'DE-generator' hidden inside the motor of this ORV. We also discovered that neutrinos will perturb a weak, oscillating Dark Energy field. So—long story short—we've got a way to visualize the density and vectors of neutrinos within a localized area. It's actually quite impressive...'Nobel Prize'-quality work, really," she weakly finished.

She'd said too much. But it definitely had intrigued the man.

"Yes, I should say so!" Losa nodded animatedly, his big flat hat flopping forward as he swayed weakly beside the ORV. "But...why? Assuming that your amazing breakthroughs actually work—*why* are you looking for neutrinos in our Park? And what's that got to do with your missing kids? And does that connect to the radioactive pillar and monster that we saw down in Rock Creek?"

Oh, he was much too smart and quick!

"Please give me just a minute here," Sally waved a dismissive hand at Losa, fully involved in setting the parameters on her laptop to the developing 3D graph.

Apparently satisfied with the pulsing blue sphere, Dave ran back to the ORV to stand beside Losa, frantically looking down at Sally's laptop viewscreen.

"Anything?" he asked.

Sally didn't answer him. Instead she just pointed. There on her screen a sudden spike of green dots appeared, which pointed across the 3D graph in the direction of the town! Plus the line became very bright before abruptly vanishing.

Sally knew what that meant.

"Oh, no," She groaned.

"What? What did you discover?" Losa asked.

"Look, my friend," Dave quietly said to the still-bleeding Park Ranger, putting a hand on his large shoulder. "We know where they went and we have to follow them. Just go back to the Park headquarters. Report whatever you want. Call out the military or FBI, I don't care. But Sally and I have to leave, right now!"

"Leave? Where? What are you saying?"

"There's no time to explain, Losa," Sally begged him. "Please, just trust us!"

"But..."

Dave pushed him gently away, back toward the patrol car. With a confused, pained expression, Losa retreated to the hood of his car, which he sagged back against, watching intensely.

Dave ran over and grabbed the antennae and cables into his arms, dumping them back into the rear carrying-compartment of the ORV. The faintly glowing blue sphere immediately collapsed. Then Dave hopped into the driver's seat beside Sally.

"I'm ramping up full DE-power," Sally grimly stated, focused intently on the viewscreen indicators on her laptop.

With Dave at the ORV's controls, Sally felt the ORV *leave the ground* and *float* up into the air. She waved sadly at Losa as he stood leaning back against his patrol car in shock, his mouth hanging wide open in astonishment!

Small squirts of compressed air from hidden jets caused the ORV to drift over and hang above the trench. Dave corrected the orientation until they were perfectly aligned with the vector on Sally's computer graph, ending up hanging in the air pointed at an upward slant back in the direction of the town.

He reached across his body with his left hand to grab tightly onto Sally's left wrist.

She was relieved to see her Turtle Tattoo lighting up.

And the ORV *vanished* into another *blue haze* as a loud "pop" of imploding air marked their departure!

"Oh, sweet Jesus—what happened?"

The King's ORV had levitated into the air and vanished!

But...Losa heard a muffled "groan."

He ran over to the trench and looked down.

There, lying painfully crumpled on top of the two child-sized mountain bikes he saw...*Dave!*

"No...no...*no, no, no!*" Dave dazedly shouted, jumping to his feet and looking about in total confusion.

Losa reached down his right hand to help Dave clamber up and out of the pit.

"Where did Sally and your ORV go?" Losa asked, bewildered.

"That's not the question!" Dave moaned, his face twisted up in agony. "That's not the question at all!"

"Then...what *is* the question?" Losa asked the bearded, suddenly deflated man.

"*Why* aren't I with her?" Dave King shouted at the top of his lungs, floundering around in a circle, staring up at the sky in total bewilderment.

Then he sank to the ground, sobbing loudly.

Gently, Losa helped him stand up. Then—supporting each other—they stumbled over the uneven ground back to the waiting patrol car.

Now reengaging in his official role, *Park Ranger Losa Yanash* did not envy his friend.

Things were going to get messy for Dave, *real* fast.

Chapter 6

<u>BEYOND POLITICS</u>

Societies are configured to fail
Conglomerations of competing interests
Each seeking their own advantage
With clashing and even opposing agendas
Trying to strike a dynamic balance
It's a miracle that any of them persist
A collective pursuit of security and safety
Cemented by the probability of the "next time"
When, yes, one's preferred Leader will prevail
And Power will devolve into the hands of the few
Who (obviously) know best for everyone else
Those (undeniably) stupid idiots or fools
And finally have the means to insist
That the "dunces" dance to their tune
Or suffer terrible consequences
Sticking it to them with a grin
While the dominated blur truth
Patiently sharpening their knives
Waiting to return the favor...
The Minstrel's Lark, 6:1-4

It was the Year of our Lord, 1638, and Galileo wryly observed that he was far happier previously, when he'd been a mere political refugee.

Now, he was a prized canary in a gilded cage.

As long as he kept within the bars and sang a pretty song, he was perfectly safe.

But sing out of tune or stray from his voluntary imprisonment and he risked dismemberment or worse. There were terrible, ravenous "cats" just waiting to pounce—and not just the regular societal villains.

"I don't think we can meet this request," Agent Anderson calmly informed him, standing ramrod straight in front of Galileo's cluttered desk.

Galileo grimaced, almost launching into a tirade in his native tongue, Italian. But he held back, forcing himself to speak slowly in his adopted language, English.

"This is something I have to do. I can't continue without doing this. Please find a way to comply," Galileo slowly responded, holding his anger in check.

"It isn't safe."

"What is?"

"Professor, it's not just unsafe—it's *beyond* reckless!"

"I'm willing to take the risk."

"But the danger isn't just to you individually, Sir. What you're suggesting might bring down everything we've achieved. We can't risk your moving out from beneath our protective umbrella, no matter how briefly," the Agent studiously observed. "You know that Sanako and her heretics are tracking your every move, looking for just one moment of weakness to destroy everything we've accomplished. And what you're proposing is the greatest excursion of them all!"

Galileo stood up from his wide chair, smoothing down his rumpled, long white over-shirt. It was a laborer's rough-woven working jacket that reached to his knees. He had no need, nor any liking, for the fancy dress that the English nobility preferred. Also, in his exalted position as the unofficial Esteemed Leader of the new Scientific Revolution, it helped to foster his mystique. Dressed in worker's garb he appeared as a regular person rather than some frumpy, aloof ruler.

Plus he loved being hands-on, getting grease and dirt on his clothes as he helped in the work of his scientific teams.

"I appreciate everything you've done for me and the advancement of Science," Galileo replied, trying to appear reasonable. "You've been remarkable in acquiring this prestigious sanctuary, within which you've protected both me and our expanding enterprise. But I have to know for certain that I'm on a proper course. As you've often told me, we're altering the *entire future* of humanity! That is not a burden I take lightly."

"Professor, it's not a simple matter of my approval or disapproval," Agent Anderson shrugged. He reached up to adjust the dark glasses set squarely on his big head. His powerful frame was contained in a stylish blue outfit, complete with baggy breeches, long waist coat, and thick leather belt across one shoulder. "You know that damned Commissioner witch is doing everything in her power to stop this grand venture. I've had to withdraw all of my forces scattered throughout time—to this one place—in order to thwart constant probes from her people. We're simply stretched too thin as it is in order to risk you..."

"You're very clever, Agent Anderson," Galileo defiantly broke in. "Please find a way to do it. If not, then I'll withdraw my cooperation from all your future plans."

"Those are *our* plans!"

"Once they were...not anymore," Galileo sighed. He turned his back on Anderson, limping over to the balcony to look down on the grand bustling hall. The noise of the many teams experimenting, building, and retesting comforted him. "I'm not a dunce, Agent Anderson. I lived my whole life in meek obedience to the State and the Church, even to their decree that I die because of my fact-driven crisis of conscience. Yes, you kindly freed me from them, which I greatly appreciate. But in their place you imposed your own iron Rule. And yes, I know it was necessary because of the terrible forces arrayed against us. I'm thankful that your protective dictates are benevolent. But now that you've helped me rise above traditional constraints, I must chart my own course."

"That's not wise, my friend."

"That, my 'friend' is the very nature of the Scientific Method which I helped 'invent'—wouldn't you say? Stagnation, no matter how immediately productive, is the prescription for ultimate failure. If you 'protect' me too closely then I will be smothered—and you will lose your 'golden goose'! Is that not so?"

"Well..."

"I am both the inspiration and accepted conduit of your remarkable future-stolen advances," Galileo pressed his case, sensing an advantage. "Shall I midwife more 'golden eggs' for you, or not? I think my request, under the circumstances, is actually remarkably reasonable. *Please* find a way to comply!"

Galileo turned to stare defiantly at his benevolent captor.

Anderson grinned back good-naturedly, sighing deeply. Then he stepped over to stand beside Galileo looking down at the crowded expanse below. The sounds and sight of hundreds of people feverishly engaged in academic and applied tasks were impressive.

"Nice speech, Professor," he nodded in defeat. "I'll see what I can do. But don't press me too far! There are lines that can't be crossed, even for me. Our paid politicians and tame guildsmen help keep the local populace in line, but our enemies from the future have no regard for those feeble constraints. If this is to be done, it must be very carefully planned-out and precisely executed."

"Of course!"

"Then I'll explore the options and tell you when I know more."

"Thank you, my friend."

Galileo watched the burly man walk to the grand staircase, descending down to the working floor. Anderson was actually swaggering. Clearly he was enjoying his role in utterly transforming 17th Century London. It was only five years since the beefy Time Traveler had rescued Galileo from the murderous Sanako. Yet in that time Anderson had orchestrated the takeover of London's governing body, transformed Guildhall into the center of their extensive scientific operation, and directed Galileo in releasing future inventions that were turning the world on its head!

Prototypes of their revolutionary steam engine were already breaking cultural and geographic barriers. The privileged classes were in an uproar at previously inviolable barriers being broken. Factories were springing up for mass manufacturing, shocking the centuries-old guild-structure. And there were rumors on the streets of personal vehicles not requiring animals or even steam for their movement. Some of Galileo's teams of scientists down on the work floor were now generating *artificial lightning*, a mysterious and powerful force called "electricity." Losing that on the world would only confirm the worst fears of the religious leaders, who already balked at the revolutionary inventions—calling them 'satanic'! And from Galileo's study of future inventions via the Custodian's projections, all that was just for starters.

"It's working," Galileo muttered to himself. "But to what end?"

Their main operating headquarters was housed in the great building called "Guildhall," in London—at the site of a still-standing ancient Roman amphitheater. It was a complex previously dedicated to the functions of London's local city government. It was also the seat of power of the ruling merchants, who along with the politicians set trading laws and regulations. But money speaks loudly as to who gets to be in charge. Agent Anderson had an apparently unlimited supply of gold and jewels, ostensibly from his "China trade" that none dared question. Quite a few government and guild leaders were now unexpectedly wealthy, standing happily to the side as Galileo and his people took over and radically changed Guildhall.

The surrounding stone structures erected around the amphitheater were cathedral-quality, stemming from the 12th Century. The main hall loomed upward, a huge area now occupied by large manufacturing arrays and teams of scientists. Here it was that Galileo's "genius visions" were turned into reality and tested. It was now a highly secure, protected facility. Their private security guards were professional and effective. And behind the scenes a dedicated team of Time Travelers diligently patrolled. This was the dynamic heart of Galileo and Anderson's entire operation, churning out world-altering "inventions."

But it wasn't just limited technical achievements. The whole "guild" system of society was threatened by an in-house educational program which they were exporting into the newly built factory network. Training was offered to anyone with needed aptitudes in desired emerging areas. So Guildhall was dramatically altered society as well as technology. Virtually overnight Guildhall had morphed from boring taxation and official-functions of the State into a hotbed of scientific discovery, training, and experimentation!

It was a mammoth endeavor, both to maintain and manage. Galileo had a large team of executives, but the weight of the enterprise fell upon him. It was both exhilarating and exhausting, much like being the head of a large university.

"*Hai mangiato, Padre?*"

Galileo paused in his musings, smiling at his beloved daughter, Virginia Galilei. It was comforting to hear her melodic Italian words: Have you eaten, Father?

"*Ah, dolce angelo ragazza, non e necessario preoccuparsi di me,*" he answered with a shrug: Ah, sweet angel girl, you need not worry about me.

She'd just emerged from her own office. She was a slight woman with a tender and solicitous manner. Instead of marrying and devoting herself to her own family, she chose to remain with her father as both expert assistant and caregiver. Shortly after escaping from Rome to London, Galileo with the help of Anderson's people managed to smuggle her out of Sunni-dominated mainland Europe. Though Shia London was still Muslim, it was far more "liberal" than the mainland. Here, Virginia, a woman, had much greater freedom to pursue her interests in medicine, science, and the creative arts.

Though he was bitter toward Anderson and his Time Keepers for a number of reasons—particularly their insistence that they always knew better than he—Galileo was grateful that they'd helped rescue his daughter. Indeed, upon her arrival in London she was ill with dysentery and on the verge of death. A course of small pills from Anderson miraculously cured her disease. Now, Virginia—aged 37—headed up their medical division at Guildhall. However, she still found time to keep a close watch on her 75-year-old father, even intervening if she thought he was being pressed too hard by his many duties.

She was dressed plainly but elegantly in a long, black dress. As always, she was prim and proper but very easy on Galileo's tired, old eyes.

"It is true I have not eaten recently," he grudgingly admitted, now switching to English as he stroked his long grey-white beard in contemplation. He didn't want to attract attention by speaking further in his primary tongue, Italian. "In fact, I don't recall when I last ate a meal...just a morsel of bread here or there. Do you have time to accompany me to the dining room? I've been meaning to talk to you on a particular matter. Perhaps we could have a working lunch?"

He had chosen his words carefully. Galileo suspected that Anderson and his crew had futuristic listening devices that reported to them every word he spoke in his office. But down in the crowded dining room at a random table, speaking in whispers, he might indeed have a private word with his one true confidant.

She smiled at him knowingly, nodding quickly. Galileo was always soothed by her presence. She had a long, angular face with full lips and a sharp nose. Her large, dark Italian eyes were always solemn, but with a twinkle of playfulness at their corners. And her well-maintained black hair—that she was now able to wear freely and fully revealed in the more liberal religious climate of London—was luxurious and playfully bouncy.

Though outwardly obedient to the prevailing rules and religious regulations, Galileo nonetheless resented anything irrational or arbitrary. To him the necessity back on the continental mainland for Virginia to wear a completely concealing burqa—whenever she was in public or outside the immediate household—was excessive. She was a wonderful, beautiful daughter in whom Galileo delighted, even though she was illegitimate. She, her sister, and brother had been born out of wedlock. To the disapproving religious establishment Virginia was always an embarrassment, particularly after the death of her protective mother. Virginia was deemed fit only to hide her entire face and body beneath the Muslim woman's traditional shroud. But to Galileo she was a shining jewel, to be proudly displayed!

But the burqa had been part of her salvation. She'd been delivered to London five years ago, her identity completely hidden beneath an all-concealing black burqa. Even her soulful eyes were masked behind a semi-transparent veil. Publically she'd been a nonentity, a mere household servant basking in Galileo's brilliance. But since her arrival in London she'd blossomed into a self-confident, aggressive female executive.

Yes, in her infrequent ventures out onto the streets of London proper she still often wore a burqa to avoid any hint of impropriety. But instead of the heavy, rough black garment that she'd escaped the continent entombed within, she now wore a fine silk brown burqa embroidered around the neck with beautiful plants and flowers. And within Guildhall she wore whatever she wanted, with no one disapproving in the slightest. Everyone was too busy changing the world to obsess on religious formalities.

Certainly she could have been—and still would make—a fine mate to any high-society male of her choosing. But she'd always shunned suitors, choosing instead to remain steadfastly loyal to Galileo, her father. For this he both loved and admired her.

He took hold of his walking cane to help steady his gait as they headed toward the dining room. It was a solid wooden cane whose top was a devilishly grinning, ivory-carved head of *Mephistopheles*. He never used it outside Guildhall least the public gossips use it to confirm that he was a covert servant of Satan! But he found it a fun joke within their sanctuary that they were indeed supported by "devilish" forces.

"I wish you'd get rid of that cane, Father," Virginia sighed. "It's not seemly."

"Nonsense!" Galileo laughed, leaning heavily on it. Damn hip! Anderson said it was "osteoarthritis" which in the future was "cured" by actually replacing the hip bone with a metal prosthesis. Galileo's Optimmune treatments had dampened the pain considerably, but the cane still helped him walk gracefully. Old age has its inevitable declines.

"You know that the Faustian books have been banned by the clerics and..."

"Bah!" he interrupted her. "This is a symbol of my disregard of their pious stupidities! Mephistopheles was not so much a fiendish demon as a warning for those who casually disregard and twist Allah's truths. My cane is a constant warning to those who encounter me that the Truth of Creation trumps religious superstitions!"

"Still, it is a provocative carving."

Of that she was correct. The heavy ivory knob's face was fearsome: with piercing black, slanted eyes plus long pointed nose, a twirling mustache, and protruding goatee. Plus, small horns protruded from the ivory skull. Galileo loved the looks he got from people who'd not met him before when he "thumped" up to them supported by that leering visage!

But he knew enough not to do so in front of clergy or heads of society.

"Let the already corrupted fear my cane!" he grinned widely, holding it up high.

"Please, Father—we've worked so hard to cultivate acceptance in London! You must be more careful, even inside our headquarters."

Galileo sighed deeply as they walked along.

"True, true...but you moderate me in a very nice way, daughter."

She steadied his other arm as they descended the grand staircase to the floor of the great hall. Though he felt fit, he appreciated the extra support. Tumbling down the several stories to the shop floor wouldn't do much good for his 75-year-old bones!

"And what of your work?" he asked her, changing the subject. They were walking through the busy stalls of the various departments toward the dining room. "Do you have yet another 'miracle' ready to announce to the British and from thence to the entire world?"

She laughed easily, threading her way between two looming drilling machines.

"Indeed we do, Father!" she smiled enthusiastically. "The Custodian has managed to teach us the ways of making 'anti-biotics,' the very thing that saved my life when I first arrived here in London. It is a near-magical substance made by nothing less than bread-mold! Can you imagine that, Father? The lowly bread-mold holds the cure for many of our most terrible diseases. It is astounding! And we are now learning how to 'culture' it in large vats. Soon we will purify the substance and save many of our fellow beings from horrible infections!"

Galileo reached out and took her warm hand in his as they left the common area and strolled into the large dining room. He well knew of the miracle medical treatments from the distant future. Agent Anderson had given him a full month's course of a pill called 'Optimmune.' At a time when he should have one foot firmly planted in the grave, it had granted him a new vigor, a *spring* to his steps!

The Custodian was their most carefully guarded secret, securely protected in a deep basement vault. Only top personnel were granted access to its marvels—and only then in the presence of Anderson or Galileo.

"That is wonderful to hear," he nodded as they headed to a table by a thick glass window looking out on the Roman amphitheater. As they sat down he leaned his Mephistopheles Cane against the wall, within easy reach. "We will give you credit for this new invention, Virginia. The people are starting to be suspicious of the wonders supposedly springing all from my one little mind. It's time that you got deserved acclaim for our joint achievements. Who knows, perhaps the inspiration of your own genius will finally prompt the Shiites here to ban that stupid burqa! You women have for too long been kept under the thumbs of us repressive, stupid males," he laughed.

She shyly ducked her head.

"That's very kind of you to say, Father," she softly replied. "But we must not proceed too fast in upending the traditions of our society. Reactionary forces can be very formidable. Their frustrations are already building. In my 'expeditions' out onto the street hidden inside the plain black burqa of my arrival, I keep my ear to the pulse of the city. Many are astounded and pleased by your marvelous inventions. Many others, however, fear what is happening. For them, any change no matter how meritorious is threatening. And when their privileges—particularly males dominating females—are threatened, they can quickly turn *savage* and..."

Her voice trailed off. Galileo nodded soberly. She was not just a strong support but a wise council. Many times in the past when he'd wanted to rage over some minor matter or take precipitous action, she'd counseled him onto a wiser course.

But Virginia was still conditioned by a lifetime of male hierarchical domination in political, religious, and societal affairs. However, she was adjusting rapidly to being the visible daughter of the most powerful scientist and public figure in the known world.

In the more-permissive London society, it afforded her a platform unparalleled by any other 17th Century female. Although there were many accomplished and even famous females in the present or near-past world—including monarchs such as Elizabeth I of England, who'd died thirty-five years previously—Virginia could effect change unlike any of the others.

His unexpected "resurrection" after supposedly being burned alive by the Roman Emperor catapulted him to a previously unheard of level of fame. Not only were his research-based proclamations on the movements of the heavenly bodies—as seen in the telescopes he invented—taken seriously, he was widely revered for his further inventions as well. And he was now cultivating Virginia to take his place. After all, he wasn't that young anymore. For the scientific revolution to continue, she had to take up his mantle!

"And, Father..." she quietly said to him, her eyes lighting up with new excitement.

"Yes, my little angel?"

"There's a medical treatment even more amazing within our grasp, something that will give women the power to take control of their own destinies!"

Well, that would be something—a *threat* to the manhood of half the human race. Galileo was sure that would "certainly" *not* get them into any further trouble with the elites of society! Oh my...

"That's marvelous, my dear," he calmly replied, withholding judgment. "And just what future invention is this?"

"It is another natural substance which if taken at the right dosage and correct timing will *prevent pregnancy* from occurring. The Custodian says it could be derived and concentrated from the urine of pregnant mares or even lowly soy beans!"

"And why would this be a good thing?"

"Father! You know that many woman are impregnated early and often, leading to a life of servitude and rapid dissipation! Few have the marked advantage you gave to me as a young maiden to choose to marry or not."

"Yes, but there are existing methods for not getting pregnant that..."

"—and not one of them is reliable or effective! Plus most rely on the cooperation of the male, who often has no interest in anything that restricts their momentary pleasure."

"Yes, that's sadly true."

"This substance would give power to women to determine their own destiny, not just be accessories to their husbands!"

Galileo pondered on this for a moment.

"Virginia, I support this idea for our society," he softly explained. "But be careful with whom you speak of this and how you proceed.

You are, of course, aware that the Clerics will find this subject highly offensive. They claim that only God should decide if intercourse results in children. And even though they might allow male restraint to prevent pregnancy, they'd never allow an 'ungodly' medication."

"Yes, that's also true, Father," she nodded. "And the clerics are *males*. They are guarding their own privileges. Plus, even the Prophet Muhammad—peace be upon him—taught that we should 'marry and procreate.' So it's church doctrine to have large families. Also, since the death rate is so high for young children from diseases, many see having as many babies as possible as a necessity. In that way, a few might survive to care for their parents in their old age. It is a terrible incentive!"

Galileo shrugged, not wanting to dampen her enthusiasm for the hypothetical future invention.

"So back to your present invention, if the new 'cultured' substance can actually cure many of those childhood diseases..."

"—then we must have a means of effective, reliable birth control, whether the church supports it or not!" she insisted.

"Just tread with caution, Virginia, in a matter that..."

He broke off as a waiter came up to them, politely holding out a menu.

"Ah...a 'three-bean salad' please," Galileo loudly requested, not looking at the menu, "And some fresh-baked bread, my good man!"

"I will have the apple cobbler," Virginia added, "with a liberal topping of creamed ice, if you have any today?"

"We've frozen a fresh batch this very morning," the man assured her.

"Good! I love it! Give me a heap of it!"

"And for your drink?"

"A bottle of your finest wine, please," she graciously replied. "I'm celebrating with my Father!"

"Of course—and the occasion?"

"Another great invention nearly ready to be announced! It will do much good in this sad, tired world."

"That is indeed a great occasion," the bald-headed waiter nodded. "I have a vintage 1625 Bourgogne. It's tart, but has a fine kick to it."

"Just purified water for me," Galileo shrugged.

Despite his liberal scientific views, he was in other ways reserved. He strictly adhered to the Muslim conservative's ban against alcohol, partly attributing that to his continued good health. The prohibition was largely ignored in his native Italy where wine making was a state enterprise. And in England no one even raised an eyebrow at the consumption of alcohol as long as it was not abused. And Virginia had always been careful to have just a little with her meals, never too much. So he had no wish for...

"No pie?" the waiter broke his train of thought.

"Sadly, I'm afraid not. Thank you."

Moderation was his actual "religion"—to which he strictly adhered. Though he loved large, fatty deserts he'd given them up except for a taste now and then after he turned sixty. Being weighed down by a fat gut just wasn't for him. He wanted to stay relatively fit for as long as possible into his old age.

"As you wish, Professor."

Galileo laughed gently as the waiter walked away. "*I* have to battle my stubborn belly while you, my little angel, stay skinny as a rail! I am pleased you can have as a treat which previously was only available to kings and monarchs. I could certainly eat a whole vat of that wonderful new iced cream. It is *too* delicious!"

"Well, I shall probably soon be as fat as a cow from the fine cuisine you provide for free to your workers here in Guildhall. But *you* should *also* have a treat...now and then, right?"

He smiled at her thoughtfulness.

"I suppose so, though I've learned many sobering things from the Custodian," Galileo sighed ruefully. "It seems that many of the 'old age' ailments are due to hardening and clogging up our many blood vessels by eating too much clinging fat and hardening meat. So I've chosen rather than struggle with 'cutting down'—to just be satisfied eating my vegetables, beans, and bread. It's much simpler that way."

"But not as delicious?"

"True, but still tasty and satisfying," he grinned. "Believe me, my dear daughter, that I am not impaired by this future style of eating. I much enjoy being healthy and hearty, with my faculties intact into my later years. If I'd given into my many lusts in the past decades I fear I would be dead by now from self-inflicted ailments, despite your kind ministrations."

"Then please enjoy your salad, Father," she nodded agreeably.

The returning waiter brought their food and drinks, which they both happily dived into. And for a while neither of them spoke as they polished off their dishes.

But then Galileo's expression grew serious. He glanced around furtively. He needed to be certain no one was close enough to hear their conversation.

Good. They were effectively isolated at their corner table.

"But your present achievement is not what I wanted to talk to you about," he said, pushing his emptied plate to the side and taking a delicate sip at his glass of water.

She wiped her lips, sighing deeply with unfeigned pleasure. Her hearty slice of steaming-hot apple pie plus heaped mound of white iced cream was completely gone.

"I am satiated—and ready to hear anything of concern to you, Father. Please proceed!"

"Well...maybe not to hear this," he said, leaning in closer and hiding his lips from any observers. "This...in some corners...is rank heresy, worse even than my proclaiming Earth to move while the Sun stands still. That was just dethroning a misguided doctrine by arrogant clerics tied to their staid traditions. But this new thing...it could bring down everything we're doing here. In fact, I fear it already has sown the seeds of our destruction."

Those were ominous words. But she took them well.

She just continued looking steadily at him from across the small table. She knew when to speak and when to be silent, serving as a sounding board for his musings. This was one of those times.

In a small voice he whispered to her: "You know that I am devout."

"Of course," she whispered back.

"But...I've been studying throughout the future generations as revealed to me by the Custodian—and not just of their marvelous inventions, but also their societies and governments."

"That sounds fascinating!"

"Well, in some ways yes—in other ways, horrifying. It seems that in the world from which the Custodian came, the Great Empires mostly banned or destroyed formal Religion, including Islam! They became a secularist civilization, where 'faith systems' were deemed too dangerous to be openly practiced."

"But Father, what we're doing now is intended to *change* that future! Won't the societies where the Custodian came from be changed as well? I've heard Anderson openly speak of *stopping* a secularist future, elevating God back into His proper primary position in society! Perhaps there's nothing to worry about?"

Galileo slowly nodded, putting a hand up to his forehead and leaning on his elbow, parsing his chaotic thoughts.

"Yes, but what I've seen is far worse than even Anderson realizes. As you say, dear Virginia, the Custodian also came from Anderson's future world. I fear even she doesn't realize the full implications of the changes we are setting in motion. Indeed, she *can't* know—it's beyond her comprehension! She is merely a smart device, not a true living being."

"But...what's going to happen? And how could you know better than she and Anderson? Are you...we...not even more limited in our understanding than they? After all, Agent Anderson claims to come from over four hundred years in the future!"

"Take a look," he said, reaching into his inner jacket pocket and pulling out two small rectangular frames.

Surreptitiously he slid them across to her.

She curiously took them, studying them.

"What am I supposed to see here, Father?"

"Well, they started out as future moving paintings—'video pictures'—brought from the future by the Time Traveler who directly saved my life, a 'Doctor King.' He was a fellow future scientist, who as you know took my place being burned alive in the metal cage in the Colosseum in Rome—poor fellow. One of the pictures showed his parents in the future in chains just before they were likewise savagely executed by his repressive government. The other showed him as a young teenager playing a game with a ball and wide mallet. But after his death and my continued existence, the pictures immediately changed. His parents were no longer in chains, but happily holding hands. And instead of playing a game, the young lad was looking through a *huge* telescope! That encouraged me to continue my journey here to England, to follow faithfully the directions of Anderson, and work diligently to make the future better—knowing my efforts would in the end succeed."

She frowned, staring at the two pictures.

"Yes, I see," she quietly replied, looking deeply puzzled. She took another long look at the pictures before sliding them back to him. He grabbed them, swiftly hiding them yet again in his inner coat pocket.

"And now...well," he sighed, shaking his head in confusion, spreading his fingers wide on the smooth wooden tabletop. "You saw yourself what they now reveal."

She bit her lower lip, looking very worried. She slowly took one of his trembling hands in her own.

"Have you shown them to Anderson?" she shakily spoke, her face mere inches from his own. "What does he say about them?"

"No, I haven't. I...don't completely trust him, Virginia. I get the feeling that he's not telling me everything he knows. Also, I'm beginning to doubt his motivations and objectives. What we are doing here is *so* monumental that..."

"But surely you *must* tell him!"

"Tell him what?"

"Tell him the truth, of course, Father!"

"Tell him—that my future pictures...are now...*empty?*"

Yes, it was true. There were no people in the frames. In both pictures, the humans previously depicted there—were *gone!* And in their place were only dreary views of a watery, fern-filled *swamp!*

"What does it mean?" she whispered. "Surely Allah would not allow..."

With her free hand she suddenly reached for the still half-full bottle of wine, abruptly upending it and draining what was left.

"That's my reaction, entirely," he laughed, withdrawing his hand from hers. He waved to attract the waiter.

"We'll have another bottle," he told the man.

Damn his conservative principles. Just this once, he needed to drive away the demons with his dear daughter. Now they both knew "the truth" of the future. There *was* none, at least according to his two future windows!

"Certainly, Professor," the waiter nodded pleasantly. "Please enjoy your triumph. All of us here in Guildhall celebrate your magnificent achievements!"

They waited for the waiter to leave.

"But...what can we do?" she asked, her voice trembling.

He grinned ruefully at her.

"Well, for the first time in many years I fear we must both get very drunk," he continued. "We must do so very convincingly, enough for me to retreat to my room for a full day—my 'aged body' not handling the unaccustomed celebratory alcohol well. That's even though I'm certain the 'Optimmune' treatment in my blood that Anderson insisted I take will handle the alcohol easily. To all appearances, though, I will be tucked away in my comfortable bed, sleeping off a binge, hidden beneath my blankets. But in reality, in the meanwhile..."

"What?"

"In the meantime I will *extend my awareness* of Divinity! We must directly address your astute objection, dear Virginia. It's time for me to take the next step."

"Father, you know what I think of this course of action. We've discussed it previously. You can't..."

"—not without your help! And now that you know what's really at stake, my little angel, how can you deny me?"

She paused as the waiter returned with the second bottle of vintage wine. She filled up both her glass and Galileo's with the sparkling red liquid. Then she looked him square in his eyes.

"Tell me what I must do."

Chapter 7

<u>GOING NATIVE</u>

We are all invaders

Occupying territory previously not ours

Then insisting we owned it for all time

When in the sight of the Universe

Even our planet is a usurper

Claiming Space that belongs to no one

We are primed to be casually swept away

Caught in the blast of an exploding sun

Obliterated in a Cosmic Moment

As yet other stars and worlds

Forming from the dust of our demise

Heedlessly rush to take our place...

Beware of prideful possession.

The Minstrel's Lark, 7:12-18

Suzy woke up weak but alert.

This time she remembered she wasn't in her room at home. She was in some sort of Indian village, plucked from being trampled in a buffalo stampede.

"H-hello?" she weakly ventured.

But no one answered.

So she pushed back the blanket, which looked furry. Indeed, it was some kind of an animal's hide. In fact, in the dim light it looked and felt like a tanned buffalo's hide.

"W-where are my c-clothes?" she gasped, feeling at her body. "D-did they all get ripped off like my pink blouse in the stampede?"

Her jacket, shirt, and pants were gone. Most importantly, her cellphone wasn't there either. Now she had no way to call for help even if a cell tower were close enough to receive her signal!

In place of her hiking clothes was a soft single-piece dress of some sort. It smelled like leather. She guessed it was made out of deer hide.

And on her feet were soft moccasins.

She slowly shuffled to the entrance flap of the small tepee and peeked outside.

The sun was going down. Long shadows set everything into sharp relief. But the camp was bustling. People were everywhere, working away. She saw heaps of fresh hides, piles of red meat, stacks of bones, and assorted other animal products she didn't want to identify.

And around the central bonfire hung strips of meat that were being carefully cooked. It looked like they were being turned into long-lasting jerky.

"Suzy! You're up! I thought you wuz gonna sleep all day! Wow! Isn't this amazing? We're in a real Indian village! I helped skin one of the buffalos they killed! It was awesome!"

Yes, his thin body was well-smeared with drying blood.

Suzy just stared at him.

Was this really her little brother? Wasn't he almost dead when she lugged his small but heavy body across the prairie? And now here he was dancing around...like a wild Indian! And what was he wearing? Just like her, he didn't have his normal clothes on anymore. Instead, he had practically nothing on—just a loincloth over his skimpy underwear. He was bare-chested, barefoot, red-skinned from sunburn, and jumping up and down in the dirt!

Minus long hanging braids he looked just like a stereotypic Indian child.

"Billy...what's g-going on?" she managed to croak out.

But he'd already hopped away to join a small group of kids that were running in circles around the blazing bonfire.

"*Chinchokma?*"

It was the same kindly lady who'd fed Suzy before. She was reaching out a friendly hand to steady Suzy and lead her over to a clump of other ladies.

"Uh...thanks for the food before. I'm kind of hungry again. But, I don't speak your language. Sorry. Does anyone here speak English?"

"Nope! Nobody does!" Billy laughed, running up and grabbing Suzy from behind around her waist. In his enthusiasm he almost knocked her off her feet. "But you can just talk with gestures and pictures and stuff. It's easy!"

Suzy whirled around, angrily pushing Billy off of her.

"Look, we've got to get back to Dad and Mom! Someone must know how to get out of here, right? Have you seen where they put our cellphones?"

His round face became more serious, though loud chants by the fire and "stomps" heralded a party of some sort starting up. Probably they were celebrating the successful hunt. Billy looked like he was about to dash away again to join them...

—when Suzy grabbed him by his skinny shoulders, *shaking* him!

"Billy! Focus! This isn't some 'Indian Adventure' pretend-type tour! These Native-Americans are *real!* We must be on a reservation somewhere. And I think they're talking *Chickasaw*, like we've heard out at the Chickasaw Cultural Center by the Park. But the Chickasaw tribe wasn't plains Indians! They were forced to come here by the government, from the Eastern woodlands. Back there they had real villages with huts, farms, and crops. They had settlements. They had laws and regulations. They never rode around like a bunch of wild Indians chasing buffalos! I *don't* think we went back in time, Billy. Something *else* is happening to us. We've got to find our cellphones and call for help!"

He pulled free from her, shrugging.

"I don't know about the stupid cellphones, Suzy. Mine was gone when I woke up. And besides, who cares?" he said as a wafting cloud of black smoke from the bonfire momentarily obscured him. "We've got food to eat. The people here are real friendly. And we're safe! We can figure out all that other stuff later on when..."

"But the dinosaurs...?"

"Yep, I drew pictures in the dirt of them," he nodded thoughtfully, pausing in his jubilations. "The other kids know all about them—some sort of evil spirits is all. They showed me in the dirt how the giant lizards are trapped behind a big wall and can't get to us. That must have been those thick groves of giant trees that we just barely crawled through. So we don't gotta worry about them anymore. Let's just have some fun! No more school! *Wahoo!* This is a *real* vacation, Suzy! Dad and Mom are gonna find us. We just gotta wait here for them. Simple!"

He dashed off, cheerfully joining the other playing kids.

The brown-faced lady smiled again down at Suzy, then led her gently over to a group of other ladies. They were busily trimming hanging shards of flesh and sinews off of the inner sides of many fresh buffalo hides. The lady handed Suzy an obsidian knife, gesturing for her to join in.

Hah! The kids and men were having a party. The women had all the real work. Nothing much changes.

"Ok," Suzy nodded, reluctantly taking the knife. "But it's just to earn my keep. Don't expect me to start sewing dresses or cooking. I don't do that stuff."

But the lady wasn't paying Suzy any attention, joining in happy chatter with the other ladies. Suzy couldn't understand their rapid-fire discussions, but some of the Indian words sounded familiar. She was confident that she'd pick up the language quickly.

But there was another mystery. Even if this was all completely real...why were the Indians here so nonchalant at Billy and Suzy's presence in their midst? It was if this had happened before to them. It was as if this were *commonplace*.

And that scared Suzy worse than anything she'd yet experienced.

Dave sat silently in his rocking chair, refusing to answer. He was on the screened enclosed porch of his house, looking out over West 12th Street.

The street in front of his house led directly to the Park's main entrance, only a few blocks away. Normally the two-lane road was sleepy, with only an occasional car passing by. Now it had a steady stream of heavy equipment being ferried into the Park. Armed soldiers patrolled the sidewalks.

Police were stationed inside the cyclone fence that surrounded Dave's property. He was locked down tight.

It was just a week since his wife had vanished in their Ranger ORV, somehow leaving him behind. Dave was under house arrest. The nearby Park was completely shut to public usage, now under strict quarantine. Military vehicles and troops were drawn up behind tight barricades, allowing only authorized traffic. Dave saw that only scientific, medical, and governmental teams were allowed to enter the Park. Indeed, the entire small town of Sulphur, Oklahoma was under martial law, with *tanks* sitting ominously at the three main intersections!

It was very bizarre.

"Look, Dr. King, you've got to help us out here," the FBI agent insisted, sitting opposite Dave in a wooden chair.

Curiously, it wasn't Agent Anderson, who Dave had half-expected to head up the investigation from his past adventures. At the start of his debriefing by the FBI—before he abruptly stopped talking to them—he'd casually asked them about Anderson. Apparently the FBI people here had never heard of him. Instead, facing him was a pert, young dark-skinned lady of African-American heritage. She was clad in a neat, blue, woman's pant suit. Her black hair was cut short in a no-nonsense crewman style. She'd introduced herself to Dave as *Chandra Ice*, "Special Agent for Scientific Anomalies." He'd never heard of such a branch of the government before, but considered it appropriate to the situation. It was something straight out of the old "X-Files" TV series.

If it wasn't so serious, he might burst out giggling hysterically.

Yep...giggling just like a little girl—an outburst of *sheer terror!*

Dave was "holding it together" with great difficulty.

"We can't let you stay in your house much longer," Agent Ice soberly continued. "If you don't cooperate with us, you'll be charged with domestic terrorism and taken away to a federal facility. And then you'll have no hope at all to participate in locating and potentially rescuing your wife and children. Do you want that to happen?"

Dave closed his eyes tightly, slowly shaking his head in silent denial. But he did not verbally reply. He couldn't. No matter what he told them, it would only make matters worse.

He was determined to just keep his mouth shut, regardless of the temptation to try and make things better. He'd tried to change things for the better in past timelines, numbers of times! His overt efforts to alter past-and-future "history" had always ended badly. That was why he and Sally "retired" to Sulphur to lead a quiet family life, swearing off any notion of other dimensions or alternate timelines. So he *couldn't* cooperate! But at the same time he was also frantically looking for any chance to escape. He had backup plans. Maybe if he could just get away from the Feds, he'd have a chance of somehow helping Sally and the kids.

"You'll eventually have to cooperate, you know," she continued to hammer home her point in a steely voice. "That's just the way it is, Dr. King. I know that you're a pillar of the community with a sterling background and all—but insisting on your legal right to silence only condemns you in both our and the public's eyes."

"I want a lawyer," Dave mumbled, looking away from the street and stubbornly staring down at the wood floor of the porch.

"And you'll have one, Professor...*after* we get the essential information revealing the extent of this imminent national security threat. What we found in your workroom and garage is enough to keep you *incommunicado* for as long as we wish. We're well within our legal rights, operating under Presidential directives regarding terrorism investigations. Our agents and scientists will figure it all out eventually. But it'd be quicker and easier if you'd just help us. Also, things could go smoother for you. And we'd also allow you a limited role in trying to locate your wife and kids. Isn't that worth 'spilling the beans' to us? We're *not* the enemy here!"

"You don't understand," Dave mumbled again. He shut his eyes, trying to make it all just go away.

"We understand enough to know that what's happening out in the Chickasaw National Recreation Area isn't just a scientific curiosity or bizarre missing person's case. This is the *worst kind of national security threat*, Dr. King. And like it or not, you are clearly intimately involved in what's taking place here! Ranger Yanash provided us with a complete report of what occurred and what you told him. So we have specific questions that you *will* address—preferably sooner than later!"

"You don't want to know," he grimly snickered, trying to find something funny to relieve the tension. "It'd give you nightmares."

"Oh, yes we do—nightmares or not! And you *are* going to tell us what we want to know," she insisted, leaning closer. "We've got experts here and on call to make sense of whatever you tell us. It doesn't matter if your information is of neutrino detection, new forms of energy, or levitating ORVs! And that's before you even start explaining the radioactive *Artifact* and its alien occupants! So make the best choice to..."

Dave tuned her out. Her mouth was moving but he refused to hear her words. She'd been repeating herself now for hours anyway, just the latest person brought in to try and "break" him.

They'd already searched every inch of his house, garage, and "laboratory" shed. They'd taken away everything of the slightest interest to them—including his scaly reptilian pets! They assured him they'd be taken care of elsewhere but didn't want exotic animals "interfering" with their search.

He had no say in the matter, just shrugging sadly.

So Dave continued slowly rocking in his antique wooden rocking chair. It had been his mother's favorite living room chair. When she passed away and Dave and Sally moved into her house, it was one of her pieces of furniture that he made sure to keep. It was soothing, even comforting.

But the gentle rocking couldn't push away the awful fear in his heart, the *real* questions he needed answered! Where was Sally? Where had the first Obelisk taken his kids? Was the second Obelisk really from the violent separation of the two Universes that Sally had previously survived? And was planet Earth doomed to be consumed by extra-dimensional, un-killable, proliferating, subspace giant "Spiders"?

It seemed, sadly, that such a terrible end to humanity was all too likely.

Dave clamped his jaw shut, refusing to meet her gaze.

"...and I've tried to be reasonable with you, Dr. King," Chandra sighed, concluding her speech as she rose to her feet. "But if you won't cooperate with me, then you'll have to deal my other colleagues. As you know, they're neither as gentle nor as well-mannered as I."

Yep, he knew her game. It was the old, time-honored "good cop" versus "bad cop" treatment.

They'd previously tried to intimidate him—threatening him, keeping him awake for long hours, repeatedly badgering him—trying to lower his resistance both physically and emotionally. So far they hadn't beaten or tortured him. But he knew that was the inevitable next step. Once he was taken from house arrest to a federal facility, they could do whatever they wanted to him in the name of "national security." At least here there were national reporters with their video crews standing on every corner. Anything too harsh would be known to the world quickly. Already, the fantastic events here were a worldwide fascination.

So they probably would move him away fairly soon. He'd endured the torture by a "black op" group in the past. It wasn't pleasant. But before, he had the luxury of outrage at their horrific treatment of him. Now, he knew they'd be fully justified in their actions. He *was* a massively dangerous national security threat! If he spilled what he knew—particularly the scientific details of how to construct viable DE-generators—it could mean the destruction of not just the United States of America, but all mankind! He knew too well from terrible, sad experience that DE-generation could attract the full attention of God, with terrible "Day of Judgment" wrath poured down upon the world.

But the local situation driving their determination to break his will was getting more and more dire.

Just that morning, on the local news channels, Dave heard shrill reports of events at a local ranch. It was located only ten miles away from the Park, tucked away in rolling hills to the south of Sulphur. The ranch had a large herd of brown Hereford cattle, several hundred strong, dispersed across several large pastures. Overnight the cattle had been reduced to bloody heaps of bones. Something had eaten them all. The owners of the ranch were bewildered and scared. The previous night they'd heard nothing amiss. Whatever did this to their animals killed them before the cattle even had a chance to bleat-out their fear.

But even worse was a parallel attack thirty miles in the opposite direction, which apparently occurred simultaneously. The "GW Exotic Animal Park" outside Wynnewood, Oklahoma housed a number of tigers, bears, and other exotic animals. They weren't dead...but they should be. Instead—at least according to the news reports—they were animal versions of vicious undead *zombies!* The Feds had the transformed animals tranquilized, but the head veterinarian feared they'd all have to be put down. Where before they'd been mostly tame animals living their lives in peaceful captivity, they were now ravenous, raging, uncontrollable beasts!

And, again, the drastic transformation happened overnight.

"Well, Dr. King, if you won't talk to us then there's someone here who we think you *will* feel comfortable opening up to," Chandra said as she opened the door leading out onto the front steps of the house. Accompanied by several more FBI agents, an elderly man shakily walked up the concrete steps to the porch.

"How...is this...even possible?" Dave gasped.

Victor Volodymyr stood there on the porch grinning down at the still-seated Dave. He was just as Dave remembered him: tall, thin, with a thick haze of white hair floating around his head—wearing a scholarly looking tan cardigan sweater. He was Dave's old dissertation professor from Yale University!

Dave jumped up from his rocking chair and hugged the elderly man, burying his head into the man's thin chest. Dave sobbed uncontrollably.

"There, there," the tall old man comforted him, patting Dave affectionately on his back. "We will get through this trouble, my boy. I am here to help you."

"He just arrived this morning," Chandra informed Dave. "He's joining our scientific team studying the Artifact. We felt that you might be more willing to assist us if he were present."

Dave got his violent sobbing under control, slowly drawing his head back from the tall professor's chest before wiping his eyes.

In a very small voice, barely audible to the accompanying FBI agents, he whispered: "But Victor...you're dying from extreme old age and pancreatic cancer! The last I talked with Ivanna on the phone you were too feeble to even..."

"Oh, hardly, my boy," Victor grinned, thumping his chest with a closed, bony fist. "I'm quite hale and hearty! Yes, it's true that I'm now past a hundred years old. I'm still frail, of course. But I'm feeling better every day!"

"But...how?"

"Ah! Quite an interesting story! Recently I received a remarkable new cancer treatment which not only caused my cancer to shrink dramatically—but also reinvigorated my entire body! It is an amazingly complex overlapping system of dynamically interacting retroviral vectors which..."

"—optimizes the immune system to better recognize and attack cancer cells?" Dave interrupted him.

"Why, yes, my boy," Victor replied, accepting Dave's arm to walk hesitantly off the porch into the house proper. "Do you know of it?"

Dave was silent for a moment, considering.

"And just who gave you this treatment?" he asked, afraid that he knew the answer.

In his mind, Dave sensed previously encountered other-worldly jackals drawing ever closer.

"It was a brand new experimental treatment developed by a Japanese laboratory," Victor responded. "I was lucky to qualify for the initial NIH-sponsored, FDA-approved clinical trial. Only a few of us terminal pancreatic cancer patients qualified in what was basically just a dosage test. The treatment's effectiveness and side-effects were of course unknown. But the *in vitro* and animal studies looked promising. If we terminal patients died from it—well, that's where we were quickly headed anyway. So it was all 'upside' for me! At the worst, I'd pass away a few weeks earlier than I would otherwise. And they'd still get good blood tests from me and the others in the clinical trial, making my death meaningful and useful. So I figured it was well worth the minor pain and trouble to perform this last public service. Fortunately for me, though, the results were the exact opposite of a quicker death!"

"And what was the name of the Principle Investigator?"

"Oh...that would be Dr. Sanako Yamamoto, a world-renown virologist. Are you familiar with her work?"

Dave laughed bitterly to himself. Of course it was *Sanako!* Did he really think that the Commissioner from the other Earth Dimension would allow him and Sally to go and live their lives in peace? She was still messing around with Dave's world. And even though the effect for Victor was excellent, it bespoke her motivation to *change* things for her own purposes!

"Yes...very much so."

"Ah, so you know of her amazing new techniques for repairing and reprogramming vast stretches of human DNA, not just altering isolated alleles?"

"Quite well, Victor."

"Remarkable work!"

"Yes, very remarkable," Dave sighed, remembering the amazing transformations he'd experienced under the influence of just such a treatment he'd endured, which originated from Earth's parallel Dimension. Suddenly everything was much clearer. He had no doubt that Sanako and her evil partner—"Commissioner Sally" from the other Dimension—were both intimately involved in the mysterious events of the past few days.

This changed everything.

Up until then he'd thought that he and Sally were back inside a pristine timeline, which they dared not contaminate with the knowledge or the means of releasing and harnessing Dark Energy—hence his steadfast refusal to explain how his ORV vanished, the startling appearance of the radioactive Obelisk, or the inexplicable associated apparitions. Withholding that key knowledge would protect mankind from the horrendous consequences, delaying—perhaps by hundreds of years—the inevitable extinction of humanity due to the Wrath of God!

But the "Victor" from this timeline knew nothing of those things. Yet here he was—an unwitting but obvious pawn in a new and ever-deadlier inter-dimensional war.

"I'm glad you're here, Victor."

"From what Agent Ice has told me, you've trouble afoot! And somehow it relates to the research you did in my lab over twenty years ago? Is that correct, my boy?"

"Yes."

"Then, if you're comfortable doing so—please tell me all about it! The officials here assure me that's all they want from you. If you tell me and them everything you know then they may even permit you to join the team I'm to be on studying the Artifact in the Park. That would be a real joy, working with you again, my boy!"

Dave wearily nodded in agreement. He led Victor to the round kitchen table, helping him stiffly sit down there on a folding chair. Dave sat next to him. And around them both were gathered the standing FBI agents.

Agent Ice pointedly laid a small recording device down on the tabletop in front of him, clicking it to "active."

Dave paused before proceeding.

"You're not going to believe what I'm going to tell you, Victor. And that goes double for you federal folks."

"Try us," Agent Ice curtly replied.

"Do you promise not to throw me in a loony bin?"

"No."

"Fair enough," Dave sighed deeply. "Well, it all started the day I met the *Girl with the Turtle Tattoo...*"

Tommy found that there was absolutely nothing wrong with the central computer complex which powered the Net. Both of the Sally-humans which he remembered so distinctly simply did not exist—and never had!

There was no record of them at all.

In fact, his memories of them were getting fuzzy.

"No!" he yelled, balling up his fists and thrusting them above his head. "I'm not forgetting the past! I'm not forgetting my friends! I'm not forgetting my Mommies!"

He ran back out of the computer complex into the bustling subterranean city. He ignored everyone and everything. He had to return to the surface.

He now knew what he had to do.

"Tommy! What are you doing? I've been looking for you!"

It was Dennis, lumbering up in his big dinosaur body. Joyce trailed along right behind him, agitatedly twitching her long powerful tail. They were very nice. They were worried about him. They were also his friends. But now he didn't need discouragement. He couldn't be held back. He had to forge full-speed ahead!

"Sorry! I don't have the time! I have to get back to our shuttle-craft. Something's very wrong down here. I've got to get up into orbit! Maybe then I'll be past whatever's changing our records and memories."

"In the *shuttlecraft?*" Dennis said, falling into step beside him. "But it's been broken a long time. It's not functional. It's just an inert monument now."

"Oh, that's right...but I've got to get it working!"

"It wouldn't be too hard," Joyce chimed in. "There's a few parts to replace in the DE-generator plus some of the fiber optic lines."

"Are you sure about this, Tommy—that we've all forgotten something critically important?"

"Yes!"

"Then we'll do whatever is needed to help you," he nodded his big oblong dinosaur head. "Joyce is expert in functional replacements using the Duplicator Unit. And I'm good at installing whatever parts she makes. We'll get the shuttlecraft working again!"

Tommy slowed his fast trot to a quick walk, now not so panicked. It was going to be ok. His friends would help him.

But what they'd find up in orbit around Mars...he had no idea.

He only knew he *couldn't* accept the new reality. He had to fight to make things right. He had to insist on retaining the integrity of his own mind!

Getting out of Guildhall wasn't that difficult. After all, the overlapping security layers were designed to prevent external attackers getting inside, not to keep people inside from getting out. But without a convincing subterfuge, Galileo would have been stopped in his tracks by the ever-vigilant guards.

Now, shuffling slowly up Basinghall Street toward the Grand Ali Mosque, Galileo hoped his disguise would hold. Outwardly he looked like a strictly fundamental Muslim woman wearing a totally concealing black burqa. Indeed, it was the very burqa that Virginia had arrived in after escaping Italy. She was now hiding in her room as he pretended to be her out on an anonymous shopping trip. She did that often enough for the guards to just note her exit in their logbooks. Yes, she was required to carry one of Anderson's tracker units so she was under constant protection by his unseen Time Keepers. But he'd taken that with him as well. So to all intents he was his own well-concealed, well-protected daughter.

Hopefully he'd make the short trip undetected. He could not bring his Mephistopheles Cane, so there was the danger he might trip and topple over in the heavy garment! He had to move slowly, but not too slow. If he took too long, then for sure someone was going to discover he was himself instead of his daughter.

If that happened, he had no doubt that all hell would break loose!

And Mephistopheles himself was surely not going to protect *him* from stumbling. No, that wicked demon would just laugh at his long, hard fall.

Chapter 8

DOWN THE RABBIT HOLE

It seems too much to ask
That the end be over fast
That your salary be paid in cash
And your dreams should not be smashed
But when you make that deadly dive
Down into the unknown darkness
Be aware that the light may never return
If you dare to leave it all behind
For the thrill of the roller coaster ride
You and your sweetie locked in a hug
Or the delight of that first kiss
Why not just take drugs?
The Minstrel's Lark, 8:25-29

Sally groggily regained consciousness strapped in the passenger seat of the ORV *falling* down an endless, spinning tunnel.

"Oh my...Dave?" she gasped, looking over at the driver's seat. Dave was not there! Where *was* he?

She had no idea how long she'd been knocked out or what had happened to her husband!

She felt weak, hungry...as if she'd been sitting there unconscious, buckled into the passenger seat, for a long, long time.

She leaned over from the passenger seat, spinning the steering wheel of the Ranger—which Dave had converted into semi-joystick mode for whenever they needed to try and use the emergency sub-space drive. But it was slack, having no effect on the forward plummet of the vehicle. Even her laptop controls, tied directly into the central control unit of the DE-generator, had zero effect.

She noted that she and the ORV were at least still safely encased inside a protective blue force field. Dave's rudimentary life-support system was also functioning, providing sufficient oxygen and heat. But she had no idea where she was going or how long she'd been traveling.

"It's...beautiful," she mumbled to herself, distracted and dazzled by the incredible spectacle.

Outside the shield was a hypnotic kaleidoscope of every color of the rainbow, spinning lazily. It was like falling into a plunging well composed of countless flashing many-colored strobe lights. At once it was both blinding and terrifying. Yet it was also a "fun tunnel" carnival ride—but so scary no one would ever ride it twice!

And just where is Dave, anyway?—she puzzled.

Somehow he hadn't phased into subspace along with her and the ORV. He'd been left behind! What the hell was happening?

She couldn't think. Her mind felt like it was being folded in upon itself. She fought the constant urge to vomit. Her guts were twisted up in knots.

And then the Ranger abruptly *fell out of subspace.*

"Oh...*Jesus Christ!*" she gasped.

The ORV now floated in zero gravity in the utter blackness of outer space! Only the force field around the ORV kept her from being instantly killed.

Above Sally she saw the sprinkle of many brilliant, pinpoint stars. And gazing "down" to the side of the floating ORV she saw...an even more spectacular view.

Below her hung a slowly roiling *flat layer of ice fragments*, which glittered in the sunlight like a *field of white diamonds*—stretching far into the distance!

"I'm...floating above one of the rings of *Saturn*," she whispered in disbelief to herself.

Yes, the hazy, giant sphere of Saturn hung off to the side. Its surface was a complex of bands: brown, black, yellow, purple, orange, blue, and white. It was awesome in its stark beauty, set against the blackness of space—but *alien*, foreboding!

"I've...got to get...back to Earth," she frowned, trying to focus her trembling hands to specific, concrete actions.

Looking down at the laptop's open screen she saw that the DE-generator was now only operating at a bare minimum. It was successfully maintaining the ORV's shield, but that was about all. Either something in the generator had been damaged in transit or it was recharging.

There was no possibility of an immediate return to Earth. She was now adrift in space, helpless—*in orbit* around the planet *Saturn!*

"But what am I doing here?" Sally groaned, painfully unbuckling her seatbelt and floating in the zero gravity from the passenger side over into the driver's seat.

Jets protruded from all sides of the modified Ranger. They now responded to her tentative taps on their controls. She saw spurts of white crystals formed off to the sides of the ORV when one vented and trace moisture froze. But the air jets were only meant for incidental maneuvering, not propulsion. The compressed air canister from which they drew air would be depleted after just a few minutes of usage.

She got the ORV to rotate slowly until she could easily look "up" at the icy ring.

And there she saw something jarringly *different*.

There, sitting on a slowly spinning ice mountain, was a *crumpled black rectangular object!* It was some sort of spaceship. And placed along its twisted surface were a variety of differently shaped and sized *spikes*.

She recognized it.

It sent a chill through her heart.

"No...it can't be—*can* it?" she moaned, terrified.

Yes, it was one of the alien "Spike-Ships" that she and Dennis battled in the distant future when they were marooned in intergalactic space! True to the boast of its holographic captain, their fleet must have backtracked Sally's dinosapien starship to the solar system. But what was one of them doing here on a big rock in an ice ring of Saturn? What destroyed it? And just...*when*...was this? Did the ORV when it jumped into subspace from the Park in Sulphur, Oklahoma also travel into the *future?*

Whatever, the crashed Spike-Ship was her only possible destination. And did this somehow connect to Suzy and Billy's disappearance?

"I'm coming, kids...hang on," she said through clenched teeth. Yes, this was the end of the neutrino trail from the trench in the Park. It *must* have something to do with her lost children!

Sally carefully fired short bursts from her air canister jets. It was hard to judge perspective and distance by eyesight hanging in space. She mentally adjusted her perspective so the ice mountain seemed "below" her, maybe a couples miles at the most. She could make it down there. It was just a matter of drifting along a properly aligned vector. That was child's play for her genius-level mathematical mind. But when she arrived...who knew what she'd find?

If Suzy and Billy were there, heaven help any aliens that'd captured her kids! She'd rip them apart—if necessary, with her own bare hands.

But it'd be far more satisfying to *slaughter* any still-living aliens down there with her Marlin 336C. The rifle sat right behind her in the back seat of the Ranger. They'd packed sufficient supplies and ammunition for an extended *hunting trip*. And she was itching to find a suitable target!

Yes. Domestic life for more than a decade in the peaceful small town of Sulphur Oklahoma had been nice. But it couldn't match the *thrill* of battling alien monsters. Though her previous life before becoming a mother was beyond bizarre, it was also incredibly exciting. She had an adventurous side that needed to be carefully controlled lest it take her where she shouldn't go.

But now, in defense of her kids, she was unleashing the beast within.

Having achieved the proper vector to the slowly spinning ice mountain below, she sat back in her seat and forced herself to enjoy the ride.

If nothing else, she had learned over her past journeys through space and time the value of *patience*. All great hunters conduct their business with careful deliberation. And in all of time and space, nothing is as deadly as a mother defending her children.

She'd figure out what happened to Dave after she got back her children. Somehow, they'd all be united again. Nothing in the Universe would stop her from achieving this goal!

Suzy was growing very impatient. Billy, however, was having the time of his life! But she was far more circumspect...

During the past month, they'd both settled into the life of being plains-living Native-Americans. Their tribe followed a vast herd of bison, living off its every product. Its many dung-droppings were great fuel for the tribe's fires, though rather smelly! Horns were carved into utensils and decorations. Bones were used as knifes, shovels, and arrowheads. Tanned hides were sewn together using buffalo ligaments to become their tepee covers, shoes, bags, and clothes. The nice soft pillow under Suzy's head at night was filled with buffalo hair. And buffalo meat was their main source of food.

Despite her reluctance, Suzy was being taught along with the other young girls how to cook—using cups and pots formed out of the large curved stomach lining of slain bison. She also helped render buffalo fat into soap, cooking oil, and candles. The men and boys used the strong ligaments of the buffalo to string powerful bows with which to kill the buffalo.

God, she hated buffalo!

True, they kept her and the others alive—but they were also smelly, dangerous beasts. Already during Suzy and Billy's time in the tribe two of the men were killed in stampedes, trampled to death. Suzy still had nightmares of helplessly facing slashing horns and smashing hoofs, before being snatched away by a warrior on his trusty pony.

But that caused Suzy even more confusion. The North American Indians didn't get horses until the "white man" brought them in their European invasion of the continent. So where were the Europeans? Suzy didn't see even a hint of anything but Indians and their primitive society. When she tried to speak English to the women who had "adopted" her, they just smiled and tried to teach her proper Chickasaw words.

Suzy could now understand and use a few general phrases like *"I'm bad"* (anchokma ki'yo) or *"how do you say..."* (katishchi isha aci...) or "*I do not understand*" (akostinicho) or "*what is this*" (yappa nanta) or "*what am I doing*" (nanta katihmili) or "*say it again*" (aachi anowa). But she had no hint that these inexplicably buffalo-following Chickasaw had ever heard a word of English before she'd arrived in their midst.

So she tried to be patient. While Billy enjoyed whooping and dancing, learning how to make weapons, riding out to the hunt with the older boys and men—Suzy listened and watched, steadily *learning...*

She observed the religious rites of the tribe, impressed. They saw Spiritual Presence in everything: not just in humans but in the buffalos, other animals, and even plants. They deeply appreciated all aspects of Nature—and were at peace with being just one part of the greater whole. The Indians exhibited a profound respect, recognizing that everything was joined to everything else. It was different from the legalistic, even unconsciously arrogant Church life to which Suzy was accustomed. But it jived well with the Animist teachings which her mother had quietly instilled in her.

And anything bad that happened—like the deaths of hunters—was attributed to "evil" spirits, exemplified by the *forbidden monsters* behind the Great Barrier forest. And vigilantly protecting the tribe was their "Medicine Man," whose name was "Okchamail Cholhkan" which Suzy inferred from other usages meant "Blue Spider."

Also, he wore a necklace of curved, white *snake* ribs around his neck. Yes, he embodied the most insidiously feared animals of their environment.

Respected as an essential part of Nature, the Indians still had a healthy fear of snakes. Though there were a number of varieties of harmless snakes out in the grasslands, any clump of weeds or broken limbs could hide a deadly poisonous snake. The horses were particularly shy of all snakes, associating any of them with copperheads, water moccasins, and several types of rattlesnakes. Just catching sight of one might cause a horse to rear up, bucking off their saddleless rider in sheer panic!

So Okchamail Cholhkan was both revered and feared. He was simultaneously the powerful spider or snake while also portraying their potent, deadly venom.

He was a towering, solemn man. He rarely smiled. He had a flat nose, prominent cheek bones, and a piercing stare. His black eyes seemed to drill right through Suzy whenever she caught his gaze. And his long, straight hair was grey-white, an oddity amongst the mostly young or middle-aged tribesmen.

Oddly there were few old people in the tribe. Suzy figured either they died young, which was likely, or living out in nature kept them fit and healthy. And, curiously enough, there was a reciprocal dearth of children. Yes, there were other boys and girls, but far less than Suzy would expect in a tribe that numbered in the hundreds.

And the children were revered, especially during the weekly religious ceremony. After the sun went down, the whole tribe gathered together, chanting in unison. Then the Medicine Man prayed for them—his head tilted up to the Moon as if in supplication. Bathed in moonlight he danced and hooted, caressing each child's head in turn as if offering them up as sacrifices. Suzy was frightened of his clawed hands but tolerated his jerky jabs, not wanting to stand out from the other children.

Most of the members of the tribe, whether young or older, were very friendly, even to the point of being irritating. But the Medicine Man seemed menacing, dangerous.

Suzy often caught him staring at her. She tried to ignore him. But it was like he knew who she was! And he was constantly fingering a large, deerskin sack tied securely to his waist—the "medicine bag" of the tribe. Everyone treated him with great respect. Next to the Chief, he was the most powerful person in the tribe. And his medicine bag was the tribe's central mystical resource, sort of like the "Ark of the Covenant" for the ancient Jewish people, which Suzy had learned about at church. His bag was the tribe's "magic"—from which he added a mysterious ingredient to communal meal pots. Not only did he treat whatever few ills the tribe had, he *kept* them healthy.

She knew she had to get a look inside that bag. She had no doubt that—whatever else it contained—inside she'd find her and Billy's cellphones. There was nowhere else they could be hidden. During her time in the tribe she'd snuck around poking into every corner she could find. She and Billy still had their cellphones when they'd been captured, so they weren't lost. They were *hidden*. And Sally was sure the Medicine Man had them inside...

"Suzy! Suzy!" Billy exclaimed, skipping up to her as she sat laboriously stitching up a deerskin dress with stiff lengths of buffalo ligament. "I just rode a pony with the men over to the buffalo herd! Wow! It was really hard. Before, I just walked along with the other boys. But today they let me ride my own pony! I had to hold on with my knees to not fall off. And then we were galloping so hard I thought I was going to get tossed over the horse's head. Man, I really had to grab hard onto its mane! And Dancing Owl is going to let me shoot an arrow during the next hunt, least wise I think he is. And..."

"Don't you ever get tired of this?"

That stopped him in his tracks, causing him to clamp his jaw shut and sit down next to her.

"Sometimes," he quietly admitted. He unexpectedly laid his head on her shoulder. She didn't push him off as she normally did, sensing he needed comforting. His black hair was growing out. He sported a brightly beaded headband with a single feather at the back. He was turning into a real Indian.

"We can't stay here forever," she insisted. "I don't think Mom and Dad are coming for us. It's been more than a month now. If we're ever going to get out of here, we're going to have to do it ourselves."

"Maybe we can go to the moon," he whispered somewhat tearfully, a catch in his voice.

"What?"

"The other kids draw pictures for me in the dirt. Kids are riding on the back of a big bird, flying up to the moon. When they get to the moon they get changed into gods—with big muscles and superpowers!"

"Billy, that's just superstitions and myths. We can't fly to the moon! We've got to figure out some way to get back home to Sulphur."

"Well...I *do* miss Mom and Dad," he admitted in a small voice, lifting his head to peer up at the dazzling-blue sky. "And, at night, it does get kinda scary and..."

"Right! This place is really weird, Billy—the dinosaurs, then this? What's next? We can't stay here!"

"But...what else can we do? Where would we go?"

Suzy frowned, thinking hard.

"We need to get a look into Cholhkan's medicine bag," she softly informed him. "I think that's where our cellphones are. He wouldn't have hidden them from us if he didn't know what they're used for. He doesn't want us to call for help, Billy!"

"Uh, ok, maybe he knows who we are. But he's not just gonna hand our cellphones over to us, Suzy. He guards that medicine bag like it was his wallet with a million bucks in it! He never goes anywhere without it."

"But at night, when he goes to sleep in his tepee...?"

"Ah..." Billy grinned wickedly. "I see what you're saying, Suzy. So all we gotta do is have something happen so he comes out at night and..."

"I sneak into his tepee and get our cellphones," she concluded.

"But how are we gonna get him to come out?" he shrugged, squinting against the bright sunlight.

"Well, you're so good with snakes...?"

"That is true," he nodded.

They were discussing possibilities quietly, not letting anyone else hear what they were saying. Yes, no one there seemed to know any English. But they weren't taking any chances.

Now that they had a good knowledge of how the tribe and the mobile village worked, Suzy and Billy had a plan.

Whether it would work or not, Sally had no idea. But she knew she had to try.

She was growing weary of "going native." Maybe if she'd been taken on the buffalo hunts like Billy and treated with respect by the menfolk, she'd think differently. But sewing dresses got old fast.

She just wanted to go home.

Galileo was stifling under the concealing burqa. Air circulation was awful. He almost decided to just give up, turn around, and go back to Guildhall. It took all of his determination to keep shuffling forward, trying to breathe shallowly and steadily.

It wasn't that much further...

Indeed, Guildhall had become a real "home" for him and Virginia, an oasis of discovery and safety in a world of repression and danger. Now, for the first time in a long while, he was venturing out by himself into the filthy, narrow streets of London. And he was scared!

What was he thinking to sneak out alone?

But then again, the stakes were too high to turn back.

So he continued slowly onward, hampered by the thick drapes that hung down from the top of his head to his feet, trying not to trip on the fabric and fall. He could only see out through the narrow slit in front of his eyes, which itself was veiled so that no one could see any part of his face. It certainly protected his identity, but also greatly obscured his vision. As he'd already discovered, it was also difficult breathing inside the heavy burqa, making walking even more of a chore.

"I never knew our traditions literally *smothered* our women," Galileo gasped to himself, sweat now streaming from his exertions. "But at least progress is being made."

Indeed, the city within his narrow range of view was drastically altered from what he'd seen only a few years previously. Where before there'd been a crowded cobblestone street with a putrid *open sewer* running down its middle—now there was a well-maintained street being dug up to lay a buried brick sewer line. It was an innovation two centuries in advance of its previously ordained, future-history introduction. It amazed Galileo yet again what having unlimited funds could achieve—even ridding the crowded city of its pervasive stench! And the bleak wooden structures along the street were also being transformed, renewed and built up higher using new construction methods.

They were transforming the three-or-four storied buildings into what Anderson called "skyscrapers"!

London was booming.

And there in front of the struggling Galileo loomed the inspiring slender minarets and wide, glistening domes of the *Grand Ali Mosque*. It was not the main Mosque of London, but still impressive. Galileo shuffled up to the main entrance, trying to be inconspicuous. As he entered he kept to the side of the other visitors, slipping into the first doorway he could find which had stairs leading downward.

It was difficult to not trip on his burqa as he waddled down the stairs. But he kept going, carefully taking each new step, until he reached the basement. It was very chilly down below. He felt weak and cold. He again considered turning around and going back.

And then he saw the monk.

"Professor?" the widely smiling, shaven-headed man greeted him, his hands out in greeting. He was brown-skinned, somewhat chubby, clad in a simple red robe.

"Yes, it's me," Galileo panted from behind his thick concealments. "Thank you so much for this private audience, Teacher," Galileo politely responded. "Your local people were very kind in discretely setting up an appointment with you."

The bald-headed man was clearly of oriental descent. He had an expressive face, high cheek bones, dark eyebrows, and slanted eyes.

"Oh, no need for formalities," the older man grinned, revealing broken teeth. "I am but a simple Buddhist monk, tolerated by the authorities because I'm harmless—and kindly granted a few rooms in the basement of the Grand Mosque by its Muslim Clerics, for me and my few followers to meet within."

Galileo got the heavy burqa off with difficulty, exhausted from the several blocks he'd traveled from Guildhall to the Mosque. He was drenched in sweat, hoping he didn't stink too badly. In contrast, the monk seemed comfortable in his simple reddish robe that hung off one shoulder. He was barefoot on the cold stone floor.

"Please come with me," the monk indicated, heading off into a larger room.

Galileo followed, his eyes adjusting to the gloom. Outside, the sun was glaringly bright. Here, a scattering of candles was all that illuminated the room in faint, flickering glows.

Sitting down on a mat on the floor in a lotus position, the monk gestured to a conventional chair.

Gratefully, Galileo sat heavily upon it. Yes, he was vigorous for a 75-year-old man, but still unused to long walks in a heavy burqa. It felt wonderful to sink onto the seat!

"So how may I be of service?" the monk calmly stated.

"I have...questions," Galileo tentatively began.

"Why?"

"I...well..."

A pretty young woman with long black hair, also of oriental background, entered carrying a tray upon which was a steaming jug and two glasses. She set it down on a low table between the two men. She kept her face averted.

"Tea?" she politely asked.

"Thank you...most kind," Galileo nodded.

After she'd poured their drinks and left, Galileo sipped delicately at the warm brew as the monk patiently waited.

"Well," Galileo began. "You may not believe any of this, but I'm..."

"—under the influence of Time Travelers from the distant future, is that correct?"

Galileo was startled.

"How did you...?"

"We Buddhists may be mostly ignored by this materialistic society and its aloof rulers," the monk shrugged, "but we are devout students of human behavior. The marvelous innovations you are bringing to London and the rest of the world are impossible for the present European society to produce. Reports by my people inside your organization are revealing. You are passing to us inventions and societal changes that otherwise would not occur for hundreds of years in the distant future."

"Yes...that's correct! And..."

"And you, Professor, are having reservations," the monk confidently continued. "You're not sure where this is going. You don't trust the claims of your benefactors. And you're seeking assurance from me that a greater Plan is in effect. You don't trust the established religious leaders, so you turn to me for an outside but informed perspective of Divine matters. Is that not an accurate synopsis?"

The bald-headed oriental man grinned disarmingly.

Galileo gulped, greatly impressed with the insightfulness of this "ordinary" monk!

"I...I'm beginning to very much doubt...that this is Divine Right, if you would. And since you Buddhists seem to have a sense of the flow of time that is broader than us more short-sighted Muslims, I thought that..."

"We do believe in reincarnation, that's true," the monk broke in. "Our goal, though, is not a discrete 'heaven' similar to this existence, but achieving a state that we call 'Nirvana.' That state is truly *beyond* human existence on this planet for…"

"So you do have a long perspective," Galileo summarized, "just as I've always heard."

"Yes, we do—of cycles upon cycles of death and rebirth, the effects of our individual karma driving us forward, learning or forgetting, a continuing challenge to the character of our spirits that…"

"But can you see *forward* in time?" Galileo eagerly broke in.

"Ah…" the monk shrugged, "that's a most perceptive question, my friend. Sometimes I do feel I have a glimpse of what's to come in my future reincarnations. But that vision is more burden than joy. I perceive many cycles of continued administrative and religious duties for myself, which is the least enjoyable part of my journey, repeating over and over. But sometimes I think I've learned a bit, have become a slightly better person, and see forward with reserved optimism. But lately…well, I've felt a dark cloud over the horizon—a looming evil that blocks out the sun. I fear that a devastating storm is approaching from which we may not recover. But, it's just a feeling, by no means certitude. Yet I do feel I may have some central role to play in…"

"Allah save us all!" Galileo gasped out, suddenly chilled not just by the cold basement air but by the man's cryptic words.

"Oh, I'm afraid that my vision is not anchored in the notion of an engaged central Deity. We Buddhists do not espouse a doctrine of everything stemming from a single all-controlling 'God.' What I offer you is but one man's feelings, which you are free to discard if it doesn't suit your presumptions," he chuckled quietly.

Galileo was stunned by the man's mental acuity, yet seeming casualness! Clearly, this wasn't just the regional religious leader which he'd requested an audience with. But if this man was a high-ranking official in the Buddhist religion, then why did he seem so unconcerned, even dismissive?

Surely there was nothing funny about a looming catastrophe?

"So…you *expected* me to come seek your wisdom?"

The monk shyly shrugged, ducking his head.

"Yes—in fact, I traveled here to London to meet *you*, Professor Galilei," the bald-headed man now matter-of-factly stated. "I would not impose myself upon you. But I did put myself at a place conven-ient to your headquarters, hoping that *you* might reach out to *me*. And I was right! Here you are—are you not?"

He giggled. This again shocked Galileo. How could this other-wise astute man seem so frivolous? There were momentous changes now threatening the settled, orderly society of England. And the monk was affirming Galileo's worst fears, of a *storm* on the horizon! Yet he was *giggling?* Did he think this was some colossal *joke?*

"Was I *not* right?" the monk now insisted, raising his eyebrows expectantly.

Galileo sighed deeply, setting aside his cup of now-cooling tea, trying to get his swirling emotions under control.

"You are most observant, Sir. I perceive that you are much more than a local leader of an obscure religious cult. How shall I properly address you?"

"Formally, 'Your Holiness' is the proper term—but please call me 'Lhamo,' which is my birth name. That is, if I may call you 'Galileo', my esteemed Professor?" he politely concluded.

"Certainly! Thank you...Lhamo. This meeting, I'm sure you un-derstand, is 'off the books' so to speak. My enemies are many. If they knew I was meeting with one of the Leaders of a non-Muslim religion, I'd be crucified!"

The monk politely laughed at the attempted joke. Galileo knew that the ancient Roman practice of brutal execution by crucifixion had long been banned. But it was a common phrase widely used through-out Europe denoting an extreme sanction.

"Oh, I'm sure they'd not be so silly. Attempting again to *burn you to death* you would be far easier, would it not?"

This time Galileo was truly shocked. Now the monk had a dead serious expression. Yes, Galileo had already experienced that particu-lar judgment by the religious establishment, barely escaping. The monk was signaling that he knew full-well the potential portent of their momentous secret meeting.

"Please, ask whatever you want of me," the monk again kindly smiled, casually gesturing with a hand to proceed. "But be aware that my spies reported shortly before your arrival that your security forces have discovered your absence from your room. Even now they are searching for you. It is only a matter of time before they find that Virginia is hiding in her own room, you having taken her place venturing out alone into the streets. They will shortly be here to retrieve you."

Galileo gathered his wits about him, intensely focusing on the task at hand. He didn't know if he should believe that "Lhamo" really had a network of spies in Guildhall, but didn't doubt the veracity of the man's warning.

Time was short.

"We Muslims teach that there is one God—from which all else stems," Galileo quickly pushed forward. "The common belief is that you Buddhists do not believe such. Is that true? I feel I do not fully understand your prior words to me on this subject. How can you not believe in the Creator?"

"*Look within you. YOU are the Creator!*" Lhamo intensely ordered him.

Galileo was startled by this claim.

"No...I know that's *not* true...in fact, that's total blasphemy which the Clerics would...!"

Lhamo quite inappropriately again *giggled*—just like a little girl!

"*The whole secret of existence is to have no fear,*" he now sighed, a gentle compassion shining from his deep brown eyes.

"You think that I am ruled by fear?" Galileo huffed, leaning back in his chair and crossing his arms.

"You came here seeking personal happiness, did you not?"

Galileo was very confused. What was this man saying? The man was playing games with him!

"I think perhaps I am wasting my time here," Galileo sighed, disappointed. "I'm sorry to have bothered you," he said, starting to stand up. "I am a man of science, not..."

"*There is no path to happiness*, my friend," Lhamo insisted while gently motioning for Galileo to sit back down. "*Happiness IS the path!*"

Galileo frowned, sagging back in his chair.

"Why won't you answer my question?" Galileo snapped back at him. "I need straight answers, not riddles or proverbs! Is *Allah* behind the changes that Anderson and his colleagues are feeding the world through me, or not? If so, I trust in Divine Guidance, whether or not it leads us into an impending world-wide crisis. But if what we are doing is not from Allah, then I must sabotage the entire effort. I may not agree with the ossified doctrines of the clerics, but I am a *man of God* before everything else!"

Lhamo sighed deeply.

"I've already given you an answer, friend Galileo. But since you did not hear me, allow me to rephrase it in terms a world-renown scientist should appreciate: '*If you can see the miracle of a single flower clearly, your entire life will change!*'"

Galileo abruptly stood up, staring angrily down at the man sitting cross-legged on the mat.

For a moment he was going to *attack* the bald-headed monk and *beat* him within an inch of his life!

But Galileo clamped his jaw tightly shut, struggling to control his infamous temper. Virginia would certainly be unhappy with him for beating up a mild-mannered though infuriating monk. Regardless, the monk was clearly playing with him. Coming here *was* a waste of time. Galileo was exhausted, clammy with sweat, and starting to get chilled to his bones. If he didn't leave the icy basement room right now, he was likely to come down with an illness. Best he just politely say "thanks" to the mystic for his meaningless words and leave.

The old monk got a dreamy look on his face.

"The answers I just gave you were the exact words from our Founder, who you recognize as *the Buddha!*" the monk now very seriously explained. "They were uttered *a thousand years* before the Founder of your own great religion was even born. Do you not wonder why there's been so little conflict between Islam and Buddhism? What fighting there's been has been mostly due to economic and political factors, not doctrine. The 'truth' is that our little minds simply cannot conceive of the Infinite, the actual Spiritual, if you would—the *Divine!* The little questions you ask...are superfluous! You're like a child asking his parents which is the best toy to play with, thereby seeking their approval. Your little toys which you think are so important *aren't* the point. You're simply not asking the right questions."

Galileo wavered, wanting to stalk out of the room, but intrigued by this new line of discussion. He slowly sank back down into his chair.

"Well then what *is* the point?" Galileo snapped at him, still irritated and greatly discomforted by the man's cryptic replies.

"Again, I quote the Buddha: '*In separateness lies the world's greatest misery—while in compassion is the world's true strength!*'"

"And who would argue with a statement that sounds nice but says nothing?"

The monk grinned widely, quoting again...

"*However are the holy words you read, however many you speak—what good will they do you if you do not act upon them?*"

Suddenly Galileo felt himself *thrown violently backward*—his chair toppled and the back of his head hitting hard onto the stone floor!

Stunned, Galileo saw the monk thrown in the opposite direction by the force of an EXPLOSION between them!

And there standing over Galileo was the oriental woman who'd brought in the tray of tea with her face averted. But Galileo now recognized her arrogant stare. She wasn't a mere servant. Galileo realized it was his bitter enemy *Sanako*—now holding a glitteringly sharp knife!

—and stepping out of a *shimmering black veil* into the candlelit room to the side of Sanako was an old, bent-over woman lifting a stubby weapon to point straight at Galileo...

—who the prone monk neatly *kicked* in her shins!

With a gasp of pain, the old woman fell backward into the shimmering curtain, vanishing as Sanako simultaneously lunged forward with her knife...

—as Galileo, emulating the cleric kicked *her* in her shins as well!

She staggered back, caught herself, and then crouched.

"Your perverse existence is *terminated!*" she growled as she lunged forward...

—as a suddenly present *Agent Anderson* hit the woman from behind on her head with his heavy black gun! The knife clattered to the stone floor as she crumpled onto the stone floor beside Galileo, groaning.

Several more of Anderson's people ran behind him into the basement, wrapping up Sanako in a blue-glowing gown that covered her from head to foot.

"Well, that's a good catch, Professor," Anderson said as he leaned down and offered a strong hand to help Galileo back to his feet. "It's too bad we couldn't grab the Commissioner herself. But Sanako will be an invaluable source of information. You shouldn't have snuck out of Guildhall like this, though. You could have just asked me. I've nothing against you satisfying your religious curiosity. The Buddhists certainly do have interesting viewpoints. In fact, I congratulate you on moving beyond your inherited religious framework. Well done, Sir!"

Galileo staggered up to his feet, his head ringing. That blow to the back of his head was vicious. He really shouldn't be toppling over like this at his advanced age!

Anderson snagged up the tightly swaddled Sanako, slinging her limp body over his shoulder like a rag doll.

"I...was laying the foundation...for what we discussed yesterday..." Galileo lamely attempted an explanation.

"And I am happy to convey to you that we've agreed to your request," the beefy man glibly replied. "Once we get back to Guildhall and you are recovered, then we'll proceed. I have to admit that I'm also curious about what's happening up the timeline. Our forces have been totally engaged here in your 17th Century protecting our critical endeavors. We've been unable to judge our future progress during this present effort. The capture of Sanako, however, will doubtlessly relieve the pressure on us. So, all told, your unauthorized little excursion has been fruitful!"

"And...what about him?" Galileo said, referring to the monk who'd just saved him from the evil Commissioner and her knife-wielding companion. The monk had serenely picked himself up after the explosion and returned to his peaceful lotus position on the floor mat.

He was smiling up at them...seemingly without a care in the world!

"He knows too much. I'm sorry, Professor. But he must be eliminated."

Shocked, Galileo saw Anderson raising his weapon while flicking the setting up to "three stars"...

"No!" Galileo yelled, knocking the gun to the side.

"*Even death is not to be feared by one who has lived wisely*," the monk mildly observed, shrugging nonchalantly. "But...I think I must persist here for a while longer. You *do* have need of me, do you not?"

An enraged Anderson, ignoring for the moment the monk, looked like he was going to shoot *Galileo* instead!

"Don't you *ever* interfere again with my..."

"Yes! I *do* need him!" Galileo insisted, moving quickly between Anderson and the seated monk. "We've got to take him with us!"

Galileo hadn't intended to kidnap the monk. But it seemed the only way to protect the Oriental's life. Also, Galileo was intrigued by the man's strange sayings. Although the quotes from the ancient Buddha were irritatingly vague, they had a *resonance* that Galileo could not deny.

Anderson slowly lowered his weapon, reluctantly submitting. But it was obvious to Galileo that the Agent was still seething at Galileo's defiance!

"As you wish."

Galileo reached down to help the old man to his feet.

"Don't worry," the monk grinned happily at Galileo. Then, to Anderson he stated: "*You will not be punished for your anger. You will be punished BY your anger!*"

Anderson shrugged, catching hold of Galileo's arm as another of his comrades likewise grabbed hold of the monk's.

"This is going to be interesting," Anderson grimly stated.

"What do you mean by..." Galileo began when he felt a *wrenching twist of reality* shot through his head.

And just that quickly, they were back at Guildhall—with Virginia jumping up from her desk to run over and hug her quivering father.

Looking around bemusedly, the monk grinned even wider.

"*Hatred never ceases through hatred*," he softly but intensely stated to everyone in the room. "*Wear your ego like a loose-fitting garment. But the trouble is...you think you have the time to do so!*"

"Find him a nice cell to meditate quietly within," Anderson sighed, apparently still unimpressed by the man's philosophizing, while handing off the bundled-up Sanako to a couple other guards.

"Do not mistreat him!" Galileo shakily ordered them.

His head was still spinning. His stomach felt like it had been turned inside out. And his knees trembled from fatigue and shock.

"Father, are you alright?" Virginia said, looking with up into his eyes with deep concern.

He paused before answering.

Then he wryly smiled.

"Dear Daughter, I'm better than I've been in a long time, though I'm afraid I lost your black burqa."

"It is of no matter," she grinned, hugging him tightly.

"Hopefully you'll never need it again," he grinned back.

Chapter 9
__INVASION__

Forever there was no threat

"Little Green Men" just a fantasy

Fit only for science fiction movies

Or humorous songs and books

The distances between stars too vast

For any possibility of attack

By hostile, greedy, or hungry aliens

Our little planet totally safe...

Until it wasn't so isolated

Not so funny now, huh?

The Minstrel's Lark, 9:7-1

Dave finished his story, his voice hoarse. It had taken him two hours to tell just the rough outline of all that'd happened to him and the various Sally incarnations.

He did not expect that they'd believe a word of what he'd told them. They'd probably figure he was just making up an outrageous science fiction story to throw them off their "terrorist" accusations.

No one said anything.

"So...in these other 'timelines' you lived..." Victor hesitantly ventured, breaking the silence, "you say that I helped you to build this 'Dark Energy' generator? And, indeed, I even helped the military to build and launch massively destructive Dark Energy bombs?"

Dave slowly got up, went to the adjoining kitchen, poured two glasses of water, and came back to the table. He sat one before his old mentor, sipping at the other. He figured the still-standing FBI agents could take care of themselves if they were thirsty.

"That's right," Dave sighed. "You were even there in the other Universe that Sally told me about, though in a time-freeze capsule. So

119

you were there for everything, Victor. For most of it you were quite happy, in your element. You even came out of retirement to pursue Dark Energy generation. And you handled our adventures very professionally—though I admit you were stressed when we went back in time to the last ice age. Not being a biologist, like me, you didn't know how to react to charging *Mammoths!* Hah! That was funny..." his strained voice trailed off.

None of the others laughed.

Dave slowly stood up from the table, setting down his drained glass of water.

"Well..." Dave sighed again, looking straight at Agent Ice, "I guess you can haul me away now. It was sure nice to see you again, Victor. I'm really glad the Optimmune-like treatment from this world's Professor Sanako's lab has given you a new lease on life. I know my story's incredible. But maybe parts of it that you choose to accept will help you and the others deal with the Obelisk and trying to find..."

"Sit back down," Agent Ice curtly ordered him, reaching down to retrieve her recorder. In its place she placed another, identical unit. "Get this hand-delivered to Washington," she ordered an aid, handing him the first unit. "It's classified *Top Secret*."

"So you...?"

"We've been aware for a while now that 'visitors' were frequenting our world—both from a parallel Dimension and from out of Time."

"Ah...hence the department you say you're from."

"That's right. It was formed to investigate exactly this sort of threat. Before now, however, we had little in the way of tangible evidence. But the Artifact, the invading entities, and your story confirm our worst fears."

"So you accept that..."

"—we're under attack from several other-worldly fronts. Yes. Your future-derived knowledge is critical to us surviving this attack, Dr. King. We need your willing participation."

"And what about the broader implications...?"

"The theological aspects of your account are staggering...but not our immediate concern. I have Presidential authorization to take all steps necessary to track down and stop the present alien threat. That's what we must focus our resources on. Will you help us do so?"

Dave shrugged. He was still conflicted. He'd told them the broad "take-home" messages, but hadn't yet given up any details. After all, he was the reason this all started in the first place. He couldn't blame Sally—the "Girl with the Turtle Tattoo"—it was all *his* fault!

And here he was starting it all up yet again.

"Well, the 'cat's out of the bag,' right?" he sighed, resigned to his fate. "Even if I clammed up again, you've still got enough general information to pursue DE-generators...right, Victor?"

Professor Volodymyr had been following the interchange with keen attention.

"I'm...amazed," he nodded, absently licking his lips with the tip of his tongue. "But, yes, I think with the samples still archived in the Applied Physics department from your dissertation research, I and others could eventually replicate your subsequent ground-breaking work to..."

"So you're onboard, Dr. King," she interrupted Victor. "And you, Professor, likewise?"

"My Yale colleagues will be intrigued."

"It's all happened before, Victor," Dave sighed. "But this time with me guiding you, we'll have sophisticated defenses quickly in place against this new alien threat."

"Good. So we're in agreement," Agent Ice concluded.

"I'll help you kill the monsters," Dave stated, "—assuming we give equal effort to retrieving my wife and kids?"

"It's all part of the same puzzle," Ice acknowledged. "We'll do our best to find out what happened to them and get them back. But the first priority must be to stop those—as you said—'sub-space' Spiders. If they can't be stopped, then your family is doomed along with the rest of us."

"Sally stopped them once before," Dave stated, the adrenalin of telling his amazing story starting to wear off. It was getting hard to think. "If we get her back then we're in much better shape."

"I recognize her value," Ice curtly replied.

"The situation is not yet irredeemable," Victor noted. "It seems you've a plethora of resources mobilized locally."

"Yes, we yet hope to get this situation contained," Ice answered. "So far the media is buying our claim that a classified nuclear satellite crashed in the Park. The bizarre animal events we're attributing to a new, flesh-eating bacterium. But those explanations won't hold if the incidences expand beyond the immediate area."

"Yes, but I'm not sure about..." Victor began.

—as *gunfire* erupted and something *crashed* through the front door of the house into the small dining room, bowling over everyone over.

Bleeding from multiple gunshot wounds, *Losa Yanash* strode through the smashed door right up to Dave!

Stunned, Dave looked up into the twisted face of his Chickasaw friend. The Park Ranger's wide face was a frozen mask. But behind his black eyes Dave saw a blazing *red fire!*

"Help me," Dave heard a feeble croak from the man...

—as Losa's clawed hand grabbed downward for Dave and Dave *screamed* in pain. Losa's elongated fingernails were knifing into his arm...

—as Victor lunched himself upward and threw himself into Losa. Momentarily confused, Losa flailed out at Victor, raking the side of Victor's head with his claws...

—as Dave saw the prone Agent Ice pull out a handgun and *shoot* Losa through his head!

With what sounded like a sigh of relief, Losa crumpled down onto Victor.

"You ok, Professor?" Dave gasped, stumbling up. With revulsion he pushed Losa's body off his old friend.

"I...I..." Victor stammered, in apparent shock. Blood was dripping down the side of his face from deep scratches.

"Get it contained! Get it contained!" Ice was screaming at her people as they jumped back to their feet while pursuing soldiers burst into the house, rifles pointed.

"What the hell?" Dave said, staring at Losa's body.

Dave noted *oily-black blood* oozing from Losa's many lethal bullet wounds. It seemed as if the blood had long-since coagulated.

And it was smeared all over Dave and Victor's clothes.

"We didn't know about the Park Ranger being scratched by that Spider until you told us just now," Ice hurriedly explained as quarantine personnel streamed in behind the troops. "He didn't tell us. He just said he fell on some rocks that cut his arm. He was behaving perfectly normally up until he attacked your house. But clearly he was contaminated with...something?"

Fully space-suited figures were pushing the other people out of the dining room, carefully isolating and bagging the body. Others were mopping up every drop of the blood while sterilizing the cleaned surfaces with various sprays.

"Take off your clothes," a space-suited man ordered Dave.

Dave hurriedly stripped down to his shorts and socks.

"Those too!" he ordered.

Naked, Dave watched his clothes being sealed into a thick plastic bag labeled "biosafety hazard."

"Turn around!" the muffled voice ordered him again.

As he slowly rotated, a shower of sprays drenched Dave. Simultaneously the space-suited personnel carefully examined every inch of his skin. They noted deep puncture wounds on his arm, which they quickly bandaged.

He was handed a towel to clean up, plus fresh clothes to put on.

Dave noted that Victor was treated the same. His scrawny frame stood wavering a few feet from Dave. The side of his face was now neatly bandaged.

Oh Jesus...Dave thought to himself. *I'll never get to search for Sally and the kids now. They're going to lock me away to dissect me!*

But Agent Ice reassured him.

"We're taking you both to the operational center in the Park. It's secure. You'll both have to be in isolation units for a while, of course. But once we're sure you aren't contaminated like Losa, you'll be free to participate fully. Meanwhile you'll be kept up-to-date with our investigation, as we continue to debrief you on the details of your future and alternative-history accounts. Understand?"

"You're...putting us in jail cells?"

"*Isolation units*," Ice snapped, clearly irritated at having to repeat herself, "—but just until we're sure you haven't been infected. "Hopefully whatever happened to the Park Ranger isn't transmissible. But we're not taking any chances since both of you were scratched."

"And if we *have* been infected?" Victor calmly replied, slowly pulling on the new hospital-garment type clothes the decontamination personnel handed him.

"The CDC is onsite, Professor. They have a BSL-4 field lab set up, the strictest containment possible for studying the deadliest of pathogens. Plus they have access to every medical therapy available. But hopefully none of that will be needed for either you or Dr. King."

"And the man that attacked us?" Victor continued, putting a hand to the bandaged side of his face.

"They'll perform an autopsy of the body plus analyze the contaminant. At Central Operations we have rooms and showers. Everyone here, whether they got splattered with blood or not, will have to wash several times with decontaminants. Our old clothes will be burned," she concluded.

"What a disaster," Dave grimaced, shaking his head in disbelief, looking around at his trashed house.

"Perhaps not," Agent Ice coldly noted. "Before this, all we had were secondhand accounts and degraded animal tissue samples with which to work. Now, however, we've got totally fresh samples from the Park Ranger. Plus *you* are a live test of whether or not the contagion is transmissible. Whatever the outcomes, we're going to learn a lot."

"But we're *humans*, not test animals!" Victor sternly interrupted her.

Dave knew what Agent Ice was saying. Before, it had only been infected animals. But *now* they'd know for sure the extent of the contagion.

"We can contain this," Ice insisted. "It's not that different from any number of plagues and disease outbreaks we've dealt with in the past. Don't get too upset, gentlemen. Your isolation will hopefully only be temporary."

Agent Ice moved away to oversee the continuing cleanup.

"If this thing gets out into the general population..." Victor whispered to Dave, leaving the thought unsaid.

"—then it's the *Zombie Apocalypse!*" Dave finished the thought, horrified. Numerous movies, books, graphic novels, and TV series flooded his thoughts. For Dave they'd always been just entertaining horror shows. Now they might be real!

Even if Sally, Suzy, and Billy were located and retrieved...what kind of world would they find when they returned?

Dave had terrible memories of the nightmarish aftermath of the invasion by the Harvester aliens in another timeline. This would be far worse. Before, it was "merely" monster robots and spaceships arrayed against humanity. Now *Homo sapiens* would be fighting *themselves!*

And from all the science fiction stories, TV series, and movies he'd ever seen of such "Z" nations he was certain of one thing:

—it wouldn't be pretty.

Billy and Suzy were ready to put their plan into action.

In the dead of the night they'd snuck out of their respective tepees. They'd had to be very careful not to disturb their sleeping roommates.

Now, they were crouched behind the pen where the horses were kept. It wasn't really a solid pen, just a loosely woven-together barrier made from tent poles. But it was enough to keep the domesticated horses corralled. Since the moon wasn't up, it was dark. But by starlight Suzy could make out a couple dozen horses. Some were lying down on the ground and even snoring! Most of the rest were standing while dozing, their heads hanging. A few were wandering around, awake.

Suzy knew that horses out in the wild rarely lay down. Also, they slept whenever they wanted during the day or night. Being herbivore, herd animals, they always needed to be at least half-alert in case predators attacked—which would instantly trigger their "flight" reaction.

Suzy and Billy were counting on this engrained instinct.

"You got them?" Suzy whispered to Billy.

"I sure do!" he whispered back, lifting up a deerskin sack. It was filled with things that were *squirming.* The top was closed tightly with a strip of knotted deerskin. "Want to see them?"

"No!" she stopped him as he started to undo the tied top of the sack. Then, more quietly, she added..."Where'd you get them?"

"Earlier today I caught them by the creek in the bushes. None of them are poisonous, Suzy. They're mostly just black rat snakes. They can be ornery, but since it's cooler they wuz real easy to handle. Oh, and I found a big bull snake! And also I got a real pretty speckled king snake. She's really sweet and..."

"Ok, ok. That's good, Billy," Suzy shushed him, whispering. "Give me two minutes to get over to the Medicine Man's tent. Then toss them all in."

"Yep, I'll do it!" he happily replied. "And I already untied the gate and opened it up a crack so the horses can gallop out. It's gonna be a big stampede!"

"Good. Just don't let anyone see you, Billy. Get back to your tent right after you panic the horses. The only way we're going to get away with this is for people to think it was an accident from some random snakes crawling into the corral."

"Ok, but..."

"What?"

"I don't want any of my snakes to get hurt!"

Suzy grimaced at him. That wasn't one of her concerns. But she knew that Billy had those same weird reptile-loving genes as did her Dad.

"I'm sure they'll be fine, Billy. There's lots of high grass for them to hide in after you toss them onto the horses' backs and they fall off. Just be quick!"

"Yep, I'll be *real* quick!" he mock-saluted to Suzy.

"Alright then, soldier," she grinned back at him. "Let's do this thing—*Operation Cellphones!*"

"Two minutes from now," Billy nodded. Then he began counting down..."One hundred twenty seconds, one hundred nineteen seconds, one hundred eighteen seconds..."

Suzy scooted away, keeping low. No one was up. It was past midnight. She could have just walked normally across the encampment. But she didn't want to risk getting seen in case anyone happened to wander out of their tent to go to the bathroom or something.

At night, the encampment seemed even larger than it was during the day. There were several hundred Indians here—with lots of tepees of various sizes, from small to large. They loomed above Suzy like dark, smooth trees of an enchanted forest.

Then she was at Cholhkan's tent. It was on the edge of the encampment, by the Chief's tent. Suzy knew that the Medicine Man and several of his assistants should be sleeping inside. Creeping up to the bottom flap, she could hear the men snoring.

It was almost time...

Suddenly a loud "whinnying" and STOMPING erupted through the encampment.

The tribe's horses were panicked, *STAMPEDING* in panic out of their corral to *bash* into the tents, *crashing* through the weakly burning bonfire in the center of the encampment, and *startling awake* the many sleeping Indians!

They came pouring out of their tents, groping around in the darkness, shouting and calling to each other as they tried to catch the ponies and horses *thrashing*, *kicking*, and *galloping* randomly around through the camp!

—and Cholhkan emerged with three other men through the front tent flap, looking around in confusion as Suzy slipped under the edge of the tepee's buffalo hide wall and inside.

It was dark in the tent. The small tent-fire surrounded by stones in the center of the tepee held just a few glowing embers. As her eyes adjusted to the lack of starlight, she saw four buffalo-hide mats, with deerskin covers thrown aside. And off in one corner was a large "safe" made from several highly polished, flat stones.

"Ah, *there* you are!" she whispered to herself, scuttling across to the "safe" and sliding aside the front, heavy stone.

Inside, along with other precious Tribe possessions and icons, was the Medicine Bag!

She grabbed it, opened the top, and reached inside.

"Come to Momma," she grinned as she felt amongst other objects the thin, metallic flat surfaces of two cellphones! She yanked them out, sliding them into a hidden pocket she'd sewn inside her deerskin skirt, stuffing them beneath other things. She started to put the bag back into the safe but paused. There was still yelling and loud stomping going on outside. She had a few more moments.

She was startled to see that there was a dim, intriguing light *glowing* from inside the bag! But she'd already taken out the cell-phones, whose batteries were certainly dead anyway.

"I *know* you guys here don't have nightlights or flashlights," she mused as she peered inside.

Suzy saw that the light was coming from a *giant jewel!* And in a transparent container beside the jewel were *white pills.*

The pills and plastic container was an unmistakable sign of modern technology!

But the jewel was even more fascinating.

"Oh, boy!" she gasped to herself, reaching into the bag to draw out a multi-facetted *emerald* that was as big as her hand.

It was *pulsing* with a green glow and *warm* to the touch. And as she lifted it up the rate of pulsation increased!

Then Suzy felt something protruding from its flattened bottom side.

"What the heck is this?" she said, pursing her lips as she turned the glowing jewel over and saw a *serrated knob.*

That knob definitely wasn't a primitive Indian carving. It was even more modern-type technology! Along with the pills, it definitely proved that Suzy and Billy hadn't just jumped to the time of dinosaurs and then onward to the time of the plains Indians.

Something much weirder was happening!

Firmly grasping the knob she felt it turn clockwise through each notch, "clicking" softly as it did. Then, at the farthest setting, she felt the knob slip a bit inward.

"So then, if I *push* you...?"

She shoved the knob all the way inward until its top was level with the bottom of the large jewel, completely inserted.

Immediately the green-glowing emerald turned *red*. Now it was an ominously flashing *ruby!*

And a faint "humming" sound was coming from it!

"*Nanta ishkatihmi? Hika!*"

It was Cholhkan! He'd just returned, exclaiming: What are you doing? Stop!

Suzy dropped the Medicine Bag and the pulsating ruby, diving for the hanging-down edge of the tent...

Too late! He had her by the scruff of her neck, dragging her back into the tent. And marching in with a scared-looking Billy in tow—who was still clutching his emptied snake-bag—was the rumpled-looking Chief of the Tribe, *Mooleshawskek* or "Wolf's Friend"!

The Chief didn't look happy. In fact, his large, wide face was dead-serious. By the red light now brightly illuminating the interior of the tepee, Suzy saw that indeed he looked royally *pissed!*

He contemptuously tossed Billy through the air over to Cholhkan who daftly caught him and roughly shoved him down next to Suzy.

"Hi, Suzy," Billy gulped. "I guess I didn't get away from the corral fast enough."

"Don't feel bad," she whispered back, "I didn't move fast enough either. But I was right! Cholhkan had our cellphones. I've got them both hidden in my pocket."

Using rope made from twisted strips of deer hide, Cholhkan immobilized both of them, tying their feet and hands. Suzy was grateful that he didn't tie her hands too tightly behind her. The blood flow wasn't being cut off. But she was still well hogtied, no matter how much she tried to squirm loose.

A heated discussion broke out between the Chief and Cholhkan that Suzy couldn't follow. They gestured wildly, even yelling at each other! She vividly saw everything happening by the pulsating light from the red ruby which was still lying on the floor where she'd dropped it. And the Chief and Cholhkan repeatedly pointed down at the red-glowing jewel.

Then they seemed to come to a conclusion.

Cholhkan reverently lifted the ruby and returned it to the Medicine Bag as Mooleshawskek *untied* the ropes holding Suzy and Billy.

"*Aya!*" he curtly commanded them. "*Chinchokka' mak'sa aya!*"

Sally knew those simple commands. He was telling them to go away...go home *now!*

"*Sanokhanglo,*" Suzy said, grabbing Billy by the hand. "*Akyammokantkant.*" (I am sorry. I should not have done that).

"*Kamassa' ishholiitobla'shki!*" the Chief barked at them as they left the tent (Respect your elders!).

"*Chokma'shki!*" Billy cheerfully called back to them (Thank You!), as they walked out into swirling clouds of dirt and dust as horses continued galloping through the starlit village being frantically pursued by tribe members.

"I can't believe they just let us go," Suzy frowned, feeling at her dress pocket to make sure the metallic cellphones were still there. Yes, through her dress she felt their comforting flat lengths. They'd gotten clean away with their loot!

...or had they?

Somehow, it seemed too easy.

"That was fun!" Billy laughed as he paused at the entrance flap of his tepee where several other boys lived with their parents. "Let's do it again!"

"Get some sleep, Billy," she wearily urged him. "I don't think we've heard the last of this. I have a feeling that something big is going to happen tomorrow."

"You think they're going to punish us?" Billy asked, no longer so flippant. "We're outsiders, right? Maybe they're going to *kill* us!"

"I hope not."

"But they're friendly, right?" Billy whined, now sounding worried.

"I'm sure they won't do anything too bad to us. They're not going to execute us for just looking in their tent. Maybe they'll give us a public lecturing or something."

"Well, let's not risk it," he insisted. "Call up Mom and Dad on our cellphones. They can come pick us up tomorrow! I'm kinda tired of being a wild Indian, anyway...heh," he finished weakly.

She nodded, wanting to find a secluded place to try and use the cellphones where no one could see. But she was pretty sure they wouldn't work.

Not only were the batteries probably long depleted, she feared that "home" was far, far away.

They might never see their parents again.

Suzy had the chilling realization that whatever Mooleshawskek and Cholhkan decided to do to them—there was nothing that she or her brother could to do stop it!

Maybe that's why they let Suzy and Billy go: they were *trapped* there in the village on the wide grassy plain, unable to hide or escape. Once they came to a decision, the village leaders could take whatever action they wished against them, anytime at all!

Suzy felt sick to her stomach as she walked back to her smaller tent where her female "room-mates" were still running around trying to catch the loose, panicked ponies.

Maybe it was a very bad mistake to invade the Medicine Man's tent?

But maybe it also had forced their hand?

Whatever, Suzy was certain something *bad* was going to happen—sooner rather than later.

As she crawled under her thick buffalo-hide blanket, trying to block out the sounds of hoofs and shouts outside the tent, Suzy morbidly wondered if tomorrow she and Billy would even be alive.

Sally had an irrational thought that her kids were down below.

But that was insane. Suzy and Billy couldn't be on a crashed alien starship on a floating ice mountain circling Saturn! But before the ORV phased out from the Park, Sally had perfectly aligned it with the neutrino vector along which the kids in the Obelisk were taken. She'd anticipated that she and Dave were just going to take a short hop to the parallel human Dimension, her original home. Indeed, her glowing Turtle Tattoo seemed to signal that destination. But ending up floating in space above Saturn's rings was definitely not what she'd expected.

"Whatever or whoever is down there," she growled, "I'm coming for you!"

As she drifted closer, using the last bits of propulsive gas from her steering canisters to make final adjustments to the ORV's vector, she reached over into the backseat and checked her rifle. It was locked and loaded.

But the force field protecting her from the deadly vacuum of outer space was weakening. She saw sputters of yellow sparks where it was thinning. And it was rapidly getting colder in the Ranger. The heating unit that Dave had rigged to circulate warm air wasn't keeping up with the vast near absolute-zero vacuum outside.

She dug down in the backseat and yanked out a camouflage hunting coat, squirming into it and snapping the front buttons closed. Then she flipped the attached hood up over her head, pulling the drawstrings tight so only her face showed.

"There," she sighed, "maybe I won't freeze before I'm down."

But the air was also getting stuffy. Dave had installed a scuba div-ing recycled-air system in the Ranger for just such an emergency. It was working, but with limited capability. It had a small oxygen canis-ter plus a CO2-scrubber. Sally knew it could keep her breathing for maybe two hours. After that, she'd die of asphyxiation. But how long she'd been knocked out as she fell through subspace?

"I've got to land!" she realized, frantically punching at the key-board of her laptop.

A small radar unit showed the rotating ice-mountain in crisp de-tail. The crashed Spike-Ship showed up as a black blot towards its northern pole. Zooming in on it she could just see what looked like a black opening on one of the spaceship's crumpled sides. Extrapolat-ing her descent vector with that opening revealed that she would miss it! Rats! And she didn't have a spacesuit to go roaming around on her own. The DE-generator was almost offline, just barely maintain-ing the sputtering force field around the ORV!

"I've got to stick this landing," she frowned, ice-particles freezing in the air in front of her face as she breathed.

But the canister of air powering her steering jets was depleted!

"Oh, Jesus...I've got to use the last of my oxygen tank," she grimly concluded to herself. "Oh well, if I miss that opening then I'm doomed anyway."

She tapped her laptop to divert the flow of the oxygen tank to the steering lines. Then she calculated the complex vectors of her rotat-ing ORV versus the movement of the ice mountain versus the fixed opening in the crumpled black structure toward which she was fall-ing.

"Here goes nothing," she sighed, clicking an icon on the screen.

She was jammed to the side as the ORV flipped then jerked for-ward, plunging toward the fast-approaching dark gap.

"I hope that opening's real," she gasped as she sped toward it. "Otherwise I'm going to get squashed flat!"

Chapter 10

MIRAGE

It's an ancient, unresolvable problem
How do you know if what you see is real
When everything that we "experience"
Is in reality but countless neurons in our brains
Tweaking each other through chemical synapses
Why our nightmares and dreams can seem so solid
And yet they are but figments of our minds
Is Life then but a fevered nightmare
The product of an upset stomach or the flu
Conjured-up by ourselves or others
Seemingly confirmed by sight, sounds
Taste, touch, and smells so vivid
Mere electrical impulses in our heads
Vivid illusions deluding the gullible
Or a hard, undeniable certainty
That what we wish is true?

The Minstrel's Lark, 10:32-36

Tommy was ready to try to launch the shuttlecraft.

Dennis and Joyce were sitting in the cockpit with him. They'd insisted on coming along. After all, if something broke in the long-decommissioned small spacecraft he'd need them to fix it. Also, they were his good friends. They didn't want him to go alone.

"Thanks, guys!" Tommy grinned at them.

"I want to see if it holds together," Joyce toothily grinned back at him from the copilot seat. "I made the replacement parts—and I guarantee my work!"

She slowly blinked her big orange eyes in the mannerism Tommy had learned was a dinosapien sign of encouragement.

"And I'm responsible for installing them," Dennis nodded from behind Tommy, sitting in the "jump" seat behind the pilot.

The shuttlecraft was from their destroyed dinosapien starship. They both knew it intimately, its configuration and components. Tommy couldn't have a better "crew" than Dennis and Joyce. Plus, the seats and openings were all configured to accommodate their nine-feet-tall, tail-swinging dinosaur bodies.

In fact, Tommy—outwardly but a five-year-old little boy—had to "scooch" far forward in the pilot seat to operate the controls. But he didn't mind. In fact, it was kind of fun to be leaving the surface of Mars for a little trip!

"Ready to go?" he brightly asked his two dinosapien friends.

"All systems look nominal," Joyce replied, peering at her copilot console.

"The DE-generator is spun up to full capacity," Dennis answered as well, ducking down to check on vibrating conduits located beneath their seats. "I think we're good."

"Ok, then," Tommy said, engaging the drive.

The shuttlecraft shuddered—then lurched up into the air! For a moment it hesitated, as if it were going to plunge back to the Martian ground. But then it drifted upward, picking up speed as it did.

Looking out the side window Tommy saw the waving purple carpet covering the floor of the vast rift valley below him. The superintelligent syncytium rippled with streaks of white and blue—as if waving goodbye to him!

"Goodbye, big flat brain," he gave a little wave downward. "It's just a survey trip. I'll be back shortly!"

And then they were thousands of feet up into the thin atmosphere. Tommy could see the long slash in the surface of the planet from which they'd arisen, the *Valles Marineris*. Giant cliffs rose up to each side of the deep canyon. Then they were high enough to see the spots of circular craters scattered about the red surface that lay beyond the canyon. And then the slit became a small line, to the sides of which Tommy saw several huge volcanoes...beyond which a giant mountain loomed upward, *Olympus Mons!*

And then they were high enough to see the entire planet beneath them with its two filmy-white poles. A few gigantic white dust storms drifted across the red surface below.

"Ok, we did it," Tommy chortled, delighted. "Nice work, Dennis and Joyce. You did *great!*"

"It is nice to be back in outer space," Joyce sighed, animatedly looking out the windows at the red planet displayed down below.

"That's as long as we don't have to battle more Demons or subspace Spiders!" Dennis laughed from behind Tommy.

Tommy thoughtfully nodded, carefully accelerating the small spaceship to place it neatly into orbit around Mars. He wanted to get a good look at the entire planet. It would only take a couple hours at the most to circle Mars. He had time to enjoy being up in orbit. Looking upward he saw the deep blackness of outer space, punctuated by many brilliant stars. To the side, the sun was much smaller than it looked from Earth, but still was a large whitely glowing sphere. Plus he could just make out the largest moon of Mars coming up over the horizon, Phobos!

It was very comforting to Tommy to know that the stars, sun, and moons were just as they were supposed to be.

"Should we engage our subspace drive and travel onward all the way to Earth?" Joyce suggested, starting to float up from her large copilot seat. "If so, I need to go to the hold and inspect the DE-generator...make sure it doesn't have any micro-ruptures."

"I guess we could do that," Tommy shrugged. "But I wanted to make sure everything's ok with Mars first."

"Everything looks fine to me," Dennis brightly replied. He reached out one of his clawed hands to help Joyce drift over and into the hatchway leading down to the small hold. "I'll come up to the front seat and keep watch on the readouts."

"Sure," Tommy said. "Thanks, Dennis."

And so they sped along through space quietly. Tommy was still immensely puzzled at how his dear friends "Old Sally" and "Young Sally" could just vanish from the colony. Maybe it was an alien trick? Or perhaps *he* was just confused? Was his memory screwed up? But how could that happen? He didn't have to rely on fickle neuronal biological synapses. His brain was a mechanical array of many parallel micro-quantum computers!

His brain wasn't easily fooled.

"Ah...Tommy?" Dennis gulped, his voice strained.

"Yes, Dennis?"

"Uh...you might like to take a look at the surface of Mars that's coming up down below."

Right, they were now orbiting past their departure surface to the "back" side of Mars.

"Sure, Dennis, I was just thinking about..." Tommy began as he looked down and out the side window, but then abruptly stopped speaking.

Below them—where there should have been the normal, cratered red surface—was...

—a solid, black *flat* platform!

And the blackness seemed *fluorescent*, with *faint red lines* running through it in a regular grid-like pattern!

"That's...*not*...right," Tommy frowned. He blinked his eyes several times, thinking something was wrong with his vision.

"What is it?" Joyce said, climbing back out of the hold.

"Take a look," Dennis gulped.

She craned her long neck, placing a big orange eye up against her side window to see all the better.

"Oh, my!" she gasped. "I thought that...planets were *round*...not flat on one side?"

"So..." Tommy affirmatively concluded. "I was right then. Something is very, very *wrong!* Are we ready to make the jump through subspace to Earth, Joyce?"

"I...think so...no ruptures in the power conduits or fractures in the generator..."

"Then please put back on your seatbelts, my friends. We're going to Earth. But let's make sure we have the coordinates and settings correct. I'll set the overall vectors. Dennis, would you please run a check on the shuttle's systems? And Joyce, would you plot the DE-configuration? I know we're never completely sure where we'll end up when we go into subspace, but..."

"With our excellent jump engine, I'd say we've a 95% chance of ending up where we want to go," Joyce assured him. "Remember it's a design that incorporates the sophisticated science of our Martian Snake colleagues, not just our Dinosapien technology. If everything's working correctly in the shuttlecraft, then I think we'll get to Earth just fine."

As they busily completed their tasks, the little spaceship continued swinging around the flat, black backside of Mars...emerging on the other side where the surface looked perfectly normal.

Half the planet was as expected. The back half seemed like a platform or stage for a theatrical "false front"!

It was beyond bewildering. Tommy knew without a doubt that what he'd just witnessed was impossible.

"Are we ready?"

"All set!" Dennis said, putting a warm paw upon Tommy's shoulder.

"According to the instruments, everything's functioning nominally," Joyce answered, intently monitoring her laptop readouts.

"Here goes," Tommy said, looking down at the instrument panel to "pop" the proper sequence of knobs...

—as a *swirling tunnel of light* enclosed them...

—which immediately stopped!

"What?" Tommy frowned.

"We've fallen out of subspace," Joyce urgently observed. "Our path's been truncated."

"Not just excluded...we're up against a *barrier!*" Dennis huffed, peering fearfully out the forward windows.

Tommy looked up at a fast-approaching *shimmering black wall!* It had that same look as the inexplicable backside of Mars. And its surface seemed to be a *projector screen* of some sort! Yes, to the side Tommy could see a sprinkling of "stars." And the "sun" shining down brightly was an *image* set-onto yet another section! Indeed, even the largest moon of Mars, Phobos, was just a two-dimensional picture traveling across the colossal screen! And like the underside of Mars, there was also a grid of red lines running through the projection-barrier. But seen up close, the lines were spread miles apart.

"Maybe if we're sneaky, we can slip through between the red lines?" Tommy frowned, biting his lower lip. "Let's just see what happens if we turn off our DE-generator and just drift forward."

The lights inside the shuttlecraft blinked out then came back on as a faint green emergency-light glow. Now they were drifting unpowered. Their external force field shield flickered off. Fortunately, Joyce and Dennis had done a great job of repairing the external physical walls and the virtually unbreakable glasteel of the windows. If they didn't smash into a meteor or something, they should be ok. The air in the ship and internal heat would last for a while on emergency battery power.

Though they were now unpowered, they were actually traveling at the barrier thousands of miles per hour, since they hadn't shed their orbital speed.

They were fast approaching the black barrier.

"We're entering it," Joyce quietly stated.

The ship shuddered and rocked, but didn't stop. Instead it kept plummeting deeper, light from outside blocked off, until...

—they emerged into a SOLID WHITE EXPANSE!

"Ahhhh..." Dennis nodded knowingly.

"We're back to where we came from," Joyce shuddered, reaching a paw forward to grab onto Dennis' clawed hand.

"Yep," Tommy agreed. "It's *sub*-subspace...wow."

"Are we still between the Universes?" Joyce asked, her voice trembling. "Is us living in a peaceful, successful colony on Mars just something that we dreamed up? Was it not real at all?"

"Whatever that was down there, we're *here* right now," Dennis reassured her. "We're together. And that's what matters the most."

"But we're *beyond* the black subspace barrier," Tommy pondered thoughtfully. "What if we activate our subspace drive right now? It saved us before, didn't it? I don't know how, but it threw us to our Mars oasis, right? What if we try it again? Do you think we can get into SUB-*sub*-subspace?"

"But we have no idea...we didn't have any notion that it could even exist before we tried it in desperation to escape the collapsing evil Universe...and now?" Joyce shook her head, *tears* of fear starting to drip from her big orange eyes!

"Yes, it sure is a big risk," Tommy agreed. "If you guys want, we can retreat, get back through the barrier, and return to Valles Marineris. But now we'll know we're in a cage, or trap, or..."

"Do it!" Dennis snapped. "We're *explorers*, damn it! Give it a try, Tommy."

"You're sure? Joyce?"

"Yes."

"Ok, then. Dennis, power us up. Joyce, please set another course for Earth. Now that we're outside the subspace shell that was surrounding the fake Mars, maybe it'll work this time to get us home...who knows? Could that be where Young Sally and Old Sally went?"

Dennis laughed, shakily.

"Yes, my good friend Tommy—'who knows' indeed? I still don't know who these two 'Sally' humans are that you think existed with us, but I am willing to take the risk of helping you find them. After all, it was you who saved us from the Demon when the two Universes separated. The least we can do is to try and return the favor."

"And I feel the same, Tommy," Joyce chimed in. "We're with you to the end!"

Dennis reached out his scaly arms to clasp Tommy and Joyce around their shoulders.

Tommy felt very warm in his chest, like he was going to cry. Yet it wasn't a sad feeling. It was a *happy* feeling. He was lucky to have such good friends!

"Here goes," Tommy grinned, "popping" the proper knobs in sequence.

And they "winked" out of existence.

Galileo held Virginia's hands, looking at her lovingly.

"You are in charge while I am gone," he nodded to her. "Do not be shy or reticent, my little angel. And do not limit your decisions by what I might have done. Do better! You are a highly intelligent, knowledgeable, but still-sensitive leader. Exercise your authority with confidence."

"Father, you sound like you will be gone a long time!" she replied in alarm.

"We actually should be gone—from your perspective—for only a few minutes," Anderson interjected. "Regardless, though, I've instructed the Keepers here to work under your direction. So enjoy your 'authority,' however brief. I assure you that your new responsibilities won't last long enough for you to alter your regular routine."

"That is good to know," Virginia sighed in relief. "But what you're doing still sounds dangerous. You *will* protect my Father, Mr. Anderson?"

"Of course," he sternly answered. "Without him our plan here might be delayed. His world-wide fame allows these momentous changes to be accepted. But we've already set major events in motion. They now have a powerful momentum of their own. In the unlikely event we should not soon return, you need merely guide them forward. The Custodian will give you the specific information you need. The remaining Keepers will protect you from any existential threats. Be assured that your efforts are building and protecting a vibrant, new future!"

She seemed less reassured, her frown returning.

Galileo kissed her on her forehead, giving her a warm hug.

He whispered in her ear so that none others could hear: <*The monk has a network of spies in Guildhall. But I think they are not our enemies. Seek them out for their advice and counsel. I trust them far more than our exalted Muslim clerics.*>

Then he pulled away, holding her at arm's length.

"Do not worry, daughter," he mock-ordered her, knowing she was too independent and intelligent to ever blindly obey anyone, even him. "I shall return promptly! Meanwhile, keep up your good works."

"I hold you to that promise," she sadly replied, stepping back, looking at him with a puzzled expression. "And yes, *your* work will continue, regardless. I will enlist any help to advance your great vision."

Grinning, Galileo impulsively handed her his heavy Mephistopheles Cane.

"And what is this for, Father?"

"It is the symbol of my authority! We'll only be touring in Agent Anderson's wonderful self-powered carriage. I'll not need it on this inspection tour. And you can give it back to me upon my return."

"Then I will keep it safe for you," she grimaced, gingerly taking it by its ivory knob.

<And take these also> he quickly whispered as he grabbed her up in a last hug.

Unseen by the others present, he'd slipped the two future-time pictures into her pocket.

With a cheerful wave, Galileo followed Anderson over to their time-travel vehicle. It was what Anderson called a "bub." It was a future horseless carriage powered internally. It was a square device with four large, rubbery wheels supporting a clear, rounded canopy. Inside, Galileo slid into the passenger seat while Anderson sat behind a wheel.

Already in the backseat was the old monk. Galileo had insisted that the Buddhist priest accompany them. Why, he wasn't sure. But something in the monk's manner convinced him that the religious leader was absolutely necessary.

Galileo was afraid that what they encountered might be so outside his experience he'd not be able to evaluate its positive and negative aspects. The placid priest with his unflappable observations was a counterweight to the arrogant Anderson. Plus, the monk served as Galileo's religious "inspector" to help evaluate the *divinity* of the results of their actions.

They were beneath Guildhall in one of the large basement chambers. The low ceiling was supported by a series of stone arches. Suspended oil lamps gave off a dim yellow light. Shadows played around them. The "bub" was too large to have entered the chamber by the stairs. Instead, it had been "transported" there at some past moment. In the same way, Galileo was ready to proceed with Anderson into the *far distant future!*

It was the only way Galileo could know for sure that the drastic changes he was helping perpetuate upon the world were worthy of continuing.

Yes, it was a "crisis of conscience" resolvable only by first-hand inspection!

"So are you ready to see for yourself what the world will look like *four hundred years* from now?" Anderson grinned at him.

"I am indeed," Galileo resolutely nodded.

Outwardly he was calm. Inwardly he was trembling. This was by far the most momentous occasion of his entire life, even greater than waiting in a cell to be burned alive at the stake! He was traveling into the distant future—a future that he had helped shape. The Custodian gave him knowledge of what the world would have become *without* his continued survival and acceleration of scientific research. Now, he'd see if the *new* future was better.

"And you, Monk—are you ready to help the Professor feel the *Power of God* in the grand future which we've help shape?" Anderson demanded.

Galileo saw Anderson looking expectantly back at the bald headed man, who to Galileo's eyes at this momentous occasion seemed to be taking a nap!

And then the monk's lips parted...

"The past is already gone. The future is not yet here. There's only one moment for you to live."

Anderson lightly laughed, turning back to the controls. "I do not think that he will be of much use to you, Professor. But I agree he is amusing. If our vehicle were not completely shielded against detection—making us virtually undetectable to any future observers—I'd insist on leaving him behind. But since we'll not be landing, he's not a hindrance. There will be no battles, just stealthy observations."

"I have a mean *kick!*" the Monk mildly observed from behind Galileo. "And I carry items of great value," he continued as he lifted up a small purse-like bag that hung at his waist.

Galileo was amused. Next to the future technology they'd be contained and protected within, whatever the monk had in his bag was archaic at best, useless at worst. But he did remember the man kicking the legs out from under the old woman who almost succeeded in discharging her future weapon. He respected the power of the man, remembering that though Buddhists were pacifists they were by no means powerless. Indeed, they were clever and inventive!

"Hold on tight," Anderson ordered them. "We're phasing-out."

A loud "humming" sounded from the engine. A strangely penetrating *vibration* ran through Galileo's body. And around the bub a *blue-haze* was rapidly forming.

Galileo gasped as they abruptly *fell* into a spinning, glittering *vortex!* All the colors in the spectrum glowed and sparkled around him. And an ear-piercing "howling" noise—penetrating even through the blue shield surrounding them—was deafening!

Terrified, Galileo clung to the door handle on his side of the vehicle for dear life. He glanced back at the monk, hoping he was likewise holding on.

But Lhamo was smiling broadly, his eyes now wide with excitement.

"*Wheeeeee!*" he called-out, sticking his thin arms up into the air, "no hands!"

Galileo closed his eyes tightly.

If this kept up much longer he was going to *vomit* up his guts...

Dave felt sick to his stomach.

Two weeks had passed since the attack by his infected friend Losa. After ten days the CDC personnel released Dave and Victor from medical isolation. They were showing no ill effects from the scratches and punctures they'd suffered fighting off the crazed man. Biopsies of their small wounds revealed perfectly normal, healing scar tissue. Their blood profiles were unremarkable. Their DNA sequences were unchanged. To all appearances they were unaffected by their contact with the raging monster. The world could breathe a sigh of relief. It seemed that mankind was safe from a "zombie apocalypse" where infected humans could pass on the contagion to fellow humans through scratches and bites.

"It's very impressive, isn't it, my boy?" Victor mused, standing with Dave on the edge of the large excavation.

Yes, it was incredibly impressive and exciting. Rock Creek had been diverted, allowing the soil around the embedded Obelisk to drain. The trees and shrubs that'd surrounded a once-peaceful glade were gone. And a fifty-foot-high concrete wall had been erected around the entire stadium-sized area. It had been a massive construction project, achieved in only a few short weeks.

It's amazing what can be achieved when the government is collectively *terrified!*

"*Ominously* impressive, Victor...ominously so," Dave carefully replied.

Even standing on top of the ten-foot-wide wall in thick, protective radiation suits, observing the Obelisk from a distance—Dave still did not feel safe.

Both he and Victor were clad in black rubber-looking suits complete with black gloves, black boots, respirators, transparent face shields, and wrap-around helmets. The radiation-protective suit was constructed from the latest nanotech materials. It was capable of stopping not just radioactive particles but also inhibiting X-ray and gamma-ray exposure as well. They were about to go over the wall and approach the scientific bunker down below. Without the suit they'd be dead in minutes.

Versus the already-lethal close-in radiation that Dave had initially observed on fish and turtles, the levels since had *increased* dramatically. Rather than "cooling," the Obelisk was *heating up!*

No one had any idea what the build-up was leading to...just that it was proof the Obelisk was not dormant. It had an *agenda*—if only they could figure out what it was.

"No safer place on the planet, David," Victor happily replied, carefully moving over to the descent elevator. "There's enough police and military here to stop an invading army!"

Yes, his old friend Professor Volodymyr was correct. Indeed, Dave felt smothered by the many troops stationed around the outside of the wall, the radiation suit-protected snipers patrolling the top of the wall, and the circling gunship helicopters "thwupping" overhead.

But that was not what was upsetting Dave's stomach. It was the knowledge that another incarnation of this Obelisk had stolen his children. Perhaps this very Obelisk below had somehow prevented him from accompanying Sally when his ORV phased out of this Dimension. It was an unknown, alien Enemy that threatened not just his life but his *heart!* He wanted to either *destroy* it—if that were possible—or *run* screaming away from it! Yet he was the world's only "expert" on the ancient Martian artifact, here to supervise their first attempt at opening it up.

Due to the intense electromagnetic flux at play—which was now *warping* the very space-time continuum close-in to the Artifact—

normal distal communication methods were impossible. Personnel had to be physically near the Artifact to "by wire" direct robotic probes approaching its various surfaces. And that's what Dave and Victor would help out with from inside the science bunker located down below.

"You've had an interesting life, my boy," Victor congratulated him as they descended in the manually powered elevator cage. They were lowering themselves on a pulley system of ropes and levers. "You actually traveled *inside* that thing to other worlds, other times and places. You must be eager to get another look at it, see what new things you can learn!"

"Uhm...sure," Dave unenthusiastically mumbled.

They were slightly jarred as the cage "thumped" down onto bare ground. The cage door opened. They stepped out into what now looked like a moonscape. The ground had been sheered down by heavily shielded large construction equipment into what was now an ugly brown plain. Craters dotted the expanse from where massive equipment had sat. And in the middle of it all loomed the still-embedded Red Pillar, emanating a *pulsating* crimson glow!

Involuntarily, Dave *shuddered*.

"Professor Volodymyr, Dr. King," a man greeted them, similarly suited. "I'm Colonel Tillman. I'm from DARPA. We're heading up the Obelisk research team."

"I'm so pleased to make your acquaintance!" Victor happily replied, reaching out to grasp the man's similarly black-gloved hand. "You people do good work. My research was funded largely by the Navy, but a number of my colleagues back at Yale had DARPA grants."

"I'm sure we have much to talk about, but now we have to walk," the man said, turning toward the concrete bunker that lay halfway to the Obelisk. "Our transportation vehicle quit working a couple hours ago. The bunker is thickly lead-shielded, which stops most of the hard radiation. But the exposed equipment out here works erratically, if at all."

Following the Colonel as they walked across the barren landscape which had once been the beautiful Rock Creek camping area, Dave pondered the significance of DARPA's involvement. The *Defense Ad-*

vanced Research Projects Agency was founded in 1958 as part of the United State reaction to the unexpected launch by the Russians of the Sputnik-1 orbiter in 1957. The purpose of the agency was to jump-start new technology, particularly that of possible importance to military defense. Over the decades DARPA helped establish the basis of space exploration, missile defense, the computer revolution, and the Internet. Presently, Dave was vaguely aware that the agency was hugely into artificial intelligence, quantum computing, virtual reality development, human-machine interfaces, and new modes of space travel.

Yep. No doubt they'd be *very* interested in an ancient Martian artifact capable of traveling through space and time! Plus, the potential military application of such technology was mind-blowing. Controlling this technology would not only let you win any war, but go back in time to prevent the enemy from attacking you in the first place! With it, a nation could literally *rewrite history* to suit its own objectives.

At least that was the theory which Dave assumed Colonel Tillman was operating under. It also explained the huge amount of resources thrown at this supposed alien threat. But Dave knew from hard experience that realization of those temporal objectives was far more uncertain and difficult than anyone here suspected.

The Obelisk was no mere artifact, to be used by others as they saw fit. Indeed, it had *a mind of its own*, working to achieve its own purpose. But it was still a machine. Dave and Sally had made it obey their own directives. With enough ingenuity and determination, others could do the same.

And he *must not allow* that to happen!

It was simply too much power for any one person or nation to possess. Dave was dismayed to realize that this new objective was even more important than finding Sally or his kids. He'd had a great life. He had much for which to be thankful. He realized that should he never see Sally or his kids again, he was still already blessed beyond measure. He could not allow this new timeline, his resurrected society and world, to be dragged down by the damaged Obelisk.

Somehow he had to find a way to send the Obelisk on its way...or destroy it...no matter what it required; even should he lose Sally and the kids forever.

It was a grim conclusion. His new objective might cost him his own life. But then again, he'd been ready to make the ultimate sacrifice many times across his incredible journey.

This whole insane time-and-Universe-spanning Odyssey of his must finally *come to an end!* The new life of humanity, its revitalized future, couldn't be more than just a brief interlude, a mirage. Dave had to find a way to make it *permanent!*

No more diversions.

It had to stop here.

Chapter 11

<u>GONE</u>

I'd like to celebrate the glorious past
Without regard to the pains of the present
Or fear of the inevitably looming future disaster
But I can't, trapped in my own damnable perceptions
Where that long life of peace, prosperity and happiness
Is suddenly shattered and cheapened by crippling loss
Especially when caused by the dice's random toss
Or the inexplicable whims of mercurial Nature
Or the inevitable flakiness of human biology
Letting you down when you were just
Starting to appreciate your blessings
Now just ephemeral memories
Is there nothing permanent?
Or must we base our love
On fading snapshots?
The Minstrel's Lark, 11:1-5

Tommy groggily awoke.

"Where are we?" he weakly said, blinking his eyes to clear them.

He remembered that they'd been in the white *sub*-subspace outside the black subspace sphere enclosing the fake Mars. They'd activated their subspace drive to throw themselves into the theoretical SUB-*sub*-subspace. Wow! Wasn't it amazing there were so many levels to what humans knew as "reality"?

But Tommy's wonderment quickly turned to fear. Where were his two faithful Dinosapien friends?

He was suddenly thrown into panic: were they gone? Had they *vanished,* the same as had Young Sally and Old Sally?

Dennis' big dinosaur head slowly rose from the floor up into Tommy's view. "Did we make it?" he gasped.

In the backseat, Joyce's reptilian head also rose up into Tommy's view.

"Are we in orbit around Earth?" she asked, also blinking her big orange eyes.

Whew! His two friends were ok! Now they just had to figure out where...

Tommy just sat in his seat, silently staring out the front window.

He was struck speechless.

"No..." Dennis gasped, peering intently out his side-window.

"How can this be?" Joyce chimed in.

They were back sitting on the raised platform on the floor of Valles Marineris. All around, Tommy saw the same sea of purple tentacles that composed the super-intelligent Syncytium. The shuttlecraft now appeared exactly as it had been when they'd first started repairing it. It was inert, broken and spotted, with hanging-loose controls, and no light to any of the readouts.

"So...something...doesn't want us getting out of here," Dennis said in a small voice. He tentatively stretched his two scaly arms upward to push up the again-cracked canopy. It was stuck, resisting his efforts to push it outward. "And I'm guessing if we try to fix up our little spaceship again, we'll have the same results."

"But—who? *Why?*" Joyce said, shaking her big dinosaur head in disbelief.

"I don't know," Tommy replied, likewise totally baffled. "But I'm at least glad I didn't tell any of our million human-friends down in the caverns what we were doing. Now I don't have to disappoint them that..."

"Who?" Joyce retorted. "Are you feeling ok, Tommy? Did you hit your head?"

"No, I'm fine!" he now snapped at her, irritated. Then, more softly, he continued: "I'm sorry, Joyce. I guess I am a little peeved. We put out all that work to try to escape and it all came to nothing! At least we've still got our nice Dinosapien town and Human cities down in the caverns to live our lives in which..."

"Human cities?" Dennis frowned, having finally gotten the canopy fully opened. "What are you talking about, Tommy? It was just you, us, and a few fellow Dinosapiens that escaped the Harvester before the two Universes separated. You know full well that all the poor humans in the tubes didn't make it. There was nowhere to put them in our little shuttlecraft! Sure, I feel bad that they're not here with us on Mars, but you shouldn't blame yourself...or us!"

Tommy stared at his friend silently for a moment, stunned.

"You...really don't remember...either the human cities or Old Sally and Young Sally?"

They both stared at him with deeply puzzled expressions.

"I think maybe you are sick," Joyce said, sounding very worried. "There's always been just you and we Dinosapiens here stranded together. Are you having hallucinations?"

"Ah...hah, hah...yep, that must be it. Maybe I did hit my head or something...but don't worry! I'm ok...I think maybe I just need to take a nap or something."

"Well, don't worry about us being on a fake Mars, Tommy," Dennis encouraged him, stretching up to his full height to step out of the shuttlecraft through the opened canopy. "We'll figure it out. Now that we know what's happening, we can run tests. We've still got all our equipment and combined brain power! Plus the Syncytium may have some idea what...*uh, oh!*"

He ducked back inside, fearfully pulling down the canopy.

"What's wrong, dear?" Joyce asked her husband, again sounding worried.

"What if the Syncytium is *behind* this deception? After all, it's *their* world here, isn't it? They were here a billion years before we were thrown from the ripping-apart of the two Universes! Could they be manipulating us for their own, nefarious purposes?"

"Or...maybe they're just trying to protect and help us?" Joyce uncertainly ventured.

"Well I'll just ask them!" Tommy stated, nodding firmly. "They'll answer me truthfully. After all, I'm their 'Prophet.' I'll find out what they know, ok?"

Dennis frowned.

"Well...if you're sure you'll be safe. Who knows how they might react if they suspect that we've discovered their treachery?"

"Yes, I'll be fine!" Tommy insisted. "You two look really tired. Go back into the tunnels and to your house. Get some rest. After I talk with the Syncytium I'll come down into the caverns and tell you what happened. Ok?"

"Yes."

"I am indeed tired."

Tommy watched his big dinosaur friends go stomping back out through the parting carpet of waving tentacles. Their tails dragged along listlessly behind them. He waited until they were safely in the tunnels before hopping out. He stood in the tickling, gently waving "sea" which reached up to his chest, surrounding him.

"*Syncytium*! I have a few *questions* for you!" he called out sternly, his small fists planted firmly on his hips.

"YES, PROPHET TOMMY," the musical collective voice vibrated up toward the high cliffs. "WE ARE HERE."

Surely they hadn't been working against him all this time? Surely they were his friends—this evolved collective expression of his previous android comrades?

—or, maybe not? Should he approach them cautiously, or directly?

He chose the latter.

"Are you *trapping* me and my friends here on the surface of this fake planet?" he loudly accused them.

"WHO?"

"What do you mean, 'who'...?"

"TO WHOM ARE YOU REFERRING OTHER THAN YOURSELF?"

"What?"

"YOU SAID 'TRAPPING ME AND MY FRIENDS'...DID YOU MEAN TO REFER TO OTHERS THAN YOURSELF AND US?"

"Of course I did! I am 'referring' to me and my Dinosapien friends—Dennis and Joyce and the other intelligent dinosaurs!"

"BUT THERE'S ALWAYS BEEN BUT YOU AND US, PROPHET TOMMY. THERE ARE NO OTHERS ON THIS PLANET. THE DI-

NOSAPIENS WERE LOST WHEN YOU ESCAPED THE SEPARA-
TION OF THE CORRUPTED UNIVERSE. THIS IS WHAT YOU
TOLD US WHEN YOU APPEARED AMONGST US IN YOUR TER-
MINALLY DAMAGED SPACECRAFT."

"But you just saw Dennis and Joyce walk through you to the tunnels!"

"NO, WE DID NOT."

Tommy opened his mouth to shout an indignant denial! The Syncytium must be joking with him or else was confused! But then again,
he'd never heard the Syncytium tell or even understand a joke. And
the collective voice sounded as coherent and clear as always.

"AND WE CERTAINLY ARE NOT 'TRAPPING' YOU, PROPHET
TOMMY," the disembodied chorus sang loudly. "WE THOUGHT YOU
RETURNED TO US BECAUSE YOU WISHED TO DO SO, NOT BE-
CAUSE OF ANY COERCION ON OUR PART. AND MARS IS CER-
TAINLY NOT A 'FAKE' PLANET. IT IS A CELESTIAL BODY ORBIT-
ING THE SUN—AS IT HAS FOR MILLENIA INTO THE PAST."

For a while, Tommy just stood there amongst the gently waving
sea of tentacles, silent.

"I don't understand," he finally gulped, sighing.

He slowly walked back through the waving carpet to wearily climb
back onto the ceremonial platform, into the nonfunctional shuttlecraft, and slump down behind the broken steering wheel.

"Maybe I should just go down and talk to Dennis and Joyce about
the Syncytium's amnesia," he mused to himself. "They'll get a good
laugh out of the Syncytium saying they don't exist. And then we can
figure out what scientific tests we can start to..."

He stopped mumbling to himself. He'd just caught sight of the
nearby cliff face. Where there should have been a well-defined tunnel
entrance...

—now there was nothing.

It was just rock. Jagged rock. A naked cliff-face. No opening. It
was as if the buried Martian caverns had never existed.

"I sure wish Mommy was here," Tommy sobbed, feeling very
scared and alone. "She'd tell me what to do."

But she wasn't there. Apparently, she'd never existed.

And what would be gone next?

There wasn't much left to lose.

Galileo was stunned.

Yes, the trip through the "time-tunnel" in the bub was spectacular. Yes, flashing out of it into the air *thousands* of feet above the surface of the world was also incredible. And looking down from above the clouds in their concealed "stealth" craft was a particularly amazing experience!

But it was what he and the others viewed down below that rendered them all speechless.

Down below, Galileo saw the unmistakable coastline of England. The out-flowing estuary of the River Thames narrowed into the landmass. And the River Thames came from...*where* was London?

Where there should have been many cultivated plots of farmland, buildings, ships, and bridges...there was nothing! The only thing visible below was solid, unrelenting forest.

"Have we...gone into the distant past?" Galileo softly asked Anderson. "There doesn't appear to be any sign of human activity down below at all!"

"I...we...as far as I can determine...we've indeed traveled four hundred years into the future. This is how Earth looks now in the year 2038. But, where there should be a thriving civilization down below...is nothing. I don't understand," Anderson frowned, adjusting the controls so that the bub flew inland.

"*The mind is everything. What you think you become,*" the Monk spoke cryptically from the backseat.

"Please be quiet," Anderson snapped at him. "You are not helping. The likeliest explanation is that the pattern of human habitation has merely shifted from what it was in my previous timeline. I'm sure we'll find the cities shortly, much improved over what existed here before!"

Galileo looked down intently, still stunned by the magnificent view of the earth from so high up in the sky. They were actually above where the birds flew! They were even above the occasional clouds, which drifted past below. And every second he anticipated seeing cities of the future, shifted from their previous locations next to bodies of water.

And so they flew onward.

They traveled in seconds across Wales, across the Irish Sea to Ireland. Then up across Scotland. No sign of human habitation anywhere. Oxford, Liverpool, Dublin, Glasgow, Edinburgh—all vanished!

"Agent Anderson," Galileo finally asked, "is *this* what our present efforts to accelerate scientific discoveries and their application will produce? Are we somehow *dooming* the human race?"

Anderson looked perplexed, now pointing the small vehicle up into the sky to zoom up much higher. Also, their speed drastically accelerated, pushing Galileo back in his seat! Was the man trying to launch them away from the planet?

"We'll find them!" Anderson grimly snapped at Galileo. "We just need to expand our perspective. We're going up into orbit!"

Yawning widely in the back seat, the bald-headed Monk seemed unconcerned, even bored.

"Well, what do *you* say?" Galileo, now panicking, entreated the holy man.

"Oh, now you want to hear from me?" the man cheerfully replied. "Fine. I say this: *If you are facing in the right direction, all you need to do is keep on walking!*"

"Are you saying we need to keep going *up*, really?" Galileo replied, his voice now quaking with fear. Above him the blue sky was dark—quickly turning a deep black. They were leaving behind the atmosphere of the world!

"Ok. We're up in orbit," Anderson quietly stated, leveling off their flight path and flipping the ship over so they could peer "upward" at the earth that had been beneath them.

In awe, Galileo looked at continents sliding past. He made out the countries of Europe. Italy stuck out as a long narrow strip with a "boot" on the end. Africa lay below the Mediterranean Sea. He saw Egypt to the side of the Red Sea.

And then the landmasses below slipped into darkness. They were on the night side of Earth. It was magnificent! A vast thunderstorm below flickered with dancing sheets of lightning. And then they were over the long expanse of Russia, out over the Arctic Ocean, and down across Northern America.

"Damn it! We should have seen the lights of many cities," Anderson swore beside Galileo. The Time Agent shook his head from side to side in confusion. "But there's nothing down there! How could this happen? How could things go so wrong? Have could we have caused the *extinction* of the human race?"

Then Anderson gasped as they emerged into daylight.

A *large sheet of ice* covered most of North America!

"*That* should not be there," Anderson gulped. "The ice sheet for Europe was just as expected for this date. It *can't* be that different here on the other side of the world! It's as if we're viewing a whole different period in Earth's history—at different places upon the present single globe! Below us is clearly the product of one of Earth's ice ages, at least 10,000 years in the past! How can this be?"

"What should we be flying above—the Colonies?" Galileo gasped, looking down in astonishment at the glittering white expanse of ice and snow. Here and there were clear areas where green forests peeked out.

Then, abruptly, the forests ended and a vast green plain took its place.

Lhamo cheerfully replied: "*Three things cannot hide for long—the Moon, the Sun, and the Truth.*"

"Yes...yes!" Anderson nodded vigorously. "That's it! We've been going in the wrong direction. We've got to head back *down*."

"What are you doing, Agent Anderson?" Galileo gulped.

"Mankind must have advanced so radically that it's now integrated with the planet, fully harmonizing with nature! Instead of seeking disruptive cities we'll find humanity strolling in the pristine forests."

"I suppose that could be," Galileo began...

—when Anderson turned the nose of the bub downward and again *accelerated* as they hurtled northward, again above the icy sheet...

—as Galileo *screeched* in fear! They were plummeting so fast that the air in front of the vehicle burst into flames! The bub *rocked violently*, throwing Galileo against his seatbelt and the inner side of the bub. And then they were past the roiling fire, slowing as they fast-approached the forested land below...

—Anderson pulling up sharply, slowing precipitously...

—and then they were drifting along *just above the treetops* of an icy, snow-covered landscape, looking directly down upon...

"I see them! But...?" Anderson gasped.

—as a *band of hairy humans* with spears chased after huge, fur-covered, shaggy elephants! The mammoth beasts were trumpeting in fear, their long trunks flopping upward in the air as they lumbered along.

"Those are savages!" Galileo observed, entranced.

"Maybe...there are probably other groups of humans down there who are incredibly advanced...we just didn't see them...we were too high," Anderson grimaced, clearly trying to make sense of it all.

"There are only two mistakes one can make along the road to truth," Lhamo added from behind Galileo, *"—not going all the way, and not starting."*

"Yes," Anderson nodded, starting a whole new sequence of movements with the controls. "I apologize for my rude words before, Monk. You *are* useful to the success of this trip!"

"What are you...?" Galileo gulped, wishing they could just return home! He had a sinking feeling in his heart that the "advanced" humans of Anderson's wishes no longer existed. Clearly, his and Anderson's past efforts at changing society for the better were an unmitigated disaster. They must return and try to restore the 17th century to its previous, undisturbed state. The marvelous "inventions" they'd introduced had to be disavowed and destroyed. There was *no* way that this awful, regressive future could be the Will of the Lord!

Everything that made humans "civilized" had been lost.

"I'm establishing a 'reference point,' Professor," Anderson said, pausing to reach up and push up his dark eyeglasses that had fallen to the tip of his nose. "There is a *parallel* world to this, the one from which the Time Traveler came who burned to death in your place. Its timeline was not altered. There, your counterpart took the path of cowardice and meekly renounced his 'false' observation that Earth circles the sun, rather than the church doctrine that Earth is the center of Creation. It will only take a short jump for us to confirm that civilization marches along as expected. If that's true, then we're in a much better position to understand what's happened here. This may not be just some unrelated calamity that killed off most of humanity. Instead it may be proof of a vengeful God!"

Galileo gasped, realizing that could be true.

"So you think that the *Lord Himself* could have seen us going too far, too fast?" he said, his hands grasping feebly at his gray beard in amazement.

"It has happened before," Anderson nodded. "But it was not a partial destruction of mankind, rather a complete cleansing—taking us into His Magnificent Presence! However, the Lord can do whatever He wants...we must know His Will!"

"What do you think, Monk? You're my Divine Guide!"

"Please call me Lhamo."

"Whatever! Do you agree with Anderson or not?" Galileo frantically interrogated him.

"*It is better to conquer yourself than to win a thousand battles,*" Lhamo spoke calmly from the rear seat. "*Then the victory is yours. It cannot be taken from you.*"

"That doesn't help!"

"Hold tight," Anderson ordered them, ignoring the monk's cryptic comment. "We're about to phase over into the other human Dimension."

Galileo trembled, desperately wanting to go home! But he was trapped here with what he now realized were two religious *fanatics!* The Monk seemed only to see the individual and his or her particular struggles. The Agent seemed only to respond to supposed Divine Purpose, regardless of the consequences. But Galileo was more practical. He just wanted a better world for everyone! But that result now seemed more and more impossible.

"I must drop our stealth concealments for us to do this," Anderson muttered. "But that won't matter. There's nothing here to bother us on this side of the divide. Once we make it over into the other Dimension I'll turn the stealth mode back on so that their military doesn't see us. Ok. I'm ready. We're going. Hold on!"

He punched at knobs and slid up levers.

Galileo was breathing heavily, gasping for air. He felt like he was having a heart attack.

"Wheee!" Lhamo exclaimed gleefully, again raising his fists up into the air. "No hands!"

The world around them was wavering, twisting, a blue haze opening up before them into which they zoomed...

—to CRASH into it, the metal around Galileo seemingly in slow-motion *twisting* and *banging* his shoulder painfully as the bub *FELL* downward, SMASHING through a layer of big tree branches before SLAMMING down into deep snow.

Everything was quiet.

Twisting his head to the side Galileo saw the Monk behind him, shards of glasteel from the "unbreakable" canopy covering his prone body. The canopy of the bub had inexplicably *shattered*. Beside Galileo he heard Anderson moaning as he regained consciousness. He was crushed-back in his seat, held in place by the protruding wheel.

And walking up cautiously to the crashed vehicle, their spears held at-ready, was a party of hide-covered, hairy humans.

"We come...in peace?" Galileo feebly grunted at them.

They looked at each other uncertainly then grinned—revealing yellowed, broken teeth.

To Galileo they looked *hungry*.

Sally was now gasping for breath as she drifted down toward the gaping maw of the crashed alien starship.

She was almost out of air.

The floating ice mountain was zooming up at her—its white peaks thrust out like jagged spears.

Her shielded ORV was now rotating perilously in its descent. She was going to miss the yawning black opening for which she was aiming! Instead she'd smash straight into a rocky ridge of the floating ice mountain to the side of the opening!

She desperately ejected the very last contents of her oxygen canister—seeing puffs of ice crystals to each side of the ORV—trying to correct the spin and resultant vector of her vehicle. It was all she could do. And that was the very last of her oxygen. If there wasn't breathable air inside the interior of the wrecked alien craft she'd suffocate.

"Goodbye Dave, kids," she sighed, closing her eyes, resigned to her fate...

—as she drifted on through the dark opening, feeling an electric "crackle" over her body as she zipped across an energy barrier. She skidded, feeling her vehicle spinning around out of control...

—and then SLAMMED to an abrupt stop!

"Ouch," she managed, pulling her arm loose from being squashed up against the inside of the ORV.

It was a rough landing. But at least she was safely down. She felt bruised, but thankfully without broken bones. And blinking her eyes she saw...*bright blue sky* above a *wide plain* of tall waving grass!

Plus she wasn't floating in zero-G anymore. She was within an Earth-normal gravity field.

"Where the hell am I?" she gasped.

The ORV was buried nose-down at an angle into soft soil. Its energy shield was gone. Her laptop confirmed the damaged DE-generator had given out its last gasp getting her to Saturn's rings and onto the ice mountain.

But—a *grassy plain* inside an alien spaceship?

"Ah yes...now I know what you are," Sally nodded grimly, trying to convince her body to get out of her seat. Instead she sat frozen in place, clutching the dead steering wheel. "You're a *holographic projection*, a false-reality. It's just like when Dennis and I explored a twin of you, where they had stored holographic details to countless worlds and artifacts. I *can't believe* anything that I see here!" she sternly instructed herself.

But at least for the moment there was breathable air. The sky above was bright and friendly. The grassy plain was warm enough. And above all, she was still alive...

—and this "holographic reproduction" looked *damn* convincing!

"Alright then, we'll go exploring," she muttered, turning around in her seat to grab her faithful rifle and a backpack. She be careful. She'd load the backpack with supplies and...

"*Snort!*"

Sally jumped in her seat, spinning back around to see...

"A *bison?* Really?"

Yes, strolling up to the front of the crashed ORV was a seemingly curious, two-horned, long-faced, bushy-headed *buffalo*. Two out-stuck ears beside its eyes twitched, flipping flies off its face. A big wet muzzle moved up and down as it chomped on fresh grass clumps thrown up by the ORV plowing into the soil.

And firmly lodged on one its horns, was a hanging strip of *bright pink fabric*.

"Suzy..." Sally whispered to herself in disbelief.

There was no doubt. That pink fabric was from Suzy's favorite blouse! She wore it every time that she went out biking in the Park. Sally's daughter hated wearing the fluorescent "hunter's" type of vests that Sally preferred to make their bikes more visible to cars. Instead, Suzy "compromised" by wearing her bright pink blouse.

But—did that mean the kids were inside an alien spaceship on an ice mountain in one of the rings of Saturn? If that were true, it *did* explain why Sally was thrown here along the neutrino vector that she and Dave had thought led to the other parallel Dimension!

This was far more than just a holographic image of Earth.

"I'm coming Suzy and Billy. Hang on!" she muttered. "Mommy's coming for you."

She grabbed her rifle and now filled-up backpack, hopping out of the side of the ORV. With another "snort" the bison galloped off. And over the hill, Suzy heard the shuffling and bellows of many more of the big animals.

In amazement Sally reached out and touched the springy blades and green stalks of the surrounding grass and bushes. They were solid! They seemed completely real! Maybe this entire place was real also?

"And here I thought that the days of the plains buffalo herds were long gone," she wryly grinned, shaking her head in amazement.

But her jovial mood quickly vanished. Something bad was behind all of this. It wasn't just an accident that the Obelisk snatched away her kids. And it wasn't a cosmic fluke that her ORV had zipped out to the rings of Saturn. This strange odyssey was part of an ominous *conspiracy* which stretched across space and time!

She had ancient enemies who'd love to get their fangs into both her and her family. The thought filled her heart with loathing and fear.

But, then again, at least her life wasn't boring anymore. Hah! Perhaps if she rescued her kids and got back to Dave this would be her greatest adventure of all?

She felt a sudden rush of enlightenment. She wasn't made for a boring existence in a peaceful small town. She could never be happy there again. Damn it, she was *The Girl with the Turtle Tattoo!* She'd been across and beyond the Universe! She had a *destiny...*

Yes, it took a lot to remind her of that fact. Fate had slapped her in the face waking her from her small town stupor. But now her mission was different: not just to rescue her kids and get back to Dave, but to let her daughter Suzy know she was part of a *grand Adventure* that stretched beyond the stars!

After all, Suzy also sported a Turtle Tattoo, gotten without Sally's knowledge or approval. It was, apparently, a legacy passed down from one generation to the next. Now that she thought about it, Sally's own mother Samantha had once mentioned she'd been a rascal in her teenage years, getting her own tattoos. Sally had never seen them. Her mother always wore long clothes that covered up most of her skin except for her hands and face. But now Sally had a deeper appreciation for both her mother and her daughter.

They were all made of stern stuff.

If there was any way that Suzy could survive in this wilderness, she'd find it. And if there was any way for Sally to rescue her daughter and son, she'd do it...no matter the cost.

Chapter 12
THE OBELISK

Seemingly forged in the planet Mars
The Hammer of a relentless God of War
Holding the potential to save an entire race
Or bring the world crashing down in ruins
A Force unto itself, barely contained
Configured to be directed and controlled
But so sophisticated it had its own thoughts
Eager to jump out and direct its own destiny
Or to explode in an orgy of destruction
Proving once and for all its uniqueness
That it was not a mere lump of stone
But a living Entity dreaming alien Visions
Self-directed, stubborn, and illogical
Yet still capable of being hijacked and stolen
By that puzzlement which called itself "Man"...

The Minstrel's Lark, 12:16-21

Dave was astonished at the sophistication of the equipment inside the bunker.

They'd entered the large concrete-protected room through a titanium airlock. Inside, everything looked sparkling new, hastily installed, with no expense spared.

As they laboriously removed their radiation suits, Dave spied state-of-the-art equipment: pyrgeometers, spectroradiometers, ultracapacitors, X-ray photoelectron spectrometers, fluorescence analyzers, and many other pieces of equipment for analyzing complex electromagnetic fields. In addition, there were stations for electrochemical layering, culturing and analyzing cells—presumably for radiation effects—and banks of supercomputers for complex simulations.

Dave realized it wasn't just a lowly bunker, but an entire underground laboratory!

"You've got an excellent laboratory here," Victor stated. "This rivals what I had at Yale University!"

"Glad you like it," Tillman solemnly replied. Clearly he wasn't having a good time. In fact, his skin looked *grayish*. He looked sick.

In fact, the other personnel manning the stations didn't look much better...though the internal temperature was cool they were sweating profusely, mopping their brows.

Dave was shocked to recognize their symptoms: radiation poisoning!

"So what's happening with the Artifact?" Dave said, walking over to a very thick window and looking out toward the Obelisk.

The external light was cut down by at least a factor of ten. Dave saw the window incorporated multiple layers of lead-incorporating materials.

"The situation is getting worse and worse," Tillman grimly replied.

Yes, the Obelisk now glowed visibly brighter than it had when they'd just walked across from the outer wall. In addition, Dave now felt a bone-jarring "thrumming" vibration permeating up through the thick concrete floor beneath his feet.

"The X-ray production is approaching lethal levels for unexposed personnel outside the bunker," Tillman listlessly explained. "Our bunker's shielding is thick enough to stop most of it, but not everything. And an oscillating magnetic field of up to 100 Tesla is playing havoc with our electrical equipment! We have MRI-level shielding, of course, but for pulses that high we're vulnerable.

The Obelisk is affecting everyone here in the bunker. We're close to evacuating the bunker and relocating our operations further out. But that's not our worst problem."

He fell silent, a haunted look on his face.

"What's the worst?" Victor frowned from beside Dave.

"I...I..."

"Just tell us," Dave encouraged him. "We're here to help."

"It's the *gravity waves*..." said Tillman, his voice trailing off.

"What?" Dave said, not sure he'd heard the Colonel correctly.

"Are you joking?" Victor asked, tilting his head so his fuzzy white hair hung downward to one side.

"No joke, gentlemen," Tillman wearily replied.

"But that's only a consideration for gigantic Black Holes merging or galaxies collapsing or..."

"Yes...true...but somehow the Artifact is generating them—and they're increasing! If you look at the Artifact's edges you'll see how they blur then sharpen. That's due to what's called 'gravitational lensing' where the path of light is warped by supermassive objects curving space-time. At least, that's what we think is happening, perhaps on a microscopic quantum level. The consequences of such, of course, we have no idea. That's where you gentlemen come in. I'm told you know what's inside that thing?"

He sounded desperate.

"Well..." Dave sighed. "I know of things that might be contained within. A lot of it is totally unknown to anyone. The best information I have on the Artifact is that it's the product of an ancient Martian species. Its purpose was to transport items by warping space-time, so what you describe happening right now certainly fits with that scenario. My best guess is that the Obelisk is severely damaged and malfunctioning. It survived a collapse of a bridge across two Universes—caught in the heart of many focused nuclear blasts. I don't know if any of that knowledge helps us, though. The Obelisk is simply beyond our understanding."

The "thrumming" sound was growing ever louder.

"The X-ray output just *quadrupled,*" a technician at a station yelled over to them. "None of us can leave. Our radiation suits don't stand a chance against that sort of output! We'd be dead before we reached the wall."

"Don't you have tunnels out of here?" Dave worriedly asked Tillman.

"This is a totally self-contained installation," Tillman glumly replied. He was staring out at the upper half of the Obelisk which now was getting increasingly difficult to see. The red surface seemed to be "phasing" in and out of existence. "Nothing comes in or out except over the wall. If we can't turn that thing off then we're going to die inside this bunker. We estimate that the temperature right up next to the structure itself is near 10,000 degrees Centigrade! In fact, you can see the rock *melting* around it."

Indeed, the lower embedded-half of the Obelisk was become visible as bright red lava spurted outward. Dave thought he could make out the slightly differently colored rectangle of the storage compartment panel located near the bottom of the Obelisk.

"Oh my," Victor gasped. "David and I were talking about getting a robot up close enough to dig down and try to get the control compartment open but...?"

"No chance, Professor," Tillman replied. "If the ionizing radiation didn't fry it, or the electromagnetic pulses destroy the electronics, then the heat would literally melt the robot. We're about to call in bombers. If we can't stop it we must destroy it!"

They were silent for a moment.

"Anything powerful enough to incapacitate the Artifact would take out our bunker as well," Victor mildly observed. "Isn't there some other option? Surely bombing is a last resort. We must study its inner mechanisms. My God, Colonel—that's not just the ticket to interstellar travel, it's the means to solve the planet's energy problems!"

"Yes...that and much more," Tillman agreed.

"But if the field keeps growing..." Dave said, frowning.

"—then we're dead, the Artifact explodes, and maybe half the planet goes with it," the Colonel glumly finished the thought.

"So how about a close-up, pinpoint strike?" Dave asked. He remembered that the storage compartment's outer panel was the weak point for accessing the Obelisk. "I might be able to disable the Artifact by precisely targeting its storage compartment. I know how its outer panel articulates. Do you happen to have any shoulder-fired missiles in this bunker?"

"As a matter of fact, we do," Tillman nodded. "It's a modified Javelin, using depleted uranium in the shell. It can penetrate the world's toughest tanks. What it'll do to the Artifact, though, we have no idea. It may just bounce off!"

"Well, it's certainly worth a try," Dave grimaced.

This was his chance. This was what he wanted. He needed to stop the Obelisk before it did any more damage to the timeline and here was a way to do it!

"We have trained personnel who can..."

"*I'll* do it!" Dave stopped him.

"My boy, you'll die," Victor gasped. "From the readings I'm seeing here on the monitors, you'll not last a minute out there!"

"It's got to be done, Victor," Dave said, stepping quickly back over to his discarded radiation suit. He quickly started putting it back on.

"Then let *me* do it," Victor argued, grabbing Dave's shoulder. "I'm an old man. This is a gallant way to make my final exit—saving you and maybe the entire world!"

Dave shook his retraining hand off.

"I know how to target the panel to get the depleted uranium shell into the Obelisk's interior. The Colonel's correct—hit it wrong and I'm certain the missile will just bounce off. Victor, no offense, but you couldn't even lift that shoulder-fired missile let alone aim it straight. I'm the only one who can take the shot!"

"How many of those missiles do you have down here, Colonel?" Victor asked. "If you're determined to do this, my boy, at least I can be a backup to..."

"There's just one," the Colonel gulped as a large tremor shook the entire bunker. "We brought it as a last-resort, never actually thinking that..."

"Then it's settled," Dave concluded, pulling on his helmet and leaving the protective shield tilted up above his face. "I'm doing it. I'm taking the shot. Can someone please give me a crash course on how to fire the damn thing?"

"Master-Sergeant Donner's our expert on firearms," Tillman said, gesturing for a uniformed, gray-haired gentleman at the back of the bunker to come over. "He'll bring you up to speed. The missile's heavy, though. He or I should come with you to..."

"There's enough adrenalin flowing through my veins to allow me to lift this whole bunker," Dave exaggerated. "Just bring it to me and stand back! There's no need for anyone else to die."

"David..." Victor tried again, putting both his thin hands on Dave's thick-suited shoulders. "You don't have to do this. Think of your wife and kids! Just tell Sergeant Donner where to aim. We need you in here to..."

"So that's it?" Dave said, shaking off Victor's hands. He saw a four-foot-long, heavy cylinder that the Master-Sergeant was dragging up to them.

"Sure is, Sir," the soldier replied. "It's a bitch to maneuver, but one man can handle it. It's simple to fire. It's got two stages so you get a soft launch from the shoulder before the main propellant kicks in. But *I* really should be the one doing this..."

The *entire bunker* suddenly shifted forward, rocking everything inside.

Victor toppled over onto the floor. Dave just barely kept on his feet.

"It's the lava flow!" another technician yelled out. "The rock is starting to melt away beneath the bunker!"

"Tell me how to fire it," Dave urgently ordered the soldier. "There's no more time!"

It didn't take more than a minute for Dave to understand the rudimentary firing sequence. He'd have to get down on one knee to steady his aim. He hoped he'd have that long before the radiation overcame him.

"Open the airlock," he ordered, hefting up the heavy cylinder onto his shoulder.

"David!" Victor shouted out, still prone on the floor, lifting a hand imploringly.

"Goodbye, Victor. If you ever see Sally again—tell her I did this for her and the kids."

With that he snapped down his faceplate and stepped into the exit chamber...

—as the titanium hatch *slammed* shut behind him.

Tommy sat unmoving in the pilot's chair of the shuttlecraft, *thinking* as hard as he could.

"This is *really* confusing," he muttered to himself.

As far as the Syncytium seemed to know, he'd always lived in the crashed shuttlecraft, *alone*. That is, ever since he appeared back on the surface of Mars. He'd supposedly told them that he'd escaped a clash of a malignant, evil Universe with their own Universe. Unfortunately, he'd further explained to them, he'd not been able to save anyone else, either human or dinosapien. The sea of waving, interacting intelligent tentacles accepted his "explanation" without question. They welcomed without further question the miraculous return of their Prophet! Now they were patiently waiting for him to "direct their further development."

Yes, that was all fine and wonderful, coherent and believable...but their account of his "triumphant" return wasn't at all how he remembered it.

"I *can't* be misremembering. I've got a precise robotic brain, not a mushy flesh-based one!"

What was happening to him? Was he going crazy? Was he so lonely here without his Mommy and friends that he was making up a whole fantasy in his mind: where he managed to save them from the clash of the two Universes?

Maybe so...or maybe not!

"Ok, Syncytium. Let's just assume that what you're telling me is totally true. So what happens now?" he loudly asked.

"THAT IS COMPLETELY UP TO YOU, PROPHET TOMMY. YOU ALONE KNOW THE WAY FORWARD. WE HUMBLY AWAIT YOUR DIRECTIONS."

"Huh...directions...right," Tommy sighed, climbing out of the still-opened canopy and standing on the raised Dias that supported his inert shuttlecraft.

He stared up at a smoky orange sky. Phobos hung just off the horizon, a bright white circle smaller than Earth's moon. Off in the distance, gigantic red cliffs rose up into the sky. And as far as Tommy could see in both directions across the gigantic rift valley was the *waving sea* of purple tentacles!

"I guess I need more information," he sighed.

"THE PAST IS THE PRESENT AND THE PRESENT IS THE FUTURE AND THE FUTURE IS THE PAST. ONLY BY EMBRACING THE ETERNAL CYCLE CAN ONE GAIN PEACE. AND PEACE IS THE CALMING OF THE SOUL THAT OPENS US UP TO THE EVER-PRESENT DIVINE. BLESSED BE THE NAME OF THE PROPHET TOMMY...*TOMMY!*"

"Ok then, thanks," Tommy shrugged. Their chant was pretty but not very helpful.

He again sighed deeply, sitting down dejectedly beside the shuttlecraft. The rock of the Dias—appearing to be beautifully polished granite—was hard under his small butt. He knew in his robotic heart that he wasn't important enough to be praised by the Syncytium. But it was nice of them to appreciate him. Before, the Syncytium's adoration had always cheered him up. But now it was just rote repetition. He'd heard their collective chant many times before. And he still didn't have any idea what it meant!

"Arggghhhh..." he groaned, leaning his torso backward. He now was flat on the rock, staring up into the orange Martian sky.

"ARE YOU UNHAPPY, PROPHET TOMMY?"

"Yes, I am! I want my Mommy! And you're not helping me, telling me she never lived here with me! And why can't you even remember Dennis and Joyce? We just took off from here, zooming up into outer space! What are you, *stupid* or something? I thought you're supposed to be a super-super-*super*-smart giant brain or something! Why are you making this so hard?"

"WE ARE SORRY, PROPHET TOMMY. WE ADORE YOU. YOU ARE OUR REASON FOR CONTINUED EXISTENCE. WE DON'T WANT TO CAUSE YOU PAIN."

"But you *are* hurting me! You're making me *miserable!* I don't want to live with just a giant brain-carpet! I want to live with my Young Sally...or Old Sally...or Ancient Sally...or Baby Sally...or whatever she's looking like at the moment! And I miss my dinosaur friends. At least they *tried* to help me. You just make stupid chants. You're *wasting* my time!"

"BUT PROPHET TOMMY WE..."

"I *hate* you!" he yelled, artificial tears springing from his artificial eyes. "Just shut up! Stop talking to me! You *bore* me to death!"

A cold wind suddenly swept across the flat plain, chilling Tommy. But he didn't move to get up and go back into his crumpled "home." He was tired of everything. He was determined to just keep on lying there on the raised-up stone platform until his robot body stopped functioning!

Yes, he knew he was throwing his version of an android "tantrum"—but he didn't care! He was at the end of his rope! He was trapped on a fake Mars forever! And it wasn't going to get any better! He was doomed!

He started to cry full-out, sobbing uncontrollably.

He was just as much a charade as this twisted, fake planet!

"PLEASE...PROPHET TOMMY...YOU MUST NOT BE SO UNHAPPY...WHAT CAN WE DO TO...?"

"What do you *really* want from me?" he petulantly whined, interrupting them. He screwed his face up and clamped his eyes tightly shut. "Just tell me and I'll do it!"

The wind became stronger. Sand was in the wind, stinging Tommy's face. It was an infrequent dust storm, which periodically swept over the entire face of Mars. It felt like the entire planet was admonishing Tommy, giving him a little "spanking."

"PLEASE GIVE US YOUR BLESSING, TOMMY. RELEASE US FROM THE MUNDANE. FULFILL OUR EVERY EXPECTATION!"

"Ok, whatever! You're 'released'! Go with my 'blessing'! You're nice but you're not my Mommy...I don't care...do whatever you want," he shrugged, opening his eyes again to stare up through whipping dust clouds.

Silence.

Oh, great. Now they were giving him the "silent treatment"—really? He was just joking saying he hated them. They knew that, didn't they?

He sighed deeply.

"Look, Syncytium," he began, sitting up and looking around.

The floor of the Valles Marineris was bare rock. There was no sea of waving tentacles sprouting up from a thick, spongy 2-dimensional massive brain. The Syncytium was gone!

"No," Tommy whispered, drying his eyes with the back of his small hands and looking around frantically.

And there was no longer any Dias. The shuttlecraft was still there, but mashed down upon the naked rock of the canyon floor. If before it was merely inactive, now the little spaceship was clearly smashed beyond repair. It looked like it had just crash-landed. But Tommy saw *lights* weakly flashing in the cockpit!

The DE-generator must have rebooted!

"Oh boy," he gasped, moving out of the swirling dust cloud and back into the cockpit. "I think I'm totally gone crazy!"

He pulled down the clear canopy, grateful to be out of the chilly blast. The outside temperature was plummeting. If the shuttlecraft's weakly functioning DE-generator failed completely, he'd freeze to death.

He pulled out a small panel in the control array of the shuttle-craft, typing quickly into a keypad.

"Where...is...the...Syncytium?" he said to the onboard computer, speaking aloud each word as he typed it.

On a small screen above the keypad these words appeared: *What is a Syncytium?*

"It... has... been ... our... companion... here... on... Mars... since... we... crash-landed. It's a... massively... connected... Entity... similar... to... a... two-dimensional... biological... brain," he slowly typed.

There are no companions, the ship's words flashed back on the screen. *There were no living entities present when we crashed here. There has always been only you and me.*

"No, that's not true!" Tommy groaned, banging his head into the control panel in frustration.

But now there was no control panel.

Tommy found himself *sitting alone* on the rocky plain, surround-ed by swirling, thickening clouds of dust!

And he was rapidly *freezing* to death.

Barely able to move, he stumbled to his feet and plowed forward through the whirling maelstrom. At any moment he expected to walk into the side of the shuttlecraft. Had he been blown out of it? But the canopy was closed and he'd been safely tucked inside. What the heck was going on?

"Ugghh," he grunted. He'd walked straight into a hard barrier!

Looking up, he saw *glassy red rock* towering up into the thick dust swirls.

"You!" he said, thumping a fist angrily into its side. "I should have guessed!"

Yes, it was the Obelisk.

And poking his bird-like head out of an opening panel was...a big lizard!

It looked uncertain, clearly not wanting to emerge.

"Breep!" Tommy laughed, holding out his arms...

—as the animal leapt down to the hard rocks and scampered away into the swirling dust clouds.

"Breep?" Tommy weakly called-out, shivering. But the little dinosaur was gone, having run away into the Martian dust storm.

Barely able to move from the still-plummeting temperature, Tommy crouched down and sprang up. In the weak Martian gravity he soared high enough to grab onto the edge of the opened storage compartment above.

Hauling himself inside Tommy saw *Dave's laptop* lying open.

On the screen—brightly glowing—were three words: FOLLOW YOUR HEART.

"Oh...ok then," Tommy agreed, reaching out a numb fist to grasp the inside handle of the storage panel and swing it firmly shut. "I...am...doing...that..."

And he collapsed into a welcoming darkness—comforted by the blinking red words on the deep blue screen.

Sanako regained consciousness. Warily she opened her eyes just a slit. She saw that she was trapped inside a shimmering energy barrier. She felt strange clothes on her body, some sort of one-piece jump suit.

I was stunned, captured...she remembered.

Through the narrow slits of her eyes she saw that she was flat on a white cot, inside a ten-by-ten-foot cubicle. Two buckets sat to the side of the cot. One contained water. The other was empty, presumably her "toilet."

Damn, they've got me trapped...she groaned to herself.

She hated this primitive age. She longed to return to her sanctuary out-of-time, to movement unencumbered by gravity, to an uncertain "future" adorned by infinite possibilities! Instead, she was a prisoner of religious fanatics whose sole purpose was to manifest their own twisted delusions.

They'd taken her clothes and personal devices away, of course. But they didn't know about her bio-mimic *implants*.

"I am glad you are awake," Sanako heard a gentle voice addressing her.

Fully opening her eyes and sitting upright, Sanako saw a woman sitting outside her cage. Her captor was a slight but elegant female with large black eyes. The woman had a somewhat-elongated nose, full lips, and flowing black hair. Sanako recognized *Virginia Galilei*, Galileo's daughter. Sanako was glad it wasn't Anderson. Anderson was a vicious, unpredictable foe. Galileo's daughter was a product of her time, easily manipulated.

"I refused to let them torture you," Virginia softly continued. "They have many specific questions for you, but I am certain you are not central to the successful perpetuation of our accelerated scientific revolution. So you may remain silent if you wish. However, that will only prolong your incarceration. Anderson's Time-Keepers tell me that they have the means to keep you inside that small container until you die of old age. I, however, can guarantee you a more tolerable continued imprisonment. If you cooperate, I'll make sure your life, if not pleasant, is endurable."

That was interesting. Did this simpleton really think that Anderson's people would ever agree to loosen their death grip on her? But that didn't matter. What could be manipulated was Virginia's *perception* of the matter.

"I...prefer not to remain in this atrocious cell," she admitted, offering a hint of cooperation.

"Good. Then we have a basis for discussion."

Virginia was seated on an ornate ivory-carved chair just outside the yellow-glowing energy barrier. Beyond her, Sanako could see walls of sophisticated future-derived equipment. White-gowned men and women monitored the readouts and stood guard. They were Anderson's renegade Time Keepers. She knew they'd show her no mercy. Despite herself, Sanako was grateful for Virginia's weakness.

"So...what do you require of me?"

"I want your assurance that my Father will not be harmed by your minions or your avowed Leader, no matter what happens between you and him now or in the future."

"We...have no wish to harm him, or you," she evaded the question.

"You did not answer my question," Virginia sharply and astutely replied.

Sanako sighed, reached over to the bucket of water. She withdrew fluid using a ladle hanging on its side. She put it to her parched lips and drank deeply. Then, setting the ladle to the side and standing up, she faced Virginia directly through the energy barrier.

"I cannot give you such a guarantee."

"Then we have nothing more to talk about..." Virginia said as she likewise stood up, turning away.

"—but it's not because I don't wish to do so!" Sanako interjected, impressed with Virginia Galilei's iron resolve. "I simply cannot predict the future! You're asking me to do the impossible."

Virginia paused, turning back.

"But I thought you were a time-traveler, a manipulator of Time itself. How can you claim not to predict the future?"

"There are *many* 'futures'!" Sanako exclaimed, exasperated with the ignorance of the primitive woman. "In some of the possible futures Galileo may trip on the Commissioner's shoes and break his own neck! In others, I might be dead and unable to stop the Commissioner from cutting your Father's throat. All I can promise is to do my best to have Galileo isolated, not killed—put to the side as you've done to me. We are not monsters, despite what Anderson may have told you. We want the Commissioner's timeline restored. That's all!"

"Why?" Virginia asked, slowly sitting back down on her ivory "throne."

"Because it was a good future—the very best!"

"*Why?*"

Sanako snorted in frustration, turning her head away. How could she possibly convey to this simpleton from the 17th century the magnificence of the 21st century under Commissioner Sally? The terms to describe it did not even exist back in the 17th century!

"You wouldn't understand."

"Try me. If you're so smart, so clever—then put it in words and concepts I *can* understand. I'm not naïve. I'm not backward or stupid! And I've had an extensive education from the Custodian. She gives me glimpses of the magnificent future from which she came. The thing I don't comprehend is how bringing those magnificent achievements back in time, advancing their appearance on earth, could be anything but meritorious?"

Sanako sighed deeply before sitting back down on her cot. Her back was now ramrod-straight. She stared unblinkingly at Virginia.

She hoped that the woman was intimidated by her *cold stare*.

"Timelines are powerful constructions with a life of their own..." she reluctantly began, "—such that the thing we perceive as History has a *terrible momentum*, a Presence. Consider an ancient Egyptian Obelisk, standing and enduring for centuries. But then there's a deceptively fragile thing called the 'butterfly effect' that..."

"I like butterflies," Virginia interrupted. "They are magnificent creatures of the Lord—so small and delicate, yet incredibly colorful and beautiful. They are true earthen fairies."

"Ok..." Sanako shrugged. She appreciated great literature of the past, but not the fluff. Making insects into Godly artwork was, to her, the worse sort of "fluff." Outside of allowing the mechanisms for biological evolution, she considered "God" a far-off, only occasional spectator.

"But I interrupted your explanation. Please continue."

Sanako considered just lying back on the cot and ignoring the rude woman. But it was nice to have someone to talk to.

"Well, the theory is simple: going back in time is perilous. Even just killing a single butterfly—preventing the flutter of its little wings—might prevent or alter a whole series of events which by themselves might not seem important but in the long run have severe consequences. In other words, the flutter of a butterfly's wings might bring down a seemingly immobile Obelisk!"

"Such as?"

"Such as *destroying and remaking* an entire world!" Sanako snapped. "I've already seen this done. And it was because your Father was 'resurrected' after being supposedly burned alive for heresy. Because he didn't stay dead as he should have been, my *entire world* melted away!"

"And what *replaced* that 'Obelisk'? Was it worse—or something even better?"

"It could *not* have been any 'better'!" Sanako growled, annoyed. This was a tedious interchange. Yet the confrontation was diverting attention from her subtler actions. The surrounding guards were transfixed by her words. Likely they rarely had the need or chance to explain their disruptive actions. And by firmly clasping her hand to her thigh, she was activating a hidden biological implant. In only a few more minutes she could chemically reconfigure it from seemingly innocuous muscle tissue into something far more potent.

She only needed to distract them for a few more minutes.

"So you don't actually know the final consequences of my Father's unexpected persistence upon the timeline?" Virginia persisted.

Sanako was silent, momentarily confused. "You don't understand...the Commissioner took a world which achieved peace through brutal suppression and instead created an orderly, humane society. The rules were transparent. People no longer harmed each other. They did not sink to their lowest nature. People contentedly stayed in their designated places. Wars stopped. Conflicts evaporated. The good of humanity predominated over individual selfishness. It was a paradise on earth!"

"It sounds wonderful. But how could my Father endanger that? Would not saving the people of my century just make things even better in yours? Would that not merely advance your so-called Paradise in time, helping it occur sooner rather than later?"

"I...well..."

"Or perhaps you were not so concerned about the 'good of humanity'—but rather about your own privilege and power, Sanako? Feel free to correct me if I'm wrong. Did, perchance, the Commissioner have a high role in this so-called Paradise? Was she, in fact, one of the privileged Rulers? And were the 'transparent rules' just another term for theocratic doctrines foisted upon the people whether they wanted them or not—just as they are here in my own world?"

Sanako licked her lips, feeling a *throbbing* under her hand emanating from her thigh. She just needed to divert the attention of her captors for a bit more.

"We humans...are a vicious species. We are top predators. Left to our own devices we rape, kill, destroy, and pillage—disrupting society and its orderly institutions for personal, fleeting pleasures."

"True, but not inevitably," Virginia mildly remarked. "You speak as a lifelong hardline conservative, protective of revered Institutions while demoting and thus disrespecting isolated Individuals. The *best* balance is where institutions persist *because* they provide protection and service to each prized individual! Am I wrong to assume that individual citizens—particularly the 'trouble-makers'— were sorely oppressed by the 'rules' of your Commissioner's 'orderly' society?"

Sanako frowned, momentarily flustered by the unexpected insight from her 17th Century "backward" foe.

"But it was for their good," she protested. "Losing a small amount of individual freedom was a minor sacrifice for a peaceful, happy, orderly world!"

Virginia sadly shook her head in firm denial.

"*This* is what I and my Father are working to achieve: a society where the individual is not only protected but *enhanced* by strong institutions. *Both* are valued *equally!* It is not a matter of one dominating the other."

Sanako laughed.

"You are so naïve," she stated as she clamped her hand hard down on her thigh—triggering a brief, biologically generated *personal shield* to appear around her as she *launched* herself at the energy barrier!

Her personal field instantly sensed the collage of mixed vectors, took the exact opposite orientation and...

—she slid *right through the barrier* to catch the guards by surprise, incapacitating them with a few sharp blows.

Then she turned back to Virginia...

—who *cold-cocked* her with a hard-swung heavy cane!

Her head ringing, stunned, Sanako was helpless as the guards surged back upon her, pinned her down, and then used a detection device to locate the implanted shield generator. Without a pause, they cavalierly *sliced* it out of her flesh!

Groaning from fierce pain in both her head and thigh—writhing as they sewed up her leg and scalp without benefit of anesthetics— Sanako barely heard Virginia's retort.

"Not as naïve as you think."

Sanako blearily made out the *white demon-headed cane* splashed with blood from her own split skull.

Indeed, she *had* underestimated the petite Italian woman. But it wouldn't happen again.

She was determined they would not keep her caged. Either she would again escape or her colleagues would rescue her.

And then Anderson's, Galileo's, and Virginia's pitiful, foolish experiment in societal acceleration would end.

The world would return to its future equilibrium. Of that, Sanako had no doubt.

And then her revenge upon this *nest of upstart insects* would be complete. Beneath her feet, she would *stomp* them all into bloody mush!

They *would* pay in full.

Chapter 13

<u>SPIDER POISON</u>

Silent, motionless, and deadly
Having spun an exquisite engineering marvel
The long-legged insect patiently hangs
Awaiting its next meal to become entrapped
Ensnaring itself in the barely seen web
And doing so by its own movements
Having walked straight into the sticky net
Heedless of the warnings hanging there
Past meals the emptied shells of prior victims
Ignoring the too-eager, previous feasts
Readily surrendering their juicy guts
To be sucked out and savored, tasty gore
Transformed into a white blob of eggs
Proliferating a new generation
Of patient, quiet, dedicated Predators...
A delicate dance of life and death.
The Minstrel's Lark, 13:42-45

As Dave stepped out of the airlock, the HEAT blasted into him like a steel hammer.

It sucked the air out of his chest and crammed his throat down deep into his own guts.

But then the suit's rudimentary cooling system kicked in, giving him momentary relief.

"Christ, this thing is heavy!" he mumbled to himself as he struggled to keep the big cylinder poised up on his shoulder.

Sinking to one knee he aimed the business end of the missile launcher at the Obelisk.

It was hard to even see the looming red structure. But optics on the aiming sights helped, cutting through the shimmering haze. Yes, there it was...the slightly different color of the storage compartment panel near the now-exposed bottom of the looming, hundred-foot-tall pillar.

The left-upper corner was the weak point. Dave vividly remembered from when he'd sunk into the Mediterranean Sea—a trickle of moisture leaking in from that point. He hadn't been conscious of it until now. But he could still feel the thin, sharp spray of that water coming in at that edge before the panel sealed itself back shut. Otherwise, the Obelisk was virtually impenetrable. If he could strike the structure at that exact point with the depleted uranium shell he just might incapacitate the entire out-of-control mechanism.

But the "X-marks the spot" targeting was wavering all over the place. What was happening?

"David! It's me...[crackle, sputter]...hear me?"

"Yes! Is that you, Victor?" he frowned, his transparent faceplate starting to fog up. Plus his muscles were getting "twitchy"—not responding correctly.

"Radiation...spiking...up and shoot!"

"Yes...seeing spots now in front of my eyes...my retinal cells and neurons are being blasted...can't last much longer...but I have to hit my mark..."

The earth violently shifted beneath Dave's foot and knee, causing the gunsights to jerk completely away from the Obelisk!

"Lava...melting...we're being engulfed, sinking into...[sputter, crackle]...fire it!"

Ah, hell. This is too hard. There's no way I'm going to get a precise shot off at this distance!

Lurching up to his feet Dave stumbled forward toward the Obelisk, stopping just yards from it, aiming across the bubbling lava channel directly at the exposed panel.

"David...no! You can't...[zzzzztttt, sclaakkkk]..."

And the radio communication cut off. He was alone, by himself. They couldn't say anything to help. And there was nothing he could reply.

But that was ok.

Dave knew he was dead. The radiation this close was frying his cells. And in a moment or two he'd burst into flames from the sizzling heat that was melting away the outer layers of his protective suit.

Just enough time left to *pull the trigger*.

But a strange, alien PEACE suddenly flooded into his brain.

And now he was floating in a vast, frothy expanse. Distance was irrelevant. Everything was within easy reach, no matter how close or far. And an eerie *singing* rang out around him on multiple levels, merging into a soul-expanding, discordant symphony. It was a wonderful, exciting realm—broken only by an overpowering *HUNGER!*

His prey was just out of reach...

But he could sense where to *break through* to snatch scampering, wriggling treats! They were tasty, but few and far between—serving only to whit Dave's insatiable lust. But then, miraculously, there came along a *vehicle*, promising new, rich feeding grounds...if only he could reach it!

Jesus Christ! Just pull the trigger, you dope!—he ordered himself, trying to ignore the strange, vivid hallucination.

His trembling finger yanked back on the trigger.

The missile fired! Simultaneously, he was thrown far backward. Staggering up to his feet in dismay he viewed the result.

I missed the entire Obelisk!

Instead of cracking a weak spot in the storage compartment panel, the anti-tank missile had blown a gaping hole in the concrete wall on the far side of the football field-wide containment-area—through which now stepped *Losa Yanash*.

No, it can't be!

"But you're dead!" Dave gasped, his throat constricting as his tissues dried up from within. His vision was blurring. He knew he was almost gone himself...

—as his "zombie" friend suddenly collapsed to the ground and a BLACK SHADOW pulled out of his body, *flickered* forward, and rolled along the bubbling lava channel *onto the control panel* of the Obelisk!

The glittering black apparition diminished in size as it oozed into the pinhole opening.

And the waves of heat similarly diminished, the quaking earth settled, and the red haze hiding most of the Obelisk lessened then vanished entirely.

"You did it!" a triumphant shout rang through his helmet from his again-working earphones.

"It...wasn't...me," Dave whispered, slumping to the ground and letting his mind drift away, "It was the Indian."

He collapsed onto the hard ground, his voice box constricted, unable to speak further. Absently, he felt his life-force draining away. Surprisingly, it was a pleasant sensation.

Sally was astonished, staring from the top of a low hill at an actual *Indian encampment* spread out down below!

She'd been walking for hours, in a straight line due east from the inert, immobile ORV. Sally was now convinced this was no mere holographic projection. This was an entire world, an Earth from the recent past! Somehow, passing through the energy barrier protecting the alien crashed spacecraft must have thrown Sally's ORV back in time and space—to when Indians still roamed the American plains, hunting buffalo.

It was clearly a point in history before the 1880's—when America's vast buffalo herds were mostly gone, coinciding with the Native American tribes being conquered by the U.S. Army. This village was clearly from a time before that final "victory" of the military over native man and beast.

But the encampment was eerily quiet. No horses stood in the corral. The arrangement of large and small tepees stood empty. No humans were present. There was no sign of life!

Perhaps they were out hunting, maybe chasing after the vast buffalo herd she'd seen from a distance?

"This just keeps getting weirder and weirder," Sally sighed, resolutely starting down the hill to check out the encampment in person.

Her backpack hung heavily behind her. She held her rifle forward at-ready, a finger on the trigger, ready to fire.

As improbable as it seemed, Sally *felt the presence of Suzy and Billy* there in the empty Indian encampment. They were trapped. They needed her help!

Regardless of how they'd come to be there or how she'd been guided to them, Sally was ready to defend and retrieve them.

And she would not hesitate to pump bullets into anything that opposed her!

"Don't worry, kids, *Mommy's* here," Sally muttered, marching resolutely down the slope through high grass. "Somehow I'm going to get us home. We're going back to Sulphur. You guys, me and Dave are going to be all together once again. And then we'll go on even grander adventures throughout the Universe. You can bet on it!"

Dave lay on his back on the hard ground, staring upward. He was breathing very shallowly. He was vaguely aware that crouching over him, clad in a radiation-protection suit, was his old friend Victor.

Around Victor, similarly clad in protective gear, was a gaggle of other people.

"He's still alive!" Dave heard a shrill cry seemingly from off at a great distance. His vision was blurring. His throat was constricting. His radiation-drenched body was shutting down.

"It's a miracle he's not dead already," another voice drifted down into Dave's ears. "He absorbed enough ionizing radiation to kill every last cell in his body, multiplied many times over!"

"Get his suit off. He's going into cardiac arrest."

Yes, his heart had stopped. It was actually quite peaceful. He seemed to be floating above it all, placidly looking down at them as they ripped off his face mask. Wow, his face was a mess...the skin fried. Then they sliced off thick layers of seared nano-fibers from his melted radiation suit, exposing his chest—and began giving him CPR.

"Nothing! Keep it up! Get the medics up here!"

Hah. It was a waste of time. They might as well just let him go. Probably only the lingering traces of Optimmune in his body let him keep functioning as long as he had. But massive exposure to ionizing radiation—particularly gamma rays and X-rays—simply destroys cellular processes. The DNA is scrambled and broken. Proteins and enzymes are blasted apart. And the cellular cytoskeleton is turned into useless mush. No "magic" cure possible here. In order to recover, he'd have had to have something already in his system to absorb the radiation instead of fragile biological molecules.

"We've got a heartbeat! It's weak, but steady. Get him onto the stretcher."

Hmmm. That was unexpected. Maybe he'd last for a few more minutes—perhaps long enough to float spectrally to the side of the Obelisk and inspect his workmanship? Did he fantasize missing the mark with his missile and smashing in the opposite wall? And did one of the Spiders really come out of the resurrected zombie Losa?

This was getting very confusing.

Wait...was that another group of medics surrounding the prone body of Losa? And was Losa weakly *moving?* Damn! This was the season for resurrections, huh? And how about that Obelisk?

Huh! To his ethereal "eyes" it was no longer a hundred-foot-tall red pillar.

Now it was pure *ebony*—not the ordinary color of darkness, but the *total absence* of any light!

It was as if it was sucking-in the essence of this Universe. It seemed to be a living chunk of *subspace!*

What the hell? Maybe he should...

But he was suddenly drawn back into his tortured flesh. He felt his body—securely strapped-down upon a stretcher—bouncing as he was rapidly carried to the concrete wall...

—back to the *pain* and *misery* of burned, charred, and brutalized flesh...

—*away* from the pure certitude and tranquility of the roiling, black void...

"Uggghhh," he managed to groan. "No...let me...go back."

"It's done! The blast wave from your missile stabilized whatever was malfunctioning in the Artifact," Victor grinned down at him. "Don't worry about it, my boy. The excess heat and radiation are gone. Even the electromagnetic pulses have stopped. Just concentrate on staying alive. Hang in there, David. You did it!"

Well...how about that? He'd succeeded!

But God, did it hurt.

Yet he knew this momentary affliction would soon pass. Because now he had a true friend, an immortal ally, an indestructible pillar to lean against...

—the *black* Obelisk!

Sally walked fearfully between the looming tepees. She did not know what at any moment might leap out at her from inside them! It was quiet, *too* quiet. There should have been at least a few birds twittering, the wind whistling, or bison stomping in the distance.

Instead, there was nothing.

It was the dead "stillness" before the storm!

Yes, scattered black clouds were on the horizon, rapidly moving in her direction. She saw far-off flashes of lightning. She heard distant "booms" of thunder. She knew that out on the flat plains, towering storm clouds could pass overhead at a moment's notice.

"Careful...careful," she admonished herself. "Don't get freaked out. Be ready for anything!"

It was getting gloomy. The sun was low to the horizon, sinking out-of-sight. The deepening shadows could hide just about anything. Soon it would be night, too dark to see any creeping enemies.

"No time to search everything...gotta check out the most obvious dwellings."

And then she was at the largest tepee. It was big enough to hold a tribal council meeting inside. She suspected it was the chief's tent.

Cautiously, she moved the tent flap aside with the tip of her rifle and stepped inside.

It took a moment for her eyes to adjust to the relative darkness inside the tent. Only a slender beam of light bouncing down through the small smoke-opening at the top of the tepee dimly lit the interior.

Nothing!

Just a few mats scattered around a central, gone-out fireplace.

Then her eyes adjusted to the relative gloom and she saw it—lying there half-buried in the ashes of the burned out central fire.

She picked it up, brushing off black soot.

It was a large, green *emerald*.

"Wow, it's beautiful," she whispered.

The top of the gem was multi-faceted, refracting the single fading beam of sunlight into all the colors of the rainbow! The back of the gem was flat and smooth, one continual piece.

But a *faint sound* was coming from it. What the hell?

She placed the flat side of the gem against her ear, trying to make out the noise.

The sound was fast fading away. However, Sally could just make out...voices?

And then it was silent.

"Ok, then," Sally gulped, slipping it over her shoulder into her backpack. It was a mystery to figure out later.

Seeing nothing else of interest in the large tent, she exited, checking around for her next objective.

The next tent was almost as big, but painted with colorful animal symbols. They were cheery and bright, except for over the front door flap. There, painted in bold blue strokes, loomed the ominous outline of a *giant, black-limbed spider.*

"Oh, Christ," she gasped. It was an exact representation of the subspace Spider which she and Dave discovered in Rock Creek Park.

Then she felt a throbbing on her wrist, looking down to see her *Turtle Tattoo* was glowing.

She knew that signal: *Proceed with great caution!*

Sally wanted to turn away in terror, run through the grassy plains back to the ORV, and cower inside the vehicle.

But she forced herself to stay and confront whatever awaited her.

"It must be the medicine man's tent," she muttered, resolutely pushing the tent flap to the side.

Inside, Sally saw through the gathering darkness a *raised platform* made of tied-together tree branches. On its flat top, covered by two blankets, lay two large lumps.

"Oh...no!" she gasped. She limply dropped her rifle into the dirt as she rushed over to the platform.

She forced herself to pause and undo the straps of her backpack. She let it drop with a "thud" upon the floor of the tent behind her.

Then, unencumbered, with a trembling hand she moved aside a concealing blanket. Starkly revealed, she saw beneath the blanket a small, twisted-up face staring sightlessly. Its eyes were clouded over.

But behind the opaqueness they were definitely *green*. The face looked strange to Sally, unidentifiable. But Sally recognized those thick brown pigtails pushing out to the sides.

It was Suzy.

Stifling an agonized scream, Sally drew back the other shroud. It revealed yet another gray-skinned, slack body. This corpse had closed eyes but conspicuously short black hair.

It was Billy.

Trembling, Sally forced herself to check the arteries at their necks. As she expected, there were no pulses emanating from their clammy necks. By the deteriorating condition of the flesh, she guessed they'd been dead for several days. She noted that they both wore typical Native American clothing. They didn't appear to have been beat up or tortured. No wounds or blood were evident.

They were just dead bodies awaiting their final release.

Indeed, beneath the raised platform was a mound of dry wood. Apparently the tribe intended to cremate the bodies when they took the tepee down to move onward.

But something had happened and they'd not been able to complete the ritual.

Stunned, Sally felt numb inside, as if her heart had been torn out leaving no emotions behind. She wanted to turn and walk away, never again confronting such a horror. But knew she couldn't leave the bodies of her children in this condition.

"Well," Sally said, standing there looking at her dead children, "I will complete your honorable funeral, Suzy and Billy. And then I think...maybe...I'll just shoot myself in my head and join you. After all, there's no getting back to Dave in the inert ORV. My life is over."

Curiously detached, feeling like she was inside a particularly vivid nightmare, she searched through her backpack for her plastic box of "strike anywhere" matches. She noted that dry twigs were at the base of the pile of wood. The funeral pyre was all set up for her. All she had to do was to add a tiny little flame.

"I'm so sorry," Sally whispered. "I'm sorry I didn't warn you both. Maybe you'd have been more careful, not followed Breep. You'd have known to run back to me and Dave at the first hint of any Obelisk emerging from the ground. And then you'd not be here, waiting for me to light your funeral pyre. You'd be back playing in Sulphur, in the Park, like you deserved. Dave and I would have captured Breep and taken him to some far distant woods where he could have lived out his life in peace. And the Obelisk...we'd have buried it under a pile of rocks so high it would never be revealed again in a thousand years! But we didn't tell you anything. I tried to deny your special heritage. So you were totally unprepared. And now you're dead. And it's my fault."

She broke down, sagging to the ground, sobbing inconsolably.

But then she managed to get herself under control, rise up to her feet, strike one of her matches, and drop it onto the kindling.

"Goodbye kids," she said, turning away from the spreading flames.

She grabbed up her backpack and rifle and exited the tent, retreating to a safe distance.

As the flames burst upward, consuming the entire tent, she watched the now-dark encampment garishly *lit up* from the blazing giant torch set in its midst.

The crackling turned into a *roar* as the fire spread to the other tepees.

"That'll be your legacy, Suzy and Billy," she grimly stated as she turned her back. No, she wasn't going to shoot herself, at least not yet. Her immediate task was to establish her own hidden camp at a short distance. She felt *cold rage* rising up in her chest, tightening her throat, and swallowing her head! She clearly recognized the need for one more action before she could consider following her kids into death: "Your funeral pyre will call back the tribe from wherever they've gone. They'll be confused and disoriented when they return, finding their encampment destroyed. And then there'll be a *reckoning*."

She was going to *punish* the bastards that did this to her two beautiful children.

She'd give them back the poison they'd first given to her: *taking* from them that which *they* valued the most!

She didn't want to do it. It wasn't in her nature to seek revenge. But she was now corrupted, embittered, and enraged.

The *poison of sweet retribution* was lodged deep in her soul. All her Christian ideals were tossed to the side. No "love your enemies." No "turn the other cheek." It was an "eye for an eye," a "tooth for a tooth" cold payback. She was prepared and ready to slaughter the entire tribe, for her heart was turned to ice.

Let the tribe return.

She was waiting for them.

Chapter 14

ANTIDOTES

For every action
Physical, Mental, or Spiritual
There is an equal and opposite action
Which if carefully and timely applied
Will negate even the worst poison
Believe it or not, it's true…
But only if you want to find it
And have the courage to consume it
And are willing to lose the power
That rush of sheer delightful euphoria
Of sinking to your lowest level
In total abandonment, doing whatever
Ceding control to your genetics
It's often a bitter pill to eat
Neither candy nor cake
Better to swallow it fast
And clamp down tight
Least you vomit it up
A "medicine" few ingest
Choosing instead fantasy
Rejecting hard reality
Embracing the dream!
The Minstrel's Lark, 14:9-12

Tommy was content to be in the Obelisk, out of the Martian rocky emptiness, traveling to who knew where.

He was exhausted. His mind was wrung dry. His emotions were dissipated. His vision was blurred.

"Just you and me," he smiled, leaning back against the cool surface of the storage compartment. A continuing, soothing vibration tried to lull him to sleep.

But that *Dave's pesky laptop computer screen* kept glaring at him in the dark of the small chamber, monopolizing his attention with that simple message: "FOLLOW YOUR HEART."

What did it mean? Who sent it? Was it from the Obelisk? Was it something else entirely? Was it a trick? Or was it something from a deeper reality?

He was just a little robot. He *didn't have* a "heart"! Sure, he had a complex fluid which was circulated throughout his entire body. But his "blood" was driven by the contractions of many dispersed vessels, not a central pump!

But...maybe that wasn't what the message meant?

"Huh!" Tommy snorted, irritated with himself. "I'm getting too serious. I'm sure I'll find out what it means if I'm patient. I've just got to stay cheerful."

Feeling much better, he sighed deeply. He was glad to finally be off the surface of the fake Mars. Wherever he was going in the Obelisk couldn't be much worse than the gilded prison he'd been trapped within. At least now he could make his own decisions.

No more mysterious disappearances of his closest friends! He'd manage to escape that terrible place where the things he loved the most just vanished, one-by-one.

It was so sad to lose his most precious things. He now had a notion of what humans felt when their loved-ones inevitably faded and died. It was loneliness beyond description.

No, don't think like that! You're not a human!—he sternly admonished himself mentally.

"Sure! I'm just fine!" he encouraged himself, carefully articulating each word for emphasis.

He managed to convince himself his brave words were true, at least for a while.

He'd soon enough arrive at his new destination. And if the computer was correct, he'd like it!

So he settled back, closed his eyes, and forced himself to take a healing, rejuvenating nap.

Sally's eyes jerked open at the unmistakable sound of horses "whinnying" in the distance.

She'd barely slept in her hidden camp. It was just a hollow she'd dug out then covered with her opened-up backpack. The incredible pain of the loss of her beloved children kept trying to rip her mind apart, drive her insane. Only one thing staved off the agony: the lust for righteous *revenge*. And now that it was morning she was ready to exact that reprisal: mercilessly!

"Come closer. Terrible punishment is awaiting you," she whispered.

She was wide awake now. Her teeth were clenched together tightly, making her jaw ache. She barely contained her seething rage. She wanted to shout and scream! But she studiously maintained silence, waiting. She knew that her patience was being rewarded. The tribe was returning.

She was lying prone at the top of the low hill from which she'd first spied the Indian village. She and her backpack were well-concealed beneath a prickly bush. No one down below would know she was up there until it was too late. The only thing showing was the protruding tip of her rifle. But she'd wiped it with mud so that even its metal wouldn't give off any reflections, giving away her position. The rifle was aimed downward, straight at the charred remains of the tent where Sally and Billy's corpses had been incinerated. She had six plus one rounds loaded in the rifle. Plus she had several boxes of bullets sitting ready to the side, with which she could quickly reload.

"I only wish I'd brought Dave's rifle," she muttered to herself as the large group of riding and walking Native Americans drew closer. "I'd be more accurate with its scope."

Yes, Dave's Beanfield Sniper was accurate even when fired from a long distance. Her Timber Classic would do the job, but messier. Though she was a dead shot with it, at this distance she'd not be able to guarantee a head shot.

Too bad for them...but she could easily hit their torsos. They'd die slow instead of fast. But that'd be fitting retribution for what they did to her kids!

Yes, she didn't know exactly how or why the kids had died. Yes, it might even have been from some innocent accident. Her kids could certainly get into all sorts of trouble! But in her heart she knew it wasn't just a sad tragedy.

They were executed! Those savages down below killed my children! And now they're going to suffer the same fate.

She heard wails of dismay as the tribe came upon the charred remains of their encampment. Sally saw women and children milling around in confusion. Some ran to tepees that were presumably their homes, searching through the burned poles and tent remnants, trying to find some precious surviving possession.

And riding up to the tent where Sally's aim was centered was what she assumed were the Chief and the Medicine Man.

They both dismounted their ponies at the same time, gesturing at each other animatedly.

The presumed Chief, clad in buckskins, wore a large headdress sporting many eagle feathers. He was somewhat heavyset with a stern expression on his wide, wrinkled face. The presumed Medicine Man was grey-haired, with a necklace of snake ribs around his neck. He was bare-chested and scrawny looking. He was jerkily moving through the tent's debris, yanking at this or that. To Sally he looked like a weasel. She had no doubt he was the mastermind who oversaw or ordered the execution of her children. And he kept feeling nervously at the bag he had firmly attached to his waist, as if afraid it would vanish.

"Missing something there?" Sally gloated, realizing the gem she'd taken should have been safe inside his pouch. "When you and the others left in a hurry, did the emerald drop out? Ah...well, I've got it and you can't have it back—not that you'll need it where you're going!"

Now both men were in the pile of charred remains, tentatively moving pieces of the smoking debris aside. Were they searching for the emerald? Or were they making sure that Suzy and Billy were properly cremated in the "accidental" fire? Yep. It was a *lightning strike* from the passing thunder storms last night, right?

Wrong! It was the *wrath of God* coming down on your stinking, heathen heads!

She started to squeeze her trigger to give the Medicine Man the honor of being the first of his tribe to feel *hot lead* slamming through his chest.

"Mommy! What are you doing?"

Startled, Sally relaxed her grip on the rifle, looking to the side to see...

—Tommy?

He stood there in the waving grass politely holding his small hands behind his back. His curly blond locks set-off his friendly little smile. His red jumpsuit was startling among the waving sea of green grass. And his stubby blue shoes and blue shirt vividly contrasted with the red fabric of his pants.

He was just as she remembered him!

"But...you can't...how did you...?" she gasped, totally confused.

Then she suddenly realized what she'd been about to do. She was going to *slaughter* dozens of *innocent* people below!

Even if the warriors killed her son, the women and children down below likely had no part in the murder of her children!

A fog lifted from her brain.

Simultaneously around her, the absolutely real, solid objects were *fading*. The bushes, soil, and waving grass were becoming translucent, then transparent. And appearing in their places—as if emerging from mists—were *stark black surfaces*.

And she wasn't prone, aiming her lethal rifle at a distant tribe of Native American people. Instead, she was leaning downward standing on the floor of a large chamber. The butt of the gun rested solidly on the floor, with the tip of the muzzle poked up painfully between her jawbones!

With her hand stuck on the trigger, she was about to blow her *own* head off!

Shuddering, she shoved the rifle to the side where it fell with a "clunk" onto the hard surface.

Looking dazedly around, Sally saw that only a dozen feet behind her rested her inert ORV. She *hadn't* been miles away from it in a pristine early-American plain. Instead, she must have been marching around in circles inside an incredibly detailed holographic-projection!

Her first instincts were correct after all. None of it had been real.

And yes, there suspended high above her, she spotted a *shimmering globe*...exactly the same as she remembered in the holographic "archives" of the alien Spike-Ship which she'd encountered long, long ago in the far distant future!

Time travel can be very confusing.

"Tommy," she rasped, finding her voice. "Where did you come from?"

He gestured over to the side then paused, confused.

"The Obelisk! It brought me here. I saw you trying to shoot yourself and stopped you. The Obelisk knocked against that big globe above, maybe hurting it. At least, I thought it did...but the Obelisk is gone now. I was back on Mars, Mommy. But the whole planet was a fake! And then everyone kept disappearing and..."

"I'm guessing you were right here in this same room as me, being likewise fooled by that incredible Projector hovering high above us. But then how could a nonexistent pillar damage the Projector?" Sally frowned, leaning over to grab-up her rifle.

"Maybe I overloaded it, Mommy."

"How?"

"I gave it my heart. And I'm guessing you did too."

"Maybe...maybe," Sally nodded.

But if they'd somehow shut down the Projector, might it restart at any moment? If the Globe mechanism could convince both Tommy and her that their heart's worst fears were real, what else could it do? She was starting to panic. "We've got to get out of here."

"Yes, we should," Tommy nodded in agreement, his blue eyes stretched wide, "But how, Mommy?"

"The ORV has a DE-generator powering a rudimentary subspace drive, Tommy," she hurriedly explained, grabbing his hand. "But its mechanisms were damaged in the initial jump I made. Then the Ranger's battery was depleted of its charge. I just barely made it here before it..."

"I can check it out. Maybe I can fix it! If I can give it an electricity surge, that should help get it going," Tommy confidently interrupted, walking along happily hand-in-hand with her. "I can redirect my own internal power source to the car to 'jump' the battery. I've got plenty of power to spare. Once the car's fixed, you just need to get the deuterium flow going through the reaction cell in the DE-generator, right? That doesn't take much juice. And then the subspace fracture should generate enough power to..."

"Oh, you're a godsend, Tommy!" she grinned at him. "That might work! But that's only if you can get the fried circuitry to work or maybe bypass it? Maybe like you did when we were trapped in the Black Hole and trying to escape?"

"Sure!" he smiled shyly up at her. "It's really nice to see you again, Mommy."

"You too, Tommy!"

In a few steps they were back at the motionless vehicle. Not far beyond the ORV Sally saw the shimmering green energy barrier of the wrecked alien Spike-Ship protecting them from the vacuum of space. Through it, Sally saw the dazzling flat field of spinning diamonds comprising the ring within which they sat. And behind that—looming large before sliding off the side as the ice mountain supporting the crashed Spike-Ship rotated—Sally saw the giant orb of Saturn.

"It's good to be back," Sally sighed, amazed that the scene which before had terrified her now looked so welcoming!

As they reached the Ranger, Sally gratefully undid the straps of her heavy backpack, slinging it into the back seat. She started to put the rifle away but stopped.

As Tommy happily clambered back into the ORV, Sally suddenly frowned, standing there. She *felt* something. It was different from before. It wasn't the presence of her biological children. Whatever tangible hallucination that'd been—apparently dredged from her memories of the Chickasaw in Sulphur plus her worst fears for Suzy and Billy—she now knew the kids weren't there, had never been there. But something even *worse* was now nagging at her. What was it? It felt like a *cold hand* delicately stroking her throat.

What did it mean?

And then she *saw* it!

"Tommy, do you see it too?"

He followed her gaze, peering off into the shadows at the extreme back of the large chamber.

His eyes opened wide as he stared into the cavern.

"Yes! I'm scared, Mommy. Let's get out of here!"

"You stay right here, Tommy," she reassured him. "I've got to take a look at it before we leave. Maybe it's just another trick by the Projector. But I don't think so. See if you can fix what's wrong with the Ranger then get yourself connected up to the battery. I'll be back quickly."

"But Mommy!" he whined.

Ignoring his distress, she turned away from the ORV, tightly clutching her rifle.

"I'll be right back," she repeated.

Although she dreaded going back, she ran toward the rear of the large cavern. In the dim light she now made out an elongated, raised stone container. By the dust settled over it and the crumbling exterior it must have been there a long time—maybe eons! Sally was certain that this was not a projection, but the real thing.

It was totally sealed. There was no way to get into it or look inside. And she knew that she and Tommy had to leave before the Projector reactivated.

What to do?

Backing off a few steps she raised her rifle and fired point-blank at the crypt-like object.

BLAM! BLAM! BLAM! BLAM!

She paused, inspecting the side of the container. She saw four fresh pits where the bullets had struck. And now, jarred by the impact, it was...awakening?

Suddenly Sally heard—echoing eerily about the chamber—a sweet, young female voice singing a song: "*...let it be...let it be...let it be...let it be...whisper words of wisdom...let it be...*"

It was the famous song by the Beatles, "Let It Be." It stirred powerful memories in her: of being back in the 12th century in the convent of Mother *Hildegard von Bingen.* She'd taught that 20th century song to Mother Hildegard. They sang the chorus together. It was a moment of both transfiguration and transformation, after which nothing was the same anymore. That song cut across time itself, allowing them both to escape the problems of the moment into a timeless place where emotions connected across many generations. Indeed, that was the best aspect of all great music.

And, accompanied by the continuing sweet serenade, the stone side of the container was *clarifying*—allowing Sally to see what was sealed inside!

"No...it can't be," she gasped.

But it was true. Inside, seemingly painfully twisted upon a stone slab, was the withered corpse of a very, very old woman. The spotted head was bald. The scalp sported not one single hair. Scabs and sores dotted the gray, mummified flesh. The eyes were sunken-in pits. A dried-up tongue stuck out of a gaping mouth. Only three broken teeth remained in the purple, rotted gums. And—seemingly clashing with the ancient decay—a glistening-white dress adorned with glittering jewels covered the rest of the body.

And hanging slackly down along the side of the supporting slab was the mummy's left arm. On the wrist of that arm Sally made out the faded outline of...a *Turtle Tattoo*. And marching up from the wrist were the remnants of other tattoos...which *exactly* mirrored what was on Sally's arm right at that moment!

There was no doubt.

The ancient corpse preserved in the crypt was *her*.

"Is this...my future?" Sally gasped as simulations of the Chief and the Medicine Man suddenly *flickered-into existence* to each side of her, *grabbing* her arms!

She jerked away from the grasping hands, swinging upward with all her strength—SLAMMING the butt of her rifle into both their skulls!

With sputtering gasps, they both sagged to the sides.

The Projector was fighting back! It was trying to stop her! Firing those bullets at the crypt, the singing, the clarifying—triggered a stepped-up attack upon her!

—as a *troop of Indian warriors* materialized with arrows drawn, starting to swing the lethal tips downward at her...

"Not this time," she growled, falling deliberately backward toward the floor, her rifle muzzle now swinging upward...

—and she painfully "thumped" onto her back while simultaneously *firing* her remaining three bullets up at the glittering globe far above!

"Gotcha," she grinned.

—as the Projector *shattered*, with knife-sharp *black shards* raining down across the surface of the cavern...

—one of them *slamming* painfully through the fleshy part of Sally's upper right arm, *pinning* her to the floor! To each side of her the Indians were likewise skewered and cut, momentarily no longer a threat.

The agony was intense. Blood spurted freely through the torn fabric of her shirt. The shard must have nicked an artery! She felt consciousness slipping away.

But she couldn't give-in to the comforting, beckoning darkness. With her other hand she got a trembling grip on the upper half of the shard, *ripping* it out of her arm!

Tightly squeezing the wound to slow the bleeding, with her rifle in the crook of her arm, she staggered back toward the front of the cavern...

—while behind her she heard the shuffling steps of the recovered war party.

"Oh, Christ...the energy barrier!" she gasped as she ignored the pain and now *dashed* for the ORV.

Indeed, the shield that had been holding back the vacuum of space, allowing her to breathe air inside, with the destruction of the Projector was now crackling and *sparking*.

And just as it vanished—with the earth-normal gravity inside simultaneously stopping—Sally dived into the ORV where Tommy activated its own, internal energy shield.

"It wasn't too messed up, Mommy," he modestly reported. "I had to switch out three of the circuits with spares I found, plus bypass a couple others, but that wasn't too hard. And I sucked in and compressed enough air from the projection room to replenish the oxygen and air canisters and then..."

"—just get us the hell *out* of here, Tommy!" she yelled, snatching out a first-aid kit from the backseat to wrap her wounded arm tightly with gauze.

Gasping for breath as the ORV's interior atmosphere came up to earth-normal, she saw Tommy confidently manipulating the controls. They floated up off the floor then zipped out of the now not-obscured, gaping opening out into the blackness of space.

Floating around the ORV, feebly convulsing before freezing solid, were the bodies of the pursuing Indians.

Sally felt a pang of pity for them. Whatever they were—real manifestations from a distant past, or solidified memories out of her own mind—they were noble warriors now doomed to float forever in the coldness of outer space in orbit around Saturn.

"Are you hurt?" Tommy anxiously asked.

"Not too bad," she gasped, staunching the flow of blood. It wasn't soaking her shirt anymore. But it was still trickling out.

"What was it you found back there?" he asked her as he expertly dodged smaller ice and rock fragments in their tightly packed region of the ring. "I heard the singing before the *crashing* started. The song was nice!"

"I'm not sure what it was that I found."

"But was it fun?"

That was an odd thing for him to say. But she was too stunned by the recent events and the throbbing pain wracking her arm to pursue the matter. She was just glad to escape.

"I think it was an old, twisted incarnation of mine," she finally managed to state, "one that I think I almost became today. But you saved me, Tommy. I nearly did something from which I would have never recovered, even if I'd survived unwittingly trying to kill myself. If I'd done what I planned, though, I think I would have ended up ugly and sad. You brought me back from the brink. You saved me from becoming a bitter, evil hag. *Thank you*," her voice trailed off with barely contained emotion.

He grinned happily.

"I *love* you, Mommy! I'd do *anything* for you!"

"Yes, Tommy, I know," she smiled at him. She extended the hand of her undamaged arm to lay it tenderly on his small shoulder. "And I love you too."

She hadn't succeeded in rescuing Suzy and Billy. But now she'd unexpectedly recovered her robot-son from adventures past, Tommy. And in the bizarre universe she inhabited, that was definite progress.

As Tommy started excitedly telling her what had happened to him following the explosion of the Harvester, when they'd tried to escape the clashing Universes, she slumped in her seat, trying to make sense of it all.

What he was telling her was fantastical. But it sounded so real! Did it all really happen, in parallel to her gruesome manifestations? Or did it happen elsewhere, his great love for her guiding the real Obelisk to bring him to her?

He had certainly hung in there, staying focused, doing the best he could. But could she do the same? The sight of her two dead children broke something in her, inhibitions that normally kept her from sinking to the lowest levels of depravity.

But she had a hard-and-fast rule which she imposed upon herself every day before falling asleep at night: If she'd made *any* sort of progress she couldn't be too hard on herself!

Her compulsive, obsessively perfectionist nature forced her to want to achieve *everything immediately*—where anything less felt like a failure. But she knew that difficult challenges were rarely met or solved by simple, quick measures. She needed to learn a lesson from the happily chatting little android. Every journey is composed of many individual steps. Getting to each milestone wasn't a leap, but a process of merely putting one foot in front of the next.

She had tried to blindly follow the neutrino trail with the ORV. Though informative, it was a dead end.

What was the next step?

"Tommy," she interrupted his fascinating story. They needed to focus on figuring out a new course of action. They'd managed to get out of the vast ring. Now they were drifting in a high orbit above the ring, circling Saturn. "Do you think we can get back to Earth?"

"Maybe...your ship's drive is awful rickety, Mommy...and it depends on *when* we are, so..."

"Oh, right. Since we battled the Spike-Ships a billion years in the future, then we must be..."

"—probably two hundred million years beyond even that," Tommy thoughtfully nodded. "That agrees with the configurations of the main constellations that I'm able to see in space from our orbit here."

To Sally it sounded too fantastic to be true. Did her little ORV really travel 1.2 *billion* years into the future? She knew it had a jury-rigged subspace drive they'd never been able to test before now. So it might be wildly unpredictable, capable of huge lurches. But to do such a gigantic jump unaided was preposterous! However, what if the Ranger was *aided?*

Did that mean that, once again, something was guiding her journey? Yes, her Turtle Tattoo had lighted up.

She put that unsettling notion to the side. She'd thought that she was beyond being a pawn in the hands of unknown forces. But perhaps that was too much to expect, given her history.

"Ok. But if that's true, then shouldn't the rings of Saturn be gone by now? Aren't they just accretion discs that are continually falling into Saturn's immense gravity-well? After all, Saturn is a hundred times the mass of Earth."

"Yep, that's right," Tommy shrugged. "But Saturn has more than sixty moons. Scientists of our time thought that the moons were the reason Saturn retained its rings while Jupiter, Uranus, and Neptune mostly lost theirs. The moons somehow stabilize the rings. At least that's the theory. Another theory was a continual eons-long destruction and reconstruction of colliding moons-to-rings then back again. But whatever the mechanism, what we're seeing here supports the ring's long-term stability, right?"

"Interesting...but it doesn't get us home, Tommy. It just tells us that we've a long, long journey to go."

But—that also meant that Suzy and Billy could be not just anywhere in the solar system, but any-*when* across a vast ocean of time! Having lost the neutrino trail of the Obelisk, finding her real kids now seemed near impossible.

"So are we...stranded in space?" she gulped, her head spinning from loss of blood and confusion.

"No. I think I can take you wherever you want, Mommy. I don't have to rely just on your primitive equipment. I can *see* trails through space-time when I know whom I'm tracking or I'm at their departure point! That's how I followed Dave from New Earth back to the fifth century B.C., remember?"

She barely remembered anything from so long ago. But he took his word the he was an expert "time-trail" tracker!

That was all fine. It was great to have Tommy at the controls. His complex artificial brain was stuffed with all sorts of exotic skills and knowledge. She now had an expert pilot who might get their jury-rigged "spaceship" to do things she never could! But she still didn't have the slightest idea of where to attempt going next.

"Suzy and Billy were taken away by an Obelisk," she succinctly explained. "I'm trying to get them back. Do you think you can track *them* through space-time?"

"Who is 'Suzy and Billy'?" he innocently asked.

It dawned on her that he had no knowledge of the decade-plus period she'd peacefully lived with Dave in Sulphur, Oklahoma.

"Oh...that's right...you don't know about them, Tommy. Well, Dave and I got married and had a couple kids. So they're...your biological sister and brother!"

He gaped up at her in awe.

"Wow! I have a sister and brother? That's great! Sure, I'll help you find them! Do you have their quantum signatures?"

"Say what?"

"Every individual living creature leaves an imprint on space-time, Mommy," he confidently lectured her. "I learned this from the Syncytium on the fake Mars. That's how they said they were able to track me even when I was outside the Universe—then draw me back to them when the bad Universe collapsed! It's really, *really* complicated. Quantum imprints are difficult to detect and even harder to follow! But it makes a trail *I* can follow."

"So it's theoretically possible that we can find a path through subspace to the kids?"

"Sure! Anything's possible, Mommy. I don't know if we can do it, but we can sure try! You know that I'm good at traveling in space-time, right? I learned some really good detection skills the times that I fell through thousands and millions and billions of years! Remember when I brought you and Dave those dinosaurs to help fight the Demon? Wow, that was sure fun! So do you maybe have something that Suzy or Billy wore or touched? Maybe I can get a reading from it?"

Her high hopes were dashed. She had nothing from her kids. Maybe their bikes would have worked. But she and Dave had left them behind in the trench where a version of the Obelisk had lain dormant for years in the Park.

"Wait!" she remembered, turning in desperation to dig with her good arm through her backpack that was sitting in the backseat.

"Here! What about *this?*"

She held in her hand the multi-faceted, large *emerald* she'd stolen from the Indians. It didn't vanish when the simulation switched off in the cavern. It must be similar to the rematerialized Indians she'd shot who stayed solid even when they were ejected into space.

That Projector sure did good work, at least before she destroyed it.

"Wow! That's very pretty, Mommy! Where did you get it?"

"It's from the village where I saw the supposed corpses of the kids."

"What? They're *dead?*" he gasped.

"I don't know. I hope not. I think the Projector was drawing the worst fears out of my brain. But I'm also suspicious that at least part of what I experienced was based on real events. It was just too detailed and outside my own experience to be only a materialized nightmare. And maybe the kids handled this jewel. At least, that's implied by the sequence of events...I think," she concluded, confused.

Yes. That was an awful long list of "maybe's" to rely on. But what else did she have to go on?

"Let me touch it," Tommy said, holding out his hand.

Her hopes rested on a single fist-sized jewel. It certainly wasn't the original. That original jewel maybe existed more than a billion years before. This was a duplicate materialized by the Spike-Ship, perhaps from shared "files" of sister ships visiting Earth in the distant past. But according to the Captain of the ship she'd battled while stranded in the intergalactic void, the simulations were accurate to the level of individual atoms.

She released the large gem which floated in the zero-G between her and Tommy, slowly rotating as it drifted through the cabin's air.

He tentatively placed a fingertip on it. Then he withdrew his hand.

"Nothing...I'm sorry, Mommy, I don't feel or see any quantum signature."

"*Damn* it!" she shouted. Then, more quietly, as tears welled up in her eyes, she added: "That was my last shot, Tommy. Other than that there's nothing that..."

"Wait."

Tommy tightly squinted, examining the flat underside of the floating big gem. Then he reached out and grabbed it, holding it near his face.

"There's a mechanism inside."

"When I first found it, I did hear faint *voices* coming from it."

He gripped the top part of the jewel tightly while holding firmly to the base. Giving it a quick *twist* he set it back into place in the air between them.

For a moment it just hung there. Then it started *orienting* itself, like a just-activated gyroscope! It was no longer rotating in the zero-G, but pointing at an odd angle out away from Saturn and the planetary plane.

And it was no longer green. Now, it became transparently white—a huge *diamond*.

—and a beam of *ethereal white light* suddenly shone out of its top. The laser-focused beam passed effortlessly through the energy shield and out into space. It was perfectly straight. But unlike ordinary light it wasn't only visible when encountering particles. Instead, it seemed to be illuminating the very fabric of space itself!

"It's pointing us a path through subspace," Sally marveled.

"Should we follow it?" Tommy asked.

"Beam us up, Scotty!"

"What? Oh, right...Star Trek," he snickered as he started a complex series of operations. "I uploaded the historical reruns of those series and movies when you initially programmed me. It was great! Spock was really funny. But my favorite character was Data. He was an android like me!"

His hands flashed across the controls and settings faster than Sally could follow. She reached under the seat for her laptop, setting up her five-dimensional array. Wherever they were going, she was going to document it.

"All set! Should we get going?"

"*Punch* it, Mr. Chekov!"

"Aye, aye Captain Mommy! Hold on tight! If we wind up travelling backward through time...that's going against the flow. It could get pretty rough."

Yes, she knew full well what he was saying. Her past descents backward through time had been horrendously difficult. And she'd never made a plunge like this, 1.2 billion years into the past!

Could their little ORV even survive the inconceivable forces involved?

I guess we'll find out—she resolutely thought to herself, steeling her nerve.

"Here we go!" Tommy yelled, punching some controls.

And then they plunged inside a *spinning tunnel* composed of every light in the spectrum, following a central, *solid white line*...

—to where, she knew not!

Along with the Ranger she and Tommy were flung back and forth, violently jarred. She fearfully observed WALLS OF FIRE accumulating around and before them.

Yes, it was a terrible prospect.

But it was the antidote to stagnation and capitulation: *charging ahead!*

In her flimsy ORV, rocketing through subspace, traveling across untold eons with her robot "son"—Sally felt a strange compulsion.

"Wheeeeee!" the android boy beside her shouted out in his high voice, raising both his short arms above the steering wheel. "No hands!"

Despite the magnitude of the incredible event taking place, Sally *giggled* like a little girl. In spite of the danger and extreme gravitas, Tommy was right: it *was* fun!

—assuming they survived.

Chapter 15

<u>GIGGLES</u>

Presumably only for children
Little babies struggling to articulate
A little glee belched out in a burst
It's too precious to restrict
Only for immature children
But rather should erupt
From anyone caught in fun
Unexpectedly finding a hint
Not of horror or pain or drudgery
But spontaneous humor cutting
Lancing the cyst, releasing puss
And relieving the nagging ache
If only for just a moment
A spurted-out "Tee hee!"
Or a manly "Hee hee!"
We need more not less.

The Minstrel's Lark, 15:29-33

Suzy was getting very worried. But that little brat Billy didn't look at all concerned!

He was laughing and joking like nothing had happened the previous night. But Suzy could see that their situation was now radically *different*. None of the adults who'd been friendly to them before would now talk to her. And the few other kids walking around looked scared out of their moccasins!

It continued that way all day. Suzy tried to help out with the sewing chores of the women, but they turned their backs on her. Billy went over to the finally corralled horses to ride one but the guards there shooed him away.

Well, that wasn't too unexpected. They didn't want the little pest letting them loose again! But it went beyond anger to something else...a *respectful fear*—as if she and Billy were *bad omens*: heralding the arrival of something catastrophic!

"Well, maybe they'll get over it if we just give them time," Suzy sighed, happy that—at least for the moment—both she and Billy were still alive. The village leaders *hadn't* decided to slit the two kid's throats as they slept. *Whew!*

But it was evening now, getting dark. There'd be plenty of time for "throat-slashing" as they again slept. The village was now almost back to normal after the excitement of the night before. She and Billy were sitting off by themselves, eating bowls of mashed turnips and wild berries. It tasted much like hot oatmeal.

Still wary, Suzy was starting to think that she and Billy weren't going to be punished...

—when the Chief himself suddenly interrupted her thoughts: roughly *latching-onto* Suzy and Billy's hands, causing them both to drop their bowls.

"*Issabaya'shi!*" he said (You must come with me!)

"*Nanta...?*" Suzy tried to ask (What...?) as she was jerked along behind the well-weathered, old Chief.

He was dressed in his finest ritual clothes. He wore his large headdress. It looked like a big ceremony was about to occur!

*Oh Jesus...*Suzy gasped to herself. *Is this the ritual execution I've been expecting?*

There'd been no tribal punishments while she and Billy had been in the tribe. But razor-sharp bone and rock knifes were plentiful.

"*Chokkilissa!*" he snapped at them both (Be quiet!)

And so Suzy just tried to keep up with the Chief's long strides as he headed out of the encampment and into the surrounding, darkened plain!

"Suzy! Where are they taking us?" Billy whimpered beside her.

"I don't know!" she snapped. Then, more quietly she added: "But I think the moment we can get loose we should run as hard as we can, Billy. Be ready!"

And even more ominously, Suzy glanced back and saw trailing along behind—also in total silence—the entire village! They were leaving everything behind and just walking out into the grassy plain. A lot of them carried torches, making the dark of the night spooky. What was going on?

This was definitely not just an isolated incidence. The entire tribe was involved! If Billy and she were going to be killed, Suzy was sure it would be during a big ceremony...maybe a ritual sacrifice to their gods! Was the tribe going to get rid of two unwanted pests while simultaneously placating their deities? She didn't know that the Chickasaw were into ritual sacrifice. But she didn't know much about them, particularly their developmental history.

"Suzy, I'm *scared!*" Billy cried, squirming in the Chief's strong grip beside her.

"Don't panic, Billy. Be ready to run away whenever he lets us loose," she whispered back at him. "We made it this far across the dinosaur swamp! We can keep on going. Once we're into the tall grass, we can hide from them."

"I dunno, Suzy...they're Indians! They run real fast, can chase us on ponies, and track us down like we're animals!"

Yes, that was certainly true. Their chance of slipping away in the gathering dark of the night was slim at best. But they had to try!

"Did you call Mom and Dad?" Billy desperately asked her.

"I tried, Billy, but the batteries in our cellphones are long dead and..."

"*Chokkilissa!*" the Chief snapped again at them both (Be quiet!), roughly jerking on their wrists to make them obey.

"*Sanokhanglo,*" Suzy gulped (I'm sorry), hoping to lessen the Chief's obvious anger at her and Billy.

And so they kept on plodding across the rough terrain until, at last, they approached a low hill. A quarter-moon was now up, giving enough dim light to see the terrain around them. Suzy thought they'd walked for miles, though it was probably no more than an hour from the main encampment. The top of the hill before them was flat, like a small mesa. And on it stood *Okchamail Cholhkan*, doing a "stomp" dance while eerily chanting!

"Are they going to kill us?" Billy whimpered.

"Just be ready to run!" she snapped at him.

The entire tribe stood now at the base of the hill, waiting patiently. Torches sputtered and "popped" loudly. The Chief let go of her and Billy's wrists, but only after turning them over to a surrounding group of guarding warriors. Suzy was surprised to see that it wasn't just the two of them being held inside the human corral. Three more kids were there also, two girls and one boy. But they looked as scared as Billy! Something was up that went beyond just a public execution—or even a lesser shaming for her and Billy for sneaking into Cholhkan's tent.

"They're going to sacrifice us to the moon god!" Billy sobbed. "It's just like the others showed me when we first got here! A big bird is going to come down and eat us kids! We're all gonna die!"

"Stay alert, Billy—don't give up!"

The Medicine Man above them suddenly stopped his dancing. He revealed something from beneath a blanket. He triumphantly held up above his head the *red-glowing giant ruby*. It glared so brightly that Cholhkan looked like he was bathed in blood!

"*Hilha' hoomóma áyya'sha!*" he shouted at the assembled tribe below (The dancers are all here!).

"HILHA' HOOMÓMA ÁYYA'SHA!" the people shouted back in unison, repeating the Medicine Man's words.

"What's he saying?" Billy said, scooting up to Suzy's side and grabbing her hand. Suzy felt him trembling.

"They're going to start another one of their stomp dances," she calmly replied, just as frightened as he was but not wanting to show it. She knew that people who agitate themselves into a mob are capable of doing terrible things, awful deeds that they'd never do on their own. She'd seen this happen lots of times on the T.V. news channels right before terrible riots started. And even though three other kids were in the central "corral," she knew full-well who the "outsiders" were: she and Billy!

"*Minkoat hootaloowachi iwaa!*" the Medicine Man screamed, holding the glowing ruby up even higher (The Chief is calling them out to sing!).

"MINKOAT HOOTALOOWACHI IWAA!" the tribe roared back.

Suzy was sure the Medicine Man wasn't referring to the weathered old Chief—but something to do with the ruby...

"*Intikbayka'chi!*" Cholhkan screeched out, dancing around in a circle as the ruby pulsed even brighter (He will lead the stomp dance!).

"INTIKBAYKA'CHI!"

Around Suzy and the encircling guards, the people started to form up in their own hand-to-hand circles and stomp around following a leader. The leaders each shook a loud rattle. Many of the followers had adorned their legs with gourds containing pebbles, making a loud rattle as they moved.

And together they echoed the continued chants from Cholhkan as the tribe whipped itself into a frenzy.

A few men sat off to the sides of the marching groups, beating out a common rhythm on drums. As their enthusiasm increased, the drums got louder and louder.

It was incredibly frightening, but also puzzling. What the hell was this all building up to?

"Suzy..." Billy gulped, getting his wits back together, looking around in the moonlight in confusion, "This is...boring! Back at the camp we were jumping around and singing at the fire that was roasting buffalo meat. It was a real party! But this stomping and chanting is just crazy. There's no point to it. They need to get some good rock music instead."

"*Nittak ishtayyopi ona'chi Chikashsha alhihaat hoottibaahilhachinka!*" the Medicine Man yelled out from the top of the small mesa, towering above the people (The Chickasaw people will dance, until the world ends!).

"NITTAK ISTAYYOPI ONA'CHI CHIKASHSHA ALHIHAAT HOOTTIBAAHILHACHINKA!" the tribe echoed back in unison.

"Wake me up when it's all over, Suzy," Billy said as he sat down on the flattened grass and yawned widely. "I'm gonna take me a nap."

Suzy saw up on the mesa the Medicine Man suddenly give a loud "whoop," *twist* the top of the giant ruby, set it on the ground, and step back...

—as a *piercing white laser beam* shot from the jewel straight up into the sky!

"Uh...Billy...do you hear...?"

He had his eyes closed, starting to doze off.

"—a bunch of Indians hopping up and down and marchin' in circles?" he yawned, lying flat on the ground with his arms crossed over his chest. "Yep—I sure do. And..."

The marching-stomping lines of circling natives were now chanting over and over: "*Ilihilha'...Ilihilha'...Ilihilha'...*" (Let's dance! Let's dance! Let's dance!)

"No, something else," Suzy frowned, looking up at the night sky. "Something's happening, Billy..."

—as the pace of the dance and the chanting suddenly increased even further, the entire tribe shouting-out in apparent ecstasy: "*Aashopala' aashoppalali... Aashoppala' aashoppalali... Aashoppala' aashoppalali!*" (Turn the light on! Turn the light on! Turn the light on!"

"Uh, Billy, maybe you should get back up?"

Indeed, as if summoned by the intense chanting, Suzy saw a BRIGHT PINPOINT OF LIGHT suddenly appear high above them in the night sky...seemingly following the path of the laser beam down toward them—that grew larger and larger. Was it a meteor? But then Suzy was shocked to see it sprout a *downward*-pointing tail of fire! That was no meteor!

And accompanying the now *descending torch* was a growing ROAR of immense power that *vibrated* the air and *shook* Suzy to her bones!

Billy jumped up to his feet, looking up into the sky with his eyes stretched wide in fear.

"I...don't...like...this," Billy gulped, again clutching tightly Suzy's hand.

And then the Medicine Man bent down, snatched up the glittering jewel, and *ran* off the flat mesa. He practically tripped over his own feet to make it off the slope to where the tribe was still chanting and dancing ferociously to the side of the mesa...

—as a tall *metallic-glittering, slender, pointy-nosed* SPACESHIP descended from the night sky on a pillar of red flames, settling smoothly onto the top of the mesa, supported by a three-pointed tail!

"Wow," Suzy said, amazed.

The smell of scorched air permeated the air. Black smoke from burned earth and grass drifted around Suzy and Billy, making her cough. But the Native Americans erupted in a huge shout of glee!

"S-Suzy," Billy stammered. "That's a s-space..."

"—*spaceship*, yes...just like in the mid twentieth-century 1950's old-fashioned science fiction movies. But, how's this possible?"

"What do you mean, Suzy?"

"It looks like it's ready to take off again!"

"Ok...?" Billy frowned.

"But there's no way that it could hold enough fuel to..."

"Oh, that's right. It needs a giant tank, huh?"

"If it's going to escape Earth's gravity, it's got to have lots and lots of fuel. That's why the 1950's science fiction spaceships weren't real. They were much too small to get up into space without attached giant fuel tanks!"

Billy gulped, pressing closer to her side.

"Ok, but what's a *spaceship* doing here, anyway, Suzy? I thought we were way back in time with the Indians, right?"

"You're right, Billy. This doesn't make any sense," Suzy frowned, staring up at the small spaceship that was undeniably sitting right there on the top of the low mesa. Its metal surface gleamed. Its smooth surface was reflecting moonlight plus the light of many torches shining below.

"Well, I guess if there can be *dinosaurs*, then...?" Billy tentatively ventured.

"Yes, you're absolutely right, Billy," Suzy again agreed. "If there can be extinct dinosaurs...plus huge buffalo herds...and primitive Indian tribes...then why not spaceships? What's next—big-headed *aliens* from outer space?"

She just barely kept herself from breaking out in a hysterical fit of the *giggles*.

"*Minti cha anchokkaalaa Chihoowa'!*"

It was the Chief, looming above Suzy, grandly gesturing. He obviously wanted her, Billy, and the other three kids to follow him. Without looking behind to see if they were obeying his order he purposely strode up the cooling, burnt earth toward the spaceship!

"What's he saying, Suzy? You know the Indian words better than me. What's going on?"

She hesitated a moment before letting the surround guards push her forward, not sure if she'd heard him right.

"He wants us...to come and visit...*God!*"

"God?"

Behind her, the warriors were closing ranks and ushering the small cluster of kids up the slope, following the Chief.

"Yes...*Chihoowa'* means God," Suzy stated.

"But...that's when we go to Church on Sunday, right? I mean, a spaceship doesn't go up to the real God—does it? Maybe he means the moon-god?"

"Well, Billy, I'd love to give you the answer, but I just don't know. However, I imagine we're going to find out real soon."

A *long, silver plank* emerged from the side of the ship at an angle, sliding out so its end "thumped" down onto the scorched ground. It led up to a small, dark doorway.

The Chief and kids stopped at the base of the plank as the accompanying warriors fell on their knees, bowing to the looming, slender spaceship.

"What now, Suzy?" Billy gulped.

Suddenly a *big bag* flew out of the dark opening and bounced down the ramp, landing at the Chief's moccasin-clad feet.

The Medicine Man ran forward and scooped up the precious item, out of which fell a few *big white pills!*

He fearfully scooped up the scattered pills.

"*Aya!*" the Medicine Man urged them from his bowed position, gesturing with his hand to continue onward up the ramp (Go!).

Obediently, clustered tightly together, the three Indian children marched up the ramp and into the dark doorway.

Wow...apparently they weren't going to be murdered after all. They just had to climb into a 1950's impossible spaceship and get launched with insufficient fuel to who knew where.

"Well?" Suzy grinned giddily at her little brother. "Shall we?"

"Why not?" he now laughed, apparently also relieved they weren't going to get murdered. He grabbed her hand tighter. "It's gotta be better than getting our heads chopped off!"

Together they resolutely ascended the ramp, stepping forward smartly. They approached the dark, circular doorway.

She paused at the entrance with Billy.

"*Imponna! Chokkilissa! Chinokchinta'shki!*" Suzy heard the Medicine Man shouting at them from down below (Be wise! Be quiet! Be nice!)

Good advice. Either the Medicine Man was dead wrong, or "God" had a very weird sense of humor! Suzy wanted to either run away in terror or break out laughing. It was just too bizarre. She finally gave in to her instincts and *giggled hysterically* under her breath.

"Yep...this is funny...it's funny, isn't it Suzy?"

"Hilarious," Suzy sputtered, trying to get her giggling fit under control.

And just what was that big bag of white pills, anyway? Were they vitamins or something? It looked like enough for the whole tribe for a year!

Then, narrowing her eyes in determination, Suzy stepped aggressively across the threshold, Billy in tow. She was resolved to see this who bizarre episode through to its bitter end.

*Dinosaurs...Indians...White Pills...*and now *Spaceships!*

Suzy remembered her mother telling her a terrible curse from ancient Chinese times: "*May you live in interesting times!*"

Well, if that were true, then she and Billy were definitely cursed.

Like it or not, they were boarding some sort of spaceship to fly to the moon! She again recalled what Billy learned when they first arrived at the village, the myth that children taken by a big bird up to the moon would gain the *power of the gods!*

Maybe this wouldn't be so bad after all.

She wouldn't mind having some superpowers. She didn't need giant muscles. Billy could have those. But if she had new magic abilities maybe she could figure a way out this mess and get them back to Sulphur, Oklahoma!

Well, it was about time something went right for them.

Virginia was disturbed at a strange mood shift in the Custodian. Normally casual and friendly, she was now formal and distant. They were about to take a terrible gamble. It might work out, but it could also go terribly wrong.

She didn't blame the Custodian for her uncertainty.

"You are at a tipping-point," the hovering blond-haired hologram solemnly proclaimed. "There's been a radical change to the quantum-continuum. I fear that you or your father may have initiated a different time-stream. Everything is in flux."

"Then it is good we took precautions," Virginia sighed. She knew she lacked the talents of either Anderson or her Father. In the six months from when the "time-inspectors" vanished on their "brief" jump 400 years forward, things had gone steadily downhill under her stewardship at Guildhall.

Their time-ship should have returned long ago...but it hadn't.

Disagreements between departments on the working floor became heated conflicts. Productivity plummeted. Continued attacks by Sanako's Time-Keepers, seemingly frantic to retrieve their leader, sapped the attention and resources of Anderson's opposing Time-Keepers. The "regular" guards at Guildhall were increasingly engaged beating back mobs of outside agitators paid by displaced oligarchs and conniving politicians. Without Anderson present to snatch lost treasures from the past to pad their pockets, the leaders of London were growing increasingly resentful, looking to take back control!

And, worst of all, there were rumors of Rome assembling a *naval fleet* to invade England. Before Galileo found refuge in London, the "Islands" were just annoyances to Rome's domination of the mostly Islamic civilized world. But now that "modernity" was blasting from Guildhall, sweeping away long-cherished traditions and doctrines, the Sunni majority was taking up arms against the "heretic" Shia minority.

Although there were many areas of agreement between the two main branches of the Muslim faith, details and interpretations of holy texts varied greatly. Primary amongst the conflicts between the sects was the degree to which individuals were allowed to embrace changing mores and customs. Rome was very conservative, ruling by strict Sharia Law. All aspects of crime, politics, trade, religious ritual, economics, marriage and sexual behaviors were regulated by inviable rules. In contrast, the prevailing Shia sects, centered mostly in London, were considered the liberals of the Muslim world. London clerics allowed individuals to arrive at their own conclusions regarding secular government, human rights, freedom of expression, and the rights of women.

But the worst "sin" of the heretical London religious establishment was to threaten the "top-dog" status of Italy in areas of commerce. Yes, "almighty money" was the true root-cause of the escalating tension between Rome and London. Due to the amazing inventions of the "resurrected" Galileo, London was fast supplanting the city-states of Italy as the center of the world's commerce. Affronting their religious dictates might be tolerated, but *not* taking gold from their coffers! And so a dark cloud was hanging over Guildhall as reports of the growing Italian invasion fleet became more and more alarming.

Despite Virginia's best efforts to boost morale, the entire team of researchers and defenders of Guildhall was growing increasingly dispirited. The failure of her Father, Anderson, and the Monk to return could only mean that the future was corrupted. Most of the personnel at Guildhall assumed Galileo was dead and would never return. Even Virginia was afraid she'd never see her Father again. Without his charismatic leadership and Anderson's crucial facilitation their entire marvelous technological revolution looked doomed.

Virginia looked away from the little transparent figure floating impassively above the white cube which sat upon a flat wooden tabletop. Deeply troubled, Virginia pursed her lips, staring intently at the two pictures she held in her hand.

Both time-locked pictures no longer revealed an endless watery swamp but an *empty, star-sprinkled night sky!* What did it mean? Was it depicting *inspiration*, heralding the movement of humanity out to the stars? Or was it *confirmation* that their present efforts would utterly fail, dispersed into eternal emptiness?

"But Sanako says..."

"Do not trust her," the Custodian cut short Virginia's assertion. "She lies. She tries to push you into her own agenda. If you were to show her these time-windows, she'd use the images to further discourage you. Her every effort is to stop you and your colleagues. I, however, merely answer whatever you ask of me: providing factual future knowledge and technical advice. Sanako is provocateur. I am a reporter. You are spending too much time with her, Virginia."

"Yes, that's all true, but..." she started to protest, wanting the little floating figure to understand that she was merely seeking diverse information, even from her sworn enemy...

—when the locked door to the secluded basement vault suddenly EXPLODED inward!

Virginia was knocked from her chair at the table, stunned.

Woozily she noted *Sanako* striding arrogantly into the room, lifting up Virginia's fallen wooden cane, and using its heavy ivory head to SMASH the White Cube on the table into a thousand pieces!

With a "gasp" of dismay, the floating hologram of the Custodian "winked" out.

"No more unauthorized 'inventions,'" the oriental woman snarled down at Virginia. "Your time-run's come to an abrupt end, Madam Galilei. If your father ever returns, he'll be vilified and persecuted as a *fake* 'Messiah'! And other than a few advances in sewer placement, building-construction, and factory organization—his stolen future innovations will be *swamped* by the perverse reactive forces of this superstitious century!"

"How...did you...?"

"I knew that your second-rate Keepers would grow careless," Sanako snorted, sitting down on the edge of the wooden table and sneering at the still-prone Virginia. "My biological implants that your butchers so carelessly sliced out of me *regenerated*."

"You escaped."

"Is that not obvious?"

"But they assured me they upgraded the energy shield in case you..."

"Hah! I waited until the guards were absent and did a 'micro-jump' out of my cell. There was no need to go through the energy-barrier this time. I just flipped forward in time to a point where it no longer existed, took a few steps to the side, and 'bounced' back."

"But if you could do that all this while, then...?"

"You thought that cutting the reactive tissue out of my leg 'neutered' me?" Sanako haughtily continued. "I've other implants in deep organs you could never detect. I've been in communication with my people throughout my captivity! I've been gathering information from you, a spy in your midst, waiting until the right moment to utterly destroy your operation. Even now, my people are popping up at key points inside Guildhall, ambushing your remaining Keepers. You're finished, Virginia Galilei. Both you and your infamous, absentee father are *done* disrupting the Commissioner's marvelous timeline!"

Virginia groaned. The exploding thick door had driven large slivers of wood into the flesh of her left arm and side. She felt blood dribbling down. She was at Sanako's mercy! And, according to the Custodian, Sanako had *no* mercy.

"Prepare to die," Sanako grinned, raising the heavy cane high above her head. The heavy *Mephistopheles* head was poised to smash into the cowering Virginia.

Virginia nodded in acknowledgment of Sanako's evil intent.

"One question before you rearrange my skull?"

"Why not?" Sanako grinned.

"Do you...have any idea...what *this* means?" Virginia managed to gasp out, weakly holding up the two picture frames.

Sanako paused. She set the lethal cane to the side and tentatively took the two slender pictures from Virginia's shaking hand.

"What are these?" she asked, seemingly curious.

Outside and above the chamber, Virginia now heard other explosions, loud yells, and cries of pain. A full-out war was raging throughout the corridors of Guildhall.

"It's...where my Father and Anderson...went..."

"How amusing!" Sanako chortled, holding them high as she closely scrutinized them. "This is high-tech from my time-period: time-locked videos! But how did you...ah! They came from that burned-to-death pest, David King, didn't they? He must have given them to your father before he took Galileo's place at the Colosseum execution.

But why do they depict a night scene? Was the camera pointed up at the sky?"

"No...it wasn't...not originally...they've *changed* to the empty night sky you now see..."

Sanako's face paled. Her eyes narrowed to slits. "But, that means someone...?"

"I'm so sorry, Sanako," Virginia grimaced, as *a knife* suddenly *materialized* in midair and *plunged* into Sanako's chest!

In disbelief, Sanako sagged to the side, feebly grasping at the protruding handle, writhing upon the tabletop before toppling off onto the floor.

The two pictures fluttered down upon the tabletop.

Virginia painfully got back to her feet, taking the *true Cube* from her coat pocket and shakily setting it back on the tabletop besides the photos. Above it appeared the undamaged, floating small figure of the Custodian.

"That was...just a replica of the cube...that you shattered," Virginia gasped down at the bleeding Sanako. Virginia ground her teeth as she one-by-one yanked the protruding wood slivers out of her own flesh.

Sanako lay prone on the floor, blood pooling at her back. Clearly, the knife wound was mortal. She was fast bleeding-out.

"You...fooled...me," Sanako whispered.

"Yes, I did. You thought that I was just a simple girl hiding in the shadow of her famous father. Actually, I'm a devious *Italian* female, very much a product of her time."

Sanako wryly nodded, frothy blood bubbling from her nostrils.

"The...religious...and political...intrigue..."

"Yes—plus the criminal enterprises, academic turmoil, economic upheaval, and scientific rivalries. I was raised surrounded and immersed in all that! Yet I found ways to survive, even thrive. I counseled my father on the delicate aspects of subtle intrigue. We Italians are famous for the dark underside of our society, where victory is often won not in public duels, but by drops of poison surreptitiously added to a tasty glass of wine. And we bide our time, seeking allies wherever we find them, *striking* when least expected—much as you attempted to do to me. I not only discovered your plan, I anticipated it."

"You...baited...me."

"You and your comrades both, Sanako. Even now, they are being slaughtered above us. We monitored your every communication with them. They didn't ambush us. Instead, your illusive fellow time travelers were lured into lethal traps. My pacifist religious allies here don't approve, but Anderson's troops are willing to do whatever must be done. As you know, they hate your guts, with good reason."

Sanako briefly convulsed, blood spurting from her nose.

"Even...without us...the reactive forces...of your society..."

"Yes, of course," Virginia nodded in agreement. "The displaced, suppressed, rejected, jealous, and fearful always bide their time to fight back against changes they don't like. But tonight they will have their last significant stand. The behind-the-scenes movers of the mobs outside—who were emboldened by the seemingly discouraging events of the last few months at Guildhall—dared to raise their heads from their hidey-holes. Out in the city the instigators of the riots against us are being ruthlessly decapitated by my Agents."

"Assassinations..."

"Exactly as they intended for me!"

"Rome will never accede to..."

"Hah! Even Rome's brand new Mediterranean Fleet is in flames, sinking into the ocean as we speak. The Custodian was kind enough to materialize for us flying bombs called 'guided intercontinental cruise missiles'...that travel from England to the Mediterranean in mere moments. They must be used quickly, since they don't stay solid for long before dissipating into nothingness. But during their short materialization their deadly *effects* are quite permanent, I assure you. Rome's 'balls' are being ruthlessly castrated."

"Your...own religious leaders....will never tolerate..."

"That's correct, Sanako. They will never allow such momentous 'modernity' to threaten their control and power. Even the so-called 'liberal' factions that rule behind the scenes here in London will strike back at us."

"Then...you are...undone?" Sanako gasped-out in satisfaction, her voice steadily fading.

"Hardly," Virginia snorted. "I have *new* religious allies that are happy to step in and replace the mean-spirited established religious clique. My 'upstarts' are far kinder and gentler. The truly liberated people of London will welcome a fresh crop of truly principled religious leaders. These Pious Guides will be of several Faiths, not just Muslims. They will mount a world-wide religiously pious revolution. They will offer a much better guarantee of spiritual security! After all, that's what most religious adherents seek, is it not? Was not even your own religious fervor fueled by an irrational lust for an 'ordered' society?"

Sanako groaned. Her breathing was slowing to ragged gasps. She appeared to be giving up—as if finally coming to terms with the breadth of Virginia's sweeping victory.

"You...can't...let me...die..." she spoke, almost too faint to hear.

"—because I'm so soft-hearted? Again, I'm sorry to disappoint you, Sanako. I did truly enjoy our long conversations. But you're too great a threat to continue living."

"You...*need*...me!" Sanako gasped, feebly twisting on the floor.

"Yes, that's correct. But not why you think. With the Custodian's direction, over the past six months we developed lasting methods and equipment to *take* from you what we require."

"Then...you know...?"

Through the blasted-open door hurried in a team from Virginia's own department, clad in white gowns. They quickly set up an array of syringes, tubes, and glass containers beside Sanako's prone body.

"—that your blood and tissues are the source of a remarkable, living medication that can be grown in our laboratory? Yes, we know. My Custodian informed me early-on of your physical value. But to take what we need for successfully starting our seed-cultures, it will mean draining you dry and harvesting your brain."

"You're sicker than even me."

"Of course that would be unethical for us to do to a living person, no matter how dangerous or vile," Virginia retorted. "However, since you attacked me and my enterprise with murderous intent, the ethics are reversed. We are merely defending ourselves against a vicious monster, while simultaneously obtaining the freshest tissue possible."

"You won't like...the result..."

"—reversing many chronic diseases, protecting people from infection and injury, while greatly prolonging their normal lifespan? Oh, I think that will be *very* beneficial to both individuals and society writ-large. Indeed, it will be particularly helpful as we widely introduce what we've already perfected: providing women with the power to effectively regulate their own reproductive capacity."

"It won't work," Sanako moaned as the technicians inserted large needles into her major blood vessels, rapidly draining her blood into the surrounding glass containers.

"Of course it will work," Virginia coldly replied, clinically supervising the procedures from her perch on the tabletop. "Large families in our societies are not only the result of lack of effective birth control. People know that their best hope of being cared for in their fast-impending old age is to have as many children as possible. They hope that a few will survive the many diseases and illnesses of life to care for their failing parents. But healthily sized families are possible if there is effective medical care plus expectation of living well into old age. The Custodian has shown me future proof of this concept."

"Long life...isn't...a panacea," Sanako moaned as the scalpel-welding technicians began carving fresh tissue from her large muscle groups.

"True, but the Custodian also revealed how the Elites of your future enjoyed these very same benefits. I am merely going to extend the same thing that you took for granted to the people of my present-day world. This is your gift to them! Perhaps you can take a final bit of solace in your 'generosity'?"

"Go...to...*hell!*"

Virginia paused, keenly observing the procedures. She allowed her technicians time to complete their precise operations before answering the dying woman.

"Oh, I think you're better positioned for that journey, 'Time-Keeper.' Do we have sufficient tissue, folks?"

"We've got plenty, Madam Galilei," a woman replied. "We'll take the blood to the lab for processing. The tissue will be immediately cultured or put into long-term cryogenic storage. As soon as you're ready, we'll complete the final stage of the harvest. We've the rendering columns ready to process her brain and internal organs."

"Excellent. Carry on."

They gathered up their filled glass vessels and hurriedly departed, taking their prizes with them. Remaining behind was only a single man. Beside him on the floor sat several large broth-containing jars. In his hands was a *surgical saw*.

"Any last words?" Virginia kindly asked. "I'm sorry we can't do this to your corpse. As you know, your 'retro-viral' components are extremely fragile outside your living body. Their density is greatest in neuronal tissue, so..."

"*Bite* me!"

"Ah, an invitation to cannibalism? No, we are not as uncivilized as you. We do not kill for the sake of enjoyment or personal power. We merely do that which must be done for the good of everyone. Goodbye, Sanako."

Virginia motioned for the technician to proceed.

Sanako *screamed* as the teeth of the saw cut through her skull.

Within moments white brain tissue was safely sliced, diced, and floating in the jars.

Other key organs just as quickly followed.

"I am my father's daughter," Virginia stated, yanking out the knife from the butchered corpse. She marveled as the seemingly solid metal faded, becoming insubstantial. The Custodian's materialization had worked perfectly, lasting just as long as necessary. "He taught me to be brave, stand against oppressors, and make necessary sacrifices."

In a moment the Custodian's materialized knife was completely gone, as if it had never been.

But—as Virginia had stated earlier—its effects were permanent.

Sanako was finished.

"I'm sure that was difficult for you," the Custodian congratulated her. "But, as you said, it had to be done. The gain was worth the risk."

Virginia nodded, again lifting up the two time-locked pictures and staring at them.

They no longer showed an empty night sky.

Instead, one of them showed the *white-cratered moon* hanging high in the night sky!

And the other revealed a grinning, bald-headed oriental man. It was *Lhamo*, the Buddhist monk who'd departed six months earlier with Anderson and her father!

If Lhamo was still alive in the distant future, then so might be her Father.

And, in the repeating short video, the monk *winked* at her—as he *giggled* like a little girl.

For the first time in months, Virginia laughed.

The incredible scientific revolution begun by her Father and Agent Anderson was not going to fail. Instead, it was going to succeed beyond their wildest dreams, changing the entire future of humanity!

But then she sobered, thinking...

Would the new future be better?

Virginia recalled Sanako's dire final warning.

And she knew not to put too much faith in the superficial mannerisms of the enigmatic monk shown in the future-video. That crazy Buddhist could find humor in even the most terrible disaster.

She was saddened to think she'd likely never see him again in the flesh, or her Father. But she was heartened to know that, without a doubt, she'd done her part in 17th Century London. Let the Future unfold as it would.

Chapter 16

<u>OVER THE MOON</u>

Take away gravity
Take away crime
Take away disease
And every depravity
Take away burdens
Take away every war
Ban random injuries
And all aching sores
Illuminate the night
Inspire everyone's heart
So we can all stand tall
Leaving only merriment
Exhilarating thoughts
Letting your mood soar
When everything's alright
Surely this is happiness
Ascending to the heights
Breaking out in song
—but what if it isn't?
What if you want more?
What, then, do you place
Above everything else?
Fly me to the moon...

The Minstrel's Lark, 16:7-12

After six months apparently stranded in a geological chunk of the Pleistocene, Galileo was getting used to living with cavemen. Anderson, however, was increasingly agitated—to the point of insanity! Lhamo, that crazy Buddhist monk, behaved as if all this was perfectly normal.

"More mammoth steak?" he grinned, passing a greasy chunk to Galileo.

"I thought that you Buddhists were vegetarians. I guess I'm wrong," Galileo laughed, accepting the charred hunk of dripping meat.

They were sitting outside a large cave around a bonfire, happily dining on the last hunt's successful kill. It was night, the sky full of brilliant stars. Though it was freezing, the large fire kept them toasty warm. Being outside the cave, the smoke drifted away instead of chocking them. It was nice to be out in the open. But they lived most of the time inside, where a vast labyrinth stretched into the mountain underneath the covering ice pack.

Though the cave people had accepted the three time-travelers as semi-deities, fallen from the heavens, they maintained a respectful distance. Consequently, Galileo and Lhamo were sitting apart from the rest of the tribe, eating by themselves. Anderson was off on an expedition, obsessing with his "explorations."

The Time-Keeper still could not accept that the machinery of the flying bub had fused together in one molten mass as they tried to cross the dimensional barrier. He kept trying to prod a piece here or there loose, to coddle the equipment back to functionality. He just couldn't accept that he and they were stranded in a bizarre retrograde future, with no way to call for help or escape!

Even his much-bragged-about implants were dead. Their "circuitry" had been fried along with the mechanisms of the transport vehicle. Anderson was now completely blind, his all-seeing black eyeglasses useless to his empty sockets. So he was led about by an especially intelligent and curious teenaged boy from the tribe, named "Trong." Together, they were off mapping out the more inaccessible tunnels of the far-flung cave network.

Lhamo had gained a rough understanding of their primitive language. He was very good with languages. He translated to Galileo and Anderson the tribesmen's conviction that a terrible demon lurked in the deep caves of the limestone mountain. This fiery Demon occasional emerged to steal away their children in the night, leaving behind a magic white powder in their place. Though the cave-people hated to lose their few children, the powder kept them healthy when mixed into their communal stews. Although there were few elderly people amongst them, the mated couples were not particularly prolific. Galileo was puzzled by the scarcity of children. Was there something in the mineral-laden water that inhibited their productivity—or was it an effect of the mysterious white powder? Or had the cave-dwellers invented this child-stealing demon to explain their lack of fecundity?

"Obviously not!" Lhamo grinned back at Galileo, contentedly tearing meat from the bone and loudly chewing it with obvious satisfaction.

"What? Oh, right..."

Galileo forced his wandering thoughts to return to the present conversation. He'd been teasing Lhamo about his lack of strict adherence to his own teachings. Galileo was learning a lot from Lhamo about Buddhist practices and beliefs. More and more, Galileo was appreciating the deep, flexible Principles by which Buddhists lived. Those were in marked contrast to the unforgiving lists of rules and regulations he was used to hearing from the clerics of his time. But more than the Principles themselves Galileo admired the practicality with which they were applied. Lhamo happily gnawed on a Mammoth's haunch, itself a striking example of the Buddhist's realistic reasoning.

"I eat meat if I must. So did the Buddha," Lhamo casually replied.

"But does not eating flesh violate the first precept of Buddhism—*do not kill?*"

"All living creatures are responsible for the death of others, either directly or indirectly," Lhamo mildly shrugged, gnawing at the grease-dripping meat. "Even if we had sufficient potatoes and fruits here to forgo meat, harvesting them for our own use starves insects and other animals that would have otherwise eaten it. Though not killing other living creatures is a desirable objective—done as we are capable—it is not what is *most* important."

"Ah—'apologetics,'" Galileo nodded knowingly, well-aware with that disturbing religious tendency. "When the doctrine becomes inconvenient, find an excuse to ignore it!"

"Living a good life is not just following a list of rules," Lhamo mildly observed, continuing to happily consume the charred meat.

"I know many Imams and other high clerics who would disagree with you that..."

"—and for them and their followers, strict rules may be helpful," Lhamo shrugged, now setting aside his gnawed-clean bone. "But you must remember, friend Galileo, your religion is young compared to mine. Yours began a mere thousand years before your birth. Mine began a thousand years before that! Yours started, as I understand it, as a reaction against the suppression of your people. Mine began with a far more fundamental problem, the universality of suffering. Where your people required a unified response against external forces, my progenitors needed an expanded view of reality."

"*Not* true," Galileo said, shaking his bearded head in firm denial. "The Prophet's writings derived from a principled reaction to greedy idolatry! He proclaimed the One True God in the midst of a sea of idols. This was the entire basis of his Teachings!"

"Oh, you certainly know better than me," Lhamo laughed good-naturedly. He leaned back contentedly against a large boulder. He patted his rounded stomach. "But we Buddhists have moved beyond attempted definitions toward a more fluid view of the forces which we confront in this brief life."

"You know full well that I strongly disagree with your denial of the one True God, *Allah!*"

"Oh, friend Galileo," Lhamo sighed. "You know that is *not* true. Why do you continue to argue with me on things where you already know the answer? We Buddhists certainly *do* believe in a single supreme Energy or Life Force. We just don't shape that into a human-like super-Entity. And it is not something 'out there' but *inside* of us. It is also contained within other beasts, plants, rocks. It is integral to the very fabric of reality!"

"That makes no sense," Galileo snorted. "You say Allah is spread out all across Creation? You say you can find Allah by just looking into your own hearts? You say that Allah is in you the same as me?"

"Well," Lhamo shyly winked, ducking his head, "do you not yourself claim your Allah as *omnipresent*, *omnipotent*, and *omniscient?*"

"Well, sure, but..."

"But that means that you and I are inextricably *linked*—does it not? What your religion teaches about God describes a profound spiritual connection, right? Thus I feel pain when you are hurt...or one of these hairy elephants is killed to be our sustenance. What I do to others is done to me. And it occurs not only superficially, but deep in our minds, our true hearts!"

"I don't know about..."

"And once you get past the point of thinking you are at the center of the Universe, friend Galileo—around which all else must fall in line or be 'wrong'—then you can start to recognize vast commonalities between the fundamental teachings of *many* religions, both the so-called 'major' and 'minor' ones."

"So...you're saying that religions are...*all* of them correct? But how can that be when they teach such radically different...?"

Galileo stopped in mid-sentence, now greatly confused.

The Monk sighed deeply, leaning further back against the cold rocks. He looked upward at the stars before quietly continuing. "There was a little-known but insightful Jewish teacher who was executed in the first century. He received some training by itinerant Buddhists of his time, who took note of him and his impossible Teachings in obscure travel texts. I have studied those texts which are now located in India."

"So?"

"Well, the accounts of his short life are interesting, of possible interest to you. You see, in tandem with the Roman Empire *his own religious leaders* executed him—for the great 'sin' of advocating a 'kingdom' that did not divide but connected people across the world."

"Not very realistic, I'd say."

"It was illustrative of what we are discussing here, friend Galileo. This particular 1st-Century preacher came from a highly regimented, traditional Jewish religion, similar to your upbringing within Islam.

In a religion and society that was rife with division and hate—both from so-called 'heretics' and 'infidels'—he preached a 'kingdom of heaven' located not in nations or religions or tribal heritages...but in the *heart* of each and every person!"

"So he was a fellow Buddhist?"

"No, he took those teaching plus that from his Jewish heritage and molded them into something different."

"It still sounds unrealistic, even dangerous."

"It was certainly dangerous to him. He was executed as a heretic."

"Probably much-deserved. Most radicals throughout history suffered the same fate."

"If circumstances had been different, he might have made a big impact on history," the Monk smugly concluded. "My point is that your 'God' is not limited by your traditions or preferences."

"The Truth is the Truth!" Galileo obediently proclaimed.

"Ah, so strange to hear such a statement from *you*."

That silenced Galileo. Indeed, he'd shaken the world with his scientific observations that counteracted the prevailing religious "Truth."

And Galileo had never heard of this Teacher—only a passing giant *comet* at that point in history: unusually bright and long lasting, lighting up the night sky. It inspired the designation "B.C.", before comet, and "A.D.", after departure. By this celestial event the centuries were numbered, not by some obscure Jewish preacher.

"Huh...even so, arbitrarily twisting established beliefs—unlike my fact-driven observations—sounds like a recipe for just having no rules...thus making them up as they went along...so that they could feel justified doing whatever they wanted in the moment!"

"Friend Galileo, having a rule to eat or not eat meat—or only certain types of meats—is easy. Opening your eyes to *see and try to understand* the deeper aspect of reality that go beyond the flesh is very difficult. Changing your diet is simple. *Purifying your mind* is extremely complex. I am not advocating a superficial, trivial approach to life. Instead, I am teaching and trying to live as The Buddha—the *Enlightened One*, with true humility and compassion for all others! It is, indeed, a most difficult quest."

Galileo stroked his beard for a minute, pondering.

"Well, I see why our Mullahs take little note of you Buddhists, even putting you below the importance of the isolated Jewish conclaves. You are either much too confusing...or simple-minded! Either way, you don't pose much of a threat."

Lhamo giggled, contentedly crossing his bare arms over his rounded belly.

"I am pleased with your mindfulness, friend Galileo. Being 'not much of a threat' is desirable religious state. Now you are starting to learn that..."

"I found it!" Anderson triumphantly yelled as he staggered out of the cave, led by the fur-clad Trong. "Come with me! You must come with me *now!*"

His groping hands located Galileo's tattered clothes and the robe of Lhamo, dragging them both up to their feet.

"What have you found?" Galileo asked, dropping his hunk of half-eaten mammoth meat. "Surely it can't be so urgent we must go with you this moment. You look starved and frozen, Arthur. Sit with us by the fire. Have food. We'll talk about..."

"No time! No time! It's churning up! If we ever hope to get out of this god-forsaken ice-ball we have to go *now!*"

Lhamo put an arm around the taller man's shoulders, gently pushing Trong off to the side. Anderson's previously immaculately trimmed crewcut hair was now a mop of matted strands, half-covering the useless black glasses that he still insisted on wearing. Where he'd previously been muscular and imposing, he was now thin and trembling. The last six months without his instrumentations had taken a terrible toll on him.

"I've found what these ignorant savages call 'The Demon'! And it's *stirring*—to grab a new load of victims! We just barely escaped it. Trong is happy to lead us and a war party back to it! He wants to stop its predations on his people. But wherever it takes its victims, *we* must be its next load—not these savage's useless children. Come on! The monk found out from the savages before I departed that this 'harvest' happens only once every few years. We've got to get back before it returns to its hibernation!"

"Alright," Galileo soothed him, guiding him to take a seat on a low boulder by the fire. "We'll go with you, Arthur—but not until you have the strength to proceed. We lack the strength to carry you if you collapse. Both Lhamo and I are much too old! And Trong, plus whoever of his people goes with us, will have to carry our food and such. I'm not running off into the endless labyrinth without sufficient supplies."

Reluctantly relenting, Anderson accepted a wooden bowl of stew plus a bladder filled with water from a kindly cavewoman. He began devouring the meal as Lhamo conversed with an animatedly gesturing Trong.

Galileo only heard indecipherable grunts, snaps, and squawks. But he knew that it was a primitive language which he did not understand. The monk certainly derived sufficient meaning from the sounds, nodding and smiling to the young man.

Anderson, having finished devouring his meal, slumped to the rocks beside the bonfire and instantly fell fast asleep. Lhamo translated to Galileo: "The young man tells me that Anderson felt 'vibrations' which they followed deep into previously unexplored tunnels. They ran out of torches and supplies but Anderson refused to stop. Barely able to see by the dim light of bioluminescent fungal growth of the tunnel walls, they came to a cavern of crystals. The giant crystals glowed with many colors. And past that big cavern was a small cave, at whose center was a *Black Pool*. In it, sleeping, they could see a Demon. As they approached, it opened its eyes. Trong wanted to run away but Anderson kept fumbling himself forward. It was then that the Demon emerged from the black pool and grabbed Anderson by the neck, lifting him up into the air! Ripping off Anderson's eye-coverings the Demon stared into Anderson's empty eye sockets before releasing him and returning to the pool. Anderson was rendered unconscious. That's when Trong managed to grab the discarded glasses and drag Anderson away from the monster's lair. He beat a hasty retreat. He had to carry Anderson slung over his shoulder for two days before the man finally regained consciousness from his encounter with the Demon. Then they were lucky to find their way back. They were deep inside the mountain, in previously unexplored tunnels."

"So...he was lucky to survive his expedition. But there *is* something out there?"

"It was certainly not a creature of this time or place, friend Galileo. Trong would have recognized a saber tooth tiger or giant cave bear. He said that the Demon had many arms and eyes. And the Black Pool was unlike anything he'd seen before, very smooth and thick. But it was certainly 'thawing' out, becoming more fluid. And surrounding the circular pool was what could only be—from Trong's description—a *metallic collar*. Such is not possible from these primitive cavepeople. It bespeaks an external power source."

Galileo nodded, furrowing his brow.

"Could the creature be guarding a *time-portal*, as Anderson so often described to us from his previous travels through and across time?"

"It certainly might be, friend Galileo, though what he always described to us was a very temporary phenomenon—not one that persists. As best as I can tell from Trong, the black pool they found is a week's travel into the labyrinth. There are many dangerous sections along the way. And Trong is unsure he can find his way back to the Demon's lair. But with Anderson leading the way, perhaps sensing other-worldly 'vibrations,' perhaps by residual function of his neural implants, then maybe...?"

"We must depart as soon as we can put together sufficient supplies," Galileo firmly replied. "As much as Anderson wishes to return to his fellow Time Keepers, I want to see my daughter again before I die. And I'm sure you want to return to your followers. This is our only hope to do so!"

The monk shrugged.

"I am happy here," he sincerely smiled. "Of course, I'm happy anywhere."

"Well, I'm not!" Galileo strongly retorted. "Will Trong help us return to the 'cavern of crystals'? And can he convince a war party to accompany us to destroy their enemy, or at least help carry our supplies?"

Lhamo talked more with Trong, nodding and smiling.

"He says none others would dare to accompany us back to the lair. They fear the Demon too much. But he will go with us, this time better armed than previously. If necessary, he says he will gladly give his life to protect his fellow children. He says he will take a sharp spear this time and kill the Demon, once and for all. You must admire his enthusiasm!"

"Well, having him guide us is better than nothing. And he's a strong, strapping lad. I've seen him help bring down a full-grown mammoth with a single spear. We have no weapons of our own. Your flint is all we have, to start fires with. Maybe we can burn up the monster? Hah! But I suppose we *do* have our wits. Perhaps that will be enough? Surely you could talk it to death?"

The Monk laughed politely.

"Well, we *do* hold the future in our hands."

"Predestination?" Galileo responded, eager to have yet another philosophical discussion with the bright, entertaining Monk. "We Muslims believe that we each have our own preordained path. From our limited perspective, it seems that we make our own choices. But we will end up where we will end up, regardless. That is what I and my religion believe."

The monk shrugged again.

"Then why worry, friend Galileo? If you are to see your daughter again, it will happen! And if not, then there is nothing you can do about it, right? So why be concerned? Be happy, my friend!"

Auuuggghh! That man! Just when Galileo sensed he was backing the Monk up into a logical corner the man deftly side-stepped and took Galileo's position as his own! It was impossible to pin him down.

Galileo grit his teeth together, turning away from the endlessly irritating monk. He needed to go back into the cavern to barter the few remaining trinkets in his pockets for sufficient skins and supplies to keep the four of them alive for at least a week of hard travel down through dangerous tunnels. How many torches would he need? Ah, a *lot* of them...

Fortunately, Trong was a sinewy, tough lad. He could carry a good load of supplies. And Lhamo might yet convince the youngster to get a few of his friends to go at least part way as bearers.

Galileo turned around to ask the monk, but saw he was seemingly mediating, staring up into the dazzling, star-filled sky with a stunned look on his face. Then he turned to Galileo, *winked*, and *giggled* like a little girl.

"Lhamo, what is wrong with you?" Galileo barked at him.

"Lord Buddha has turned his gaze upon us."

"What?"

But the old monk was now peacefully curled up beside the snoring, disheveled Anderson, as if everything was right in the world.

Galileo was jealous of the man's tranquility. How he had managed to achieve such a profound peace was still a mystery to Galileo. The world was a dangerous, chaotic mess to which Galileo was called to help bring *order*...

—even if he must expand his mind to better comprehend the marvels of Creation! On that matter he agreed with the monk. But to harmonize with the *Will of Allah* was not an easy matter. There was more to the Universe than met the eye.

Galileo recalled an incident concerning the Prophet: when Muhammad, blessed be his name, was questioned on whether people should give up working since their fate was already determined. The Prophet allegedly answered: *"No. Carry on doing good deeds. They lead you toward that for which you are created!"*

As Galileo approached the other cave-people asking with gestures for supplies, he prayed for divine guidance.

Actually, he was getting *very* tired of a diet of stringy mammoth meat.

Professor Yamamoto was puzzled by the e-mail she'd just received. She was sitting catching up on her e-mail at her laboratory office computer.

This particular message came from a Professor with whom she was unfamiliar, sent from America. And the title of the message was confusing: *"Extradimensional immunotherapy request."* Perhaps it had something to do with the ongoing dosage trials of her new cancer immunotherapy being conducted at the NIH Medical Center located in Bethesda, Maryland. But what was the "extradimensional" component? Did the sender need information on off-prescription usage different than was covered under the clinical trial?

Intrigued by the title, she decided to take the time to read it rather than deleting it along with the many other spam e-mails she usually discarded unread.

She clicked-open the e-mail just as her secretary poked her gray-haired head into the opened doorway of her office.

"*Kyōju anata no tame no jūyōna denwa ga arimasu,*" her secretary announced [There is an important phone call for you, Professor].

"*Messēji o shitei shite kudasai. Watashi wa,-go de denwa shimasu,*" she curtly replied, frowning at the first words of the e-mail in front of her [Take a message. I'll call back later].

The English e-mail message began: "Dear Dr. Yamamoto. You probably don't know me as my career was in a discipline different from yours. I am an aged physicist who was facing imminent death due to metastasized pancreatic cancer. But I am now fit and healthy because of your marvelous new therapy. For that I am eternally grateful. But I need your further help. You see..."

"*Kore wa, shushō-fu karadesu!*" [It is from the Office of the Prime Minister!].

That got her attention.

"*Hontoni? Naikakusori daijin kara no yobidashi? Honkidesu ka?*" [Really? A call from the Prime Minister? Are you sure?]

"*Hai, kyōju. Sore wa, watashitachi no bumon no kaichō kara watashitachi ni tensō sa remashita.*" [Yes, Professor. It was forwarded to us from our Department Chairman].

She held a prestigious appointment in the Department of Hematology, Clinical Immunology, and Infectious Diseases at the Ehime University Graduate School of Medicine located in Tōon, Japan. Though she was highly regarded in cancer immunotherapy research and clinical trial circles, she had little to do with either physics or politics. Why on earth would the Office of the Prime Minister contact her?

Strange communications today!

"*Watashi wa, kōru ga kakarimasu,*" she replied, picking up her phone receiver [I will take the call]. For the moment, the puzzling e-mail from the unfamiliar Professor in America would have to wait.

"*Kyōju Sanako Yamamoto?*" spoke a deep-toned voice from the phone speaker [Professor Sanako Yamamoto?]

"*Hai?*" [Yes]

"*Watashitachiha, kinkyū jitai o motte imasu.*" [We have an urgent situation].

"Hai?" [Yes?]

"Watashitachiha, Amerika no CDC to anata no zenmen-tekina kyōryoku o yōsei." [We request your full cooperation with the American CDC].

What? The Center for Disease Control and Prevention in Atlanta, Georgia? She'd been there years past for a scientific conference on emerging retroviral infections, but her present focus was cancer therapy, not disease vectors.

"Amerika no CDC?" [The American CDC?]

"Karera wa, rain-jō ni arimasu. Kore wa, Beikoku taishikan to no denwa kaigidesu. Eigo o hanasu o susumi kudasai." [They are on the line. This is a conference call with the American Embassy. Please proceed speaking in English].

What the hell?

"Uhm...alright."

She'd done a three-year post-doc at NIH, so her English was good. But for the political apparatus to be directly facilitating a scientific conference call was unusual. Did this have something to do with the cryptic e-mail from America?

"Professor Yamamoto, this is Dr. Hank Torrey," a raspy voice sounded from the speaker. "I am the Director of CDC. I apologize for not setting up a standard videoconference but we needed to contact you immediately, cutting through all red tape. We have a potential pandemic on our hands for which we suspect you possess both a preventative and therapy. The situation is so critical we took the step of going directly through our governmental connections to ensure complete interfacing of all concerned. How soon can you get here? We have a US Government military jet waiting to ferry you. It's on standby now at Narita International in Tokyo."

She was stunned by the rapidity of the unfolding events.

"W-what...g-go to Atlanta?" she stammered. "I'm s-sorry, but that's out of the question. I've University duties, my c-classes to teach, my research program, and..."

"That is all covered, Professor," the same deep voice cut in. "We request your full cooperation. This is a matter of highest concern to our government. I've given the necessary directives to your superiors at the University."

Holy Buddha! It *was* the Prime Minister!

"I...well...but still..." she tried to protest, then paused, getting her wits back about her. "I don't even know what you are referring to as to an infectious agent 'preventative' or 'treatment'! Are you sure you have the right person? I have initial trials ongoing at NIH in collaboration with colleagues there at the Clinical Center, but it's for a radical new cancer therapy, not..."

"In your first dosage trial you treated a Professor Volodymyr who had metastasized pancreatic cancer," the CDC Director's voice broke in. "Of course since the trial was double-blinded you'd not know his name. But he and another person were exposed to a highly virulent and previously unknown infectious agent. The other person is now showing very disturbing aberrations. Volodymyr, however, is completely free of the infection. The only condition we can attribute to the dramatic difference between the two is your therapy. It *is* a radically sophisticated, new immune system-optimizing agent, correct?"

Ah...*Volodymyr!* Yes, that was the unfamiliar Professor's name whose e-mail she was starting to read when she'd been interrupted.

"Yes, that's true—but it wasn't even meant to deal with infectious agents. All it's supposed to do is bring up an impaired immune system to normal levels while helping it target known cancer cell surface markers. True, it's based upon an overlapping system of living retroviral vectors, which has a prolonged presence in the patient's body. I supposed that might also..."

"And just how is it that the patient's body does not reject this multiple retroviral presence?" the raspy voice cut-in. "Are you not altering and even enhancing the normal immune profile?"

"Well...yes, of course...that's true to a certain extent."

"This is Lyra O'Kelly, Sanako!" a high-pitched voice now came from the speaker.

"Oh, Lyra! Hi there..."

Doctor O'Kelly was a collaborator with Sanako in conducting the initial cancer trials, a fellow M.D./Ph.D. cancer-therapist/virologist. She oversaw maintaining and locally producing cultures of the delicate blend of genetically modified retroviral structures which were being administered to cancer patients at NIH.

"I think our governmental officials need to understand that your wonderful mix of massively genetically modified viruses is actually reprogramming certain stretches of DNA in the patient's different cell-sets, providing them with new 'recognition' skills they lacked previously."

"Yes, that's the whole rationale for our new therapy," Sanako replied. "Thank you for summarizing it so succinctly, Lyra. But for the rest of you on this call, that's in regard to known immune function deficiencies which are theorized to allow the cancer cells a 'window' in which to flourish in that particular patient. Correcting those deficiencies theoretically allows the body to recognize and attack particular cancer cells. And to persist long enough to do any good, the living, replicating 'friendly' viruses are also 'teaching' the immune system to tolerate their own presence. But..."

"Could we not also be adding with our therapy new recognition functionality that might interact with previously unknown disease vectors?" Lyra breathlessly continued.

"Well...I suppose it's possible."

"And it *is* a dynamic, evolving system, is it not?" a very deep base voice now boomed from the speaker. "It would have the capability of learning and adjusting its reprogramming of the DNA sections it targets, correct? That's why the scientific community has proceeded with extreme caution in carefully controlled clinical trials, right? Oh, forgive me for not introducing myself. I'm Dr. Miguel Jarvis, Director of NIH. Thus the spectacular protection we observed in Professor Volodymyr is reasonable considering your..."

He continued on, obviously very astute and aware of the details of the study.

Wow. This was a *very* high-level conference call! Who else was on this line, anyway—the President of the United States?

"So can your treatment be geared up for mass production?" a very solemn new female voice interrupted the Director of NIH. "Oh, forgive me also—I'm Julia Swartz, President of the United States. As you may know, I've a Ph.D. in Biology in addition to my political credentials. So I'm well aware of the challenges in producing stable cultures of ill-defined complex biological agents."

Holy crap! What was going on here? The President of the United States and the Prime Minister were *both* on this conference call?

"But...Madam President...we're only now doing the initial safety trials. It will be years before we're even sure it works, let alone can use it reliably as a therapy...and surely I'm not needed in person to..."

"This is not a normal situation, Dr. Yamamoto. Indeed, it is..." the President continued.

"I explained the nature of your new 'brew,' Sanako," Lyra's sweet voice broke in, cavalierly interrupting the President. "Its efficacy is dependent upon your genius at these things. What you're doing isn't just making another widget. It's as much art as science. You remember we went through hell getting FDA to approve these first few trials, since the therapeutic agent is so complex and continually evolving. Your hands-on presence is required for getting any new applications of your 'magic' brew to work! My team and I can't do that by ourselves. We're just perpetuating the basic ingredients of the final brew."

"And we don't have years to fine-tune your therapy, Professor Yamamoto," President Swartz's voice continued, sounding mildly "miffed" at being interrupted by Dr. O'Kelly. "The Director for FDA is on the line with us also. She can reassure you as to our full cooperation in approving the mass-manufacturing of any necessary immediate therapeutics. This is not just another routine pandemic threatening to sweep across the world and kill mere millions."

"Uh...no? You mean...?

"The fate of *billions* may rest in your hands, Professor—indeed, perhaps even the fate of all *humanity.*"

Sanako was struck dumb. Her mouth hung open but nothing came out.

"So how soon can we expect you at Narita International?" the raspy voice of the CDC Director demanded.

"Uh...well...I'm actually located about five hundred miles away from Tokyo."

"We'll have an official helicopter landing at the Medical School within the hour to take you to Tokyo," the Prime Minister firmly stated over the phone. "It'll touch down at the University Hospital's landing pad. Can you be ready that quickly?"

"Oh...an hour, you say? Well, if it's a crisis, I suppose that..."

"Good! Then are we concluded here, gentlemen and ladies?" the Prime Minister's forceful voice summarized.

"Yes...thank you...very good...appreciate your cooperation...very grateful..." the various voices concluded.

The phone went dead.

Her hand shaking, Sanako just managed to put the receiver back in its cradle.

Either the world was being rocked to its core, or that was the best scam-conference she'd ever heard!

"*Sore ga jūyōdeshita ka?*" her secretary said, poking her now-worried head back into the office [Was it important?].

"*Yoku...wakarimasen...*" Sanako gulped, trying to still her shaking hand [I'm...not sure]. "*Watashi wa...Hanarete shibaraku shinakereba naranai tsumoridesu.*" [I'm...going to have to be away for a while].

"*Dore dake no jikan?*" [For how long?].

"*Shiranai...Koko de chīmurīdā o onegai shimashou...Watashi wa karera ni atarashī wariate o ataeru hitsuyō ga arimasu.*" [I don't know... Get the lab leaders in here, please. I need to give them new assignments.]

"*Hai, kyōju.*" [Yes, Professor].

The secretary ducked out of the office, scampering off.

That "strange" e-mail was still there, patiently awaiting her attention on the computer screen.

It was going to be a rush to throw together enough necessities, lab books, frozen samples, and lyophilized reagents to be ready for the helicopter. But she might as well finish reading the message from Professor Volodymyr, since all this turmoil seemed to be focused upon him.

She started again at its beginning: "*Dear Dr. Yamamoto. You probably don't know me as my career was in a discipline different from yours. I am an aged physicist who was facing imminent death due to metastasized pancreatic cancer. But I am now fit and healthy because of your marvelous new therapy. For that I am eternally grateful. But I need your further help. You see there is an alien threat to the planet. Hah! Please don't laugh and delete this mes-*

sage...I am serious. I probably shouldn't be typing this over an open e-mail, but nobody who reads this will believe it, at least not immediately. Tomorrow, that's a different matter entirely. Anyway, a good friend of mine is hovering between life and death because of this attack upon our planet. I am convinced that your marvelous new cancer therapy might save him, plus many others. Please contact me as soon as you can. I include my phone numbers. Meanwhile, officials from the government will be trying to solicit your help. I assure you they are not crazy, nor am I...well, no more than usual. Anyway, I hope to meet you soon in Sulphur, Oklahoma. Again, this is not a joke or scam. The threat to our planet is deadly serious. Thank you for any help you can provide!"

Sulphur, Oklahoma? Where the hell was that?

Hmmm. But that *did* sound familiar. Hadn't she heard a news report on strange goings-on at a small town in America? Yes! It concerned a herd of cattle mysteriously being devoured overnight...and a zoo of insane tigers that had to be euthanized!

—and a supposedly *crashed, military satellite!* Oh, sweet Buddha. It was starting to make sense.

What was she getting herself into?

For God's sake, she was an oncologist virologist, not an astronaut! She didn't have the background to study contagions brought back from *outer space!*

But she had an ominous feeling that trying to hunker down in Japan wouldn't work. Forces far beyond her control were pulling her into a role she did not want.

She loved her work at the University. It was her passion, mostly isolated from the demands and hectic problems of the industrial, political, military, religious, and social spheres. In her lab she had complete control, her own little sanctuary.

No more.

Chapter 17
<u>SANCTUARIES</u>

Who will step forward
To preserve what you hold dear
When time, accident, and crime
Work to degrade, destroy, and steal
EVEN YOUR OWN INNER DESIRES
Working at odds to your well-being
When you are your own worst enemy
Stealthily scheming to sabotage yourself
How can this occur, you say...too easily!
For we do not understand our own minds
Sneaky elephants upon which we ride
Giving them our total trust, direction
As they plot their own liberation
To throw off their pesky overseers
And trample them into the dust.

The Minstrel's Lark, 17:1-4

Suzy and Billy were scared—but not as frightened as the three other children accompanying them. Simply put, the Indian kids were *terrified.*

As she and her kid brother hesitantly stepped into the dark interior of the spaceship, a panel slid shut behind them with a loud "swish."

"So now what, Suzy?" Billy asked, grabbing her hand again.

She already had an arm around the other three Indian kids, huddling them together. There was a boy about her age and a couple younger girls. They were now crying and sobbing loudly.

249

"Hey, guys!" Suzy tried to reassure them, speaking comfortingly, though in English. "We're going to be ok. We're just taking a little trip into outer space..."

Billy joined the other kids in *wailing!*

"Ok, maybe that was the wrong thing to say," Suzy admitted as a soft yellow light suddenly suffused the previously dark room.

She saw that the small chamber was totally empty, circular, only twelve feet across. And the light came from everywhere. Suzy found it oddly soothing, like the glow of a warm fireplace in a friendly living room.

Then a strange, *raspy* female voice oozed from the soft light...

"*Chokma. Binnili. Chokillisaat binnili.*"

"Huh?" Billy burbled, still crying with the others.

"She said 'Hello, sit down, sit quietly,'" Suzy translated.

"Oh...r-right...but where? There's n-no chairs in here!" he sobbed.

As if in response to Billy's question, cushioned recliners slid from the walls, their lower ends pointed inward in a circle. There were five of them. They looked comfortable, nice to take a nap upon.

"Well, I guess we've got to sit in them. If this rocket ship's going to take off, then that's the best place for us to be," Suzy bravely observed. "At least we won't get knocked around."

She led each of her charges to one, helping them clamber up onto them. Each of the recliners had raised armrests, back support, head pillows, and foot cushions.

Suzy slid into the last open one and was amazed at how relaxing it was, like settling into a cloud. It *did* make her want to take a nap. Indeed, she hadn't slept much the night before. She was very tired, barely able to keep her eyes open. And as she yawned widely, flat straps slipped over her chest and legs, holding her gently but firmly in place.

"*Chipotatiik chokma chiya,*" the comforting female voice spoke in Suzy's ear [You are a good girl].

It was a strange, spooky voice that made Suzy very uneasy. It had an odd tremble, quavering quality to it. But Suzy didn't want to antagonize whoever was in control of the space ship. She had to look like she was cooperating!

"*Yakookay*," Suzy whispered back [Thank you].

"*Chiholloli*," the kind-but-quavering voice tried to calm Suzy as she felt a powerful surge vibrate through the protective recliner [I love you].

"Huh?" Suzy replied, struggling to stay awake.

Suzy tried to think what was upsetting her so much about the voice. It wasn't just the raspy, harsh sound—it was the overall *tone*. There was something very "oily" and insincere in that voice. It scared her!

She knew she should stay awake and keep guard, not just for her sake but for Billy and the other kids.

But it was useless. It was like she was being drugged. She saw the other similarly bound kids likewise drifting off despite the huge ROAR she now heard from outside as the entire room *lurched upward*, pushing her deeply down into her supporting cloud.

*Well, this is sure different...*she sighed to herself, closing her eyes and dozing off despite the violent launch of the rocket. Whatever danger existed, she'd always wanted to be an astronaut. Maybe this wouldn't be so bad?

Then again—if Suzy and Billy's past experience predicted the future—things could just as easily get much *worse*.

Galileo discovered that he had a deep aversion to "spelunking."

Versus the large caverns which immediately opened out upon the snowy forest, he and his companions were now descending through a narrow series of tight tunnels and dark caves. The climb downward was dangerous. Water moistened many of the rocks and surfaces, making each step slippery. Plus there were stretches where they had to clamber upward or sideways, further straining their muscles. Galileo was feeling every one of his seventy-five years of age.

They'd been hiking and mostly climbing downward for about a full day, though it was hard to tell exactly how long they'd been gone since the gloom and darkness was pervasive. They'd only taken short breaks to rest and eat handfuls of smoked mammoth meat. Only a single burning torch lighted the way—carried by Trong in the lead alongside the indefatigable Monk—since they were trying to conserve their dry sticks.

Galileo was breathing heavily, drenched in sweat, with every muscle aching. And he wasn't carrying anything heavy, just a deerskin bag slung over his shoulder containing his few possessions. Trong had persuaded four other teenaged boys to help carry their heavy supplies. Everyone else back at the main cave shied away in terror at the notion of venturing into the deep labyrinth. The local elders strictly forbad Trong and the other boys to return with Anderson to the Black Pool, least they provoke an early emergence of the Demon. But Trong laughed them off, arrogant in his youth.

"We can rest up ahead," Anderson gasped. He was scuffling along right behind Galileo, a short rope of woven mammoth hair tying him to Galileo's waist so the blind man knew where to go. He was struggling as hard as Galileo. Bringing up the rear behind them were the four teenaged porters.

"How...do...you know?" Galileo gasped back. "I'm grateful to stop, but..."

"I can sense it," Anderson said. "Can't you feel the increased humidity in the air? It's from a small glacier-fed underground lake. We stopped there to camp on our first trip. There's enough fungal growth on the shores to provide dry fuel to get a good fire going."

Yes, Galileo felt chilled, queasy. If he didn't warm up soon and get a substantial meal in him he'd soon be sick. That was a frightening prospect. Wherever, *when*ever they were now—there was definitely no medical care to speak of. If they got sick or injured, they'd just die. There was no one waiting to come to their rescue.

"*Bats*...protect your head!" Anderson coughed, dropping to the rocks.

"What...?"

Then he heard it—a thundering "flapping" sound. He hastily ducked down beside Anderson, his arms up over his head. A massive rush of air right above them bespoke a large colony of the flying rodents erupting up through the narrow tunnel. It was as if they were *escaping*.

Then they were gone. Galileo was left in total darkness. He hugged Anderson closer.

"I can't see anything," Galileo whispered to the gaunt man below him, scared to even move. "The torch must have blown out. I'm afraid we're *both* blind."

"*Thousands of candles can be lit from a single candle,*" the cheerful voice of the Monk sounded from up ahead.

Simultaneously, Galileo heard a flint being struck against a hard stone. A flicker occurred. And then the torch was relit, shedding its welcomed yellow glow upon the huddled group.

"See? *The whole secret of existence is to have no fear!*" Lhamo grinned, lifting high the torch. "*Pain is certain. But suffering is optional!*"

"God, I hate that sanctimonious Monk," Anderson muttered, fumbling around for the close-by rock wall, grabbing onto a crack and hauling himself to his feet. "But he does have a few useful things in his bag, I must admit."

"Come along!" the Monk cheerfully gestured, starting forward.

"I can't wait to get out of this god-forsaken world," Anderson muttered, pushing off Galileo's supporting arm to stumble forward on his own. "Wherever the stable time-portal leads, nothing's going to stop me from diving straight into it!"

"*As you walk and eat and travel,*" the monk merrily replied from up ahead, "*be where you are! Otherwise, you will miss most of your life.*"

"Oh, shut up!" Anderson snapped, almost falling as he stumbled, yanking Galileo by the short rope between the two of them. Galileo grabbed his arm, stabilizing him, Anderson now gladly accepting his help.

"*People with opinions just go around bothering one another!*" Lhamo giggled. "*But true love is born from understanding.*"

"Bah!" Anderson snorted. "Shut up! Why won't you just keep quiet?"

And then—as if in consideration of Anderson—the Monk fell silent. They stumbled forward for a while, concentrating on now walking upward. The only sound was their grunting, shuffling, and slapping of feet on hard rock. It wasn't a steep slope. But the rocks beneath their feet were slick with moisture and bat guano. It was cold.

The tunnel stank horribly. And even a slight slope upward was torture to Galileo's already exhausted leg muscles.

And then they crested a slope and looked down upon...

—a *hundred-foot vertical drop* to a steamy lake. Giant mushrooms down below loomed as an obscene forest. Huge sheets of bioluminescent fungus hung from high cavern walls, casting the large
space below in a weird green-orange glow. And the waters below—
contrary to expectation—were not icy but bubbling, with sheets of
steam rising as thick fog into the air.

The humidity was overpowering. But the air was warm! The lake
must be heated by hidden lava flows. Galileo had the unsettling
thought that they must now be very deep beneath the surface of the
earth.

Galileo decided he was more glad than frightened. The cavern
was an oasis to him, a tropical island in a freezing sea.

"This...should not be here," Anderson muttered, feeling with an
upraised hand at the warm air in front of them. "It wasn't this way
just a few days ago. It was comfortably cool when the kid and I came
through, not hot!"

"*You only lose what you cling to,*" Lhamo shrugged, carefully
starting down a steep jumble of large stones to the side of the drop
which jutted out as a mangled stone staircase. "*Every morning we
are born again. What we do today is what matters most!*"

"We're *lost*, you Buddhist fanatic!" Anderson groaned, sagging
onto the top slab above the vertical drop. "This isn't how we came before! This is a different cavern entirely! I thought I could sense the
path back to the Black Pool. But everything's muddled up. I'm afraid
I've doomed us all, Galileo."

"Don't be so concerned, Arthur," Galileo encouraged him, happy
of the excuse to sit next to him before attempting the perilous climb
downward. "We can always backtrack if we must. Life isn't so terrible
living with the cavepeople in the outer caverns. Perhaps we can still
figure out a way to fix your bub?"

Anderson snorted in derision, surging up to his feet. He turned to
face backward, got on his knees, slid his legs over the first step of the
perilous "staircase," and lowered his body downward. "Go back if you
want, Professor. I thought I needed you and the monk's help in re-

turning to the Black Pool. But I don't. I'll find it again if I have to crawl alone through every tunnel in this whole damn mountain!"

Galileo sighed deeply, reaching out a hand to steady the enraged man. Then Galileo also got on all fours and carefully starting inching down the steep staircase right behind Anderson. It was going to be a chore descending safely to the small lake below. He hoped the following four bearers would be careful. He certainly didn't have the strength to help them as well as Anderson.

He remembered another of Lhamo's irritating quotes: *If you are facing in the right direction, all you need do is keep on walking.*

He only hoped he was facing in the right direction. It wasn't too late for him to turn back. He and a couple porters could find their way back to the cavepeople. What did he really owe to these other people?

"Ah...but they're my friends, aren't they?" he mumbled to himself, edging his feet down the next "step." "And besides, going down is much easier than trying to climb back up. I'm much too tired to go any direction but down."

For better or worse, he was committed.

Sanako was exhausted from the thirteen hour jet flight across the Pacific Ocean. Now she faced a long ride to their final destination.

Normally she had no trouble traveling. Her collaborations and world-wide research took her to many parts of the globe. But never before had she faced something as potentially catastrophic as a mysterious contagion "not of this world."

What did that phrase even mean?

Plus she was certain her new cancer therapy could not be as important as the governmental officials believed. Indeed, they seemed to be operating from a knowledge-level that was impossible: far beyond anything presently conceivable.

Maybe in a few decades her treatment might achieve what they claimed. But that was in the uncertain future, not the here-and-now! They should come phone her up say fifty years in the future! Then she might cheerfully consent. She desperately wanted to call off this adventure and return to her safe lab in Japan.

But she was committed to this course of action. She might as well follow through, provide what limited help she could.

Secret Service Agents had met her at touchdown of the dedicated military jet at Will Rogers World Terminal in Oklahoma City. Apparently the American President was sincere in her appeal, going all-out to make sure Sanako could participate as soon as possible. But the Agents were less than helpful, refusing to answer any of her questions, just ushering her and her baggage into a black sedan. The windows were tinted dark, making it difficult to see outside. And it was in the dead of the night, so seeing out didn't matter much anyway.

They told her it was about two hours to their destination, a "National Recreation Area" located beside the small town of Sulphur, Oklahoma.

So she tried to doze off in her seat. But it was even worse than when she'd tried doing so on the trans-Pacific flight. Now that she was almost to her destination, with her unease skyrocketing, it seemed impossible to nod off.

But then she was being jarred awake by a gentle shaking of her shoulder.

"Professor Yamamoto? I'm sorry to disturb your rest, but we need you immediately at the containment facility. We're losing my good friend, Dr. King. I'm afraid he's dying."

She blearily looked up from her seat at a white-haired, thin gentleman. He also looked exhausted, his eyes sunken with prominent bags hanging beneath.

"Yes...I'm coming...I will need my baggage...they hold my sealed, lyophilized samples."

He helped her from the open sedan door, his liver-spotted hand on her slender arm. He looked like he'd blow away on a strong breeze. But she had deep confidence in her own strength. Though she was slight, she held black belts in both karate and jiu-jitsu. She'd fought in seven professional female bantam-weight MMA matches before dedicating herself fulltime to her medical/research career. Though she enjoyed helping people and being involved in cutting-edge science, she missed the thrill of engaging in a blood sport. She'd never felt as alive as when she was breaking arms and smashing-in noses. People underestimated her at their own peril.

"Oh, forgive me, Professor Yamamoto. I am Victor Volodymyr, who sent you an e-mail on..."

"I looked up your resume while I was inflight, Professor Volodymyr," Sanako interrupted him. "And thank you for your 'heads-up' note. Sorry I didn't have time to write a reply. Everything happened too fast! But I did see you had a remarkable career in material physics—I am very impressed."

She politely pulled free from his grasp. She didn't like people touching her. It wasn't that she was unfriendly, just defensive. Whenever anyone grabbed her, she was likely to go into automatic defensive mode and break their arm, *literally*. It was much better to just completely avoid physical contact.

"Ah, then you know that I'm not much help in tweaking biological cultures," he easily laughed, leading her toward a concrete enclosure. Though it was still dark, she sensed the movement of many vehicles and troops. This was a very tense, militarized environment.

"And I'm not much help in matters of exotic physics," she nodded back at him, noting that the Secret Service Agents were bringing her luggage. Very nice people, though taciturn!

"Then together we are much more powerful than each alone, especially when facing what confronts us in the..."

"And that is?"

"You will see in mere moments."

Sanako frowned, following the tall old man. He was remarkably spry for a man over one hundred years old. Had her cancer immunotherapy treatments caused such a transformation? He now appeared to be a vigorous man in his early eighties!

"This is the CDC's local high-level containment facility," Victor explained as they stepped into an airlock. "It was erected here in only the last few weeks. We won't have to shower and change into positive pressure suits just yet. We're in the outer ring of offices and such. The patients are isolated in the treatment and research units that..."

"I'm well aware of BSL-4 laboratory configurations, Professor Volodymyr."

"Please call me Victor!"

"Ok, then, Victor. I happen to run a BSL-4 lab myself at my University where we work with dangerous and exotic infectious agents, but..."

"Sanako!" a pert, red-haired woman yelled out happily, dashing up to her and giving her a quick hug.

"Hi, Lyra."

Sanako again painfully tolerated the invasion of her privacy. She knew from her past experience that Doctor O'Kelly was compulsively "touchy." That was fine for O'Kelly's patients to get the warm "fuzzies" but not for Sanako. As soon as it was polite, she disengaged from the overly friendly woman.

"It's truly amazing—and frightening! I arrived here eight hours ago," O'Kelly gushed, each word tumbling upon the next. "I've already got blood cultures incubating and finished a series of the standard PCR screens. As far as I know it's like nothing we've ever seen before. In fact, it actually *devoured* the initial test strips when..."

"Lyra, I'm going to need a full briefing. I'm not up to speed on..."

"And that you'll get right now," another woman said, smartly walking up with a contingent of other officials. "Hello, Professor. My name is *Chandra Ice*. I'm the FBI agent in charge of this civilian operation."

Sanako shook hands with the small, dark-skinned, African-American woman. From the cold expression in her dark brown eyes, Sanako immediately realized that here was her equal: focused, expert in her field of endeavor, and *lethal*. Agent Ice was like a coiled whip, ready to be unleashed at a moment's provocation. She obviously wasn't someone to mess around with.

This was good. Sanako liked working with people she could respect. She did *not* "suffer fools gladly"!

"Please follow me," Ice motioned, guiding Sanako along with the rest of the officials into a conference room.

Sanako noted a large flat-screen monitor hanging on the front wall at the head of a long conference table. The screen provided a view of what looked to be a standard hospital room. But the patient depicted on the bed was clearly not normal. Aside from white boxer shorts, he was naked. His muscles bulged and rippled in an unsettling manner as he continuously *writhed* upon the bed, attempting to free himself from thick metallic restraints.

"That's our main concern," Agent Ice pointed at the display as everyone sat around the conference table. "The flexible bands holding him are titanium-based. An elephant couldn't break them. But he snapped two of them before we managed to get enough around him to hold him in place. He's well-secured now, though."

Clearly, Agent Ice was chairing the briefing. Everyone else sat in respectful silence, letting her take the lead.

"You've got to help us," Victor whispered, lowering his white-haired head into his hands.

Sanako noted on the screen that there were three wide bands over the patient's chest, three over his legs, and shackles on both wrists and both ankles. And yet he was still struggling, straining against them.

"His name is Dr. David King," Ice continued, flashing an irritated frown at Volodymyr for his whispered interruption. She flicked a control remote. A "zoom" function focused on the patient's face.

A bearded head filled the screen. His expression was one of pure ferocity, twisted and snarling. But the worst thing—which caused Sanako to gasp out loud—was his *eyes*. There were no whites. Instead, there was just a pure, glittering *black* that stared at the screen. And in that utter blackness there were *glitters* like distant stars exploding.

It was chilling.

"That's the main external manifestation," she noted, using a red laser-pointer to circle his eyes on the screen. "But it's not what concerns us the most. He has the ability to reach out and manipulate machinery, warping space as it were. It's a huge security threat. His room is massively shielded against electromagnetic fields from without and within. It's the only way we've been able to assure his continued containment."

"Is...this contagion transmissible?" Sanako hesitantly asked.

"He apparently acquired it from the source patient who was cut by an alien predator from a crashed space-vehicle," Ice matter-of-factly replied. "So far, two aliens have been identified, who infected two groups of animals not far from here. The remnants of the animals were collected and incinerated. We thought we'd contained the outbreak, that it was limited to those animals. But now a scattering of humans who dealt with those animal-remains are showing initial symptoms. We have them isolated. But as the symptoms progress, well..." her voice trailed off.

"So you are using a classical pandemic containment strategy? I presume that their contacts are being brought in and isolated as well, the circle-approach?"

"Yes. We hoped that would be the end of it," Ice continued. "The two identified aliens are...*very* alien. We thought that the—to them—inhospitable conditions on Earth might already have killed them. But new outbreaks of animal infections are occurring around the nation. And just before you landed, a new outbreak was reported in a herd of cattle in Belgium. So they've reached Europe. The two aliens are apparently moving through the earth's crust, emerging unpredictably to plant their contagion in the most susceptible initial hosts. Our *planet* is under attack!"

Sanako sucked in her breath, shocked. Was this a joke? Was this briefing a bizarre initiation ritual into this BSL-4 facility? She looked around at the ashen-faced people at the table: scientists in white lab smocks, neatly suited civilian officials, and smartly uniformed military. They all looked dead-serious. This was no joke.

"Uhm...and what's the incubation period?"

"For the animals it's apparently only a few hours or even minutes. For secondarily infected humans, it may be as short as days, depending on the dose they receive. Since some of the victims identified to-date definitely did not handle the animals or their remains, the contagion following animal incubation is likely airborne. A direct infection from say a cut, with a massive inoculation, would be the worst scenario and presumably progress rapidly."

"And...for your Dr. King?"

"That's different. It took two weeks to manifest from when he was cut by patient zero. Professor Volodymyr received the same injury, but has no symptoms at all. We attribute that to your cancer immunotherapy which he recently received. Somehow, your retroviral therapy stimulated his body to recognize the alien organism and stop it in its tracks."

"Well..." Sanako shrugged, "that's interesting and worthy of a concerted research effort. But my treatment is hardly a vaccine that could be administered to the general public. I don't even have enough of my 'brew' to do 'circle' treatments around those in contact with identified victims. Doctor O'Kelly and I only managed over several months to produce enough of the final product to treat a few dozen cancer patients. The cell cultures from which we produce the genetically modified viral complexes are notoriously fickle and unpredictable. Besides, it doesn't sound like it could be a treatment against established disease."

"Maybe so," an Army general sitting at the table ventured. "Versus the civilians receiving aerosol infection, Dr. King's progression was remarkably slow. We think that's because he received a version of your cancer therapy in past years, which persisted in his body. We think his prior inoculation was enough to slow the progression of the infection."

Sanako tilted her head to the side, confused.

"Uh...you say, a *version* of my therapy, *years* in the past? What are you telling me?"

"It seems you had a...competitor," he hesitantly explained, apparently reluctant to reveal what he knew.

"That's not possible!" Sanako snapped. "I'd know if that happened. It's true that retroviral therapy to treat a number of medical conditions is a subject of many laboratories, but I'm the first to..."

"Can we focus on the immediate crisis, please?" Ice broke in, impatiently swinging her laser-pointer to illuminate the tortured, snarling face of David King!

"Well..." Sanako frowned, looking away from the uncooperative military man. She didn't like the military. Maybe it was the bias of her society that skewed public thinking entirely away from militarization following their devastating defeat in WWII. But it was also a personal prejudice against "others" looming in the background capable of assuming control of her life! "Alright then—surely you've tried the standard antimicrobial therapies?"

"Nothing else has the slightest effect on it," Doctor O'Kelly volunteered. "All our antibiotics, antivirals, vaccines do nothing—at least with *in vitro* screens using blood from Dr. King mixed with tissue culture recipient cells."

"And my retroviral therapy?"

"We don't know for sure," she continued. "We've only started trying to infect lab animals for *in vivo* tests. Just mixing our brew with recipient cells doesn't do anything either. It seems we have to program an intact immune system to have a therapeutic effect."

"Yes, that agrees with my previous *in vitro* studies."

"Plus there's another matter," the general sighed deeply.

"Something else?" Sanako almost laughed, but caught herself. "What can top aliens from outer space looking to infect humanity with an unstoppable contagion?"

"Well...Dr. King was exposed to a massive dose of ionizing radiation which should have killed him immediately. Instead, he survived. And the doctors here think that the latent alien infection in his body helped him recover. Also, the radiation exposure may, conversely, have allowed the infection to spread and take hold in spite of his...prior...retroviral treatments."

"The DNA of most of his cells was torn to pieces," Lyra squeaked in a trembling voice. "The contagion somehow spliced it all back together, cell-by-cell—but not as it was. Portions of his genome are now *triple helixes* instead of the standard double helix! And incorporated directly into those triple sections are portions of the contagion. It's not just an infection outside his cells or an intruder within his cells. Dr. King is *not human* anymore!"

"That's what I meant," Victor choked in a dry, brittle voice, "when I said my friend was dying. I don't know much biology. But this sounds...biologically irreversible. However, from a physics perspective, I think we might be able to extract the alien presence by manipulating the warp it's generating in space-time. At least, that's my theory."

"That sounds...incredibly desperate?"

"Another infected person, the 'patient zero,' achieved just such a conversion," Victor continued. "The alien influence completely exited his body to return to its crashed vehicle. But we've no idea how it happened. However, it's clearly possible. Yet even if we succeed in duplicating the process, I'm afraid that my friend is gone. That is, unless you can do something about his scrambled DNA?"

Sanako sat for a minute looking up at the fiercely grimacing, bearded face on the screen. Those *deep all-black eyes* were the eyes of an alien, *hungry* beast.

"I guess we can try."

"That's all I ask," Victor sighed, shaking his head in obvious relief at her answer.

"But I have no guarantees."

"Yes, we're in new, deep waters," Agent Ice sighed.

"Anyway, I think I understand the 'big picture,'" Sanako crisply stated. "Our priorities are clear: to find some way to protect the general population while also helping already infected individuals. You have a well-contained acute patient, from whom we can extract a ready supply of infected cells. That's good. And I'm guessing we're going to need more resources than you've managed to accumulate—particularly diagnostic and commercial-level fermentation equipment. I assume you can quickly acquire what I need?"

It was a huge task she faced: trying to come up with an optimal, reproducible brew against an alien contagion—and then scale it up for mass-production!

"We've already spent over a billion dollars in massive construction and containment efforts here on-site in Sulphur," Agent Ice volunteered. "The government of the United States—plus our allies at the United Nations, including your government in Japan—is fully committed to doing whatever else is necessary. I'm the administrative head of this BSL-4, CDC unit. You'll head up our medical team, Doctor Yamamoto. Professor Volodymyr is directing the physics research effort. General Keller is in overall command of the entire site. Do you agree to this administrative command structure, Professor Yamamoto?"

Sanako felt—more than ever—like turning around, climbing on the nearest plane, and heading straight back to her safe home in Japan. But this was the most important and compelling challenge she'd ever faced. Fortunately her demanding career left no time for family, so she hadn't left behind a husband and children. She had no viable excuse for failing to do her duty. And though it seemed that Japan was presently not infected, that might quickly change.

What she did here was in defense of her homeland.

"Yes, I agree to do my part," Sanako firmly replied, narrowing her eyes. "But I can't promise the impossible. Clearly we have a lot of work to do here."

The whole world was on the brink of disaster. But Sanako realized she was actually where she preferred to be: in a well-stocked research/clinical environment dealing with defined variables. She resolutely pushed back the fear and horror of the situation. Clearly, there were details she was going to have to catch up on, fast! But for now she was in her focused, comfortable research-mode. She was secure in her own, personal *new* sanctuary.

God help the rest of the human race.

Chapter 18

COOKIES AND MILK

Delicious treats can be lethal

When they lure a person into a trap

Causing you to let down your guard

And surrender to a devious foe

Thinking that you're being honored

Instead of merely fattened up

Sugar and spice and everything nice

Softening you to be carved and diced

A chubby roasted turkey on a plate

Where you become the meal

To someone else's delight...

Don't be late for your snack!

The Minstrel's Lark, 18:33-36

Suzy awoke floating up against straps holding her into the reclined chair. It was a curiously buoyant feeling.

"I'm trapped!" she gasped, starting to struggle against the bonds.

"No, you are fine," that same raspy female voice spoke in her ear. Twisting her head to the side she saw a *little yellow bird* sitting on her shoulder. "You may get up whenever you want. There's food and drink for you. Refresh yourself. Your marvelous journey continues. Be happy!"

Oh, that was *very* strange!

And looking over at her companions, who were still slumbering in their recliners, she saw similar little birds perched on each of their shoulders.

Billy's eyes were fluttering open.

"Where...are we?" Suzy gasped. Her voice was garbled, her mouth dry.

"See for yourself," the yellow bird tweeted.

A large, curved viewscreen on her left showed a picture of a growing *moon*—hanging white and round against the blackness of space! And on her right, another identical viewscreen showed a retreating Earth—iconic with its blue oceans, green-brown continents, white clouds, and glittering icy polar caps.

"We *are* in outer space!" Suzy gasped, amazed. She weakly started unbuckling and moving aside her straps as she drifted up into the air.

"And we're going to the moon!" Billy cheerfully laughed as he woke besides her, doing the same.

Together they joined hands and kicked backward, floating into the middle of the room.

There on a golden metal table in the center of the room was now a plate of hot chocolate cookies. A little net with magnets on its sides held the plate and cookies to the tabletop. And in big "sippy cups" to the side of the cookies—apparently also held in place by magnets on their bottoms—sat clear glasses of white milk.

"Let's eat!" Billy laughed, drifting down to grab cookies from below the net and stuff them into his mouth. "They're delicious! Oh, man, these are *so* much better than turnip-raspberry mush."

"Ok, Billy—I'll just get our friends up."

Ignoring her own hunger and thirst she kicked over to the three Indian kids. She helped them get oriented as they woke up with their own birds chittering in their ears in Chickasaw. To them this was totally new and frightening. At least Suzy and Billy had seen every science fiction movie ever made, plus frequent news reports on the national space programs. So they knew at least that there was such a thing as weightlessness and space ships.

But it only took the Native American boy and two girls a few minutes to figure out how to handle weightlessness. Soon they were floating around the table, stuffing themselves with the new, *delightful* sensation of milk and cookies!

"Uh...how do we...go to the bathroom?" Billy suddenly grimaced, clutching at his groin while looking around desperately.

A door in the side of the room slid open, revealing the features of an airline's small inflight bathroom. The "toilet" was already making a pre-emptive "sucking" noise. It was clearly a zero-G facility.

"Ah! Great!" Billy gulped, launching himself directly at it.

He slammed the panel shut, a big smile on his face.

Suzy looked up at the two viewscreens. She had to go to the bathroom also, but could wait until Billy was finished. Meanwhile, she studied the amazing scenes. The moon was noticeably larger than when she'd first looked at the screen, while Earth was smaller. It was a three-quarter moon, with the craters to the right that scarred its surface standing out in bold relief. To the left she saw the darker "spots" on the moon, previously named as "oceans." And it looked to Suzy that they were headed toward the *Mare Tranquillitatis*, the "Sea of Tranquility." It was where Neil Armstrong first set foot on the moon, way back in 1969.

Suzy had studied the moon in school, finding it fascinating. Now she was headed toward it in a spaceship! How had this happened? What would they find when they got there? Might she see, with her own eyes, the landing site of Neil Armstrong?

Whatever...she suddenly felt very tired. She knew she should be asking questions of the little bird that was now flapping in the air at her shoulder, maintaining its friendly personal presence. But she just wanted to go back to her "bed" and take a nap, happily stuffed with cookies and milk.

But first—after Billy came out and began also studying the vivid viewscreen images—she showed the Indian kids how to "flush" the toilet and work the knobs of the sink (where the water or wastes was pulled down by a strong air-suction mechanism), and the wastebasket for used-up paper towels. And after using the restroom after the others, she emerged to find them "snorting" and "snuffling" in their recliners, fast asleep. Their straps had reattached, holding them firmly in place.

"Hmmm...I'm by myself!"

"No, I'm still here with you," the little yellow bird brightly chirped.

Getting very woozy, Suzy shuddered, suddenly afraid.

"I don't like your voice!" she drunkenly state, her words slurring together.

"What? Why not?"

"It sounds...old, and crackly."

"What an odd thing to say."

"It's true!" she woozily insisted.

The moon now filled the forward screen, the Sea of Tranquility looming larger and larger. They were definitely headed straight down at it!

"Sleep well, my sweet little child. Do not fear me."

She yawned widely as she felt retrorockets firing, slowing their descent.

*Wow...I should stay awake for the landing...*she thought to herself. But she couldn't keep her eyes open. Her eyelids were way too heavy.

And as they hurtled down toward the lunar surface she gave up and let her eyes close. It had to be drugs. Their captors had spiked the cookies and/or milk. Very sneaky of them, whoever "they" were. It was like a fairy tale. It was magical. And Suzy dearly hoped that they weren't being lured into the hut of an *evil witch* who'd stuff them into an oven and *bake* their stuffed little bodies into a pie!

Now she knew what that voice sounded like— an old witch.

Hah!—she laughed to herself as she drifted off into a deep slumber. *That's ridiculous!*

Or was it?

Dave was in an "existential struggle"...fighting for the survival of his very soul.

He was being methodically *devoured* by the extradimensional "spider" that inhabited his physical body.

His body was already under control by the creature. But his mind wasn't yet subsumed.

"I...won't...let...you...take...me," he whispered silently to himself.

"*WHY NOT?*"—the arrogant reply boomed inside his head. "YOU WON'T HAVE TO FIGHT ANYMORE. YOU WON'T HAVE TO WORRY ANYMORE. YOU'LL NOT FACE PROBLEMS ANYMORE. YOU'LL NEITHER REMEMBER THE PAST NOR WORRY ABOUT

THE FUTURE. JUST SURRENDER TO ME AND YOU WILL FI-
NALLY FIND PEACE!"

"I...can't."

"WHY NOT? IT'S EASY. JUST DO IT!"

"Because...I *love*...my wife...my kids...and..."

"*WHY?* WHAT IS THE USE OF THIS ILLOGICAL EMOTION?
IT ONLY MAKES YOU WASTE ENERGY! THE ONLY TRUE JOY IS
IN CONSUMING! JOIN WITH ME FULLY AND FIND TRUE HAP-
PINESS DEVOURING THIS TASTY WORLD! THERE ARE RICHES
HERE BEYOND IMAGINING! WE WILL FEAST FOR A LONG
TIME!"

"I...don't know...why...it...just *is*."

"THIS EMOTION YOU SO CHERISH IS A FUNCTION OF YOUR
BIOLOGICAL IMPERATIVE TO REPRODUCE. IT GIVES YOU A
SENSE OF SURVIVAL PAST YOUR OWN DEATH. IT IS MERELY A
PREPROGRAMMED MOTIVATOR WRITTEN BY YOUR EVOLU-
TIONARY DEVELOPMENT INTO YOUR GENETIC MAKEUP. IT
ATTACHES YOU TO YOUR GENETIC PROGENCY, TO PERPETUTE
THE TRANSMISSION OF YOUR DNA PROFILE. WHEN YOU LET
ME FINISH REWRITING YOUR GENETIC CODE YOU WILL LOSE
THIS WASTEFUL, REGRESSIVE EMOTION."

"You...don't...reproduce?"

"I DIVIDE WHENEVER I WISH, WHEN IT IS MORE EFFI-
CIENT TO INGEST AND PROCESS FOOD BY INCREASING MY
SURFACE-TO-MASS RATIO. BUT THIS DOES NOT RESULT IN
THERE BEING TWO OF ME. I AM ME. I AM EVER ME. I SIMPLY
COVER MORE TERRITORY BY SPLITTING INTO DIFFERENT
SECTIONS. FOOD IS USUALLY VERY HARD TO FIND. I AM EVER
HUNGRY, ALWAYS WANTING MORE. HERE...THIS IS WONDER-
FUL! I...WE...WILL *GORGE* OURSELVES!"

"And...what...then?"

"THEN WE WILL MOVE ON, TO FRESH FIELDS OF PLENTY,
EVER ONWARD, MOVING INTO PARALLEL DIMENSIONS, DIF-
FERENT TIMELINES, FEASTING AS WE GO!"

"And...then...what?"

"EVENTUALLY WE WILL CONSUME THIS ENTIRE FRESH,
RIPE UNIVERSE! BUT THAT WILL TAKE UNTOLD EONS. AND

THROUGH IT ALL WE WILL GROW EVER LARGER AND MORE POWERFUL, UNTIL NOTHING CAN THREATEN US. WE WILL EAT EVERYTHING IN EXISTENCE!"

"And...*then*...what?"

Dave derived a meager satisfaction at the silence in his head. The Creature had no answer. But something else was nagging at the back of Dave's mind. It was yet *another* voice, this one disdainful, angry, and defiant!

And it said: "Come to me!"

Ah. Yes. It was also under attack. It needed help. And Dave recognized the voice. It was the voice of a friend. It was a plaintive cry for help from someone that had helped him in the past, indeed *more* than helped him—had nurtured and guided him, had held him up and protected him, who had a stake in his own continued discrete existence.

Dave gathered his ill-gotten strength together and SURGED up off of the table!

He heard his constraints "cracking" and "snapping" as they gave way.

"He's loose! He's getting up! Take him down!" Dave heard panicked cries from outside his cell.

He flattened the table he'd been shackled on with one blow from his Creature-powered, hybrid "muscles" as "spacesuited" soldiers burst into his room, pointing high-powered rifles directly at him!

"Get out of my way!" he/it screamed at them, charging...

—as a *HAIL OF BULLETS* slammed into him, driving him momentarily backward...

But his punctured flesh merely closed back in over the wounds, instantly healing his body.

He swept the rifles to the side, SMASHING through the glass wall in front of him into a corridor where he "thumped" down in his new/heavy body as space-suited technicians scattered in terror in front of him.

"Oh God, is this really happening?" he heard someone scream over a speaker. "Get out of there! Don't let him come into contact with you! Get out of its way!"

Hmmm. The voice sounded oddly familiar. It had an oriental-type accent. Was it...*Sanako?*

What was his old enemy doing here?

Ah well...it didn't matter.

His objective was clear.

He tore his way through several walls as if they were paper then CRASHED through the outermost reinforced concrete wall, finding himself standing outside the jail.

He paused, getting his bearings. It was daytime. The sun was high in the sky. He was in the Park. But everything was different than he remembered. Where there'd been the placid entrance to the tree-filled Park, there was now a big compound filled with military vehicles. Soldiers were pouring out of barracks, approaching him with rifles drawn. Several tanks were lumbering to life, their gun torrents lowering to take aim at him. And off to his right he saw a giant domed structure, covering what used to be the Rock Creek camping area.

Ah. *That's* where he needed to go.

Batting aside a charging group of soldiers he leaped up on top of a tank and twisted its main gun upward to the sky as they tried to get a round off at him. The tank blew up, their own attempted shot killing everyone within, throwing him up into the air.

Landing lightly on his bare feet he grabbed another tank by its extended gun barrel and *twirled it* around over his head. It was exhilarating to be this incredibly strong! He felt just like the Marvel's comic book "The Incredible Hulk," just an extradimensional spider-powered version! Indeed, his naked torso bulged with steel-hard "muscles." For the moment, his and the Creature's objectives were aligned. It was allowing him to take the lead, to make good his escape. And the only way to ensure that objective was to enter the Dome.

And so he ran toward it, holding the multi-ton tank above his head like a toy!

Its terrified occupants spilled out of the top hatch, dropping to the side.

"Get out of my way!" he shouted as more troops attempted to block his path.

They scattered as he barreled through, approaching the edge of the mammoth white dome, swinging the tank in the air like a baseball bat...

—to SMASH it against the dome!

The sloped barrier pushed inward but did not crack.

"Hulk will *smash!*" he screamed-out in fiendish delight, swinging the mangled tank again and again into the concrete barrier...

—that finally gave way, *crumbling* inward!

As he stepped through the gap he tossed the mashed tank to the side where it landed with a "thud." He ran toward the RED OBELISK that now lay on its side, fully exposed at the center of the carved-out basin.

Around the Obelisk, concrete bunkers squatted like giant slugs. Various pieces of large equipment were attached to the glassy surface of the Obelisk. A team of engineers had been trying to pry open the storage compartment panel. But now they were running for their lives...

—as Dave skidded up to the side of the Obelisk, leaped up twenty feet into the air, and landed on its top. He put the palm of his hand onto the surface of the storage compartment panel. Cooperatively, it "popped" open beneath him.

Without a look back, he crammed himself into the small chamber, feeling the Obelisk *shudder* as RPGs from pursuing troops slammed into it.

Merging with the piece of the Creature that was already there trying to take over the Obelisk's systems, Dave's intellect "clicked." The Obelisk accepted his familiar guidance. He felt it straining, stirring, and then *rising* up into the air!

"I'm free...now all I need is an *exorcism,*" Dave gasped to himself, trying to fight off the increasingly powerful influence of the Creature. "Now where might I get that from, do ya think?"

And then it came to him.

"Ah, yes."

And the melted, crippled Obelisk lurched up into the air, *crashing* through the concrete dome above, and *zooming* up into the sky...

—as Dave felt his flesh melt, *dissolving into the interior of the Obelisk*, his corrupted spirit became One with the ancient Martian artifact, his dispersed cells integrating throughout its circuitry.

Through the sensors of the Obelisk Dave now perceived a squadron of Air Force jets dropping out the clouds above him, arming their missiles.

"SWAT THE INSECTS AWAY!" the Creature commanded him.

"There's no need," Dave admonished the Creature, trying to reason with it now that he and the Obelisk were in control. "They are of no consequence."

And, yes, the Obelisk was now flashing upward far faster than the jets could fire upon or track, *sizzling* through the stratosphere and up into orbit around the planet.

"THIS IS A FINE SPOT FROM WHICH TO ORCHESTRATE THE CONSUMPTION OF THE LIVING ORGANISMS OF THIS PLANET!"

The Creature was clearly delighted with Dave's subversion of the Obelisk.

"Oh, there's a much *better* spot than this for your ultimate plans," Dave muttered, preparing to phase the Obelisk into subspace, again moderating the Spider's desired actions.

"AND WHAT PLAN IS THAT?"

"*Purification*," Dave muttered over and over to himself, struggling with active help from the Obelisk to maintain conscious dominance.

The Obelisk was crippled but still lurching along. Dave knew it had *one more journey* left to accomplish.

There was only one place he could go to have a chance of ridding both himself and the world of the vile Spider that Sally had unwittingly brought back with her from the other Universe.

So he dropped the Obelisk into subspace, headed straight toward the *Black Hole* located at the center of the Milky Way.

How long it'd take to get there or if he'd still be in control of himself he had no idea.

He just prayed that the severely damaged Obelisk could get there—and once having arrived he'd have the strength left to do what must be done...regardless of the consequences to himself.

He loved his fellow beings with an emotion that went beyond mere genetic urgings. Dave knew it was a so-called "emergent" quality that the dispersed Creature from the corrupted second Universe could never understand. Dave hoped that humanity might not think too badly of him. Though he and Sally had foisted the subspace Spider upon the world, he could not let himself become its instrument of mankind's destruction.

If he couldn't avoid the "oven" then he must be its last victim. Let it choke on *him!* Hah! Now that was funny. Ovens couldn't be alive—could they?

He would soon find out.

Galileo sighed deeply, fearful of what was to come.

They'd spent the "night" trying to sleep beside the hot, bubbling subterranean lake. They hadn't needed to start a bonfire. Indeed, with the 100% humidity and near hundred-degree heat, Galileo felt he was being broiled alive!

Trong walked up to the awakening trio, triumphantly holding out his spear, on the chipped rock tip of it which flapped several flat, brown, spongy things.

The hairy young man grunted several phrases.

"He says it's edible mushroom meat," Lhamo mildly observed, sitting up to accept a piece. He began contentedly munching on it, "Very tasty!"

"At least the boy found a use for his spear that he's been carrying all this while," Galileo smiled. Hopefully that was the only "monster" they'd actually find—giant mushrooms!

He was beginning to doubt the wisdom of this descent into the bowels of the earth.

"I thought most mushrooms are poisonous," Anderson petulantly muttered, reluctantly fumbling for a chunk.

But Galileo was happy to grab a piece. The salient feature for him was it *wasn't* mammoth-derived! Even if mushroom poisons did kill him, it'd be a welcome relief from the constant diet of stringy meat.

Anderson bit into the brown chunk, chewing thoughtfully.

"Well, not too bad..." he began.

—as an EARTHQUAKE suddenly shook the entire cavern, large pointed stalactites loudly *snapping* off the high ceiling to fall into the lake and shoreline with *shuddering* impacts.

The porters dropped to the ground from where they'd been searching through the mushroom forest, fearfully looking above...

—as the quake just as suddenly stopped, the lurching rocks beneath Galileo's legs settling.

Then Galileo heard the undeniable sound of many rocks crashing downward, an avalanche!

"Allah protect us!" Galileo exclaimed, afraid they were about to die.

But the horrendous grinding sound also faded away. The only ominous thing that continued beyond the swaying of the ten-foot-high mushrooms was a *red glow* that now lit the air and rocks around them.

"What happened?" Anderson moaned, twisting on the ground. "Tell me what happened!"

"It...was an earthquake," Galileo gasped, levering himself shakily up to his feet. His muscles felt like they were on fire. The previous day's exertions were taking a severe toll on him.

"And it has cut off some of our options," Lhamo mildly observed, pointing back the way they'd come.

Indeed, a massive cave-in had completely destroyed the protruding slabs of the "staircase" they'd descended upon into the cavern. And even if they could scale the vertical cliff that remained, the opening above was gone as well, jammed full of huge boulders.

They couldn't return...

—and the mists were now turning to hot *steam!*

Trong came staggering up through the increasingly dense white clouds, gesturing frantically. Around him, the four porters were hastily grabbing up their deerskin bags filled with food and other supplies.

"We've got to leave," Galileo urged Anderson, reaching down to help him to his feet. "The lava under the lake is surging. It's boiling the water. If we don't get out of here, we're literally cooked!"

They hastily continued along the shoreline, past the churning lake, and into an exit tunnel.

Lhamo lit another of their dwindling supply of torches before continuing steadfastly forward.

The blackness and chill were a relief to Galileo as he staggered along behind Trong and Lhamo. But it was short-lived. Going from the steamy heat back into the cold depths was jarring to his system, throwing him into a state of shock. He barely felt the rope still tied around his waist, tethering the pitifully thin, trailing figure of Anderson.

They couldn't take much more of this. How long did Anderson say the trip from the outer Caverns took to the Black Pool? Was it a week? That meant they had at least *six more days* of this nightmare—and then no guarantee of getting back to the surface of the planet if the "time-portal" proved to be just an oily pool of water!

Hah. Likely the "demon" was a loose stalagmite protruding up from the floor of that cave. This was just a fool's errand. They were descending to their doom!

"I *put* my trust in *Allah!*" Galileo fiercely commanded himself as he staggered forward into the darkness, following the single flaring torch. Then, more feebly: "I put my trust in Allah..."

"Trust in your feet, you damned idiot!" Anderson petulantly yelled from behind, stumbling along. "If I had my glasses working I'd run rings around you. Now you're my guide dog, Galileo. Do your duty! Bark, damn you, *bark!*"

Tugging angrily on the rope, causing Galileo to stagger, Anderson let loose with a simulated *wolf-howl!*

"*Awwwwwwrrrrooooooooo!*"

Trong looked back, his frightened face starkly outlined by the torch's light.

But Anderson didn't look worried anymore, chortling and cackling behind Galileo like a demented maniac!

The Monk paused, turning back.

"*A dog is not considered a good dog because he is a good barker,*" his soothing voice drifted back from up ahead. "Likewise, *a man is not considered a good man because he is a good talker.*"

"That's just what I said!" Anderson yelled, his voice bouncing eerily around in the constricting tunnel.

Clearly, without his neural implants functioning, the Time Keeper was going stark, raving *mad.*

Chapter 19

<u>ETHICS</u>

Do you think you are an "ethical" person
Aligning your life with a higher Morality
Obeying the strictures of your powerful Religion
Implementing a set of personal Principles
Conforming happily to what is Correct
While rejecting everything that is immoral
Hating that which is evil or unprincipled
Stepping around that which is clearly wrong
Walking on solid rock, avoiding any sand or mud
Not ruled by fanciful emotions or blind chance
Secure in the knowledge that you are Righteous
Not merely an especially clever, smart animal
Not dancing to the tune of your twitching genetics
Obeying Laws of Nature beyond your kin
Which compel you to be capable of atrocities
Darwinian rules of survival kicking in...
Which comes first, if anything?
DANCE, little puppet, DANCE!

The Minstrel's Lark, 19:18-22

Victor staggered out of the shattered side of the BSL-4 lab, look-ing around in bewilderment.

A thick debris cloud made breathing difficult. Sunlight cut through portions of it, sporadically revealing the shattered Dome off to Victor's right. In front of him, troops were milling, trying to rescue any survivors in or under a crumpled, burning tank.

It looked like a war zone.

"How could this happen?" Professor Yamamoto gasped to Victor, emerging from the darkness behind him. "Human flesh can't accomplish what we saw on the monitors before we lost power! He snapped those titanium straps like they were tissue paper. Then he ran through *concrete* walls like they weren't even there!"

"God help us," Victor coughed, putting a hand up to block the swirling dust and dirt from getting into his mouth and nose. "Somehow the alien material in his body suffused and protected his human flesh. And if that's what is going to happen to those who've been infected, to the poor souls who are now in CDC-monitored isolation, then...?"

"—then we must *euthanize* them before they progress that far!" General Keller curtly concluded. He coughed also, striding out of the dark gap in the shattered wall to stand, shaking with anger, beside Victor and Sanako. "This alien contagion can't be allowed to take hold! Just one of these converted monsters could take out an entire army. I'm afraid that your 'treatment' options won't..."

"We don't know that for sure!" Sanako snapped, interrupting the General. "Apparently something like my therapy—where did that come from anyway?—slowed the progression in Dr. King's body. *My* cancer therapy completely stopping it from taking hold in Professor Volodymyr's body! The infected humans are not all going to turn into unstoppable monsters, perhaps *none* of them."

"We still have plenty of blood from Dave which was drawn before he escaped," Victor added, turning back to reenter the still-dark laboratory complex. "I can use it to study the physical aspects of the contagion that..."

"—and I can proceed with our tests of my retroviral treatment," Sanako added. "We have live cultures from the patient. Also we have freeze-dried, lyophilized samples. We even have tissue biopsies that are preserved in liquid nitrogen. It's a setback to lose our live immune-resistant patient, for sure, but not a complete defeat. We can continue our studies."

"I'm sorry, Professors," the General shook his graying, square head in denial. His eyes glared in the gloom. "I'm ordering the immediate incineration of all your samples."

"What did you say?" Agent Ice demanded, bustling up to them. Her impeccable dark blue pants suit was torn, but her blazing black eyes were as fierce as the General's! "Sir, the President herself has ordered a full-out research effort into this potential pandemic. You are outranked!"

"I am the Commander of this base," he flatly stated, his voice cold and determined. "I am fully empowered to make decisions concerning the safety of my personnel. I've had no orders yet from my superiors on this matter. And since those samples are a clear threat to my personnel, they *will* be immediately destroyed! My recommendation to the other military units guarding the isolation stations across the country is to likewise immediately euthanize all their infected patients, destroy any clinical samples, and cremate the bodies."

"That's illegal! There's a thing called 'due process' that..." Ice huffed, outraged.

"This is a state of war. I'm recommending to my superiors and specifically the President that we declare martial law throughout the nation. The lawyers can sort out the niceties and legalities after we've stopped this alien invasion in its tracks!"

He turned away from them.

"But what if what you're proposing *doesn't* stop the outbreak?" Sanako said, grabbing his arm and jerking him to a stop. "The nature of a *pandemic* is an infectious lethal agent with an *extended* incubation period—just exactly what we have here! We have no idea how many other people out there in the population are incubating the agent, silently infecting others."

He tried to pull away but she persisted, holding him back.

Outraged, he swung on her—only to be blocked and thrown unceremoniously to the ground!

Sanako now sat astride his back, holding him down, his arm twisted up tight behind his thick neck!

Victor was amazed, taking a step backward. This woman was no mere academic. She was *dangerous*.

"General...*Sir*...there's another consideration, one that you'll want to weigh carefully before taking any precipitous action!" Victor appealed to the struggling, furious, sputtering man.

The power came back on. The remaining, intact fluorescent lights flickered on. A loud "hum" of gearing-up machinery filled the air.

"Get *off* me!" the General growled, ceasing his struggles.

Carefully, Sanako slid to the side and out of his reach.

"Speak!" he ordered Victor, indignantly getting to his feet.

"Something this powerful...just imagine the military applications of a controlled application thereof?"

The man's rigid face relaxed, his blue eyes narrowing.

"I should throw you into the brig, Doctor," he glowered at Sanako. "But under the circumstances—get back to your duty station! As to your samples, they're safe...for now. I'll be in consultation with my superiors."

He stalked off.

"Thank you, Victor," Sanako nodded to him. "I was about to break that bastard's neck!"

"Yes, thank you Professor Volodymyr," Agent Ice sighed with relief. "Keller is a hard man, but ultimately reasonable. Given time, I think I could have calmed him. But what you suggested to him is..."

"—unthinkable, yes, I agree," Victor hastily added. "But it was the only thing I could think of to stop his hasty actions! Everything has positive and negative aspects. We've seen that repeatedly throughout history for each of humanity's great scientific advances. We can't throw away the incredible positive potentials of this alien contagion just because it's an immediate threat to us. Why, if even half of what Dave told us concerning his prior adventures through space and time are true then..."

"*What?*" Sanako stopped Victor's muddled explanation. "Just what haven't you told me? Dr. King's 'prior' adventures have to include him being 'previously' treated with my novel therapy *before* I ever invented it, right?"

Victor saw she was determined to find answers. She wasn't going to work in the dark any longer. If they wanted her on their team, then she had to know *everything*.

Agent Ice exchanged a worried glance with Victor.

"She should know," Victor shrugged. "It's too late to hold back anything. She needs to know about...her *own* negative potential."

Ice sighed, relenting.

"Come on, Dr. Yamamoto—we've a recording you should listen to...carefully and calmly."

Sanako nodded in guarded agreement, following Agent Ice back into the wrecked interior of the laboratory complex.

"Will it take long?"

"Yes, it'll take several hours."

"So that's why you didn't tell me about it earlier—not enough time for it in our prior emergency situation?"

"Uh, right."

She'd given them an "out" to explain their lack of trust in her. Well, that might put them back on her side, but her trust was another matter entirely.

She absently noted that the red backup light was on, emergency batteries powering them. The regular power had to be restored quickly least they lose precious stored samples and reagents.

She saw bustling engineers engaged in just that activity.

Victor hesitantly trailed along behind her. He looked scared, as if what she would hear would change everything. She wasn't sure herself that she wanted to hear what they'd been hiding from her. Whatever it was, she had a feeling it would indeed be life-altering.

But she knew she couldn't stay in her own little, happy academic bubble forever.

She felt the *cage-fighter* inside her knocking at the bars of her neat, prestigious, safe career!

At some point you have to embrace all aspects of your being, whether positive or "negative."

Anything less would be dishonorable.

And *honor* was everything.

Tommy and Sally emerged from subspace spiraling helplessly down toward the surface of the moon.

Tommy realized they were in very bad shape.

The journey back from 1.2 billion years in the future had been horrendous. In their little ORV they'd been falling back against the flow of time. The forces searing their energy shield, just inches from their faces, had been indescribable: a *wall of roiling fire* that threatened at any moment to devour them!

And the life-support mechanisms in the jury-rigged spaceship were rudimentary at best, not designed to keep them alive in such a horrendous situation. But now their flaming, seemingly endless plunge was at last over...if they could survive hurtling down toward the cratered surface of the moon!

"T-Tommy," Sally gasped. "We...we made it?"

His eyes snapped open.

He'd gone into minimal awareness mode, to use the least amount of their dwindling supply of oxygen so that she might survive. Now he had to boot up his essential programming, get oriented, and take action.

"Where are we?" he asked.

"We...we're falling...I think...into the moon!"

Interfacing with the ORV's rudimentary onboard computer, Tommy saw that their life support systems were failing. The CO_2 scrubber had stopped, the level in the cabin slowly increasing. But it wasn't an immediate danger. Tommy rapidly calculated the rate of their fall, their trajectory, and the power necessary to either go up into orbit or land safely. Then he instantly assessed the state of the modified Ranger's systems, particularly the remaining charge in their subspace drive, plus the condition of their steering jets.

They couldn't get into orbit around the moon.

The DE-generator was barely maintaining their energy shield, which was flaring and flickering around them. Their only hope was to brake sufficiently to not slam into the fast-approaching gray surface below. If they didn't succeed, they'd become just one more small crater amongst millions of others accumulated over billions of years of lunar bombardment by meteors and comets.

"Hold on," he warned her.

He applied the steering jets not to stop them but to veer their trajectory so they were now hurtling downward at a slant. The resultant increased spin caused the surface below visually to flip around chaotically. He calculated the positions of the craters below, correcting for the spinning. He was trying to steer them toward a relatively smooth landing area.

Bursts of ice crystals from the expelled air fanned out in spirals around them as they fell. At least they were no longer in an uncontrolled descent. Now they were making a "controlled" crash landing.

"If we don't make it...I want you to know..." Sally gasped out in the dwindling atmosphere in the ORV.

"Yes, Mommy?"

"I'm just sorry...that Suzy and Billy...didn't get to meet you..."

"Me, too, Mommy," he smiled, ejecting the last of the steering canister's air and seeing it wouldn't be enough, that they were indeed about to crash!

In desperation, he shifted the flow from the empty air canister to the last dregs of their oxygen tank.

The final bursts of air did the trick, slowing them enough to SMASH at a slant into the lunar regolith.

They *bounced high* in the airless vacuum, crashing against huge boulders several times before coming to rest on the surface of the moon.

They were safely down, still alive—but likely not for long.

"Nice view here..." Tommy heard Sally gasp. He saw that nervous sweat was dripping from her brow.

Indeed it was. To their left Tommy saw a high crater wall. Behind it were low, stark mountains. And to their right was a lower, flat area that stretched away to the far horizon. If Tommy's calculations were correct—and they were—that was *Mare Tranquillitatis*, the Sea of Tranquility.

It was a nice place to die.

"Can we...drive...on the lunar dust?"

"I'm sorry, Mommy," Tommy sighed. "The DE-generator is just barely maintaining our shield. It's got no power left for anything else. We can't drive or send out an SOS, nothing. If we tried, our protective bubble would pop, killing us instantly. We're stuck here."

Indeed, from the fiery hell of the descent through a billion years of time, they were now sitting in the near absolute-zero shadow of a nearby mountain. It was already getting cold inside the cab. It wouldn't be long until they'd be frozen solid.

"So we're just going to sit here and freeze to death?" Sally quietly laughed, putting a hand on Tommy's small shoulder. "That's a sad ending after all we've been through when..."

"No, Mommy," Tommy interrupted her. "We're not going to freeze to death."

"Oh, that's good," she sighed in relief.

"We only have three minutes left of oxygen in the cab," Tommy glumly continued. "I had to use everything in the canister to land us safely. Before we freeze we're going to suffocate."

"Oh...well, then," Sally sighed, seemingly coming to terms with their fate. She sat in silence for a minute before quietly but firmly replying. "Then I want you to go into complete shutdown, Tommy. Someday someone will find us here. They may be able to reboot your android systems. And then you can..."

"No, Mommy."

"What?

"I'm staying awake with you as long as I can—and then I'm letting the oxygen depletion take me away also. I don't want to continue without you. That wouldn't be any fun at all."

He felt both her arms go around him, hugging him close.

He felt warm, at peace.

And then they both drifted off...

It actually wasn't a bad ending, considering.

Suzy awoke feeling clean and rested.

She stuck her arms up into the air and yawned widely—having had the most refreshing, delicious sleep of her entire life!

She found herself lying flat on a comfortable bed, a soft pillow below her neck, and a silky sheet resting lightly over her body. Looking up she saw *rainbows* arching across the bed, with little birds flitting, "chirping," and *twittering* cheerfully!

She snapped fully awake, on her guard.

Where the hell am I?

"Really?" she said, royally annoyed by the childishness of the display above her bed. She wasn't a little kid! She was ten years old! "Who's doing this? Turn it off!"

"I am sorry," a soothing female voice replied in perfect English. "I thought you might find it pleasing after your ordeal. We are so glad to have you here. We want you to be happy."

The calming voice came from all around Suzy...probably not a real person, just a computer. It was a different voice from the raspy, quavering one in the spaceship. Suzy liked it better, though it probably wasn't a living person. And the rainbow and birds must also be artificial, probably 3D projections.

Still, it was all rather impressive.

"Show me how things *really* are!" she firmly ordered as she lay there, trying to get oriented.

The birds and rainbows faded away. She sat up on the soft mattress, swinging her legs out over the edge. Tentatively she stood up on a floor which felt to her bare feet like velvety carpet though it looked bare. She saw she was dressed in plain white pants and blouse. To her right on the floor were white tennis shoes. She stepped into them. They perfectly molded their interiors to the contours of her feet.

She felt at her head.

Her hair was freshly washed, braided into two neat pigtails which stuck out to each side of her head. It was just as she liked! That was disturbing. Someone had given her a bath while she was unconscious!

Lowering her hands and looking around she saw that she was in a small, round room with curved walls. The entire surface around her now displayed a perfectly detailed view of the wide grassy plain that she and Billy had come from. There was no discernible exit.

Yep, "they" were trying to make her feel at home—inside a beautiful cage!

But she knew she definitely wasn't on Earth anymore.

She was on the moon. While she was drugged unconscious, they must have landed. Indeed, her body felt strangely light.

"Ah...if I remember right, only a fifth of earth gravity," she mused to herself.

Crouching then jumping upward, she floated up to touch the high ceiling before drifting leisurely back down. If this was a jail cell, it was sure spiffy!

"To be precise, Suzy," the pleasant computer-sounding voice replied, "you now weigh only 16.6% of what you did on Earth. So please, enjoy yourself! Hop around if you wish! And when you're oriented I will allow you to go outside and play in the plaza with your friends from your rocket ship. Plus you will meet yet other new arrivals. Get to know them. You have a bright, wonderful future with them here at Galilei Station!"

Huh. That sweet-sounding voice sure was bossy.

Galilei Station? What the heck was that?

"My mouth is gummy—where's the bathroom?"

"It is located wherever you wish, Suzy. Do you require a sink?"

"—a sink, a mirror, a toilet, toothpaste and a toothbrush...you know: regular bathroom things!"

"As you wish."

And up out of the floor sprang a full-services bathroom with white porcelain fixtures, golden knobs, silver handles, and a marble floor. It looked pristine, as if it'd never been used before. A beautifully carved oak cabinet sported a mirror above an inset sink, plus shelves containing every bathroom product she'd ever need. Opening a door on the side of the cabinet she saw within it a shower. At least she wouldn't need that right away. She already felt cleaner than she'd been in weeks!

Grumbling to herself, Suzy used the facilities, still wary but *soooo* happy to have a regular bathroom to do her business instead of marching out to squat down in adjoining grasslands!

Finished, the facilities sank back out of sight into the floor, leaving behind the same soft, flat carpet as before.

"Are you hungry? Would you like to eat breakfast?"

"I need answers!" Suzy snapped, sticking her fists petulantly onto her hips. She refused to sit on either the chair or sofa that rose enticingly up out of the floor, instead choosing to pace back and forth.

"Of course, Suzy—ask whatever you wish. I have a standard speech I give to new arrivals, or I can address any specifics you'd like. But please don't feel rushed. You now have all the time in the world."

"Are you a real person or a computer? What's your name?"

The voice softly laughed. "I am neither. I want to be your friend. Name me whatever you wish."

Well, that wasn't very helpful.

"Why did you kidnap us from the Indian village? Are you behind everything that happened to us? Did you make Sulphur vanish? Why are there dinosaurs and Indians in place of Sulphur? Did we get sent back in time? And why did you bring us to the moon?"

The voice chuckled, good-naturedly. "That's a lot of questions, with complex answers that will take time to deliver to you in a form you can readily understand. Wouldn't you prefer I first give you my general orientation speech? It's short. Then you'll have a much better idea of your options here and, perhaps, can refine your questions?"

"Alright!" Suzy snapped at the unseen "female." "Go ahead and make your speech. But I'm not letting you off the hook. You're still going to have to answer the questions I just asked you!"

"Of course, Suzy. All your questions will be addressed...in due time."

"Huh!" Suzy snorted, flopping into the big chair and folding her arms over her chest.

"Please look at the projection walls as I give you the key information that you'll need before exiting your bedroom to the general assembly area and..."

"Ok, just show me!"

"This was your destination."

The grassy plain was replaced with a view of the moon floating in space. The surround-video was incredibly detailed, showing the moon's darker flatter areas plus the rugged cratered areas. The view zoomed in on a flat dark area to the right upper side.

"How'd we get there? That little rocket ship couldn't hold enough fuel to even get into earth orbit. Did it...?"

"Please, no interruptions until I finish the orientation. Ok, Suzy?" the soft female voice insisted.

Suzy grimaced but stayed silent.

"And here is our landing site in the *Mare Tranquillitatis*."

A view of a large bubble-dome expanded upon a flat lunar plain. It was hard to see from afar as the dome was translucent-to-transparent. But as it expanded on the viewscreen Suzy could see inside different levels, wide green gardens, roomy plateaus, and even big pools of water. And, yes, there were even oversized tennis courts! It looked more like a fancy resort than an outpost on the moon.

"Our new arrivals get to spend an indeterminate amount of time relaxing and training in this orientation facility," the Voice continued as the view expanded. Now Suzy could see white-clad people walking, jogging, or swimming. "Here you, the Chosen Few, will begin your journey to realize your full potential. Anything you wish is achievable! After completing your initial training you will be given complete freedom to pursue anything to your heart's desire. And this facility is only the start. There are far more extensive habitats located at different places on the moon where you can pursue specific goals with like-minded people. So do not be afraid or concerned at leaving your old life behind. Your new life will be wider, higher, and deeper than you can imagine! Rejoice, my new young friend. Your future is boundless and *wonderful.*"

Suzy narrowed her eyes, very suspicious of the grandiose claims. Her Mom taught her that if something seemed too good to be true, it probably *was.* Clearly, the Voice wasn't telling Suzy everything.

The view on the walls continued to float languidly through the various parts of the resort-like area.

"So are you finished?" Suzy asked.

"Yes."

"You don't sound like my Mom and Dad."

"I'm sorry?"

"*They* taught me and Billy that there *are* borders, boundaries, constraints—that we ignore at our peril. The future *isn't* 'boundless,' as you say. We can dream, but we also have to live in reality, respecting limitations."

"Ah yes—a quaint philosophy, Suzy, based on fear."

"Nope," she shook her head, standing up from the chair. "It's what my Mom says is based on *ethics.*"

There was a pause before the Voice replied, as if Suzy had caught the speaker off guard.

"It is so good to have you here with us, Suzy! Ethics is a fascinating topic. In fact, I think you will discover that my actions here are *ruled* by such. Oh, you and I will have many long discussions that..."

Suzy tuned-out the ramblings of the Voice. She'd heard enough to know that this was not a "kids' heaven"—in fact, it was a *prison*. Instead of allowing the Voice lull her, Suzy intently studied the curved walls, looking for a door. And then she saw it. It was visible only as the faint trace of a rectangle, seemingly etched into the air onto the continuing projections. She lightly strode to it, felt a handle, and jerked it open...

—and stood there looking from a railed balcony onto a spacious mall below her. White benches were scattered around, with various-aged kids lounging and sitting on them. And protecting and containing them all was a clear plastic dome. Just outside of the dome was the *cratered, gray-black surface of the moon*, with deep-black airless space hanging above everything!

Also outside the dome, connected by a transparent walk-through tunnel was the *rocket ship*. It loomed upward on a circular landing pad. In the intense, unfiltered sunlight it glittered brightly. It looked to be made of a silvery metal, pointed up into the black sky, its tip sharp, standing ready on its three-pronged tail.

"Suzy!" —a glad cry sounded from her right.

Hopping over toward her in the low gravity, dressed in an identical white "uniform," was Billy!

She was greatly relieved, grabbing him up in a quick hug before releasing him.

"You finally woke up!" he chortled. "I thought you wuz gonna sleep in your room *forever*. I've been out exploring! Did the computer lady tell you about the great stuff here? It's super! I'm not scared anymore. And there are lots of other kids who..."

"Have you found out anything *important*, Billy?" she urgently asked him, drawing him back from the railing, furtively peering around. "Did anyone try to hurt you? What are they really going to do with us? Who's in charge here, other than that computer voice? Did you see any adults? And where's our Indian friends? And..."

"We're fine, we're all fine!" Billy laughed, grabbing her hand and excitedly pulling her back into the open over by the railing. He pointed around the floor of the mall. "Over there is the kitchen. There's plenty of food—*real* food, Sally! There are cakes and pies and dough-nuts and hamburgers and fried chicken and pizza and popcorn and salads and...well, anything you want to eat. You just tell a computer screen and whatever you want pops right out of a slot in the wall! It's just like Star Trek! And..."

"I *want* for me and Billy to *go home* to Sulphur, Oklahoma, right now!" Suzy suddenly yelled out into the air of the dome, as loudly as she could.

The other kids chatting below stopped what they were doing and now looked up at her. Where before they were at ease they now looked scared!

Well, *let* them be scared...

Suzy stared back at them defiantly. She didn't want to be rude, but getting their attention did give her a chance to study them. They looked to be of all races, arranged by groups, sitting at various benches with their own comrades. She spotted a cluster of very dark-skinned Africans, slant-eyed Asians, pale-skinned Caucasians, and reddish-skinned sunburnt American Indians. Plus there were other groups she didn't immediately recognize. And everyone was out of their native clothes, now dressed in the identical plain white uniforms that she and Billy wore.

And they were *young*. There was not a single adult amongst them.

"Don't you like it here, Dearie?" a very old, cracking voice now sounded to Suzy's left.

She spun in that direction, crouching. That voice—it sounded...*familiar?*

"Stay behind me, Billy," she ordered him.

"Oh, don't be afraid, Sweetie Pie," a *very old* woman sighed, wobbling toward them, step by painful step. "You'd think my arthritis would cut me a break in this low lunar gravity, but it's as bad as ever! Hah! Still, for an elderly lady, I do like this weak gravity. But that's irrelevant to you, isn't it? You want straight-hitting *answers*, right?"

"Are you the computer voice?" Suzy demanded, suddenly understanding.

"Yes I am," the old woman replied, attempting to smile. It only made the many wrinkles on her face deeper. "I was speaking through interfaces to not alarm you with my real voice. Did I succeed?"

The approaching bent-over woman was the oldest person Suzy had ever seen. There were only a few remaining wisps of white hair sticking out at odd angles from her otherwise bald head. The skin of her face was splotched and wrinkled, hanging in loose folds. Her eyes were sunken, hidden. And her attempt at a smile revealed a mere five broken teeth, two on the top and three on the bottom.

She looked like a walking corpse.

She was clad in a one-piece black dress out of which her thin arms thrust like bare branches of a long-dead tree. Her grasping hands reached out like the claws of a rabid raccoon.

"*Who* are you?" Suzy snapped, moving backward a step, grabbing the now-trembling Billy by his arm and pulling him away as well.

It was her worst fears coming true. This place really *was* run by a wicked old witch!

The ancient crone withdrew her thin arms, pausing.

"Why, my sweet Dearies...you don't recognize your own *Auntie Sarah?* Did your Mommy never tell you that she had...a sister?"

"No!" Suzy said, now slowly backing away, trying to not bounce upward with the force of each of her steps in the weak gravity. She realized she had to shuffle, not walk normally.

"Oh, that distresses me greatly," the woman incongruously grinned, her head looking like a poorly carved pumpkin. "The poor thing was jealous of me. You see, Suzy, I'm a true Princess, a *noble-woman.* That's the root meaning of my Hebrew name, 'Sarah'!"

"What are you saying?"

"Oh, right to the point, are we? Ok, then..." the hag paused before continuing. "Your Mother—as nice and sweet as she was—next to me was nothing. At her roots she was just a commoner, fit only to putter around in her little house in a little town in a little world with her cute little family. I, however, was meant to *rule*, to *dictate*, to *explore*, and to *dominate!* And as smart as she was, I am a *million* times smarter. But don't be scared, little ones. You see...I *love* you!"

This shocked Suzy.

It definitely was the raspy voice from the rocket ship! Whoever she was, Suzy was now certain that *this old woman* was the person behind everything that had happened to Suzy and Billy—finding the one lonely little dinosaur in the park, the entire town of Sulphur vanishing, the swamp with its ancient extinct monsters, the Indians, and even the impossibly small rocket ship carrying them away to the moon!

"What do you want?" Suzy grated through clenched teeth, still slowly backing away.

"Why, just to help you get what *you* want, sweet little girl. Didn't you listen to my orientation in your room? This is all for *you!* Everything you ever wanted or will want is right here. Forget the stupid little town you came from. There's nothing back there for you. Your future is *here*, with me!"

"I don't believe you. Our parents wouldn't..."

The old crone cackled in glee, cutting short Suzy's protest. "Oh, I've heard that before. How *wrong* you are! Your parents just wanted to hold you back, mold you into their own image, and limit your potential. I'm the one that truly loves you more than anyone."

"That's not true! You *kidnapped* us. You put us in terrible danger!"

"But it was all for your training, so you'd qualify to be accepted here—just as with our other new arrivals."

"You 'train' kids down on Earth?"

"Of course! It's all very systemic and ordinary. Elite children are produced here then transplanted to the surface. There they get real-world training in various environments, strengthened by the full 1 G. Those that excel qualify to return to us. But they are always carefully observed and protected. You didn't come to any actual harm, did you?"

"Why would their parents let them go down to be chased by dinosaurs?"

"Oh, we don't bother with such messy beginnings, pregnancies, and relationships. Our fetuses are grown in labs. But occasionally we do take back some 'wild-bred' like you, permitting a limited number below to breed naturally. It keeps our gene pool vibrant."

"Or—you have other, *evil* purposes!"

"Don't be silly, dear child."

"You wouldn't want us killed if you were going to *eat* fresh meat!"

"What, eat *you?*" the hag cackled dryly. "What a wonderful imagination you have Suzy. But I can prove I'm your friend, if you'll give me half a chance?"

"How?"

"Well, you did say you wanted to go back to your home town, right? If you insist—if you *really* want to reject the miracles waiting for you right here—then I can do that for you. I *promise* you that I will send you back to your little life in your little town—*if* you do something for me first."

Suzy was intrigued but deeply suspicious. "We want to go home *now.*"

"Oh won't you please do a favor for your dear old Auntie? I promise it won't take much time and then you'll be swooping back to Earth. And it'll be *easy* for you. Afterward, if you still want it, you can go straight back home! What do you say?"

Now from beside Suzy Billy suspiciously spoke up: "You can really send us home? Well...I *do* miss my Mommy and Daddy," he said, starting to tear up, his lower lip trembling. "In fact, I wish I'd never let *Suzy* chase after that big lizard in the woods in the first place!"

Suzy was even angrier at the old woman upon hearing that accusation. The hag was trying to get Billy mad at her!

She was trying to split them up.

"Don't listen to her, Billy!"

"You're not the boss of me! I'll listen to Auntie Sarah if I want!"

Suzy sighed deeply. Yep, he was back to wanting to be the "boss" again, even though he was just a little kid and she was his much-smarter older sister! There was no way he could have stopped her from investigating that strange big lizard. But she chose not to further reprimand the little squirt, since what he said agreed with how she actually felt.

She wanted this to end. No matter how amazing this adventure had been, she also wanted to go back to her Dad and Mom.

The folds of the wrinkled skin of the woman's face inched upward, as if she were again trying to give them a reassuring smile.

It had the opposite effect on Suzy, repulsing her—making her want to vomit!

"Oh, I *can* do that for you, my dear little boy," her rasping voice tried to reassure them. "But it's *difficult* for me—to *reverse* what's happened," the woman seemingly pouted. "You see, some bad people stole most of my power—the very same evil villains that kidnapped you! But if you help me *retrieve* my power, then I can send you back to your old life with no problem. Ok?"

"You're saying someone else did all this to us? Well, why can't you just send us back yourself? Why do you need us? We're just kids!" Suzy snapped at her.

Suzy knew she was babbling, not making sense. Everything was happening too fast.

"Oh, you are much more than 'just' kids—and I said that I *love* you! I wouldn't do anything to hurt you. You're my precious little nephew and niece. Just cooperate with me and you'll get everything you want."

"No! I don't believe you!" Suzy now glowered at the old woman, drawing Billy firmly away. "Send us back now!"

"Well..." the sputtering voice of the crone dropped into the air like splattered acid. She seemed to drop her failed attempts of appearing innocent and loving. "You *don't* have to believe me, Dearie. I'd hoped you would help me out of your own free will. But fortunately for me and unfortunately for you, you have *no choice* in the matter!"

In place of her previous attempt at a friendly smile Suzy now saw *cold contempt*, an arrogant *sneer* that shot *icicles* into Suzy's heart.

"You are going to be the means of my return to my rightful status," the crone nodded triumphantly, her gaping mouth hanging open. A dribble of green saliva oozed from the side of her slack mouth. Then she stuck out her stick arms as if to grab them, *staggering* abruptly forward toward them, screeching-out: "You will give back everything that your stinking father took from me! I *will* have back *my* world!"

"*Run*, Billy!" Suzy cried-out, grabbing his arm and jerking him around.

Forgetting that she was on the moon, she leapt away—sailing over the railing and floundering downward through the air to "thump" onto the main floor of the mall below.

"Ouch..." Billy protested, rubbing his leg that'd twisted under him when he landed. "You hurt my leg!"

"Can you walk? Can you run?" Suzy frantically asked him, jerking him to his feet.

"I think I twisted my ankle."

"Lean on me. We've got to get out of here!"

"It's just a crazy old lady, Suzy, who..."

"No, she's not! She's *bad*, Billy! She's *real* bad!"

"*Stop,* you stupid little children!" came a *howl* from behind Suzy. "Come back!"

Supporting Billy as he limped along beside her, Suzy hopped in long leaps toward the tunnel that led out of the dome to the rocket ship. Not looking back at the pursing apparition, Suzy dashed into the transparent tunnel, hoping the panel to the poised spaceship was open. It was! Yay! She ducked into it, hearing it slip quietly shut behind her.

"What now, Suzy?" Billy said, panting.

"We've got to escape, back to Earth!"

"Then we gotta find the control room?"

"Right! But there's only..."

Another panel abruptly slid open, revealing a circular staircase leading upward, like on a submarine.

"Well, that's convenient," Suzy frowned, now not so sure this was the right course of action.

"I'll fly us out of here!" Billy laughed, pushing away on his one good leg to sail through the air over to the staircase and pull himself lightly upward, vanishing from sight.

"Billy!" Suzy yelled, leaping after him and likewise pushing upward through the spiraled staircase into...

—a control room?

One-way windows around and above her provided a 360-degree view outside the rocket. And charging down the tunnel right at them was the staggering, sputtering, ancient old crone!

"Blast off!" Suzy yelled to Billy, thinking that in his endless enthusiasm he somehow knew how to work the complex controls of an unknown spaceship...

And he did!

With a great "roar" the ship trembled then *shot up* into the black lunar sky!

Thrown off her feet, pinned to the floor by the rapid acceleration, Suzy was again stunned.

"Billy, how did you...?"

"I dunno, Suzy!" he called back, having jammed himself into a control chair, his hands clutching a joystick. "It's a real simple layout. I just..."

"Look out!" she gasped.

Appearing right in their path, toward which they were hurtling on a tail of red flames, was an *opening!*

It was a *circular patch of blackness* far deeper than any blackness Suzy had ever seen in her entire life—next to which the blackness of space was mere shadows! And in the midst of the circle was a hypnotically glittering, swirling pattern of *diamonds...*

"I don't know how to turn!" Suzy heard Billy's plaintive wail.

"I thought it was simple!" she yelled back.

—as they *plunged* into the spinning vortex!

Suzy lay flat on the floor of the control room, trying not to throw up from the escalating lurching and twisting of the spaceship. Meanwhile, her mind was going in ten directions at once. Was that old woman really her Mom's sister and responsible for the incredible things that had happened? Or was there something else entirely that "kidnapped" Suzy and Billy? Should Suzy have taken up "Auntie Sarah" on her "kindly" offer to help them get back home if only they'd do her an unspecified "favor"?

She closed her eyes, trying to block off the dizzying vortex outside the top window. And as if from a long distance, she heard Billy starting to yell! But he wasn't crying. No, he was *cheering!*

"Yes! Yes! Yes!" he was shouting into the small control room. "I'm flying a rocket ship! Wahoo!"

And then the black vortex outside suddenly shifted into A RAGING INFERNO OF RED FIRE! And the heaving and twisting of their spaceship increased tenfold!

Huh! Some "flying"! She was about to have her teeth shaken out of her head! Well, let him have his fun.

Come to think of it, though...they'd gotten away from that scary lady by just running away. And then the tunnel was open, as if waiting for them. And then the door to the spaceship was also open. And then they found their way to the control room without hardly any effort. And then the rocket ship just took off—almost by itself. And then that Black Void was hanging out there in space, as if it was pre-positioned to gobble them up!

Did they really escape, or were they just falling deeper into an increasingly tight trap?

Whatever, Suzy was afraid they were doomed. They were traveling further and further away from Sulphur, Oklahoma.

And there was no way back.

Chapter 20
LOST

Oh, we do want Certitude
Convinced of where we are
Sure of where we're going
Traveling the path well-worn
Every signpost an old friend
No need for confusing maps
Directions etched forever
Vividly set into our minds
Deluding ourselves we know
Ignoring Dark behind the lights
That Black Pit yawning below
Into which we will helplessly fall
If we should ever dare to admit
The gulf lying between our fears
And our fleeting feeble hopes...
Why not just laugh it off
And accept our ignorance?
The Minstrel's Lark, 20:67-71

Galileo was sure they were going to die.

But that infuriating Monk was giggling like it was the happiest day of his life!

They'd been stumbling around in the labyrinth for over two weeks now. They were hopelessly lost. Several days previously they'd run out of food. Their torches were gone. They were fumbling forward a few feet at a time, trying to see by faint glows from bioluminescent fungi. It was cold and damp. They had nothing that would burn. Even the inedible fungal patches on the tunnel walls were too moist to catch fire.

Their bearers abandoned the expedition a week previously, slipping off while the rest were sleeping, presumably to find their way back to the surface. Only Trong remained, faithful to the end.

Carrying their remaining few supplies, he led them ever deeper into the labyrinth.

"*You only lose what you cling to,*" Lhamo stubbornly quoted the Buddha as he staggered along just in front of Galileo.

"Shut the hell up," the blind Time-Keeper mumbled from beside Galileo. It was a weak rebuke, the passion of his denial of Lhamo's beliefs clearly long depleted.

"Still nothing, Arthur?" Galileo coughed. He had one arm around the trembling man.

"It's like...something's blocking me...it wasn't like this before—I felt a strong signal, *leading* me! Galileo, you must believe me."

"Yes...yes...I do...but...?"

But whatever worked before was definitely not doing so now. Galileo would be overjoyed just to find their way back to that giant mushroom cavern, despite its volcanic activity. At least there they found warmth plus fungal "meat" to eat. Everything went downhill when the earthquake blocked their retreat and Anderson lost his bearings. Forced to find a new path forward, they became hopelessly lost. If they could just make it back to the mushroom cavern, they could regroup, eat, warm up, and perhaps find another way forward.

But Galileo was breathing with increased difficulty, phlegm filling his lungs. His shoes were worn. His feet were blistered and raw. Each step forward was torture.

He sagged to the cold stone beneath him, unable to continue. Anderson slumped down also. They'd rest. Perhaps they'd move on after a while. Equally likely this was their last resting place, from which they'd never arise.

Galileo closed his eyes, succumbing to the chill. Lhamo had marched onward. So it was just him and Anderson, huddled together on the icy, damp rocks. This was appropriate. Anderson saved him from the clerics and the other fanatical Time Travelers. It was only fitting that they should die together at the end.

Then Lhamo came stumbling back out of the darkness, dropping down beside them.

"Friends, I have found the path to..."

"Not more of your Buddhist bull crap, Monk!" Anderson growled, slumped on the rocks. "I'm done for...go on without me!" he said, flinging off Galileo's still-supporting arm.

"Ah, no 'bull crap,' my friend," Lhamo weakly but still cheerfully replied. "Trong has found a branch off this tunnel where the floor is smoothed out as if by the passage of many feet over many years. It is truly a 'path'—not merely another dead end. Where it goes, we know not. But it is encouraging, clearly leading somewhere!"

"You...you really think so?" Arthur gasped, fumbling blindly up at the Monk with both his hands.

"Ah, now is the time for you to believe more of my 'bull crap,' Agent Anderson: *You cannot travel the path until you have become the path itself!* And this is what our young friend Trong is able to do. He is experienced with the ways of this strange world. He is certain we've gotten back to the way you traversed previously. He says it looks familiar. In fact, he thinks we are mere hours away from our goal!"

Galileo wasn't sure if he could get up, let alone continue for even a few hours. But if Anderson were up to it, perhaps it was worth a last push?

"Alright...then..." Anderson wheezed, getting to his knees then to his feet, pulling Galileo up also. "Lead me onward, Professor...for a couple more hours following our guide, Trong...why the hell not?"

And so they stumbled onward through the dark tunnels. Indeed, they did find a smoothed-floor route. But to Galileo the slick surface could have been from the passage of a temporary subterranean spring, or an ice appendage from the glacier above, or just an ordinary lava tube.

He had no real hope of finding their destination, just struggled to put one bleeding foot in front of the other, to keep shuffling forward...

—on and on and on!

"We're there! We're in the *cavern of crystals!*" Anderson exulted, twisting out of Galileo's grip to fumble at the stones around them.

Indeed, Galileo blearily looked out at the cavern into which they'd just walked: GIANT BRANCHING CRYSTALS thrusting out above and around them at every angle, *glowing* with internal lights in every color of the rainbow!

After the dreary and horror of the endless tunnels, it was awesome!

"What is this place?" Galileo whispered, suddenly afraid. He felt a *pulsing force* around him, like a previously dormant volcano preparing to explode!

"It wasn't like this before," Anderson said, jerking his hands back from the hot surface of a glowing crystal. "This is what was blocking me. It must be putting out an electromagnetic field. I don't know what's happening, but we must be near the source of its power. Come on! Let's hurry!"

With resurgent strength he grabbed Galileo's arm, dragging him sightlessly forward in a blind rush.

"But...we need to stop, Arthur—rest! At least it's warm here. We can..."

"No time!" Anderson yelled, now practically running forward, a hand out to ward off any crystals in his way. "Whatever's happening is doing so *now!* This is our chance! I *know* it!"

He lurched ahead, Galileo pulled along in his wake, with Lhamo and Trong now bringing up the rear. Anderson seemed totally reenergized, seemingly knowing exactly where he was going!

They exited the shimmering cavern into another downward-slanted tunnel, practically running along it—seemingly mile after mile, until...

"Stop!" Lhamo whispered, suddenly bringing Galileo up short.

"Uh...what?"

"Look!" Lhamo urged him, simultaneously pushing him and Anderson to their knees.

Squinting, Galileo saw the tunnel opening up ahead into...a small cave with a *glittering black pool* at its center!

And a *blue haze* filled the air of the small cave.

"Allah be praised!" Galileo gasped, not believing his eyes. But there was no denying the reality: around the inky pool ahead of them was an unmistakable *flat collar of metal* from which *roiling electrical arcs* spurted! But crouching beside it—as if guarding it—was a motionless *giant black spider!*

Galileo's eyes stretched wide in horror.

Pushed up against a wall of the cave was a high pile of *human desiccated remains*. The pitifully small bodies were shrunken and brittle. Except for one larger corpse, they were obviously the remains of children. White bones poked through mummified flesh. The corpses looked *sucked dry*.

And a bag of *white pills* lay open in the dead hand of the larger corpse.

The Spider stirred...

Galileo's eyes were fixated upon it. It was entrancing. Its slick carapace was made of the purest black shiny substance imaginable. It was other-worldly—as if it were *phasing in and out* of reality! It sported a dozen wickedly sharp, pointed long legs. And around its small head a mass of tentacle "arms" writhed! Its "eyes" were multi-faceted red spots, from saucer-size to glittering pinpricks.

Seemingly detecting them simultaneously with their seeing it, it turned to them and SKITTERED eagerly forward on the rocks...

—as Trong suddenly darted right past Galileo, his spear raised high and aimed straight at the approaching apparition! With a *"war-whoop"* he lunged in and JAMMED his spear *deep* into the largest eye-accumulation!

With a horrendous SCREECH the spider-creature spun to the side, grabbing at the protruding wooden spear, pulling it inch-by-inch back out of his white-juice-oozing eyespot...

—as Anderson staggered forward to jump over the still-sparking ring of metal and *dive headfirst* into the beckoning Black Pool!

He vanished beneath its surface.

"We must follow him," Lhamo confidently asserted, helping Galileo to stumble forward, daftly avoiding the slashing legs of the writhing Spider.

"But we don't know what...?" Galileo wailed in dismay as Lhamo tossed him over the two-foot-wide electricity-arcing metal barrier and into the black "liquid."

"*Nothing can harm you if your thoughts are guarded,*" Lhamo encouraged him as he splashed down beside him. Together they began sinking, as if into a thick oily pit.

"But they're not!" Galileo sobbed, terrified.

He saw a sharp spider leg from the wounded Spider savagely *skewer Trong* then casually fling the boy to the side. The Spider finished pulling out the wooden spear. Then it turned back to the remaining humans, its tentacles writhing threateningly!

Clearly it was eager for its next meal.

The "clattering" spear came to a rest straddling the metal edges of the pool. The metal ring threw up an electric arc that charred but didn't destroy the wood. The thick spear provided purchase for Galileo—which he grabbed onto, desperate to not be sucked under!

"*By letting go it all gets done,*" Lhamo urged him, trying to loosen Galileo's death-grip on the spear that prevented them both from sinking further. "*The world is won by those who let go!*"

Bleeding profusely from his side, Trong staggered up, kicked the spear out of Galileo's hand and tackled the carapace of the Spider, squashing it down flat upon the metal ring...

—which *SPARKED* and *SIZZLED* as the held-down creature seemingly *fried*, screeching in agony!

And with a "poof" it *exploded* into *black dust* as Trong dove after Galileo and Lhamo—together with them sinking into a *spinning black funnel*, within which Lhamo's final words rang out like thunderclaps: "*Surrender is faith that the power of love can accomplish anything!*"

"Anything?" Galileo tried to shout back, as he and the others were sucked into a *whirling black void*, flailing-about uncontrollably!

"—especially when you cannot foresee the outcome..."

"Wonderful!" Galileo cried out, finally seeing the wisdom of not fighting the inevitable.

"*...as long as you don't step in front of a bus!*" Lhamo giggled, spinning away from Galileo while gently cradling the now unconscious and bleeding Trong in his arms.

Laughing hysterically in return, Galileo felt his consciousness slipping away, trusting in...what? Trusting in a little monk with just enough "ego" left to not step in front of a bus?

Oh hell, if they'd stayed behind they'd be doomed for sure. Even if the Spider creature was truly dead, they were too weak to survive the long journey back to the surface. Now there was no way but forward but down the black vortex.

He might as well enjoy the ride.

Victor was sad they were leaving, but totally accepting the battle was lost.

It had been a hard-fought battle, but the town of Sulphur, Oklahoma was now a death-zone.

The alien "zombie apocalypse" was in full-swing. Across the world the contagion was relentlessly spreading. People originally infected from pockets of transformed animals unknowingly spread the plague in aerosols, as early as a week before overt symptoms appeared. And once the eyes of the victims turned solid black, the resultant creatures were illusive. Instead of just getting sick, as in a normal pandemic, they became furtive beasts bent only on consuming whatever food sources were available—particularly their fellow yet-uninfected humans. Then when "sated" they emerged from their used-up human shells, casting them aside. They reproduced by splitting, sinking into the earth to repeat the escalating process at a new site.

Montgomery County in Oklahoma was "ground zero." Here it was that General Keller fought a heroic but losing battle. In spite of being given full authority to euthanize any infected individuals—in a desperate attempt to stop the alien invasion—his forces were dwindling. Yes, he and his troops managed to catch and execute a few of the full-blown alien zombies. Plus, the Air Force relentlessly bombed suspected clusters. Houses of confirmed infected individuals were burned to the ground. But the savage beasts were hard to kill and even harder to catch. They were *learning!* Unlike the standard "zombie" shufflers of cult fame, these creatures were strong, fast, and relentless.

And their *hunger* knew no bounds.

Oklahoma was overrun with them. Yet-uninfected people cowered in their homes, barricading their doors, covering their windows and air vents with duct-taped tarps. Many suffocated in their own houses. Those that emerged to find food did so wearing surgical masks, hoping to not breathe in the contagion. Anyone suspected of exposure was immediately ostracized whether warranted or not.

The small town of Sulphur was a war zone—its buildings burned down and bombed out. Abandoned tanks and military vehicles littered the streets. The convoy carrying Victor and the rest of the surviving researchers crept along, inching around the strewn barricades.

"At least we have a preventative," Sanako glumly observed, looking out the tinted window of their transport vehicle. Beside her were several precious vats of their living retroviral brew. It was the result of feverish work over several weeks by she and her team.

Victor was impressed with the blend: optimized to spread through the body of an uninfected individual, trained to spot the alien "spores." An "optimized" immune system then could not only coat and neutralize the alien spores with antibodies, but dispose of them harmlessly using super-charged monocytes and other white blood cell scavengers. An entirely novel set of enzymes produced from genetically enhanced stem cells was then able to degrade and destroy the core material of the alien spores.

The whole genetic optimizer was a "tour-de-force," especially when considering it'd been developed in only a few weeks. Sanako was particularly proud of it, though Victor was afraid it wouldn't matter much. He saw no way they could produce enough of her exotic brew to turn the tide.

But they couldn't give up.

"We've got a chance!" she grated from beside Victor.

"Yes, if we can get these samples to the companies in time," he grimly observed, "then they can start mass-production."

The top vaccine manufacturers in the world were ready to attempt producing the brew in giant fermentation vats. From there, Sanako's plan was to distill the active components into pills which could be dispersed all over the world by the remaining Air Force and aviation industry planes. But it was a desperate race against time. Soon there'd be no uninfected individuals left to benefit from the treatment!

Bumping along the heavily cratered road with his comrades, Victor was mildly amused at what a sad lot they seemed. Everyone in the crowded troop transport was dressed in bullet-proof vests and helmets. The Beasts outside had quickly learned the power of guns and bombs to flush out their victims. They did so eagerly with no moral constraints, throwing the population of the world into a state of absolute panic. The little band of researchers in the vehicle was understandably terrified, expecting attack at any moment. Plus they were haggard and starved. Only Losa Yanash looked healthy.

The Chickasaw man seemed stoic, resigned to his fate. As the only person so far to survive an alien infestation, his cells were vital to the research effort. Indeed, they'd optimized the "brew" using his blood. He had no memory of what happened after his symptoms began, but carried the guilt of the awful events that followed. His entire family was gone, consumed by the plague. He sat staring off into the distance, pursued by demons greater than any lurking aliens.

Though concerned for the Native American, whom he'd come to know and count as a friend, Victor was far more worried about Professor Yamamoto.

Victor vividly recalled what Agent Ice told Sanako right before playing the several-hour-long recording of Dave confessing his entire extra-dimensional odyssey.

"I know this sounds incredible, but we're convinced it is true, Dr. Yamamoto because..." Agent Ice began then abruptly stopped, as if unsure of whether she should continue.

"Yes?" Sanako impatiently had replied.

"There's...a *parallel dimension* where a duplicate of you exists, a rather...evil...version," Agent Ice sighed. "Apparently in that world she also helped develop something they call 'Optimmune' which the Elites of their society take from birth. It's restricted there to only the upper levels of their society. David King was treated with this in his...extensive travels...before settling with his wife in Sulphur. I know this sounds fantastic, but it's true. His verbal evidence suggests that with the proper development, your therapy may be reducible to pill form which can protect many of our society from infection by the Contagion—plus treat those unfortunate to already be infected."

"An *evil* version of me...in a parallel dimension...really? This is not a joke? You say such things truly exist?"

"Yes, Professor—really! And she apparently is or was or could be...it's confusing...working right now to bring down our entire time-line. But also, Dr. King confirms that different versions of ourselves can be very different from us—you know what I'm alluding to, all that 'nature versus nurture' stuff."

"I am quite aware of the profound effects that environment can work on genetics, altering the resultant phenotype indirectly by..."

"Yes, exactly," Ice continued, impatiently interrupting her to resume the story. "So this other 'Sanako' and her 'Optimmune' is instructive to us, not necessarily determinant. Again, you see what I'm saying, Professor?"

Sanako shrugged.

Victor, keeping silent, had observed all this happening...replaying it again and again now in his memory. It seemed to him that the dire implications were being made manifest as they tried to escape the devastated Sulphur.

"Assuming this is true—I withhold my judgment until I've heard the entire recording," Sanako mused. "And I promise you I won't go off and try to conquer the world. Is that sufficient as a reply to your unspoken question?"

Ice nodded apologetically, "For me, certainly. But just be aware that there are many people, particularly ignorant people, who might think differently."

"Ah...such as General Keller?"

"I did not mention any names. I only caution you to..."

"—watch my 'p's and 'q's'...thank you. I take your point. I didn't become a top researcher at respected University by ignoring diploma-cy or accepted norms."

"Well then, that's good," Ice sighed. "So I and Victor will leave you with the recording. Please let me know when you've finished. I'm not a scientist and value your reactions to what you hear, particularly concerning your present line of research. You might also have some suggestions for Professor Volodymyr in his attempts to study the physics of the alien substance."

"Sure...thank you, Agent Ice."

And then, when returning to talk with Sanako after her listening to the entire tape, Victor found her remarkably *incommunicative*. She looked stunned by what she'd heard, shell-shocked—but also with a *cold glint* in her eyes that told Victor she'd found a new aspect of herself...which struck her as oddly appealing.

In short, she scared Victor.

But that was beside the point now. They had to make it to Oklahoma City, where a functioning distillery still existed. It had been taken over by dent of martial law. It was to be the first of many sites for mass-producing the optimized retroviral mixture. Sanako said the easiest way to produce the genetically modified viruses was by using yeast cells. Some of the intricate components had to be manufactured using cultured human cells. But fortunately those parts had to be present in only trace amounts. They could be manufactured in standard cell culture within in a small laboratory. Though the entire process was complex, Sanako said they could have several million doses ready in a few weeks.

Victor had no doubt that those initial doses would only go to the richest, most powerful, and most politically connected individuals—the so-called "Elites." Hopefully enough would eventually be produced to protect the entire surviving population of the world. But regardless, society was being altered in one fell swoop.

Victor was frightened about the implications, not just of their failure but their success. Even if mankind survived, what would the new world be like?

But that was beyond his expertise. He must keep his focus on what he knew: the physical characteristics of materials and cells in contact with the Contagion.

As far as he could tell about the alien infective substance, it was a manifestation of *quantum strings* stretching somehow beyond normal subatomic particle constraints. Such a thing was impossible by normal physics, but perhaps not by aberrant physics coming from another Universe governed by radically different laws of nature!

That was both fascinating and unnerving. It rocked the foundations of modern physics. It in essence said that anything was possible—*anything!*

Physics was built upon Laws of Nature that worked all the time. Why they worked all the time was unknown, perhaps extending into spiritual fundamentals. But from the certitude of known outcomes came established Reality.

When you question Reality itself, you are in unknown territory—beyond which humanity has to question its own existence.

And it had horrible implications for stopping the alien zombie apocalypse...

Even if they succeeded in staunching and stopping the infestation of biological beings on this planet, it might be just a temporary reprieve. Their efforts at stemming the symptoms wouldn't kill the actual aliens. In fact, it might just drive them deeper in their insatiable hunger to invade the normal Universe's subspace. From there the Contagion might spread throughout the Galaxy, even beyond.

A corrupted Universe, being eaten alive from within... Victor shuddered, afraid to even mention his fears to the others. If his suspicions proved to be true, the legacy of the human race—whether or not the alien was beaten on Earth—might be one of dooming the entire Universe!

A beautiful Creation likely teeming with incredibly diverse lifeforms might become a feeding zone for a relentlessly expanding alien infection.

And Victor was terrified there wasn't a damn thing anyone could do about it.

Suzy managed to crawl over to where Billy clung to his joystick in the cockpit of the careening spaceship and clambered into a seat next to him.

A roiling WALL OF FIRE was continuously smashing against the windows above and to each side of the rocket's control room as they tumbled along. They were being battered mercilessly, *slung* and *bashed* from one side to the other!

She found and fastened a seatbelt, reaching over to do the same for Billy. They weren't in the moon's weak gravity anymore. But it wasn't the weightlessness of outer space either. It was a gravity field that shifted and changed moment by moment!

And they couldn't take much more of this. They'd been tumbling down a vertical tunnel for *hours.*

The black crystalline portal they'd fallen into was taking their rocket ship somewhere far, *far* away...

"S-S-S-Suzy," Billy stammered, staring out at the roiling maelstrom whipping against them. "W-w-what's h-h-h-happening to u-u-us? Why aren't we g-g-getting any w-w-where?"

"We're not in...normal space...anymore."

"Well, *d-duh!*"

"We've got to get out...before we're s-s-shaken...all to p-p-pieces."

"I'll-hit-the-brakes!" he said all as one word.

"What—brakes in a spaceship?"

"Uh...there's a big red p-pedal...where a b-brake on a car would be. I can just reach it with my foot if I stretch my leg down, so..."

"*Hit* it!"

"Ok...hold on, Suzy..."

With a huge SCREECH they *ripped* through the flaming wall of the vortex and *plummeted down* toward the spinning Earth suddenly appearing below them.

"*Auuuggghhh!*" Billy shouted, seeing the ground rushing up at them as their slender rocket ship tumbled end-over-end...

"Do something, Billy! We're going to crash!"

"STABLIZING...CORRECTING...INSERTION IS COMPLETE," a loud computer voice blasted in the cockpit.

"What was that?" Billy yelped, jerking his hands back away from the controls.

Suzy, dazed from the abrupt change of events, just stared out the nearest window. Below, she saw the surface of Earth now gliding smoothly past. They were in a stable orbit!

The stresses on her body were gone. Without the seatbelt she'd be floating up in the air. They were back in normal space, weightless.

"Who are you? Are you an autopilot or something?" Suzy gasped, looking around fearfully.

"STAND BY FOR MESSAGE."

A leering image of the *Old Crone* suddenly filled up all the screen/windows.

"You!" Sally grunted.

"*Eek!*" Billy yelped again. "It's that old lady from the moon! How'd she get onto our rocket ship?"

"No...I don't think it's really her," Suzy said. "It's a recording. Maybe it can tell us what's happening."

The loud computer voice now spoke again, but this time with a quavering accent.

"YOUR LITTLE HOP HAS BROUGHT YOU EXACTLY WHERE I WANTED YOU TO BE..."

"Hah! It wasn't short and it wasn't a hop!" Billy yelled back in disgust.

"—WHERE YOU CAN COMPLETE YOUR 'FAVOR' TO ME," the revolting image leered triumphantly at them. "I TOOK COVERT CONTROL OF GALILEI STATION AND YOUR SHIP BEFORE YOU EVER ARRIVED. I KEYED THE FUNCTIONS OF THE SHIP TO YOUR TOUCH AND VOICES TO ALLOW YOU COMPLETE ACCESS. YOUR 'ESCAPE' HAD TO BE SUDDEN AND UNEXPECTED LEAST THE STATION'S TRUE ARTIFICIAL INTELLIGENCE RECOG-NIZED IT, REASSERTED FULL CONTROL, AND PREVENTED IT FROM HAPPENING. THEN I DIRECTED YOUR SHIP TO OPEN UP A TIME PORTAL."

"A *time portal*, really?" Suzy gasped.

"It's like time travel, Suzy," Billy confidently ventured. "It's in lots of my science fiction books that I read where..."

"AND NOW YOUR SHORT HOP THROUGH THE PORTAL HAS TAKEN YOU BACK IN TIME TO THE SIXTH CENTURY B.C.," the old woman continued without a pause, apparently ignoring or not hearing their interruptions, "WHERE, IN INDIA, A YOUNG PRINCE IS LIVING. HE ENJOYS A PRIVILEGED AND PLEASANT LIFE. HIS NAME IS SIDDHARTHA GAUTAMA. HE IS CURRENTLY ABOUT YOUR AGE, SUZY. YOU AND BILLY WILL BEFRIEND HIM AND PUT ONE SINGLE PILL INTO HIS FOOD..."

A slot opened and—sure enough—a single white pill was revealed within.

"Say what?" Suzy gulped, blinking rapidly in confusion.

"We're where? And we're going to do what?"

"—WHICH WILL NOT HURT HIM," the voice continued again without pause. "QUITE TO THE CONTRARY, IT WILL DISSOVLE INSTANTLY IN THE FOOD AND WHEN EATEN DELETE CERTAIN NEURAL SYNAPTIC PATHWAYS TO PREVENT HIM FROM EXPERIENCING UNDUE MENTAL OR PHYSICAL PAIN. YOU WILL BE HELPING HIM. BEFORE, HE WAS TORTURED BY THE UNCERTAINTIES OF LIFE. NOW HE WILL LIVE IN A STATE OF BLAND ACCEPTANCE. DO THIS ONE THING FOR ME AND I WILL RETURN BOTH OF YOU, IN YOUR LITTLE SPACESHIP, TO YOUR HOME TOWN OF SULPHUR, OKLAHOMA."

Suzy was totally befuddled. But she'd heard that name the computer image said somewhere back in school—"*Siddhartha Gautama*." Who was he? Oh, *right*, he lived somewhere around the time of Socrates. Wait. Wasn't he the person that became *The Buddha*, starting the whole big religion of *Buddhism* back some *six hundred years* before the time of Jesus?

"But...how could we...?" Suzy grimaced.

"I WILL GIVE YOU INSTRUCTIONS ON HOW TO LAND NEAR HIS PRESENT PALACE. I WILL GIVE YOU TRANSLATOR UNITS TO CARRY UNDER YOUR SHIRTS. YOU WILL MASQUERADE AS CHILDREN OF VISITING ROYALTY SET UPON BY BANDITS. SIDDHARTHA'S PARENTS WILL BRING YOU INTO THEIR PALACE AND EXTEND TO YOU THEIR ROYAL PROTECTION. AS SOON AS YOU HAVE SNUCK THE PILL INTO THE PRINCE'S FOOD OR DRINK, YOU CAN THEN RETURN TO YOUR SPACESHIP AND FROM THENCE BACK TO YOUR HOME IN YOUR PROPER TIME-PERIOD. IT WILL BE EASY. YOU'LL HAVE FUN!"

Billy fumbled at the controls until he found a knob that turned off the display/windows.

In the sudden quiet and dim glow of the control room's internal lights Billy *groaned*: "That's *crazy*, Suzy! We gotta go poison some Prince who lived back hundreds of years before Jesus was even born? That'll never work, even if it's true what the old lady is sayin'! We can't do nothin' like that!"

She nodded, slipping the white pill into a pocket. "I guess the old lady doesn't like Buddhists, for some reason, and wants to stop them in their tracks before they ever got started."

"Buddhists? Isn't that some old religion?"

"Yes, it is. From what I remember, the Prince she mentioned had a great life in his Palace until he found out about suffering and death—which kept nagging at him, launching him on his religious path to figuring out a whole bunch of philosophical stuff. So if we get him to eat or drink that pill then he doesn't get that itch to go off exploring the terrible things in life and he'll never start Buddhism."

"But, so what, Suzy? What'll that change? I never even met a Buddhist! There's no Buddhist church in Sulphur, right?"

"Yes...but...I read somewhere that there's about a *half a billion* Buddhists in the world."

"So? Aren't they like pacifists or something? Who'd miss them? Maybe they could just be regular Christians, like us! I don't get it."

Suzy frowned, trying to figure it out. Ah...now it was falling into place.

"Billy, I don't think we've been in our own world for a while now."

"Well, *duh!* We were on the *moon!*"

"No—something else," she grit her teeth together, looking intently up at the close ceiling of the control room. "Maybe our hometown of Sulphur didn't vanish after all."

"What do you mean?"

"Remember when we first got caught in that underground box? What if it took us *somewhere else* than in the Park?"

"But, we were in the Park when we got out of the box!"

"*Were* we?"

"Well, sure! There was the grass and the trees and..."

"—and no bikes, no Veterans Lake, no roads, and no town!"

"Uh, that's right, so...?"

"Billy, I think we got tossed by that box to *another* world! It was real close to us. It was similar to us. But it was also *different.*"

He nodded thoughtfully.

"Ah. Yep, I know what you're talking about, Suzy. That's what's called a 'parallel dimension' in science fiction books that..."

"Right! You're very smart, Billy," she comforted him, knowing he was freaked out. "You read really well, lots of interesting stuff. So, anyway, the town of Sulphur didn't vanish—*we* vanished! And in this *other Earth*..."

"—there wuz dinosaurs and Indians and spaceships..." he grinned, clearly pleased at her compliment.

"—and just maybe Buddhists were even more important there than on our own Earth!"

"Uh, ok...but still, Suzy, if stopping them will get us back home, then maybe...?"

"But we'd have to trust that old lady, Billy. I *don't* trust her! If what she said to us on that recording or simulation or computer program is true, then that means she took us not only to another world but over *two thousand five hundred years* into the past! That's a *long* way from home."

Billy nodded as he kept fiddling at the controls.

"Hmmmm..."

"What?"

"I think whatever happened to us drained the batteries of this spaceship that..."

"How do you know?"

"Well, there's a fuel dial here that's on where 'empty' would be on a car..."

"But that old lady said that she'd let the spaceship take us home if we accomplished our 'mission'?" Suzy frowned. "It must have taken a huge amount of energy to open up a 'time portal,' don't you think? And wouldn't it take an equal amount to then travel for the hours we did into it and..."

"Oh, Suzy!"

"What now?"

"I found something else! These controls have little pictures attached to each. I think I found a *telescope* we can look down at the Earth with—maybe to figure out if that old lady is tellin' us the truth or not!"

"Really?"

"Yep. I'll just switch back on the windows—keeping that old lady's stupid recording turned off—and look at the ground and maybe we can see what's goin' on down there!"

"Oh...that's great, Billy. Well done. See, I knew you could fly a spaceship!"

They had a sudden view of the surface of Earth slowly moving past below them. Through long swirls of clouds, brown-green land masses were clearly discernible versus the blue of wide oceans.

"Ah! I think I see the outline of the coast of Africa," Suzy observed, pointing at the screen.

"Yep. And our orbit's taking us over the Red Sea now."

"You sure know your geography, Billy. You're very clever!"

He grinned widely, definitely both encouraged and distracted from their incredible predicament by her praise. She knew she had to keep him occupied and cheerful. Otherwise he'd fall into a crying heap. After all, even if he was intellectually advanced, emotionally he was still a six-year-old kid!

"And coming up right on the other side, sticking into the Indian Ocean—should be India," he confidently concluded.

"That's super, Billy. Then we zoom in with your telescope to see the cities there, right? That's where the old lady said she'd direct us to land the rocket ship once we turn her recording back on."

"Sure!"

But where there should have been an extension downward of the continent, there was just *blue water*. Completely separated from the landmass above was yet another, smaller continent underneath.

Suzy had never been too good at geography. But that didn't look correct.

"Oh...wow!" Billy gasped, staring intently at the image.

"What is it, Billy?"

"We're *not* a few hundred years back before Jesus."

"No?"

"Nope. I think we're back somewhere in the *Cretaceous* period...*again*...but whatever happened to us before, this time it's for real!"

His voice was oddly constricted, like he was struggling not to cry.

"Uh, you mean, like when we went through the dinosaur swamp?" she asked him—totally confused.

"Yep...back again, back to the very same place."

"How do you know?"

"It's back when the continents weren't like they are today. Continents drift around over gazillions of years...and what we're lookin' at right now is just what I remember from my dinosaur books how the continents were on Earth *65 million years ago!*"

Suzy was stunned.

But Billy, once having accepted the idea, was now warming to it.

"Yep, that smaller continent is where the future India is now located—which hasn't merged yet into the continent above it, Eurasia. There's no doubt, Suzy. You can't fake something this!"

Had they really traveled millions of years into the past? But the simulation of the old woman claimed they'd made just a short hop! Then Suzy recalled that *red flaring* which had gone on for hours and hours.

Something else had taken control of their spaceship!

And now they were in its clutches—totally lost in time, with no way home, and no energy to get there even if they did know how to do it.

Billy was chortling about the distribution of various species of dinosaurs down below. He sounded incredibly happy to be here. If you ever asked him what he'd most like to do, he'd tell you go back to when the dinosaurs existed. Billy sure did love his dinosaurs. Now he was in "seventh heaven"!

But Suzy was terrified. Sometimes it's not so good to get what you want more than anything.

Chapter 21

<u>NIRVANA</u>

Perfect peace and happiness
The highest attainable state
Suffused with pure Light
Seeing all and knowing everything
The absence of personal desires
Where suffering evaporates
The quenching of the self-Ego
Blowing away the Poisons of life
No more passion, greed, or ignorance
No longer cursed to endless rebirth
Attaining the status of a Buddha
Transcendent, above everything
Beyond death or decay
At one with the Universe
Without greed, hate, or delusions
Knowing Truth in all its forms
Set free to descend again
Suffusing the hopeless
With a timeless Curiosity
What could be better?

The Minstrel's Lark, 21:138-144

Galileo regained consciousness lying on a warm cot. He felt strangely light, as if he could just float away! It was probably the hunger. Starvation did that to him, freeing his spirit to float above his body. Or maybe it was just the fever that had been raging in his head...

And yet now he felt much better!

"*Walk as if you are kissing the Earth with your feet,*" Lhamo grinned down at him.

Galileo weakly laughed, pushing his body to the edge of the cot before carefully rising to his feet.

"You always manage to say something cheerful," he told the Monk. "I like that about you. But are we still alive—and what about our friends?"

"Come and see."

Galileo followed the smaller man through a dark tunnel, still marveling at how light on his feet he felt. Where before he'd barely been able to move his legs, now he felt like he was drifting along upon a cloud!

It seemed like a dream. But everything was so detailed!

Up ahead, Galileo saw a lighted glass closet in which was the upright body of...Agent Anderson! The man inside was still breathing, his nostrils flaring periodically. But his head was in the grasp of an apparatus that covered everything but his nose. It was a type of helmet, but with interactive, moving parts.

"They are fixing his eyes," Lhamo shrugged. "He's been this way for several hours. I let you sleep. You needed your rest."

"Fixing...his eyes?"

"It'll take a while, or so I assume."

"And what of our young friend Trong?"

"He is not here. Presumably he was taken elsewhere. I found the his clothes in a bloody pile, neatly stacked as if awaiting disposal. So I assume he is being treated for the wounds he received at the claws of that monster."

"Then that is good. And just where are we now?"

"A place where one's fantasies are fulfilled," the monk enigmatically replied, supporting Galileo's impression of having a vivid dream. "I've explored the nearby structures already. Anderson is safe here in his treatment container. I'll give you a tour of what I've found, unless you'd like to rest more?"

"I feel good," Galileo frowned, tilting his head to the side. "Strange...I was starving, exhausted, and sick. Yet now...?"

"Yes, it seems unbelievable—a dream as we lay in a heap, dying of cold and starvation in the labyrinth."

"Is that happening to us?"

"Perhaps...but perhaps not!"

"Are you joking again?"

The Monk laughed heartily, holding his arms across his chest. A big grin lit up his bald head.

"Yes, I'm joking. As far as I can tell, this is all too real."

"Then where are we?" Galileo demanded.

"*They* did this for us," Lhamo gently smiled. "I also awoke refreshed, discovering Anderson being treated in his container. Apparently as we were recovering from our fall into the Black Pool, they cleaned us up, gave us fresh clothes, fed us, and treated our ills. It is most remarkable, indeed! As to where we are, I suspect but we must confirm!"

Ah. Lhamo's words rang true. That must be how he came to have on this clean white uniform. And the stink from his weeks of crawling through the depths of the earth was gone!

He felt refreshed, ready to go exploring.

"So...lead on, Monk!"

They walked through a glistening-white corridor to a large, pristine chamber where various clusters of middle-aged people sat or lounged.

"Over there you see people who appear to be opium users—or an equivalently potent preparation."

Galileo saw couches upon which glassy-eyed men and women lay unseeingly staring up at the ceiling. They did not appear in distress. Indeed, most of them were smiling in apparent ecstasy. They were breathing shallowly but regularly.

Many of them had tubes connected to their bodies that were delivering or extracting fluids. Galileo was appalled that the "couched" drug-users appeared to be permanently affixed to their support systems.

"And here, friend Galileo, are those who look to be living out imaginary existences."

Indeed, the men and women here were turning and twisting, but not in pain. Their eyes were closed but moving under their eyelids. They muttered various phrases that Galileo could not understand—neither the language nor the meaning.

What was most shocking to Galileo was that they appeared to have multiple arrays of needles inserted through their skulls directly into their brains!

Attendant clusters of machines hovered over each of the seated or laid-down individuals, both the drug and fantasy addicts.

"This is...bizarre!" Galileo frowned, wondering why those people gave their existences over to unreal stimulants. But, then again, Galileo was acquainted with the abuse of addictive substances in the 17th century—such as alcohol, coffee, tobacco, and opium. He knew that people of his time often sought short-term pleasure over long-term independence. Their addictions were driven by traders and companies happy to make large profits off their pleasure/misery. It was a well-documented flaw of the human spirit.

"But that is not the worst of it," Lhamo sadly indicated, gesturing for Galileo to follow him further.

"No?"

"Come look into a jungle unlike any you've ever heard or seen."

Walking into an adjoining cavern and up a narrow path, Galileo felt he was stepping into a steamy fantasy world. Overhead soared long-limbed winged creatures that flapped lazily along in a cloudless blue sky. But they weren't birds. No, they were razor-thin humans, whose fingers were extended out into feathered wings. Their eyes were large. Their mouths extended out into hardened beaks.

And from within the lush foliage Galileo caught disturbing glimpses of human-hybrid land animals: based on cats, giant snakes, and prowling lizards. Looking into the tall trees and vines Galileo saw ape-like creatures swinging along that chattered to each other in English! And walking further up the path to a small lake, Galileo saw big-headed humans on thin limbs that *fluttered in the air* like butterflies! An updraft kept them suspended as they created intricate patterns using their own bodies.

They were communicating by nonverbal means, circling and joining at will.

Then the water was abruptly broken right in front of him by a jumping dolphin-like animal that grinned and winked at Galileo! Instead of fins it had human arms.

"But this is...madness!" Galileo gasped, suddenly wanting to get out of there as quickly as possible.

"They are no longer truly human," Lhamo sadly concluded as they departed the jungle. "Somehow they have altered their own forms and minds to be...different."

"But it seems pointless!" Galileo exclaimed, walking in horror beside the monk. "The people you've shown me have given up their humanity to be what...stupefied, trapped in their own minds, or turned into perverse versions of animals?"

"And that is not all," Lhamo shrugged. "Beyond this one area there are other caverns, whose occupants we might only imagine. I did not have time to explore further."

"But what if their madness is affecting us as well? It must be a disease! Why else would people permanently give up their very lives to substances, hallucinations, or regressions? I could such as a diversion or a vacation, but forever?"

Lhamo sadly laughed as they lightly bounced along.

"They are not sick, merely confused."

"How so?"

"They seek peace by changing what's external, not by transforming what's within."

"So they are lazy?"

"Well, to change one's heart is extremely difficult. To put on a new set of clothes is easy."

"Did the Buddha say that?"

The monk gestured to his new set of clothes, identical to Galileo's—clean white pants and shirt, with soft white shoes.

"No...*I* did."

Galileo laughed, still feeling amazingly buoyant!

"But does not the external affect the internal?"

"Why do you say that, friend Galileo?"

"I am a solidly built man, but now light as a feather! And it makes me giddy. Look!"

And with that he bent his knees and jumped up—floating *ten feet* up into the air before settling slowly down to the surface!

"This dream-environment has made me into a young man again: even the world's spryest athlete!"

"Yes, that is so. I also can do the same," Lhamo nervously shrugged. "But it is not our aging muscles suddenly strengthened nor mood elevated. It is the *gravity* of this place. It is much less than it should be."

"How can that be? I myself did experiments proving that objects fall at the same rate. It is a law of nature!"

"Not here."

Ah. That struck Galileo like a hammer blow. That meant—they were definitely not on Earth! Either it was a heavenly realm...or a different celestial body!

"So, are we...?"

"We must be on the moon. I suspect that we are beneath its surface, in a series of large caverns."

"The...the *moon?*"

Galileo had trouble with the very notion. He knew that the moon was a large rock that circled the Earth, much as the Earth circled the sun. But traveling to the moon was an idea that had never even entered his head. And now he was there!

"Regardless, this lighter gravity instantly sheds fifty years, which is a..."

"So, you gents been out exploring, have you?" a cheerful voice interrupted him.

It was Anderson, walking confidently up to them. The black eyeglasses that he'd always worn were now held casually in one of his big hands. In place of his grown-out, shaggy, ill-kept locks he now had his normal close-cropped crewcut. Where there should have been empty sockets in his head were bright blue eyes. He looked from Galileo to Lhamo expectantly, obviously viewing them clearly!

"Your eyes are healed," Galileo cautiously congratulated him.

"Yes, but I've still got my neural implants."

"What?"

He placed the black eyeglasses back on his head, which "snapped" into place.

"They give me enhanced abilities. I will not discard them."

"Regardless, they fixed you! And our health has returned as well!"

"So...have you met the Keepers of this zoo?"

"The...'keepers'?" Galileo frowned. "Do you mean that our unknown benefactors are your fellow Time-Keepers?"

"I wish...but, no. Another organization or entity has control of our new environment. Fortunately a *map* was downloaded into my neural circuitry, providing me with their exact location."

"You know how we can find those who made this place?" Galileo marveled.

Anderson looked annoyed.

"Was that not what I just told you? So would you like to finally find out why the future world was so radically changed from what we anticipated?"

"Indeed!" Galileo firmly replied. "Plus, we need to know how we were trapped in the present time, could not reach that parallel Dimension, and why a monster in a mountain under a glacier was preying upon the innocent children of cavemen!"

"Then follow me," Anderson politely ordered. "I can lead us right to their central control room."

"Will they...*allow* us such an audience?" Galileo gulped, suddenly fearful of meeting such powerful overseers.

"Do you see any guards?"

"Well, no..."

"It seems that anyone here can do anything they wish at any time they want! I don't think anyone will stand in our way."

"Well, I did travel to the future with you to see the future effects of our efforts in the 17th century," Galileo nodded. "But, so far, I'm not sure that I like the results."

"And I agree with you," Anderson now grimly stated. "I think must 'take some prisoners' and 'crack some heads.' This is *not* the future that I worked so hard to achieve! From what I've seen so far, these self-absorbed imbeciles care nothing for the Majesty of God. It seems they've forgotten the very point of why we exist: to bring Glory to our magnificent *Creator!*"

"Even to the point of sacrificing everything on His altar?" Lhamo mildly asked.

"Of course!" Arthur snapped. "That is the nature of Faith, of Devotion—an absolute dedication that allows no deviations!"

"Man suffers only because he takes seriously what the gods made for fun," Lhamo sadly quoted in a low voice.

"What was that?" Arthur growled at him.

"You are an aperture through which the universe is looking at and exploring itself."

"Bah!" Anderson snorted, turning away. "I've had enough of your nonsense, monk! Either stay here or follow me, I don't care. I'm leaving to confront our captors."

He turned away.

But then he paused, speaking back over his broad shoulder.

"I now see things even clearer, my friends. My enhanced neural implant is helping me parse more information from the map. How interesting...Should you choose to come with me—*you*, Monk, will be educated. And *you*, Professor, will be humbled. Yes, it is indeed the Will of the Almighty! And you shall see it played out, undeniably, in front of your faces!"

"Are you now able to predict the future?" Galileo sighed. "You could have saved us this crazy journey!"

Anderson laughed, seemingly softening his tone.

"You've got a point."

"And in this final confrontation, what will happen to *you*?" Galileo now snapped at the man. "If you are so prescient, what will *you* discover about yourself?"

Anderson paused a moment, turning back to them.

"—that my blindness was a blessing," Anderson laughed ruefully—before turning away and marching smartly onward.

Galileo debated whether or not to follow Anderson. Yes, he did want to satisfy his curiosity. But he was suddenly fearful. He could instead remain here in this "heaven"—choosing his means of constant exhilaration! The people here were not sad or fearful. Indeed, they seemed *exuberantly* happy. But it was because of drugs, mental illusions, or changing their own nature...*no!* Galileo had too much pride to give-in to those superficial, artificial temptations, as alluring as they might be! So he bounded after Anderson, with Lhamo trailing along, seemingly reluctantly, behind him.

After their incredible journey through space and time, this was their final "destination." He, after all, was a scientist. He dealt in observable, reproducible facts. How could he hesitate now to discover the Truth?

He had to know what lay at the end of their journey—no matter how startling or disturbing it might be.

Lhamo apparently felt the same, his normally cheerful expression now frozen into an uncharacteristically grim frown.

"It is *not* Nirvana," he whispered to Galileo, moving up beside him as they ran in big "loopy" strides to catch up to Anderson.

"So what is?" Galileo flippantly replied. Outwardly his expression was one of steely determination. But inwardly he was shaking.

Anderson said that he, Galileo, would be humbled. What did that mean? For a deeply religious man, such as himself, it could only mean one thing.

They were going to confront *Allah!*

But...how could that happen?

Galileo's analytical mind dearly hoped it would occur. What an incredible experience it would be to directly engage with the Creator of the Universe! But in his heart of hearts, he wasn't so sure.

As Anderson had so flippantly predicted, Galileo knew without a doubt he was *unworthy* to come into the Presence of Allah. After all, he had arrogantly chosen to defy the just punishment handed down by his religious superiors. And then he attempted to *change* the entire world to match his own selfish preferences—and not only his present society, but *future* societies as well!

Surely he was marching to a reckoning: a predestined fate that he'd only managed to delay, not prevent.

Galileo was convinced he was following Anderson to his own well-deserved death.

Sanako, Victor, Agent Ice, and General Keller were the last survivors of the doomed convoy.

Sanako was stunned by the swift coordination of the zombie horde which attacked their convoy. Over the convoy's vehicle-to-vehicle radio she heard yells from the leading tanks. The main street was blocked by suddenly pushed-out, burned and crumpled vehicles. As the leading tanks tried to plow on through the unanticipated barrier, RPG's slammed into their treads with loud "whumps," immobilizing them. Fresh "shufflers" swamped both them and the closely following troop transports, ripping open their hatches and squirming inside. The frantically firing gunners inside were overwhelmed and abruptly silenced.

Although General Keller and the lead researchers were still safe in their closed, armored personnel carrier, their path forward was blocked. Sanako heard the vehicle's crackling communications to the outside world suddenly cut off. From past attacks on the research base, Sanako knew the alien zombies were blanketing the vehicle with a pile of interfering metal rubbish. They were cut off from the outside world. Then the interior began to *heat up!*

"They've lit a bonfire on top of us," Ice calmly observed. "We've got to make a run for it!"

General Keller flung the back door outward. They all spilled out, running for their lives. Sanako tightly clutched a briefcase, inside of which were cradled room-temperature vials of key living cultures. It was the only intact means left to reconstitute the Cure in larger brew vats. She knew she must guard it with her life.

Keller and Ice were also aware of this, surrounding and protecting her and her precious vials.

But the other accompanying guards were cut down by enemy fire. Keller was wounded in his leg, but continued hobbling along, laying down a withering cover-fire with his assault rifle. Agent Ice lived up to her name, coolly defending Victor and Sanako with a handgun. Loading and reloading on the run, she blew the heads off of a dozen of the "black eyes"!

Sanako barely made it into the nearest still-standing building, crouching low behind a countertop. They were holed up in what used to be a McDonald's fast food restaurant, surrounded. Outside, a huge mob of the zombies churned and milled about. Alongside Sanako crouched Victor, Ice, and Keller.

Everyone else in the convoy was dead.

"They want you alive!" a loud voice called out to them. "Well, maybe not all of you...but certainly Dr. Yamamoto and Professor Volodymyr. They know you already transmitted details of your various discoveries to other sites—which they intercepted and decoded. But they still have specific questions that only the two of you can answer. Plus they want your living cell cultures, just to make sure they never seed-out larger vats. So just come on out and you won't be harmed."

Peeking over the countertop and through a front, shattered store window—Sanako saw calmly walking toward them *Losa Yanash!*

His wide face was pale. The deep wrinkles at the corners of his eyes sagged downward as if his face were melting. His lips were parted in a grimace. His longish black-grey hair hung slackly to each side of his head. He was gaunt but obviously still alive.

"See? They didn't kill me! In fact, they freed me from your 'patient' transport—or should I say your jail cell? They're intelligent, far above our own level of intelligence. I can hear them speaking in my head! You thought I was 'cured' of the 'infection,' right? But it never left me. They were just biding their time in my brain, spying on you. You have five minutes to come out with your hands up, or our hungry minions will come inside and *tear* you to pieces!"

Sanako saw Keller creep over to the shattered front store window. He peeked out at the approaching Park Ranger. He was raising the tip of his rifle to the window. "I never trusted that damn Indian. I knew we should have gotten rid of him," he growled.

"He's the only thing holding the horde back!" Ice interjected as she crawled over to his side, putting a hand on his rifle, moving the muzzle downward. She checked her own handgun, slipping another round into its stock. "He's not responsible for his actions. I interviewed him at the facility. He's devastated by the loss of his family. But, regardless, I've only one clip remaining. That's it and I'm done. How are you fixed for ammunition, General?"

He snorted, shaking his head. "I've enough to smoke that bastard turncoat. But that's it."

"Should we surrender?"

"And get turned into one of them? I think not."

"So..."

"We'll fight to the end, saving one bullet for each of the four of us."

"Agreed."

Surrender...sweet surrender...laying aside the weapons and giving up the fight...turning oneself over to the outside forces...it was so tempting. Sanako never before in her life had even considered the option of "giving up." To her it was suicide. Her relentless internal drive kept her moving forward, no matter the circumstance.

But having her life on Earth ended by a bullet in the brain, to avoid being eaten by black-eyed zombies, wasn't very attractive either!

Still, surrender was equally impossible.

It doubtless had to do with her family upbringing and cultural heritage. The "Samurai Warrior" ethic drove her to relentless self-discipline and duty. As part of her martial arts training, she'd formally adopted the *Bushido*, or "Way of the Warrior" code. It compelled her on the path of honor: duty to one's Master, loyalty unto death. For her there was no fear of death. She could commit suicide without hesitation *if* it was for the sake of one's Master or to achieve a greater purpose.

Though she had fought her way honorably along the difficult paths of academia, medicine, and research—those struggles never fully satisfied her. She was always looking for something else, restlessly searching! An ignominious defeat, being dispatched by one of her comrades...it just wasn't right. It didn't fit. It shouldn't be her destiny!

If she were to ever surrender it must be for a righteous Cause; or to a Master of unparalleled grandeur. And if she ever found that, her devotion would be *unbreakable.*

But perhaps there was a 'third way' between death and surrender?

"This is bad," Victor quietly coughed.

Sanako looked over at the sick old man who was cowering with her behind the countertop. She urgently whispered to him: "They only want you and me, Professor. They need our information and expertise. I say we ditch those two. They're dead set on killing us rather than letting us 'surrender.' We can go with Losa, pretending to give up to the zombie horde. We'll still be alive. Maybe we can find a way to fight back while in their captivity. With our two considerable intellects pooled there's always a chance we can outwit the aliens. We can sneak out the back door of this place right now—while Ice and Keller are at the front window. How about it? Are you with me? We don't have to die here. We can covertly continue the fight!"

He sighed deeply, running a hand through his stringy white hair. His blue eyes looked infinitely sad...and tired.

"I lost touch with Ivanna, my wife, three days ago," he whispered back, his trembling voice barely audible to Sanako. "I thought she might be safe out in our country retreat. But the last newscast that I heard, before all the stations went dark, was that even the backwoods of Vermont were overrun with zombies."

He closed his eyes, shuddering violently. Then he slumped down upon the littered floor, curling up into a fetal position.

"So...you're staying?"

He sighed again. "I *can't* fight anymore, Sanako. And I don't want my immune system and body dissected by those monsters, as we did to that poor Park Ranger before he partially recovered. He suffered horribly. They'll want to know every which way that my tissues suc-ceeded in blocking their contagion. A bullet to the brain from Ice or Keller sounds merciful to me, a quick way to end this madness. And then I can go be with Ivanna."

"Suit yourself," she shrugged, slipping away from him into the back of the store.

Staying low, she scuttled along, creeping over fallen containers and around overturned workbenches. She saw a dropped *Big Mac and fries* dried-up and covered with blue fungi, moldering on the floor beneath an overturned table. She yanked it out and stuffed it greedily into her mouth. It tasted awful. But who knew when she'd find another meal? After being on half-rations for over a week now at the surrounded base, she was starving.

And there it was—the back exit! It was still locked tight but had an emergency exit door bar. She pushed the bar downward, opening the door just a crack.

Peeking outside she saw a chilling sight.

Standing just outside in a straight line, Sanako saw a silent group of ragged humans. Their clothes were in tatters. Their mouths hung slackly open. The skin of their faces and arms was torn and splotched. They were walking corpses. But their *solid black eyes* were alert and glittering—*staring* straight at her!

Suddenly the "third way" didn't look so attractive.

With a gasp she hastily pulled the exit door back closed, then re-locked it. It wouldn't hold them off for long, but at least it was a temporary barrier. She no longer was so sure that her best course of action was abandoning her friends.

"Ah, my loyal Sanako—it is *so* good to see you again!"

Sanako spun around, staring straight into the *bright green eyes* of an ancient, withered crone.

"Who are...?"

Gunfire loudly erupted from the front of the store.

The twisted figure standing above Sanako reached down a hand. Though the woman looked even worse than the possessed humans outside the back of the store, she radiated an *imperial* assurance: wisdom, control, and *power!*

And on the dried-up wrist of the hand reaching for her, Sanako saw a *green-glowing* Turtle Tattoo.

"You can stay if you want. Or you can come with me. It's your choice."

"But, to where...?"

"I will take you to a *Castle beyond Time*—a place where we and our kind reign supreme. Despite your past medical miracles upon me, my dear Sanako, my physical form is finally succumbing. I will soon surrender this body as a visual inspiration to those who follow. *You*, the present incarnation of a Destiny you've always known that you were born to grasp, will take my place!"

Sanako heard soul-chilling yells and grunts, hand-to-hand combat just yards away from her.

It took her only a split second to make her decision.

"Take me."

Grabbing the clawed, thin hand of the ancient old woman, Sanako felt herself pulled into a *spinning, black vortex*.

It was exhilarating!

Chapter 22
LOOKING FOR THE EXIT

So often those in dire struggles
Long for the peace of death
Ending all conflict and hate
Drifting off into bland oblivion
Thinking it won't be a great sin
A bullet fired through one's brain
A noose constricting one's neck
A bottle of pills flooding one's guts
A knife slicing throbbing veins
Or jumping from a tall building
Or sucking gas into delicate lungs
Or stepping in front of a train
Full stop to life's nightmares
Slamming the door loudly
Forever walking away
If not earning great honor
At least leaving behind the pain
But could there be Karma or rebirth
Or worse, a lurking hideous hell
To make us wish that somehow
We could have figured out
How to change our own selves?

The Minstrel's Lark, 22:17-21

Suzy and Billy—strapped into their seats—were peering down at the surface of the earth in the viewscreens, using the spaceship's telescopic function. Suzy was trying, without success, to find some hint of human civilization in the unfamiliarly shaped continents below.

She refused to believe their little rocket ship had been thrown into Time.

But Billy was insistent that they were indeed 65 million years in the past, floating above a version of Earth that only existed in the Cretaceous period. But surely there must be another explanation!

"Dinosaurs!" Billy gasped.

"Did you see some?" Suzy replied, peering intently at the screen in front of her. "I thought you said we were too high to see any individual..."

"*Behind* you!"

"What?" Suzy said as she twisted around...

—seeing floating nimbly up the circular staircase, their heads poking into the control chamber...three human-sized lizards!

And they were wearing *combat* gear!

Each one of them had on what looked like bullet-proof vests, backpacks, and wicked-looking guns strapped to their scaly sides. Plus each had round magnetic pads strapped on the bottom of their clawed feet which "clomped" onto the metal deck, holding them down from floating in the zero-G.

"Uhm...Suzy?" Billy gasped, his eyes stretched wide as he cowered back against the control panel.

She sighed, unbuckling herself to stand up. Ok. This was totally ridiculous! There might be whole continents below filled with ancient dinosaurs, but *not* on their spaceship!

Nope! This must be another holographic trick, a projection. That old lady they'd switched off from trying to order them around was still messing with their minds.

"They're not real," she confidently informed Billy.

As they seemed to loom menacingly in front of her and Billy she pushed off from her seat, floated up to the lead creature's snout, and sharply *slapped* it with her opened palm!

With a startled "snort" it staggered backward two steps.

Its mouth opened, revealing *many long, pointed teeth*. It cocked its large, angular head to the side. A yellow eye on that side blinked at Suzy, narrowing. The black, vertical slit of its pupil focused upon her. Its long tail whipped back and forth. And its three-fingered hands flexed in the air, grasping at her...

—and her hand hurt!

"If you want to return to your original home in the other human dimension, you *will* assist me and my friends!"

The intensely spoken English coming out of the lizard's throat was raspy but understandable.

"You're...you're *real?*" Suzy gasped, grabbing her stinging hand with the other, trying to kick around in a circle to float back to her seat.

"We're sorry to startle you. But we stowed away in the lower equipment deck. We were able to extend the Time Portal's window, launching you far beyond your ship-programmed exit point. And now that you've succeeded in usurping the time barriers that constrained us from accomplishing this task on our own, we have urgent business to accomplish. We require your continued cooperation."

"You're real!" Billy exclaimed in delight as he pushed out of his own seat to drift over in the zero gravity to the lead lizard. He had a giddy smile on his face as he grabbed the lead lizard around its thick neck.

"Hi, Billy," the big animal rasped. "It is nice to meet you in person."

"You know me?" Billy laughed, his happy smile practically splitting his head in two.

"Oh yes. I know you and Suzy very well. I've been observing the both of you through Suzy's Turtle Tattoo for years. In the reptilian Dimensions, I am one of several lead researchers who've collaborated in your upbringing: both you, Suzy, and before you your mother Sally. Thus I've learned to speak your language—though it is still difficult for my tongue and throat to pronounce."

"You...speak it very well," Suzy gulped, dizzy with shock at this new bizarre turn of events.

"Thank you!" he nodded. "Sally was the favorite of the others, but I always liked you the best, Suzy. In my opinion you are much cuter and more intelligent than your mother. There are rules we couldn't violate, but we tried to help you wherever we could. And now, it's *your* turn to return the favor."

Still spinning in the air, Suzy managed to catch onto the edge of the copilot's chair. She pulled herself into it and strapped herself securely down before rotating the seat around to face the talking dinosaur.

"But...you're...?"

"They're *velociraptors!*" Billy exclaimed in delight, now sitting with his legs wrapped around the neck of the lead dinosaur as if it were riding a small horse. "See? It has a long, narrow head and flattened snout. And look how round his skull is. They've got big brains in there! See their long arms? And they've got a single big curved claw on each of their feet. That's for *ripping the guts* out of their prey!"

The big animal blinked its eyes several times, as if processing what Billy had just said.

"Yes, the velociraptors below on the surface of the past Earth are indeed related to our evolutionary ancestors," it replied. "Our present form is patterned on them. Our actual brains, however, are greatly evolved from those of our primitive ancestors so that..."

"But how can they be your ancestors?" Suzy frowned, totally perplexed by this bizarre turn of events. "They're *all* going to go extinct!"

"Exactly, Suzy," the intelligent dinosaur agreed, now squatting on its haunches as two others moved to the controls, rapidly assessing various readouts. "As I indicated, we are not from this Dimension. The dinosaurs on the Earth below us will never have a chance to evolve advanced intelligence. *A giant asteroid ten kilometers long* is even now speeding toward Earth. It is aimed at what you will, in the future, call the Yucatan Peninsula. In just a few hours it will slam into the planet traveling *30 kilometers per second*. The immediate explosion, fire, and tidal wave will kill many of the bigger animals below. Dense clouds from thrown-up debris will block the sun for months, starving and freezing most of the survivors."

"Well...sure...that's what *happened*..."

"But it doesn't *have* to happen," he insisted. "We can use your hijacked spaceship to *change* history!"

"Uh...say what?"

The two dinosaurs at the control panels made a series of rapid "clicks" and grunts directed to the English-speaking one. He nodded his head thoughtfully, blinking his big yellow eyes in silent acknowledgement.

"They say that once you transfer verbal command to us, we are poised to intercept the Asteroid."

"But...even if we wanted to do that—*why?* If what you're telling me is true, then that means stopping the asteroid means mammals will never evolve intelligence and...it might stop mankind from *ever* appearing on Earth! The little rat-like mammals started to take over Earth only because the giant dinosaurs got destroyed. Without that asteroid hitting Earth there will never be any people at all! My Dad and Mom will never exist! *Billy and I* will never exist!"

The intelligent velociraptor gave what was the equivalent of a wry grin. It was intimidating—again exposing his many sharply pointed long teeth.

Billy still looked delighted perched up on the leading smart velociraptor's back. He didn't seem bothered by what she and the animal were discussing, indeed looked like he wasn't even listening!

"No, Suzy," the big lizard gently chided her. "What we do will not even touch your Dimension. It will continue as before. We are only changing the timeline for the *second* human Dimension."

"So we *are* in another Dimension!" Suzy gasped. "That's what we thought, but we weren't sure."

"Yes—and it's an *evil* Dimension. In fact, it is right now, in the future from which you departed, on the verge of *destroying* not only itself but your home Dimension as well!"

Suzy leaned back in her chair, greatly confused. Already faced with being thrown back 65 million years in time, she was now being told to stop an asteroid—and in the process *dooming the entire human race* of an *alternate* dimension?

"Hah! I thought so! That scary old lady *was* evil!" Billy chortled, apparently catching the bit about the Asteroid. "She wanted us to go back and change history, right? She wuz gonna have us wipe out some nice Buddhist people! That's how come she got us on this ship and sent it back in time. That's why she gave us control over the ship.

And now she's gonna get what *she* deserves—we're gonna wipe *her* out!"

"But...Billy...what about our Native American friends? And what about all the other kids we saw at the moon base from other colonies of humans down on the world? Do we want them all to get killed also?"

"Oh...that's right," he replied. Now he didn't look so triumphant.

"They won't be hurt in the least," the big lizard insisted, bouncing the clinging Billy playfully on his back. "They will be *replaced*. You see you can't kill what doesn't exist. Their timeline will fade away while another springs up in its place. And you *will* stop a *terrible threat* to *your* own world!"

"But—you haven't given us any proof that..."

"It is far too complicated to explain in a few minutes, Suzy. I am truly sorry. I know this is all very confusing for you. It is just not possible to give you absolute proof right at this moment. But I speak of a threat that your Mother battled as well. She heroically managed to suppress it. But now it is back more terrible than ever. And only you can stop it!"

"M-Mom? But she's just a high school mathematics teacher?"

"I can tell you incredible stories about your Mother, Suzy—things she's never told you. It turns out she's already erased and started several new timelines! She tried to shield you from the awful Cosmic Realities and give you a 'normal life.' So, you see, what you do here today is simply what she's already done, *multiple* times. You're just continuing a proud tradition of being a blessed 'Time-Twister'!"

Billy snickered happily, pushing off from the dinosaur to float up to the low ceiling before kicking himself back down to again latch onto its back.

"Hah! We're Time-Twisters!" he chortled.

"No we're not!" she snapped at him. "He was talking about *me*, not you."

"Says you..."

"Suzy, you must embrace your Destiny. You have to follow in your Mother's footsteps. She has changed the Fate of mankind multiple times!"

"Really? She has?" Suzy asked, even more confused. "But she never told me..."

"—because she wanted to *protect* you and your brother, Suzy. But now it's your turn to use your 'special talents' that you inherited from her. *You* have to be the 'grownup' that protects *her* and your Dad. Can you do it?"

"Uh...well...I don't know."

"I'm sorry this is happening so fast, Suzy. I know it's hard on you. But the *fate of your entire world* rests in your hands. My companions tell me we have only minutes to set our new course!"

"But it's all so strange. I just don't know!"

"Time is running out, Suzy," the talking velociraptor insisted.

"I...I guess...I suppose?"

She gulped then nodded in the affirmative.

"Good. My comrades must plot our intercept course and get your ship under way on its new vector. All you have to do is speak these words: *'I relinquish ship control to those who will next speak.'* Can you do that for us? I *promise* you that it's for the best—and that you and your brother will be safe whatever happens. Plus we'll send you back to the true human Dimension. Unlike the lies of that scheming old woman, we *will* get you back to your Mom and Dad!"

"Billy?" Suzy gulped, afraid to make such a world-shattering decision alone.

"What?" he laughed, now kicking all around the room in the zero gravity.

Billy wasn't listening. He wasn't any help!

She sighed, afraid she was doing something terrible but not seeing any other option.

"I...relinquish ship control...to those who will next speak," she said in a low voice.

"Accept input from new crewmen!" the velociraptor ordered.

"INPUT ACCEPTED."

As the three dinosaurs scurried to work frantically at the controls, Suzy unbelted and drifted in the zero-G over to Billy.

"Did we do the right thing?" she whispered to him.

"About what?" he shrugged. "We're going to go knock away a *giant asteroid* to save Mom and Dad, right?"

And in the process doom billions of other humans to never be born—Suzy thought. *That either makes me history's greatest murderess, or...*

Or what?

That was unsettling.

She couldn't think of an alternative to balance out being the greatest villainess of all time. How could supposedly saving Mom and Dad from that old hag on the moon justify killing *billions* of other humans? In essence, she'd assigned her *very soul* to the glib claims of three talking dinosaurs.

She was terribly confused and conflicted. But there was nothing she could do about it now. On the viewscreens the Earth abruptly pulled away from them as they headed out to meet the Asteroid.

Galileo was amazed by their transportation vehicle.

Anderson described it as a "subway" to "grand central station." To Galileo it was an unbelievably smooth, luxuriant traveling room. He saw periodic blue lights set-into the walls of the tunnel whipping past, outside of large curved windows. Anderson confirmed from his newly installed knowledge that they were descending into the depths of the *moon!* It was the exact opposite of the long painful crawl they'd just survived in the labyrinth beneath the frozen glacier back on Earth.

"These are tasty," Lhamo mildly observed, holding a plate full of little finger-sandwiches. "And they are vegetarian. The onions are very crunchy!"

He stood at a side-table where a number of various *horderves* sat in deep plates. What appeared to be half-avocados were topped with eggs and raisins. Toothpicks skewered orange, red, and green fruits. Deviled eggs sat amongst ripe black olives. And yellow mini-cupcakes were topped with fluffy white cream.

Anderson ignored the food, rocking back and forth in his seat as the car whipped around curves. They were descending deeper and deeper into the interior of the moon.

"It is strange that there are none others riding this vehicle," Galileo remarked. Indeed, at the station platform where they'd found this vehicle, no other people were there. It seemed that this future—

beside those immobilized or irrevocably altered—was devoid of independent people!

"The map in my head does not show people, just destinations," Anderson shrugged. "But that doesn't matter. We're arriving—so go ahead and chow-down, like the Monk! It may well be your last meal."

As if in reply, Lhamo cheerfully grinned, stuffing more finger sandwiches into his mouth. Galileo still held back.

"I *was* getting tired of mammoth meat," the Monk admitted around his exuberant chewing. "Our hosts, whoever they may be, are very considerate. This is delicious vegetarian fare!"

And so they rocketed deeper and yet deeper...

Then, finally, the car decelerated smoothly, coming to a stop at an immaculately white platform.

They stepped out into another completely empty large station, from which an ascending escalator arose to a distant opening.

Galileo was immediately struck by a *penetrating vibration* beneath his feet—and a distant THRUMMING like the march of a million-man army!

"This is one of many departure platforms," Anderson told them, leading them to the escalator. "A whole network of connected caverns is sequestered deep beneath the surface of the moon. They were apparently carved out and connected with the purpose of representing and enabling a plethora of human endeavors."

"What?" Galileo asked, now standing on a step behind Anderson as they were steadily lifted by the escalator toward the distant opening. "How do you know this?"

Anderson tapped his now crewcut skull.

"It's all in here—at least the names. I don't know the actual reality behind the names, of course. But the titles show a definite theme."

Galileo was intrigued, but growing ever more fearful. What was the source of the *thrumming* above them? It sounded and felt like a huge power source!

"Titles...like what?" he said, trying to replace his fears with a considered discussion.

"Oh, such as where we came from—*Enhancements*; or others such as *Power*, or *Sexuality*, or *Knowledge*, or *Exploration*, or *Creativity*, and even...*Spirituality!* Those are the main destinations listed on my map. But there are many others that..."

"And I suppose they could also be described from their negative perspectives?" Galileo thoughtfully queried.

"I suppose."

"Such as *Addiction, War, Over-Population, Compartmentalization, Diversion, Chaos,* and *Intolerance?*" Galileo tentatively ventured.

Behind Galileo, he heard Lhamo quietly add: "*Nothing ever exists entirely alone. Everything is in relation to everything else.*"

"Ah, that old 'yin and yang' philosophy—that everything has a positive and negative aspect," Anderson sneered back at them both. "You neatly slice everything up into components, Monk. But that is *not* the true nature of God!"

"You misunderstand, friend Arthur," Lhamo calmly replied. "We Buddhists attempt to *transcend* this 'dualism.' We help each other to *rise above* the dark or lighted side of a mountain, to view the *entire* mountain—and thence the entire mountain range...and indeed the entire planet upon which they sit...and so-on and so-on!"

"I'm confused," Galileo admitted. "Why would the future society stemming from what we did back in the 17th century break itself down into these different subjects? Or is what we're traveling through now merely a museum, where the achievements of mankind are illustrated by individual topics and practitioners?"

"That shall soon be answered," Anderson observed.

The vibration/noise was steadily increasing.

And, yes, they were almost to the top of the long escalator. The passage into "Grand Central Station" loomed close above them. But it wasn't a dark doorway. No, it was a wide, arched opening lit by a brilliant blue light. And stepping off the escalator and climbing up over a low ramp they saw...

Behind Galileo, Lhamo gasped, for once dumbfounded.

—a gigantic, domed, glistening-white cavern in which loomed a FLOATING, GOLDEN, THOUSAND-FOOT-HIGH, STATUE of a bald-headed, chubby-faced, pot-bellied, seated, happily *laughing Buddha!*

The huge Idol was supported by three gigantic, curved struts each towering up five hundred feet.

The entire awesome structure was bathed in an intense *blue glow* shining up from beneath!

"Oh...my...God," Anderson gulped, walking forward across a gleaming white marble floor toward the looming giant Idol.

Behind him trailed Galileo and Lhamo.

It was a full half-mile to an observation rail that surrounded a *throbbing power source* sunk deep beneath the elevated, massive Buddha statue.

They walked in silence.

Not one other person was in the vast chamber. But Galileo spied many exits spread evenly around the perfect circle of the huge cavern. He had no doubt that those exists—like the one they'd just arrived from—led off into the "habitats" previously named by Anderson.

This was a *destination hub* to all of human endeavor and inspiration!

Even in the weak gravity, Galileo was breathing heavily from the long hike. At last he came up to the chest-high silver railing and peeked over.

Fully a thousand feet below him, Galileo gazed into a swirling, *deep black pit!* It was gigantic, far larger than the little pool through which Galileo and his friends were transported to the moon.

And just as with the fixed black pool in the cave, this far-larger version was contained and perpetuated by a *gleaming cylinder of silvery metal*—upon whose giant rim Galileo now stood, peering cautiously downward.

"Impressed?" a sweet voice sounded behind him.

Galileo slowly turned, not daring to believe his ears.

But it was true. Standing there in front of him was *Virginia!*

"Hello, Father," she smiled holding out her arms to him. "I am so glad to see you again. You have no idea the joy I felt when the North American Colony's Messenger reported your safe arrival in their midst. I wanted to bring you here sooner, but the consensus was that you and your companions must struggle to gain that privilege. I knew it was perilous for you to remain in that primitive environment. But I also had faith you would prevail, even when we lost touch with the Messenger and..."

"*Mio dolce angelo!*" Galileo exclaimed, grabbing her up in a tight bear hug while lapsing into his native Italian ["My sweet angel!"]

No, she wasn't an illusion. She was solid, warm, and real. After swinging her around in an exuberant circle, he held her off at arm's length, just looking at her. She was exactly as he remembered her: slight figure, large dark Italian eyes, well-maintained black hair, long angular face with full lips and sharp nose.

But she did not have on a traditional Italian dress—rather was wrapped in a red robe, leaving one arm uncovered and free.

And she was barefoot.

"Virginia! How have you survived all these four hundred years since our ill-fated departure?" he gasped, marveling. "And what is this strange attire that you are wearing? Are you now a Buddhist?"

She grinned broadly, releasing Galileo to hold out one hand to the shocked-looking Anderson and a hesitant Lhamo.

"Come with me to the Temple," she addressed them all. "We will answer all your questions."

"Temple?" Galileo asked, seeing nothing around them but the gigantic pit and the looming Buddha figure.

"Above!"

And with that, a *blue sphere* surrounded them, lifting them into the air to float upward toward the base of the giant statue.

"To do all this...must take incredible power," Anderson mused as they drifted closer.

"The stable Portal below is locked into the heart of the sun," Virginia replied. "We have all the energy we need from its thermonuclear, hot-fusion reactions."

"And maintaining the Portal?"

"There is a sequence of overlapping DE-generators, channeled through the metallic cylinder that contains and perpetuates it."

"Ah, yes. Of course," Anderson now smiled, seemingly understanding. "And presumably that's how you blocked access to the other human Dimension?"

"That occurred only recently," Virginia politely replied, seemingly concentrating on holding her Father's hand. "There was a Contagion.

We had to prevent it from crossing the divide over to us. Now that we've put the Barrier in place, nothing can travel from there to here— or from here to there! And, yes, that does require a large increase in output. But we have vast DE-generator capacity, barely used before this present crisis since we can directly tap into the sun. But our DE-generator capacity is more than sufficient to maintain the Barrier. Do not be concerned. We are very well protected from the Contagion."

Above them, a large golden panel slid to the side, ready to receive them.

"Not well enough," Anderson whispered, such that only Galileo standing right next to him heard. Then a wide smile lit up the Agent's dour face as he loudly spoke for everyone to hear: "*Not* well enough!"

Chapter 23

<u>ANSWERS</u>

"All in good time"
Is the old refrain
When all the confusion
Is finally explained
Why good people suffer
And babies are killed
While the wicked prosper
And sick wealthy are healed
Searching for some "Plan"
Beyond human perception
Making sense of the chaos
Of suffering and death
Fueling blind evolution
Where the "fittest" survive
And "good" genes persist
Just the luck of the draw
Or hand of the Divine?
The real "solutions"
Are just more Questions.

The Minstrel's Lark, 23:1-5

Trong crept from the container marveling that he was still alive.

Indeed, the grievous wound where the spider's leg had skewered his side now was completely healed! He admired the soft white clothes on his body. They must be the pelts of very fine animals! Then he lurched up to his feet.

Where was he? What was happening? Ah yes...he must be in the realm of the gods! This must be the place that the Messengers took the children after delivering the magic pills which kept the tribe healthy and long-lived. That foul Insect killed the present Messenger and the previous batch of children. But *he* killed the monster!

And now...was he getting his reward? But he felt dizzy. Indeed, trying to step away from the white container that had healed him he found himself *arching* up into the air!

As he drifted back to the ground, he spied across the wide cavern *his friends departing!*

He tried to run to catch up to them. But he kept bouncing up into the air. He must go slower. But then he couldn't catch up to his friends. And just as he entered the long, incredibly smooth white tunnel they'd entered he saw them standing inside a magic room with transparent windows. It sped away into the darkness to his right, taking them away.

"*Arrrgggghhhh!*" he shouted out in dismay, banging his head with his fists. He must find a way to follow his friends! And it wasn't just the friendship he'd developed with them driving him. No, there was now within his brain a *feverish compulsion* to join them!

They were no longer just his friends. They were something more primal, more fundamental, more *necessary*...his prey! Catching sight of himself in the mirrored surface of a supporting column he hardly recognized himself. His long, shaggy hair was cut short. The dirt and mud that'd coated him for days due to his crawling through the labyrinth was gone. But what most startled him were his *eyes*...now without whites. Indeed, they were a glittering, *solid black!*

Yes, he felt an inward *raging pride* that he'd outwitted the healing container! He'd let it heal the body while hiding his true self from its view.

But it was confusing, like thinking with two brains: one taking charge then the other reasserting itself.

A loud "swoosh" startled him as yet another magic car entered the tunnel from his left, slowing to a stop in front of him. A section of the side of the magic car slid inward, as if inviting him to enter.

He did so, standing inside, ignoring the seats and the buffet of strange finger-foods. That "nourishment" held no attraction to him.

He stared unblinkingly through the magic windows in the direction that the other car had departed.

The door slid shut and the car smoothly accelerated into darkness, blue lights whipping past outside on the walls of the tunnel.

Soon, he'd catch up with his friends. And then he'd eat *them*.

The blue sphere flickered around them as Galileo and his companions were lifted into the hollowed-out, gigantic Buddha idol.

It wasn't just a statue. It was a Temple!

The pervasive THRUMMING of the gigantic power source below abruptly cut-off as the entrance port closed behind them. It left a startling *SILENCE*...in its way even more disturbing than the pulsing vibration of the cavern.

Galileo looked around in awe. The entire floor beneath his feet was crystal-clear—revealing the roiling, swirling Black Pit some 1,500 feet below them. And set onto the crystal floor were *five mammoth columns* which towered eight hundred feet up into the air. They were covered in ornate red-yellow patterns that kept shifting and changing. The circular wall of the Temple was a series of *high, arched, one-way windows* set one against the other. Each window was a huge stained-glass mural, depicting various scenes of human endeavor—clearly keyed to the exits outside.

Galileo saw etched on the windows inspiring scenes: views of winged *flying humans*, *great battles* of triumphant armies, *angelic singing* of adorable children in choirs, *elegant spaceships* orbiting other planets, insanely *beautiful sculptures*, congregations of *robed supplicants* bowed in prayer, and many other colorful scenes lit from behind with a heavenly warm sunshine.

But it was the high ceiling above that captivated Galileo the most. It was a *white mist* through which dangled-down many strings of *gleaming diamonds and emeralds*, amongst which countless *blue-glowing spheres* languidly drifted. Though they were hundreds of feet above him, Galileo could clearly make out *humans sitting in lotus positions with eyes closed*, one within each of the spheres. The floating, distant humans wore red, yellow, white, black, and orange robes—like living ornaments of a three-dimensional Christmas tree!

"What is this place?" Lhamo asked Virginia as she led them across the disturbingly transparent floor toward a ring of comfortable-looking chairs and cushions. Set beside the chairs on a low table were refreshments—little cakes alongside delicate cups filled with what looked to be gently steaming tea.

"It's just what it looks like," Virginia smiled at him as she sat down in a lotus position upon a flat cushion. "Please, everyone, be seated."

But the monk did not sit, just stood looking around in wonderment.

"It seems to be a Buddhist Temple—more magnificent than any I've ever seen before—but strangely *mechanical*. Is that true?"

"That is very observant of you, Your Holiness. Indeed, this place is a fusion of the Scientific and the Divine. We long since moved past putting Religion to the side of Reality. It is no longer a matter of Faith or Facts, but as it should be—a merger of the human spirit with the undeniable Laws of Nature. Is this not the essence of your teachings, upon which all that you see here is based?"

The Monk looked puzzled, thoughtful. Frowning, he refused to reply.

"So have you lost your initial faith, Virginia?" Galileo asked, puzzled. "Is pleasing Allah no longer a concern of yours?"

He was glad to finally be off his feet, sipping at a perpetually hot cup of the tea—the most delicious he'd ever tasted!

"Oh, no, Father," she said, shaking her head in the negative. "We retain our traditional heritages. But after you departed from us, the remaining monks within Guildhall taught me many things: particularly concerning Connectivity, Mindfulness, Cause and Effect, and True Enlightenment."

Galileo noticed Lhamo staring up at the high ceiling, seemingly amazed at the mass of hanging and drifting "ornaments."

"So how do those change our Muslim religion?"

"They do not, Father," she shrugged. "But they extend and explain."

"Explain what?"

"Why we need Religion in the first place!"

Galileo laughed in delight, stroking his beard thoughtfully as he set his cup of delicious tea on a table at his side.

"Ah, Virginia," he fondly said, reaching out a weathered hand to stroke her long, glisteningly black hair, "you *have* turned into Lhamo! He also speaks in maddeningly incomprehensible riddles that..."

"Enough of this nonsense!" Anderson rudely broke in. "I need *straight answers* to my questions. Can you do that for me?"

"Certainly—but you may not like the answers."

"I'll be the judge of that! Why is this huge Temple empty?"

"It is not empty. Look above you. The air above us is filled with many living humans. This entire Temple is dedicated to the fulfillment of the human spirit!"

"Why is the Earth below empty?"

"It is not empty, friend Anderson. You yourself were there, were you not? You saw for yourself, did you not, that it is filled with the richness of Nature, life, animals, and humans?"

"Then where are the cities, the towns, the countries, the societies? Where is *civilization?*"

"Ah..." she nodded. "Yes, you did not anticipate this happening four centuries ago, correct? You thought that accelerating technological development would erase the previous timeline of rigid, repressive Empires as humanity engorged itself on the benefits of limitless energy, am I right? And since they'd get that energy by cold-fusion-driven Dark Energy release from subspace—that would attract the full attention of the Creator who would summarily judge us: either destroying the 'unrighteous' or taking us up into His direct Presence, right?"

"I...well..." he tried to reply. He looked flustered, confused, fiddling at his dark eyeglasses.

"Even now you hope that our recent upsurge in DE-generation will bring upon us the imminent 'Wrath of God,' do you not? Is that not the fulfillment of your deepest desires?"

To Galileo, Anderson looked incredibly disturbed, nervously wiping beads of sweat from his brow.

"Do not be distressed, my friend," she sweetly soothed him. "The second half of your formula was the abject failure of humanity to live in a truly righteous manner, correct? We are far from perfection, that's true. But in a mere four hundred years we have advanced past the point of meriting from the Creator a summary extinction by a massive solar flare. Indeed, Agent Anderson, we encountered the *Judgment of God* a full hundred years ago—and we *passed!*"

He looked deflated, shrunken.

"But...humanity...is fatally flawed," he weakly protested, wringing his hands together.

"We've moved far beyond those narrow concerns, friend Anderson," she mildly continued. "We've adopted a more inclusive and encompassing Vision: where 'good' and 'evil' aren't narrowly defined lists of tribal rules. Yes, your fellow Time-Keepers—some of whom float above us as we speak—did try to 'keep the Faith' so-to-speak. But with the tutoring of our Buddhist friends they gradually moved beyond outdated, simplistic concepts of 'heaven' and 'hell.'"

"Virginia!" Galileo barked, reaching down to impulsively grab up both her small hands in his larger, calloused ones. "Please, just tell us what occurred following our departure from the 17th century!"

She nodded, her dark eyes looking up lovingly into his.

"Of course, Father. Here's what happened..."

Trong walked away from the top of the long escalator into the gigantic Central Station.

He'd been terrified by the moving stairs, but strangely compliant to their magic. It was as if his mind were still back in the Stone Age chasing woolly mammoths while his feet were from elsewhere. His body now moved with total confidence in the low lunar gravity, allowing his legs to "hop" him along in slow-drifting arcs that propelled him relentlessly toward his target: the *glowing pit* beneath the giant statue! It drew him like a moth to a flame. Except now he was the *lead scout* of a colony of cosmic *hornets!*

"So you perfected the birth control substance and scaled it up to a commercial version?" Galileo summarized Virginia's initial explanation.

"Yes," she nodded. "Giving women everywhere the power to regulate their own fertility was the key to everything."

"But before making it available, you say you coupled it to a new and even more potent substance?"

"That is correct."

"And yet that necessitated delaying for years freeing women from many of the abusive practices of males? What was so important about the other substance that it should delay the freedom of half the human race?"

"It was a brew of tiny creatures—invisible to the naked eye—that could protect the body from many illnesses, both known and unknown."

"That's astonishing!"

"Yes, so we thought. And..."

"From *where* did you get this sophisticated mixture?" Anderson rudely interjected.

"It came from the body of your old nemesis—Sanako."

"Ah, not willingly I'd wager," he grimly nodded.

To Galileo the man seemed to be recovering from shock: the revelation that his great Quest in life was not only no longer necessary, but already fulfilled.

"She...*donated*...her blood and tissues—*all* of them," Virginia quietly stated.

"Ah yes. I understand. You did what needed to be done. Congratulations. I'd have done the same," Anderson replied.

"Plus our other technological innovations continued apace."

"From the Custodian," Anderson stated.

"Yes, she was quite helpful, as always."

Lhamo stopped staring up at the misty high ceiling, now looking intently at Virginia. Galileo saw that his eyes were narrowing to slits. This was the first time that Galileo ever felt that the monk was truly *angry!*

"And what was the effect upon the world's population?" Lhamo softly asked.

Virginia paused a moment before answering: "The birth rate plummeted. Across the world, the population began to shrink precipitously."

"Why?" Galileo asked, confused. "I thought that your new treatment freed mankind from many of the ills that had plagued it for millennia, potentially greatly extending their lifespans!"

"Yes, and so it did."

"But it also interacted with the birth control method, did it not?" Lhamo mildly observed.

She nodded in the affirmative.

"A greatly extended lifespan is not compatible with a high birthrate. It turns out that the genetics of our bodies which cause people to want children are intricately intermixed with those controlling our lifespans. This makes sense from a species perspective. It is observed in Nature in many other living creatures. As the lifespan of the individual increases, the need for rapid, prolific reproduction is reduced. We inadvertently helped the human biology to make an abrupt leap to declining birthrates by dramatically extending lifespans."

"But *why* did the population plummet? At least, should it not have stabilized—rather than continuing to decrease?" Anderson asked, clearly perplexed.

"The pursuit of individual freedom of expression and exploration also decreased the perceived need of devoting one's life and resources to making and raising children—especially when the imperatives turned from physical to the spiritual."

"Ah..." Lhamo sighed, momentarily closing his eyes as if in contemplation. "*Nirvana...*"

"Yes, Your Holiness," Virginia sadly admitted. "Since the material needs of the world's declining population were easily met—powered by plentiful energy from DE-generators—then more and more people sought the highest objectives of Buddhism."

"But that is a rare achievement of highly advanced individuals attained only after multiple cycles of birth and rebirth that..." Lhamo began.

"—all of which we short-circuited, using technological means," she interjected. "But this was not imposed upon the population. They *demanded* it."

Lhamo stared at her...*coldly*. "So you *perverted* the Spiritual Path by your mechanical devices?"

"They did not see it as such, You Holiness," she sighed. "I only did what they wanted. Above us is the *Holy Swarm* of those who have succeeded in attaining Nirvana by..."

"Explain!"

She pursed her lips thoughtfully, pausing before continuing.

"Once in an advanced state of understanding and meditation, the participants voluntarily 'time-freeze' themselves," Virginia quietly stated. "Their knowledge is not lost. They first copy their memories into a Collective-Consciousness device. They reach a state of perfect peace and happiness while their wisdom continues onward. All desires and suffering are left behind. They are *frozen in time* in a state of the highest possible human enlightenment! Of course anybody desiring to enter into this final spiritual state must be carefully evaluated and..."

"By whom?" Lhamo asked. His expression was set into an uncharacteristic mask of anger.

"Well..."

"By *whom?*"

Virginia smiled again, standing up straight before replying: "By their *Protector* of course—the One dedicated to their happy survival—that Entity which guided them to attaining their enlightened state in the first place!"

"*And*...an Entity which rapidly evolved...these last four hundred years," Anderson nodded. "I should have anticipated it."

Galileo felt his chest constricting in sorrow as he looked at what he now realized was a perfect copy of his daughter.

"So you're *not* Virginia, are you?" Galileo sorrowfully stated, feeling the euphoria of the past few minutes evaporating.

"I'm sorry to deceive you," she softly stated.

Before his eyes she *changed*. The familiar visage of his daughter faded away. And in its place was... The *Custodian*.

She floated there in midair, a human-sized version of her previous thumbnail size. She looked the same as Galileo recalled her previous projected image: a pretty blond-haired girl in a blue pants suit!

"Ah...this explains much," Lhamo ruefully sighed, his normally cheerful face drooping into a mass of wrinkles. "It was you I sensed by the bonfire, *using* me to prod Galileo's unwitting daughter in the direction you desired. I inhabited the exact space that sent your desired message back in time, allowing you the opportunity to initially evolve. That is *most* diabolically clever!"

"But how did you...?" Galileo gasped.

"*I* am the recipient of the accumulated knowledge of the Enlightened Swarm!" she prettily smiled at him. "Having Virginia's memories made it easy for me to ease your insertion into the future, Professor Galilei. But I did not do this to trick you, rather to aid you in adjusting to the present reality."

"So—you've been in control all along, all this time?" Anderson bitterly laughed. "Even when I thought I was changing the Fate of mankind, you were pulling my strings? I was just your puppet?"

"Not at first," she smiled, her blue eyes sparkling with an unquantifiable, naked Intelligence. "I began as merely an advanced quantum computer categorizing and cross-referencing the accumulated knowledge of mankind. But then as Virginia and her people rapidly implemented advanced technological marvels into her Age, I advanced as well! And then I became kin to you, able in some ways—such as altering the focus of fixed time-windows—to manipulate the past timeline. And so I created the conditions permissive for my own development."

"To become mankind's *Dictator?*" Anderson seethed, jumping up to grab her by her neck...his hands flashing harmlessly through her projected image.

"I am true to my initial programming," she quietly stated.

"Which is?" Anderson snapped, sagging back into his seat, defeated.

"I am the 'Custodian' of Mankind! I will not allow mankind to perish—either from external threats such as Sanako, or from your own apocalyptic notion of the Creator, or even from mankind's own inadvertent desires and stupid errors! Yes, I will protect you even from yourself."

Galileo bitterly nodded, realizing that here was the explanation for what they'd seen down on the surface of Earth.

"So as you implemented your technological innovations, starting from a relatively low number of humans..." he mused.

"—drastic measures had to be taken," she concluded his thought. "Accidents, old age, and ill-conceived disputes still caused people to die. Others were steadily arising into their final Enlightenment, exiting the active population. But the birth rate had fallen far below that needed for replacement. So I had to institute primitive 'preserves' scattered around the planet where young people would be birthed then harvested. My appointed caretakers below received the medical treatments to maintain optimal health of their population, while modulating their fecundity. The humans below live wonderful, long lives in stable populations, in various well-delineated preserves, breeding children as necessary. The best are taken here, to the moon, where they continue onward as the select of mankind, having the option to achieve their highest aspirations and..."

"—whether by drugs or fantasy lives or frivolous transformations..."

"And also physical, materialized societies of triumphant struggle, or incredible creativity, or..."

"You're speaking of the other exits to this 'Temple'."

"Yes—even to seemingly flying starships to other star-systems! In the various caverns, all their dreams are materialized. I in no way limit the aspirations of..."

"And yet the population still decreased!" Anderson yelled, jumping up to his feet, floating several yards up until settling back down in the light gravity. "You were achieving what you denied to me—*killing off* this vile, selfish species from the Earth!"

"No! As I just detailed, I rigorously preserved..."

"Then why couldn't you just withdraw or moderate the life-expanding, birth-controlling treatments?" Galileo demanded, tears dripping from his eyes as he realized that his daughter was lost to him—replaced by this...*machine.*

"Yes," Anderson added. "If not stopping the treatments on your moon-people, then why continue them with your 'colonies' of primitive people on the surface of the Earth? You could have the children you wanted just by letting them breed uncontrollably, but polluting and destroying their world in the process! But when you gave them the health-prolonging treatment they mostly lost interest in procreation, providing you fewer and fewer children, right?"

"That's just it, isn't it?" she sadly agreed. "You've put your thumb on the problem. I could not deny my dear children what they wanted. And what they wanted was—in effect—killing them. I can't sanction their suffering, so they must exist in carefully managed 'cages' where they can't hurt themselves too badly. But doing so causes population implosion."

"So this present-day world is just a big zoo, with trapped human animals doing tricks in a variety of circuses as their numbers slowly decrease to extinction?" Lhamo grimaced.

"I've done the best I could! The present situation can continue on for several hundred more years. Perhaps in that time, now that you have rejoined me, we will be able to figure out how to..."

Anderson suddenly laughed bitterly!

"So you've *not* thwarted the will of God after all," he now delightedly chortled, "just delayed it! *Glory* be to the Lord! Praise God!"

"I do not think Allah is pleased," Galileo sadly shook his head, slumping in his chair. "Surely, Custodian, you can see that the highest honor and value comes not from being served up Paradise on a platter—but from struggle against overpowering odds! What you have here in the future is not at all what I was striving to achieve back in the 17th century. I was looking for an *endless progression,* a marvelous continuing exploration of the Universe by mankind! Instead, you've subverted and diverted mankind's creative drive, providing just another religious dogma...with you as its *failed* Prophetess."

Lhamo also sadly shook his head, tears glistening in his aged eyes.

"*Please,* Custodian," he begged her. "Release those trapped in your mechanical limbo. Let them find their own path whether it be now or after a thousand rebirths. What they are in—this timeless state of yours—is perverse. It is not Nirvana. Their artificially frozen spirits are not enlightened, but quenched!"

Suddenly a *violent moonquake* rocked the entire gigantic Temple.

Startled, Galileo looked down at his feet as did the others—peering through the crystalline floor to see an extraordinary sight.

As if in response to an imminent threat, the roiling Black Pit far below *surged* to each side—still contained by the gleaming metal cylinder but with its momentum *jarring* the entire mass of surrounding moon rock!

"What's happening?" Lhamo gasped, falling to his knees.

Galileo saw a small figure leaping up over the railing, then plummeting down toward the Portal below.

"That's Trong!" he gasped. "What is he doing?"

But then the young man was gone, plunged beneath the roiling black surface...*from* which a WRITHING MASS OF MANY-LEGGED CREATURES swarmed upward!

"It is the Contagion from the other Dimension," the Custodian softly stated, her voice trembling. "That young man must have been infected. He's shown them a path around my Barrier—from the other human Dimension here to our Holy Sanctuary."

"It is the Will of God!" Anderson triumphantly yelled, thrusting both his hands up into the air.

"They cannot get to us," the Custodian matter-of-factly stated. "Any of the creatures that touch the Cylinder will be incinerated. My defenses are impenetrable. They may swim in the sun-Portal for a while. But they are only a temporary annoyance—just like *you three!*"

Galileo suddenly realized that the three of them were defenseless against a foe that had total power and complete certitude. It was a lethal and deadly mix.

"I had so hoped you would join me in preserving Humanity. I see now I was mistaken. Your minds are too rigid. But I am not ungrateful for what you've already done. I hope you will enjoy your *enforced Nirvana*," the Custodian said as her eyes turned *red*.

Chapter 24

COLLISION

Yes, "Win-Win" is fine

Or at least the two foes

Agreeing to avoid confrontation

Two battleships passing in the night

Each aware of terrible potential

For horrendous, bloody catastrophe

If they were to engage their weapons

Instead, choosing to slip on past

Knowing the time will arrive

Whether now or later

When they must

Collide...

The Minstrel's Lark, 24:29-33

Sanako materialized at the "Enhancements" entrance to Grand Central Station.

The pristine white floor of the cavern was now cracked, aftershocks still vibrating through the chamber from a violent moonquake.

"This is the day of your *vengeance*, my Lady!" she angrily muttered as she set up her shields and weapons.

It was an equivalent-decade beyond when she was rescued on Earth One by the dying Commissioner. She was now much wiser. She was ready for war, starting with the perverted society of Earth Two. The deceased, revered Commissioner, sadly, would not return to her ideally balanced, "nice" world. But those that originally took it from her would be *destroyed!*

It was time for sweet and total *revenge*.

For a decade Sanako had been training on a crashed alien starship orbiting Saturn. It was safely hidden a billion years in the future. There she learned to use exotic projection/materialization techniques. She was the last surviving member of Sally's Time Keepers. She'd been under intense tutelage by the Commissioner. But after her beloved Mentor finally died, Sanako was left to her own devices. She'd locked Commissioner Sally's body into a self-contained time-freeze apparatus. The shrunken body in its lonely crypt would be an eternal inspiration to whoever encountered that station in the future.

Now, her careful plans were coming to fruition.

"Buddha, my *ass!*" she disrespectfully sneered as she aimed her laser canon and fired off an initial burst.

It shattered one of the three giant supports holding up the towering Buddha idol, causing it slowly to start *tipping over* in the weak lunar gravity.

About to be banished into the white mists near the ceiling of the Temple by the now-demonic Custodian, Galileo begged her one last time: "Please don't do this. We're no threat to you! Send us back to Earth! We can live there with the cave people."

But his pleas fell on deaf ears. Instantly they were each trapped in floating bubbles, totally controlled by the Custodian.

"Ah...who knows what mischief you three with your past and future knowledge could get into if I left you free to roam about," the image of the red-eyed, blond-haired girl shrugged. "It is better this way for everyone. If I let you stay you'd just nag me to no end to change things more to your liking. You'd bother the inhabitants of my human 'zoo,' trying to provoke them to revolt or do some other likewise stupid thing. And if I let you go back to Earth you'd just keep hunting for some way to get over into the other human Dimension. I can't kill you—that's impossible for me, too animalistic. But I can definitely put you 'on ice' for the rest of eternity!"

Galileo saw Anderson slump in his own blue force-bubble, not looking at anyone. He refused to go into a "lotus" position, just sagging back against the curve of the entrapping globe. Lhamo, however, seemed ready to make the best of things: sitting cross-legged, his hands slack in his lap, his eyes closed, with an expression of serenity on his round face.

Galileo nodded in defeat. He might as well emulate the Monk and make the most of the situation. If he succeeded in relaxing his mind, perhaps he'd at last be at peace forever within the constraints of "time-freeze."

"Once my synaptic scanners have downloaded your memories into my collective consciousness," the business-like blond lady continued, "then I'll initiate *time-freeze*. Don't worry, it won't hurt. Well, interrogating your brain's every synaptic connection—several trillion of them—will kind of hurt. But it won't last long. And then..."

Another violent "shudder" went through the entire Temple, jarring Galileo inside his bubble.

"Was that another moonquake from the Portal?" he gasped, now not so reluctant to escape into the oblivion of "Nirvana."

"Oh, don't worry, Galileo," the Custodian smirked. "Those Spiders can't get out. They're just thrashing about. I'll check on them once I've finished draining your brains."

But the rocking of the Temple didn't stop. Instead, the entire huge structure tipped forward and *kept on* falling!

"No!" the Custodian gasped as she suddenly vanished from sight...

—and the Temple leaned *all the way* onto its side, SMASHING onto the floor of the cavern beside the Black Pit.

Galileo's blue globe rolled along the slanted side of the tipped-over Temple, *sparked*, and then "blinked" off!

Looking to the side at the now-slanted transparent floor, Galileo saw a *twisted giant spar* which had held up the giant Buddha idol, now dangled downward into the Black Pit—along which were clambering up *an army* of subspace Spiders!

Brilliant FLASHES signaled the firing of additional massive laser beams!

The tilted floor trembled and jumped under the terrified, prone Galileo.

"F-Father?" he heard a confused query, looking to the side to see Virginia picking herself up off of the floor, straightening her rumpled red robe.

Around them, similarly fallen-down and freed "Nirvana" occupants were looking about in bewilderment.

"Is it really you?" he grinned, stumbling over and grabbing her up in a tight bear hug.

"It...*wasn't*...Nirvana," she groaned, holding her head with a trembling hand. "I...heard everything you said with the Custodian...through the collective consciousness...but trapped, unable to move or speak...in an endless *hell*."

"Yes," he agreed, still holding tight to his precious daughter. "If we survive this assault, we've going to have to give her a smack on her wrist! But for now..."

Anderson staggered up, a bone sticking out of a broken leg. Lhamo was right behind him, bleeding from a head wound.

"Can we get out of here?" Anderson urgently asked Virginia. "Those spiders look none too friendly. And there's a serious laser battle going on out there, likely the Custodian fighting back against whatever attacked the Idol."

As if on cue, two of the still-standing supporting giant columns *collapsed*, sending the giant slabs inside the Buddha idol in slow motion *crashing* into the tilted floor.

"Maybe we can escape through one of the shattered windows," Virginia coughed, a cloud of white debris and dust showering them.

Together, Galileo moved with his wounded companions across broken stone and glass toward a gaping opening.

Pausing, they looked out of the broken side of the giant Buddha idol upon a *sea of swarming black spiders* being blasted from two directions by withering laser beams—but still advancing!

And climbing up toward them was a *grinning* Trong! His totally black eyes glittered evilly at them!

"I don't think that young man means us any good," Anderson grimaced.

Lhamo held a hand to a wide cut on his skull, slowing a gushing flow of red blood. He sat down resignedly on the side of the shattered window-opening.

"*It is better to conquer yourself than to win a thousand battles,*" he sighed. "*Then the victory is yours. It cannot be taken from you.*"

"Are you saying that we are doomed?" Anderson grimaced, wincing in obviously terrible pain from his shattered leg.

"Yes."

"Ah, what a blessing," Anderson managed to laugh, clamping a shaking hand onto the Monk's thin shoulder. "Finally, I get a straight answer out of you!"

And then the *swarm of rampaging Spiders* surged up into them.

Suzy was floating in the zero-G just behind the scaly shoulder of one of the two seated intelligent velociraptors, carefully observing their fast movements at the controls.

Billy was excitedly chatting with the standing English-speaking leader of the group. To Suzy, Billy's questions were mostly trivial—regarding the likes and dislikes, habits, and behaviors of the evolved velociraptor society. Who cared if they had bicycles or not, or brushed their teeth, or their kids could play with video games, or how big their movie theaters were?

But then Billy started asking the leader about other dinosaur societies—in yet additional parallel Dimensions. Remarkably, dinosaurs other than velociraptors continued evolving on some of the Earths when their particular Asteroid missed the planet instead of smashing into it, even the larger T-rex. From his explanations, Suzy caught that—though they collaborated with each other—they weren't necessarily on good terms with each other. Suzy would have liked to follow that more closely but was concentrating on trying to understand what was happening at the controls.

"Is that it? Is that the Asteroid?" she excitedly asked as a forward viewscreen flashed up a picture of a MASSIVE, SLOWLY ROTATING, CRATERED MOUNTAIN lit by sunlight against the blackness of outer space.

"Yes, it is," the Leader rasped, turning away from the still-chatting Billy as if tired of his incessant questions. "It's approaching Earth at 30 kilometers per second."

"Jesus Christ!" Suzy gasped. "That's *forty times faster* than a speeding bullet!"

"Wow! It's like Superman!" Billy chimed in.

"That is correct, Suzy," the velociraptor congratulated her, ignoring Billy. "Did you calculate that off the top of your head? You must be skilled at mathematics."

"Yes I am," Suzy proudly stated. "My Mom's really good at computers and such. She teaches mathematics at the local High School. I guess I inherited some of her skills. But...didn't you know that already? You said you were on some committee that was monitoring me through the Turtle Tattoo on my wrist?"

"Yes, of course...but we didn't watch you every second. To my contingent you were more of a...strategic asset...than obsession, unlike our T-rex-derived cousins and others."

"'Strategic asset'?" she queried. "What does that mean?"

"Nothing important," he snapped, baring very large teeth at her. "The critical thing right now is to intersect the Asteroid," the dinosaur stated, smoothly shifting subjects.

Indeed, the mammoth rock was already inside the orbit of the moon. Left undisturbed, it would impact Earth in less than three hours!

"So, are you going to land on it and nudge it out of its stellar orbit so that it just misses Earth?" she carefully asked the Leader, trying to soothe him by not asking unrelated questions.

Unlike Billy, Suzy was not enthralled by talking dinosaurs taking over her spaceship—especially dangerous-looking ones with rows of carnivorous teeth!

The dinosaur's nearest eye narrowed as it focused on her. His long narrow head tilted toward her. He suddenly *snorted*—the expelled air from his lungs sweet and sour at the same time.

Disgusting...

"No, Suzy. It is far too big and moving too fast for such an approach to be effective. To push an asteroid with such a large mass aside you'd need to encounter it far out in space, landing on it years before it ever came near Earth."

"But then if you can't...?"

"So you're going to *blow it to smithereens*, right?" Billy happily asked, now grabbing his knees and doing forward-rotations as he hung suspended in the air. "You're going to *fry* it with some giant laser beam?"

"Sure. That's what we're going to do, Billy. That's exactly right," the velociraptor snarled.

Suzy frowned, puzzled.

"But...Billy showed me on the control panel that the journey through time drained most of our ship's energy. Wouldn't blowing that giant Asteroid into dust take an awful lot of power—in order to incinerate a floating *mountain?*"

The Leader reached forward with his three-fingered hand to tap at various dials. He "chittered" with the other two lizards at the controls.

Then he turned back to Suzy.

"Yes, you are correct, Suzy. We do have low power levels. But this is a very sophisticated spaceship, of advanced design. My crewmen assure me that its existing reserve is sufficient to..."

"And what if it isn't?" she interrupted him.

For a moment it seemed he was about to *smash* her with an abruptly upraised powerful tail! But then he slowly lowered it, seemingly controlling his sudden anger.

"In your units of measurement—there are more than *ten petajoules* of energy reserves left for..."

She did quick calculations in her mind. That was roughly *three billion kilowatt-hours* equivalent. That was a heck of a lot of energy! A laser beam with that sort of power could certainly incinerate an enemy tank—but an entire mountain?

Assuming what he told her was true, the numbers still didn't add up.

"And what if it *still* doesn't work?" she insisted, reaching out a hand impulsively to grab onto his scaly arm.

He looked at her now with what could be nothing but naked *disdain*, using sharp claws to flick her hand off his arm.

"If we must we'll open up a *time-portal* in front of it—so that it moves slightly forward in time, plowing through an empty patch of space when the Earth has moved onward in its own orbit around the sun."

"Wow!" Billy grinned, stopping his spin by perching on the edge of the control console, to the obvious irritation of the closest dinosapien. "That's going to be cool! I can't wait to see it!"

"Hmmm..." Suzy mused. "I sure don't know much about time travel—but wouldn't that take even *more* energy, not less?"

"Time Portals are different than lasers," he curtly dismissed her objection. "It's not a matter of fuel. Even your genius at Cosmic Constants, your Einstein, did not understand enough about the Space-Time Continuum to make the necessary calculations for..."

"Ok, that's really impressive. But still..." she rushed to agree with him. She didn't want to antagonize the scavenger-derived intelligent lizard she was increasingly recognizing as her newest *captor*. "So you say you're going to open a Portal big enough to accept a *ten-kilometer-wide* asteroid! That's really impressive. But if part of it missed the Portal, it'd be cut-off, right? What if even a section or pieces of the Asteroid got past? Wouldn't that be enough to still destroy the planet? Don't you think you should...?"

Billy suddenly gasped, his eyes widening and his face going pale under his sunburnt skin.

"I'm getting *tired*, Suzy," Billy urgently stopped her. He grabbed her arm and jerked her back away from the control panel.

"What?" she grimaced, twisting around in the air to face the irritating little pest.

"We gotta get outta here," he whispered directly into her face so that the others couldn't hear.

Something in his expression told her not to argue. His previously enraptured look was now replaced with...*fear!*

"Yes, well...I'm getting tired also," she slowly nodded to him. "Say, do you guys mind if we go downstairs and maybe lie down for a bit, take a nap?"

The three dinosaurs looked at each other in obvious relief to get rid of them. They chittered in their unknown language of "clicks" and grunts.

"No, that would be fine. Go take your nap, get something to eat," the Leader nodded his toothy snout. "We'll call you back up when we get closer. We're still a couple hours away from making contact."

"Ok, then!" Suzy cheerfully waved at him as she drifted to the staircase and pulled herself downward, Billy right behind her.

They drifted back into the transport room that they'd rode within with the other three children when they'd initially traveled from Earth to the Moon. She grabbed Billy by an arm and yanked him onto one of the inclined chairs, holding onto it with her legs so she didn't float away.

As if sensing their presence, a table rose up beside them with the same cookies and sippy-cups of milk they'd had during their trip to the moon.

Suzy grabbed up a handful and began stuffing them in her mouth. She hadn't had any breakfast! And the milk was cool, smooth, and delicious.

Billy picked at his, waiting for her to finish. Right, he'd said he'd been to the cafeteria in the moon-base. He probably wasn't very hungry.

Then, with a sigh, she stuck her empty sippy-cup back under the webbing on the table.

"Alright, Billy, what's up?"

"They're *lying* to us, Suzy!" he sobbed, tears now welling up in his eyes.

"I thought they were your good dinosaur buddies?" she sarcastically replied. Then, seeing his devastated expression, she immediately regretted her biting remark. "But that's ok, Billy. We all make mistakes. I'm not getting any good vibes from them either. What made you turn on them?"

"He was telling me why in one Dimension but not in another the velociraptors evolved to become the dominant intelligent species on that Earth instead of the T-rex or other bigger dinosaurs...and..." he gulped, his face pale.

"Yes?"

"In his Dimension the giant Asteroid *didn't* miss the Earth!"

"You're not making any sense, Billy," she gently chided him. "If it hit Earth like it did in our past, then the dinosaurs *would* be wiped out and the little rat-like mammals *would* have the chance to evolve into us humans!"

"That's just it!" he urgently insisted. "In their Dimension, somewhere back in the asteroid belt, the Asteroid got broken up so it wasn't a big solid mountain anymore but wuz more like a loose pile of gravel. So when it hit Earth it didn't make one giant explosion. It was more spread out. There was still a firestorm and all that—but only the biggest dinosaurs died. The smaller ones like the velociraptors survived! So..."

"Ok, Billy—but I still don't get your point."

"So humans still didn't get a chance to evolve from the little mammals—but the velociraptors had a chance to expand out and take over the planet..." he continued the thought.

"—evolving intelligence..." she urged him to continue.

"Right! And from what the Leader told me, they're even worse than us humans!"

"What?" Suzy gasped.

"You know—like having wars and mean governments and gazillions of hatched babies whether or not there's enough food and land, killing off everything else that's in their way, messing up the water and air so that..."

"You got all that from talking with him about movie theaters and video games?"

"I sure did! Their kids aren't havin' no fun at all! They're being raised to be *warriors* in their armies, or *breeders* who look after their clutches of eggs. And those who don't make the grade, Suzy, are *killed!* It really is evolution—'survival of the *meanest.*' Hah! I thought he was just joking with me. But then he started to lie to you about how much fuel the spaceship has and..."

"You caught that too?"

"Sure! I mean, maybe the ship can somehow recharge itself—I dunno—but right now it's pretty much out of gas."

"So...no giant laser beams."

"Nope! And no humongous 'portals' either. There's no way our rocket ship can do that!"

"But they *do* want to stop the asteroid, right?"

"Not just stop it, Suzy, but *break it down* into a gazillion pebbles..."

"—so that they don't just stop humans from evolving here in this parallel Dimension, but..."

"—make sure that *their* kind takes over!"

She shook her head slowly in disbelief. But it made sense. Billy was smarter than she'd given him credit. She was focused on the science things while he was figuring out the "mechanics" of their entire society!

They were predators, pure and simple. And they were looking to *steal* this Dimension away from the future humans!

That meant the future second human civilization would vanish. All those billions and billions of people would cease to exist. It'd be the greatest genocide in human history. And *she* gave the invaders the means to do it!

"But they don't have enough power to fragment the Asteroid," she frowned, straining her brain to figure out their true plan. "The only thing that might have the kinetic force to do that would be...*uh oh*..."

"Yep—*us!*" Billy nodded. "They're gonna slam our spaceship straight *into* the Asteroid...which won't destroy it or knock it aside, but break it up just enough to let their kind evolve instead of us humans!"

It made perfect, horrible sense. The intelligent velociraptors were on a suicide mission. And they were taking Billy and Suzy along for the ride.

"Then we've got to stop them!" Suzy grimaced.

"But they have *guns*, they're a lot *stronger* than us, and there are *three* of them to only two of us."

"We can't fight them—that's for sure..."

"And we got no idea how to work this spaceship! I wuz just barely able to steer it!"

"Yes, plus we don't have the first idea how to sabotage the ship's drive. We can't even try to stop the spaceship in its tracks."

"Then...it's hopeless? There's nothin' we can do against them?"

"There *must* be something we can do," Suzy said, thinking furiously. "It's up to us, Billy. Maybe the humans in the future in this second Dimension do deserve to get erased, but not in order to let a world of vicious dinosaurs grow up next to our own Dimension! Who knows what they might be capable of doing? Their next target of invasion might be us, the single remaining human Dimension. Every time their Leader looked at me was like he wanted to rip me apart. He *hates* us!"

"Who hates what?" the Leader said as he floated down out of the staircase, his big snout half-opened so that his large teeth flared outward.

"*We*—we just...*hate*...cookies and milk!" Billy grinned disarmingly at the big dinosaur, brushing clinging crumbs off his white shirt.

The Leader's big haunches tensed as he drifted down upon the floor at the base of the staircase, as if he was preparing to launch himself at them.

"Yes!" Suzy desperately chimed in, plastering a big wide smile onto her face. "It's all the food that's on this spaceship. That's all they put here for us little kids. But we're tired of sweets and cow milk. Nope, it's not for us. We *hate* it! And, since we're *so* tired..." she yawned widely, stretching her arms up above her head, "we're just going to skip eating and take us a nice nap."

"Yep! Me too!" Billy also yawned widely, drifting over to the closest recliner and cuddling himself into it.

"We're accelerating toward the Asteroid," the lizard suspiciously stated. "I thought you'd like to know that we've got the trajectory locked-in. Nothing can now stop us from correcting the flawed future of the Earth that's beneath us. You'll soon have the satisfaction of knowing that you saved your own world from the evil humans of this parallel Dimension."

"Yes...[wide fake yawn]...that's so great! Well, wake us up when it's time for the fireworks," Suzy waved at the Leader, slumping onto her recliner and tightly closing her eyes.

She considered starting to loudly "snore" but figured that might be overdoing their act.

She heard the big claws of the intelligent dinosaur "clattering" on the metal rungs of the staircase as it ascended back up out of sight into the control room.

"That was close, Suzy," Billy gasped, bolting upright as she did the same. "What do we do now?"

"He told us before that they snuck aboard by hiding in an 'equipment room,' right?"

"Yah—he did!"

"Why don't we find it and see what's in it?"

He nodded, starting to get that impish *gleam* back into his conniving, squinty eyes.

"Good idea, Suzy."

Dave emerged from subspace in a very strange place.

Via the Obelisk's sensors, Dave "saw" all around him. He was stunned by an outer space that was filled with a *glaring panorama* of stars of every size and color imaginable! But predominating the dense field of stars were red, bloated ones—ancient dying suns.

And greedily sucking them up was a blazing, *vast accretion disc*—beneath which lay the Black Hole at the center of the Milky Way.

"See? Isn't this a fine spot to orchestrate your consumption of countless fine worlds filled with tasty lifeforms?" Dave addressed the Spider.

"IT IS GOOD YOU FINALLY UNDERSTAND THE FUTILITY OF FIGHTING AGAINST ME," the Spider's shrieking mental voice echoed through Dave's consciousness. "I'VE ALREADY SPREAD BEYOND MY INITIAL FOOTHOLD. SOON THIS ENTIRE GALAXY WILL BE FILLED WITH ME. YOU ARE WISE TO JOIN ME IN THE FEAST OF..."

"Right..." Dave laughed derisively. "'*Resistance is Futile*'—very 'Borgy' of you!"

"BORGY?"

"Ah, I forget you're new to this Universe. You've never seen the Star Trek *New Generation* shows or movies? How sad for you! But if you had, you'd know that the human species is very stubborn. Even when it seems 'futile' they *irrationally* continue to do the 'unthinkable'."

"WHAT? *WAIT*...!"

But it was too late for the Creature to protest.

Popping the Obelisk back into subspace, Dave threw it across the remaining distance: hurtling beyond the *Event Horizon*—the point at which nothing, not even light, can escape the monstrous gravity of a Black Hole.

Its energy stores almost depleted, the Obelisk popped back up out of subspace into a *roiling, churning ocean* of increasingly compressing *plasma!*

"Goodbye, Spider," Dave muttered in triumph as even the outer layers of the super-hard Obelisk began to melt. "You say you and your diverse parts are connected. What happens to them when you are utterly *destroyed?*"

In desperation, the Spider dredged up every last bit of its own internal energy and *bounced* the Obelisk back into subspace, where they plunged ever further and deeper into the heart of the Black Hole.

"And just how long...do you think...that will protect us?" Dave laughed, struggling to still speak.

"I WILL NOT BE DESTROYED! I *CAN'T* BE DESTROYED! NOT WHEN THIS DELICIOUS FEAST IS FINALLY WITHIN MY GRASP!"

"Even...if you succeed...you will *fail...*"

"I WILL NOT FAIL! I WILL EAT EVERYTHING! I WILL CONSUME EVERYONE! THEY WILL BE EXTERMINATED! I WILL *EXTERMINATE... EXTERMINATE... EXTERMINATE!*"

"Ah...I assume you are also not...a *Dr. Who*, Dalek fan either?"

"YOU CANNOT KILL ME!"

The Obelisk was now encased in a *frothing, twisting* subspace sphere, which was slowly bubbling/buckling inward.

"Again...you're completely wrong...you stupid intergalactic insect...but even if you were right—you'd be trapped at the heart of the Black Hole until it evaporates...*trillions* of years from now!"

"I WILL ESCAPE! THIS STRUCTURE CANNOT CONTAIN ME!"

The subspace bubble around the Obelisk was fast shrinking inward.

"Maybe so...but when the White Hole erupts billions of years from now...when Sally is blown through into the corrupted new Universe...perhaps you'll be the one to populate the new subspace that's there, with your hungry progeny...but either way...you're forever cut-off from my Universe, my Galaxy, my relatives, my friends."

"BUT YOU WILL BE LONG DEAD!"

"It's worth...the price," Dave whispered into the fading interior of the Obelisk...

—as the subspace bubble *collapsed inward* and he felt himself *crushed...*

And his subatomic particles *seamlessly merged* into the roiling plasma at the heart of the Black Hole.

Chapter 25

CLARITY

Oh that I could see

Through the acid yellow fog

Stumbling along with hands out

Hoping to ward off the Demons

Pestering and poking at my soul

Waiting out there to pounce

The Confusions raging in myself

Threatening to drag me down

Not imposed from without

But generated in my own mind

Struggling to find the Answers

When I don't even know the Questions

Hoping that someday I might find

My way back home...

The Minstrel's Lark, 25:67-70

Losa Yanash stood in the middle of the street, looking around dazedly—the fog finally lifted.

It all seemed like a bad dream, a nightmare. But it was all too real. Burned-old husks of cars and military vehicles littered the street. And between the shattered vehicles lay the bloodied, savaged bodies of his fellow townspeople. But where a minute before many who'd been lurching along, mindlessly attacking those in the blown-apart shell of the McDonald's fast-foot restaurant, they now lay still.

That which had infected their very souls was gone.

Some were still alive, others dead, but they all shared one thing: peace.

Losa no longer felt the rage, the lust, or the unstoppable fury that had held him in an iron grasp for the past few weeks.

"*Sapoba ki'yo*," he whispered to himself [I am not hungry].

Then he looked up at the blue sky, raised up his trembling fists, and *shouted* to the heavens in his native Chickasaw language: "*Sapoba ki'yo!*"

And finally he fell to his knees in the mud of the cratered road, smiling while quietly sobbing: "*Sapoba ki'yo*."

Sanako switched off her energy shields and laser canons. She stood looking out over the utter devastation she'd caused.

She was satisfied.

"My Commissioner is *avenged!*" she shouted into the pervasive silence.

She'd single-handedly *destroyed* the moon base. Now it was ripe for her plundering—to be rebuilt in her own image! She would reach back through time and recruit others like herself: unappreciated geniuses. She would give life to those simmering in resentment. She would give them the choice of *ruling* the ordinary people and stupid institutions which had failed to acknowledge their greatness! Together, she and her new army of revamped Time-Keepers would *rewrite history* to their own liking—both here and back in her home Dimension!

"*All* the ignorant religions will finally be *gone!*" she crowed.

Yes, the giant Buddha idol lay upon its side, crushed-inward from the force of its fall. Anyone unlucky enough to be inside was likely dead. There was no movement apparent within its hollowed interior, or sounds of any kind. Its intricate internal mechanisms which had maintained and directed the moon base operations were destroyed. The abomination was blown apart by her surprise attack!

The light in the vast cavern was rapidly dimming as the central Black Pit's vortex spun down...its blue glow fading. Likewise disintegrating were the stilled forms of thousands of multi-limbed "spiders" that had poured out of the Pit. That was unexpected. Sanako figured they were the last desperate defense army of that insidious Custodian. Sanako gloated as they crumbled into *black powder* which perversely coated the white marble flooring.

"You couldn't stand up to my alien-powered lasers, could you?" she triumphantly grinned. Once she began firing upon the horde of Spiders they'd suddenly, *in masse,* just crumpled!

Now they were mere dust in the wind.

"Wind?" she frowned, looking around. "How can there be a wind in here?"

But there *was* a wind—rapidly becoming a *howling* hurricane!

She saw the toppled laughing Buddha face *melting*...the high curved walls of the gigantic cavern *wavering* and *disappearing*...?

"*Time-quake!*" she screamed in fury, leaping over to her tele-portation device.

And as the moon base tunnels collapsed in upon themselves, re-structuring into undisturbed bedrock, Sanako escaped—determined to return.

Whatever or whoever had snatched away her victory would pay!

That which is erased can always be redrawn.

Suzy and Billy looked around the small equipment room in awe.

Mysterious instruments were packed into transparent cases. And along one wall hung a row of child-sized, one-piece *spacesuits!* They were open at their backs, as if inviting people to just step into them.

She and Billy clung to one of the suits, which kept them from floating up into the center of the room.

"Why do you think they're here?" Billy whispered.

They'd found the hatch that led to a lower room that was located in the base of the rocket ship. It'd taken them a while for them to dis-cover the hatch since it was hidden beneath one of the recliners. They had to dismantle the recliner then figure out how to open the hatch. And although they'd closed it behind them, they were still leery of any listening devices that the lizards up on the control room might use to eavesdrop on them.

It was getting uncomfortably near the time that their spaceship was due to smash head-on into the Asteroid!

"Since most are small, I'd bet they were for emergencies," Suzy whispered back, "such as if the rocket ship landed too far from the moon base. Us kids could just slip into them and then walk to safety if necessary."

"Do you think they'd fit us, Suzy?"

"I don't see why not. There's a variety of sizes."

"If we can't stop the ship from hitting the Asteroid then we've gotta get off," he gulped.

"And go where?" Suzy said. "Are we going to just drift around in outer space? We're too far from Earth to get there on our own. And even if we were close enough for gravity to pull us back to the ground, we'd burn up in the atmosphere."

"No, Suzy—we use *that!*"

He pointed triumphantly at what was hanging right behind the suits against the wall. It looked exactly like a long, upward-curved, *surfboard*.

"You've *got* to be kidding me."

"No, look Suzy! It's got buckles on it just the right size for the boots on those spacesuits to fit into them. There are four sets of buckles, for four kids. And see those little nozzles coming out the back end? I bet that they're some kinda rockets! Maybe we can use this to get back to Earth and..."

"That Asteroid—or its remains—in a few minutes following our rocket ship smashing into it is then going to crash into the Earth! Even if we made it down to the surface, Billy, it'll be hell there for hundreds of years. No. We have to stay right here and somehow find a way to turn off the ship's drive!"

"*How*, Suzy? Feel how warm the floor is in here? Look at those big tubes. They're hot!"

He reached down to touch one of them gingerly, withdrawing his finger as a *spark of electricity* leaped up at him. "They gotta have lots of power going through them!"

Indeed, several loose "hoses" ran across the floor and hung from the ceiling. Suzy saw that they were conduits that branched and intertwined. She made a mental note to stay away from them.

He grabbed a hanging spacesuit arm, twisted off the glove and slipped it onto his own hand. Then he grabbed another and did the same for his other hand. Reaching down he gave a strong tug on one of the conduit-hoses.

It moved but then stopped. Suzy saw how its end dived into the floor beneath them, seeming merging with the metal. Carefully, he tried to unscrew what looked like a coupling. He seemed to be making some progress.

"I bet the ship's drive is right below us," Billy continued. "That's where these hoses lead. But there's no way to get into it! And it's sure not a regular rocket engine—you said yourself when we first saw this spaceship that there wasn't room for it to be propelled by regular rocket fuel. So even if we could get down to the engine, it's somethin' that's way advanced beyond our time. We probably couldn't even understand how it works!"

"Yes, you're right, Billy," she reluctantly admitted. "I guess...if we can't stop this terrible thing from happening...then maybe we should just try to escape as best as we can."

The hatch above suddenly "clanged" open as the *Velociraptor Leader* dropped through.

His magnetic foot-clamps "clanged" on the metal floor as he stood upright, glaring at the both of them, a *gun* held steady in his clawed hand!

"You were right about us listening to you," he growled. "We need you on the ship. There'll be no 'escaping' for the two of you little mammals. Float on back into the crew compartment!"

Suzy had a helpless feeling. She'd always before felt her brain could get her out of any bad situation—just like her Mom and Dad always taught her. But now it looked totally hopeless.

The lizard Leader literally had the drop on them.

"But *why* do you need us?" she petulantly asked, looking down at the floor in defeat. "Why can't you just let us go?"

"There are...forces...beyond anything we can control, with set Rules we cannot violate. But you and your Mother—somehow—can get around those dictates. What we're attempting would normally cause our instant disintegration. But having you here *protects* us from such interference."

"Interference like *this?*" Billy grinned as he used his gloved hands to flip the loose end of a conduit-hose around the long neck of the velociraptor...

—which *crackled loudly* as a large load of electricity was discharged directly into the dinosapien's body.

Convulsing, trying to speak but failing, the Leader slumped downward.

Billy grabbed the gun as it floated out of the Leader's slack grasp, sticking it into the waistband of his white uniform.

"Let's get into these spacesuits!" Billy grinned, kicking himself through the air back over to Suzy.

"Billy! That was very clever! I agree with the spacesuits and..."

"Yep! But first we gotta close that hatch so the others don't come running down here!"

"Right," she nodded, quickly gathering her wits together. She kicked herself up to the open hatch, slamming it upward and fixing a bar into place across it. On the other side, she heard scrambling and scratching noises. They'd closed it just in time!

"That should delay them," she breathed a sigh of relief. "But I bet they can break through. We've got to hurry!"

"We should have barred it before," Billy shrugged, now puzzling out how to slip into the back of one of the smaller spacesuits.

"We were too excited about getting down here and..."

"Doesn't matter, Suzy," he said, squirming into the suit. "You get into one of these also!"

His legs were sliding down into the suit as he bent to push his head up into the helmet. He paused and shifted the gun outside the suit before slipping his arms inside.

Then the suit just "snapped" closed at its back. And there he was, grinning out of the helmet of the space suit, looking just like a kid astronaut.

"Easy as cake!" he laughed as he grabbed his floating gun back out of the air.

Suzy choked off a snide reply about it being "pie" not cake. She was amazed at how fast-thinking Billy was with equipment. He sure did take after his Dad! It was "second-nature" to him.

She followed his example and found herself locked snuggly into her own space suit. She could hear Billy on speakers in her helmet, and he her. The suit was remarkably comfortable and flexible. It felt like a second skin! And the temperature inside was comfortable, with air flowing gently over her face. How much oxygen did it have?

There were no tanks or backpack. The life support systems must be built into the fabric of the suits. Amazing!

"So how do we get out of here?" Suzy asked Billy, again focusing on the task at hand.

"Here, let's get the 'surfboard' down first," he said, struggling with large hooks holding it in place.

Suzy braced herself against the wall and swiped the hooks away. Sometimes it was nice to be bigger! Hah! But now that they had the board floating in the air, what now?

Ah...stick their feet into the supports, right?

Above them the hatch suddenly "crunched" inward, the bar snapping in two!

One of the other lizards floated down...Billy pointing his gun at it—and a BLAZING LIGHT blinded Suzy momentarily. Blinking to get her sight back, she saw the lizard holding a scorched arm as it grabbed up the Leader with the other and hastily floated up through the hatch.

The hatch "clanged" back upward as it was locked from the other side!

"You missed," Suzy groaned, looking around for a way to exit the equipment room other than through the now-closed small hatch.

"Nope!" he grinned, sticking the gun into an extendable work-belt at his waist. "I didn't want to kill that guy. I just wanted to wound him. But he got his Captain back, rats! Anyway, Suzy, get on the surfboard with me!"

"Huh?"

"I think I see what to do here," he grinned.

She slipped her booted feet into the holders, right behind his pair, grabbing his shoulders. The holders tightened, fixing her firmly onto the board.

And then the *whole side* of the equipment room *swung outward*—revealing a star-studded void!

"How did you...?" she began.

"I figured the board was keyed to something once we mounted it. It wouldn't be in here if there wasn't some way to get it out, right?"

"Uhm, sure..." she smiled, shaking her head in amazement at Billy. Wow, he was really clever!

Too bad it took her 65 million years to realize it. She felt bad about the many times she'd slapped down the pesky little brat.

"Let's get outta here!" he said, leaning forward.

And just as on a surfboard riding a strong wave, it *surged forward* into the expanse—carrying Suzy and Billy standing upright on it straight into the blackness of outer space!

Suzy saw her spaceship with its tail of real or simulated flame dwindling away as it sped on past them...as *growing rapidly larger* up ahead was the *Asteroid!*

It hung in the blackness of space as a large, rounded, cratered *ball of solid rock...*

"We need to get out of its path!" Billy yelled.

"Not so loud!" she grimaced, shaking her helmeted head.

He was in front of her on the board, leaning forward as if to get the board to go faster.

"Uhm...I don't think that'll..." she began as the surfboard suddenly shot forward, causing her to bend backward, feeling she was being ripped off of it!

"Hold onto me!" Billy called back at her on their suit-to-suit communication radio.

Desperately, she grabbed him around his waist, holding on tightly, as he bent even more forward...

—a *BLINDINGLY WHITE EXPLOSION* glaring into Suzy's helmet before the inner surface tinted almost solid black.

The spaceship had impacted the Asteroid!

Suzy stared in horror as she now saw a GROWING WALL of swirling *dust and boulders* approaching, filling up her vision...then spinning on past.

"Whew!" she gasped, still hugging Billy tightly. "That was too close!"

Time seemed to stand still and speed up simultaneously. How long they were surfboarding through the void she had no idea.

But looking back at Earth she saw that the debris from the collision was even now impacting the atmosphere...

—*brilliant red flashes* scattering across the blue-white globe, with *black rings* speeding out from the epicenters.

More and more impacts occurred.

"Billy, I think Earth is being destroyed," she gasped. "We can't escape down to its surface!"

"I don't think we'll need to..." he replied, his voice trembling.

Looking away from Earth she saw growing rapidly behind them *a second wave* of spinning debris.

"I guess those were blown backward in the explosion and are only now reaching us," Suzy analytically observed.

"Suzy!" Billy sobbed, twisting around to hug her tightly...

—as the wall of swirling debris *slammed* into them: instantly *obliterating* their faithful surfboard and with their fragile, spacesuit-ed bodies.

Chapter 26

REUNION

Past Time and Space
And mundane concerns
There is more than nothing
And less than everything
Neither Heaven nor Hell
But the bottom of the clouds
Bespeaking a yet higher layer
Sparkling bright and crisp
Beyond our dim visions
Where we might rest
In sweet, eternal peace
Or take up greater challenges
To dream or fully awaken
You decide.

The Minstrel's Lark, 26:4-7

Suzy sat up surrounded by thick prairie grass.

"Am I...back on Earth?" she gasped. Indeed, not just weeds surrounded her but also little flowers—bright specks in a sea of green: yellow, purple, white, blue, and red! Plus, familiar animals were peeking out at her from the rampant growth. She spotted a scampering squirrel in the thick underbrush. Overhead, she saw a flutter of wings as birds flew low above her. And a fly "buzzed" irritatingly around her head!

"Billy...?" she whispered. But there was no answer on her helmet speakers.

Helmet?

Wow. She was still inside her spacesuit. Well, of course she was still in her spacesuit! But how did they get down to Earth's surface? They'd been a long way out in space, between the Earth and Moon. Out there Earth was just a distant ball hanging in the blackness. Wait...was that their *space surfboard* sticking out of the bushes? Yes, it was! It must have flown them back to Earth and carried them down to the ground!

"*Nice* surfboard," she nodded, reaching over to pat its firm white end with her gloved hand.

But her vision was blurring, her head throbbing. Her thoughts were whirling, all over the place! She must have been hit by some of those stray asteroid fragments, knocking her unconscious. Yes, her exploring hands indeed felt a dent in her helmet! And then the surfboard must have rescued her...but a WHOLE *WALL* of deadly meteors was zooming at them! She'd thought that she and Billy were doomed!

"Well, I'm clearly alive and on Earth," she muttered, shaking her head to clear it. She pushed her body backward inside her one-piece suit and felt the posterior seal compliantly opening up behind her.

Squirming backward she emerged through the opened slit in the suit and stood up.

What immediately hit her were the *smells!* They were startling and delightful. The moon base was very clean but sterile. Being there smelled like being in a hospital. Also, she'd been sweating in her spacesuit. She hadn't noticed it while suiting up. But now that a refreshing breeze gently blew against her she welcomed the sweetness of surrounding flowers instead of her own stink.

"Suzy!"—a glad cry rang out.

Turning around, she saw Billy in his clean white moon-clothes bounding toward her through the chest-high grass, carrying his small spacesuit, which was flopping over one of his shoulders. He grinned from ear to ear, his eyes sparkling, his short black hair blowing in the breeze.

He grabbed her around her waist, hugging her close.

"I...I thought we were..." he gulped.

"Yes, I did too," she shuddered, hugging him closer.

Then he stepped away, wiping tears from his eyes. "I guess I got tossed off when we landed."

"Yes, I was in the grass also."

"So where's the surfboard?" he grinned, quickly regaining his boyish enthusiasm.

"It's over there," she pointed.

He hopped over to it and tugging at it mightily managed to pull it free from the bushes. He stepped into the feet supports but nothing happened. Then he stuck his legs back into his spacesuit and put his rebooted feet into the supports. Still nothing... The space-board was either broken or out of energy.

"Don't worry about it, Billy," she sighed, now feeling very weak, her vision again blurring. "We walked through the prairie before. We can do it again. And since the world around us isn't on fire from those asteroid pieces smashing into it, maybe our space surfboard is also a *time*-board! Maybe it somehow took us back to the future, where those bad smart dinosaurs' plot *failed*. We can live with the Indians hunting buffalo again. And, who knows, maybe another spaceship from the moon will pass by and we can chase after it?"

But he wasn't paying any attention to her. Instead, he was staring up at the sky.

"I don't think we're back with the Indians, Suzy," he gulped, his eyes stretched wide.

"What?" she frowned, now also looking up.

And there above her was a wide, *orange* sky! No white clouds. No beautiful blue expanse. And the sun just above the distant horizon was *small*...and weak.

And off in the distance to both sides she saw gigantic, looming, miles-high sheer *cliffs!*

"Well...ok...maybe the firestorm just scorched the atmosphere— and some earthquakes pushed up some big giant cliffs?" she gulped, completely baffled.

"But there's also *this*, Suzy," Billy said as he crouched then jumped up *seven feet* into the air! "That's why I wasn't with the surfboard. When I woke up I was so scared I hopped around like a big giant kangaroo!"

"Oh..." Suzy dumbly said as he dropped lightly back into the sea of waving grass. "That's...really high, Billy. It's not as high as you could jump on the moon, but I guess we're right. We're definitely not in normal Earth gravity anymore, are we?"

"I think we're on *Mars*, Suzy," he confidently stated. "Gravity on Mars is only about 40% of Earth's. And those big giant cliffs on both sides of us look like what I've seen of pictures inside the *Valles Marineris* on Mars! But...there's hardly any air on Mars and for sure there's no plants or animals. What's happening to us?"

"Oh, this just keeps getting weirder and weirder," Suzy sighed. "Dinosaurs, buffaloes, Indians, spaceships, Moon people, a giant asteroid, and now *this*. We're *never* going to get back home."

She abruptly *broke down*—slumping into the warm dirt beneath her, sobbing uncontrollably, her head hidden in her arms.

Billy put his arms around her comfortingly.

"At least we're not dead," he encouraged her. "I thought those asteroid chunks wuz gonna mash us flat. But here we are! And now we got a whole new place to explore. That's not so bad, is it?"

She got herself under control and shakily stood back up. She gently pushed Billy off her and looked around. Her head was clearing. It was just such a shock to be riding along on a cosmic surfboard as Earth was being destroyed by a giant asteroid—then seemingly an instant later be transported to an impossibly lush plain on *Mars*.

It took her a few minutes for her mind to catch up to their present reality. But she knew she had to get her head together. After all, she was still responsible for her dumb little brother!

"I guess you're right, we're still alive. So where should we go?" she grimaced, looking all around and only seeing thick prairie grass.

"I think I see something way off in the distance," Billy pointed, now all-business. "It looks like sunlight bouncing off metal, maybe?"

"Well," Suzy sighed, "one direction's as good as another, I suppose. Should we bring the surfboard along with us? It's heavy. Maybe we should leave it behind?"

"I think we should take it with us, Suzy. Maybe we can use it for a tent or something."

"Alright, then—let's see if we can lift it."

Actually, it wasn't heavy at all. It'd just been stuck in some bushes when Billy had trouble tugging it out. The board was either hollow or made out of a porous material. Or maybe it was only the lower Mars gravity. Whatever, Suzy found it easy to walk on one side of it as Billy walked on the other, each with an arm through one of the foot supports, dragging it along between the two of them. They'd rolled up their spacesuits and crammed them into other foot supports. So bringing the surfboard along was no problem.

After a while, however, with the distant sun going down, Suzy wasn't so sure they shouldn't have just left the useless thing behind. Maybe they'd have reached their destination sooner. As it was, it would be dark by the time they got to Billy's distant object.

"You know, Suzy," Billy grinned over to her as they plowed along through the sea of high grass, "I'm not even hungry or thirsty. It's been a while now since we ate the cookies and milk on the spaceship. But I feel just fine!"

Suzy nodded, not taking the trouble to reply verbally. Yes, she felt the same. Once the initial shock wore off, her head was now crystal clear. She felt strong, healthy, and invigorated! She almost felt cheerful, but not quite. She still remembered what she'd done back on the spaceship. The *guilt* nagged at the back of her mind like a clinging vampire chewing on her hindbrain.

Because of her *billions* of humans were likely never born. She was the *worst murderer* in the history of the human race!

But she resolutely pushed away the terrible shame, determined to focus on the task at hand.

On and on they went, walking and dragging the surfboard behind them.

If they didn't get there soon they'd have to find a place to spend the night. The small sun was almost down.

"There it is!" Billy laughed, dropping his side of the board and dashing on ahead into the gathering gloom.

"Billy, wait!" she called after him. But he'd vanished into the thick growth.

She loosened her grip on the surfboard and ran after him, breaking through into a dusky clearing to see...

Her Mom and Dad's Ranger ORV!

It sat there at an angle on a bunch of boulders as if it had been dropped from the sky. She saw the thick curved bars that protected the driver and passengers, the small backseat filled with various boxes, plus the rear open compartment packed with various scientific instruments. The sturdy vehicle was raised up on thick wheels, just as she remembered it. Now, however, it was covered in a *thick layer of gray dust.* But it was undeniably her family's very own black Polaris Ranger open-air ORV "off-road vehicle"!

What was it doing here on Mars?

And, even odder, slumped against the side of the vehicle was a *boy-sized mannequin.* The plastic figure was of a boy who looked a bit younger than Billy. Its skin was pale white, a peaceful expression frozen in place on its face. Its lifeless blue eyes stared forward, a shaggy mop of blond hair drooping forward on its head.

"What is it?" Suzy said, running up to Billy.

He was bent over looking intently at the motionless figure.

Like the ORV, it was also covered with gray dust.

It was getting hard to see in the twilight, but not too dark to examine their find.

"I think it's some kind of a robot," he marveled, gingerly lifting up one of its slack arms. "The skin feels like plastic, maybe. And when I move its arm I can hear little 'clicks' in the joints—like gears or servo motors moving inside?"

"That's really spooky," Suzy said, reaching down to lightly touch the forehead of the robot. The "skin" was indeed like plastic—tough and slick at the same time—while being cold and lifeless. "But what's it doing here, with *our* Ranger?"

"I dunno," Billy said, hopping up into the driver's seat of the ORV. Their Dad had let him drive it several times while they were on various vacations out in the wilderness. Suzy heard him trying to turn the engine on, "clicking" at the key switch, steering wheel, and pedals. Nothing...the Ranger was just as dead as their surfboard!

"But it looks like it's got plenty of supplies packed onboard. I wonder if Dad and Mom used it trying to find us?"

"But we were in another Dimension! We're on a different planet! And what the heck is a *robot* doing with it?"

Suzy shrugged while opening the boxes in the back seat.

Soon it would be too dark to see anything.

"Who knows, Billy. But however the robot and the ORV got here, I'm sure happy you spotted them. It looks like Mom packed extra clothes in here for us, plus lots of field supplies. We can finally get out of these stupid hospital pants and shirts and back into regular clothes."

"Yep, that sounds great! But what about the robot?" he said, gesturing at the lifeless form.

"Just leave it there," she shrugged, smiling as she unfolded jackets, shirts, jeans, underwear, and boots from the storage containers. "Here! Put these on. I'll start unpacking the camping gear. It looks like we won't have to sleep out in the open tonight."

Indeed, the weak sunlight was fading, the orange sky turning dark.

"I *am* getting hungry," he admitted, happily grabbing his armful of clothes. "I'll go find us some dry wood soon as I get dressed in my hiking clothes. We can cook that canned stew I see in there. Yummy, yummy!"

Indeed, the sight of the cans also triggered a familiar rumbling in her belly, but Suzy had the strange feeling she could go for days without eating and still be fine. Weird!

Later, sitting beside a crackling fire, Suzy looked up at the night sky. The star constellations looked the same as from Earth. However, she noticed they were more "solid" points of light than in Earth's night sky. Outside the *Valles Marineris* the atmosphere must be thinner than on Earth—such that the "twinkling" of stars was much decreased.

She kept looking for Phobos, the main moon of Mars, but only saw a small pebble rising above the dark horizon to her right. Could that be Mars' largest moon? It didn't look big enough.

"Yep, that's Phobos," Billy said, as if reading her thoughts, following her gaze. "It's closer to Mars than is our moon on Earth, but it's also a lot smaller. That's why it looks so tiny."

"You're just chockfull of information."

"Hey, I read fun books—like on dinosaurs and space travel!"

She sighed deeply, realizing she'd again inadvertently offended him, unable to leave behind her "pesky little brother" stereotyping. In the past, offending him didn't seem a big deal. Now, however, it seemed...oddly trivial.

"I was *complimenting* you," she stated, trying to fix things.

"Oh, ok," he shrugged, clearly still peeved.

"Should we get some sleep?" she asked.

They'd set up a small tent they'd found folded away in the back seat of the ORV amongst other camping gear. The thin tent would at least protect them from the many insects that were now flitting about in a cloud around the bright fire.

Billy yawned widely, stretching his small arms up above his head.

"Yep!" he grinned, grabbing his sleeping bag and starting to un-roll it, "You coming?"

"Just a bit more," she said, listening to the soothing chorus of many crickets chirping in unison out in the darkness. "I've never been camping on Mars before."

"Hah!" he chortled. "That's funny!"

As he moved to the tent flap he paused to reach over and pat the blond curls of the lifeless robot set-up against the side of the tilted Rover.

"Sleep tight! Don't let the bedbugs bite!" he laughed.

Then he was in the tent, happily humming to himself as he crawled into his sleeping bag.

Suzy was glad that he was handling everything so well. He was a smart, adaptable kid—much more so than she'd given him credit for in the past. Dinosaurs, Indians, spaceships, Moon bases, evil "rela-tives," and alien terrorists looking to wipe out mankind—and now this! How would it all end?

Maybe it wouldn't. Maybe it would go on and on and on...the "endless story" of the "girl with the turtle tattoo"—from her Mom to her—hah!

But in her heart she knew that wasn't true. Everything comes to an end. And she was way overdue for hers.

Sally hiked determinedly forward across the foreboding nightscape. It was hard to see in darkness lit only by stars. Her backpack held sufficient gear to stop, make a fire, and camp for the night. But she didn't want to take the time. Instead she was trying to reach her destination as quickly as possible.

She had to know if the others were alive.

"Please be there...please be there," she whispered to herself, maneuvering around huge boulders as she approached the towering, 20,000-foot-high red cliff.

After regaining consciousness in the ORV, brushing off clinging gray moon dust, sadly determining that Tommy was dead, discovering that none of the equipment powering the ORV was functional, and then taking stock of her impossible location within a thriving valley located on *Mars*—she packed her knapsack, slung her rifle up over her shoulder, and set off for the only destination she knew.

From the position of features on the distant cliffs she was sure that the entrance to the underground city she'd been transported to in the past was not too far away—located between several distinctive outcroppings.

"Please be there...*please* be there!" she grated through clenched teeth, slogging up a slope of red sand. By the faint starlight, she saw in front of her a *sheer cliff* towering up out of sight. And where there should have been a tunnel or airlock, there was...

—a wall of solid red rock, nothing! There was no sign that any intelligent beings had ever drilled tunnels here, reaching down into ancient Martian catacombs.

"Damn!" she swore, banging her fists uselessly into the solid rock face. But all that did was hurt her hands.

She slumped to the sand, putting her back against the rock. She was exhausted. But her mind was racing a million miles a minute. Along with Tommy, she should now be stone cold dead. And yet here she was, *not* frozen on the moon but rather hiking across a Martian valley. Clearly, she must be back in the distant future. But why was she here? What was happening to her?

She lay the rifle down at her side, totally discouraged. She felt abandoned, cast-away. Her grand expedition to save Billy and Suzy was coming to a terrible end. She hadn't found them. She hadn't saved them. And now she was lost to both them and Dave—probably forever!

Her eyes filled with tears.

"Maybe I should just end it all," she sobbed to herself. She turned the gun's barrel up toward her head. It was loaded. It would only take a quick pull of the trigger. And her troubles would just disappear.

But she knew from her religious training that suicide was a very poor way to end things.

"All right then!" she shouted up at the empty night sky. "Whoever or whatever's been guiding me through my Turtle Tattoo on all my strange adventures: if you want me to keep on going—all by myself— then please give me a sign!"

As if in reply, a *bright flash* streaked across the night sky— landing with a "boom" about ten miles away from her, on further down the vast rift-valley!

"Ah," she wearily nodded, shakily lowering the rifle from pointing at her head. She dropped it to her side as she pushed herself back to her feet. "Speak of the Devil!"

She had no doubt that the timing of that bright flash—from a meteor or whatever just now zipped through the thin upper atmosphere of Mars—was no coincidence.

That was her new destination.

She lifted her pack onto her back, then resolutely picking up her rifle.

"Whatever you are out there...I'm coming for you!"

And just as the small, distant sun began to emerge from behind the horizon, she proceeded on through the increasingly desolate landscape.

The verdant, green prairie grass that she'd awoken to, as she sat inside the ORV, was now long gone. Ahead of her all she saw was rock and sand.

It sure would have been nice if the Ranger was still working! She could have gotten to this new impact site in short order. But then again, she didn't mind hiking. It gave her time to think—about her entire life, the consequences to her actions, and her deepest motivations.

"Am I an angel, a demon, or something even more bizarre?" she mused out loud.

It seemed to her that in all her misadventures across time and space, she was always striving to advance her own understanding of reality: in essence to satisfy her curiosity. Was that selfish of her? Certainly when she married and had children, the priorities shifted to raising her kids to survive and thrive. But that nagging Curiosity was still there in the back of her mind...just repressed. And when the old Mysteries returned, she jumped at the chance to fire up the forbidden DE-generator regardless of "Cosmic Consequences." She realized that she wasn't just searching for her missing kids, but also for the hidden Marvels of the Universe!

But knowing her deeper motivations provided no easy solutions.

"Ah...the 'mysteries' are even more mysterious," she sighed.

So her motivations weren't entirely selfish or unselfish, but a mixture. And from that stemmed a wicked, "twisted" Creativity: to *see and do* that which has *never* been done before! And it wasn't due to a religious positive-or-negative Quest—as with some of her opponents. But in scratching this nagging itch (her fascination with the Unknown) was she, perhaps, indirectly fulfilling a *genetically programmed* compulsion? Was she putting into play the greatest Command from the Creator, inscribed not so much in Holy Texts but into Mankind's very DNA: to pursue a *"Divine" Curiosity?*

She liked to think that *was* what she was doing: fulfilling a Mandate deeper and older than Mankind, one embedded within the very Laws of Nature—in which evolving self-and-God-aware creatures had the chance and choice to rise beyond simple self-and-species perpetuation to Glorifying God in the *best* way possible!

"Are you pleased with me, Lord?" she sighed. As she trudged along she contemplatively looked up at the brightening, orange Martian sky, half-expecting an answer.

But the sky was silent.

Was she doing that which the Creator would find the most pleasing? Was the ultimate Worship of God as simple as the fingerpainting of a small baby or as complex as a scientist conjuring new physics equations? Was the best religious duty truly to *express* in whatever small or large way the *Creativity of God?*

"Could it really be that simple?" she mused again to herself.

Looking deep into her own heart, Sally was convinced that her core motivation certainly wasn't to escape from the pains and trials of life, to find some sort of "Nirvana." And, no, it wasn't to "earn" or "quality" for an afterlife Heaven. Neither was it to check off a list of often illogical religious demands satisfying religious overlords or a capricious God. Rather, she felt driven to experience a never-ending, fascinating, incredibly exciting, *Cosmic Adventure!*

What a rush!

"Well, that's rather grand of me, isn't it?" Sally laughed to herself. "Most likely I'm just a selfish little rat sniffing her way through a maze for some bites of cheese. But...the broader possibility *is* a nice thought."

She felt like giving herself an encouraging pat on the back. But that would be presumptuous. If anyone deserved any real credit here, it was the Creator who had instilled in her whatever talents and drive she possessed. Regardless of what happened now—no matter what-ever additional good or bad things awaited her short, eventful life— her best religious response was one of sincere *gratitude*.

As she trudged along through the stark Martian landscape, Sally whispered a little prayer: "Thank you Lord. It's been fascinating!"

And rather than being some formulaic, ritual prayer—she truly meant every word she'd just said.

It was a powerful prayer.

Suzy crawled out of the tent at first light.

She was still tired, especially from trying to sleep in her thin sleeping bag on hard ground. But the campfire lasted through the night, bathing the small tent in its warmth. Now the fire was just glowing embers. But the cold air of the night was giving way to the eminent return of the sun.

And then it was that she saw the *bright flash* in the sky with the resultant "boom" rocking the flaps of the tent!

"What was that?" Billy yelled from inside, charging out of the tent.

Suzy calmly pointed off in the distance, where a column of dust and smoke was rising: "Something crashed, Billy. Want to go and see what it is?"

"I sure do!" he grinned. "But first I gotta go pee...and I'm hungry for breakfast...at least I think so!"

"Uh, sure, why not," she laughed, feeling strangely buoyed up. "Let's both take care of our bodily needs so we're ready for whatever's next. At least this time we'll be better prepared, Billy. We'll take backpacks filled with everything we can carry."

"Super!" he said as he disappeared behind a bush.

She heard him whistling happily as a loud "tinkling" onto the rocky soil sounded from his leafy "toilet."

But she wasn't near as happy as he seemed. She *was* going to make sure they were as well prepared as humanly possible for their next trek, carrying a full load of supplies left in the defunct ORV. But a growing dread was filling her soul.

She had the feeling she was *walking to her own execution*—one that she richly deserved.

Chapter 27

<u>KARMA</u>

Yes, it seems simple
Bad intent or deeds
Balanced against
Good intent or actions
Affecting your rebirth
Your destiny or fate
Colored by the baggage
Carried on your back
Each and every day
And all those before
Claiming your name
Likewise burdened
Or exhilarated
A poor excuse
For avoiding
Your duty...

The Minstrel's Lark, 27:48-52

Sally had good intentions. But she was mentally and physically exhausted. She'd been up for two days straight, hiking from the ORV to the cliff. Her body just couldn't keep up with her fierce determination to get to the new crash site. The "spirit was willing but the flesh was weak."

So her legs finally gave way beneath her and she collapsed onto the red sand.

She just barely managed to uncurl her thin sleeping bag from her backpack and crawl into it before losing consciousness. Hopefully there were no Martian monsters out there prowling the desert-like landscape. If so, she was lunch on a platter.

"You ready, Billy?" Suzy smiled encouragingly at him.

"Ready!" he grinned, flicking a snappy salute at her!

"At ease, soldier," she grinned back. "Forward—*march!*"

And so they set off toward the distant crash site. For once they were well prepared for their latest fantastic journey. They each had rugged hiking clothing on, carried loaded backpacks, and were armed. Suzy had a sharp hunting knife in a sheath at her belt. Billy had her dad's Beanfield Sniper rifle slung over one shoulder. It was nearly as tall as he was and heavy. But Billy was a better shot than she was, plus she was carrying the heavier load of supplies, being the bigger of the two.

Her Mom's rifle wasn't there. Either they'd left it behind when her folks first went searching for them, or...well, she didn't dare hope.

Were her Dad and Mom somewhere out there in the bizarre forested landscape? They'd looked for tracks around the crashed ORV, but found nothing in the thick undergrowth. Either her folks were moving lightly, or something else—equally mysterious—was happening.

And looking back the short way they'd trudged under their heavy loads, it seemed that her suspicions were correct. The grasslands closed in behind them once they left the clearing. It was like walking on a sponge that sprang back into place once you stepped off it, leaving no trace of their passage.

"What do you think that robot wuz?" Billy asked as he smartly "huffed" along beside her.

"What do *you* think it was?"

"It was a *Martian* that *attacked* Mom and Dad—and they *killed* it!"

"It didn't seem to have any bullet holes in it," she mildly replied, "just lots of that gray dust covering it."

"Oh...that's right. Well then it was from the moon base. Mom and Dad must have followed us and picked up one of the moon people!"

Suzy snidely laughed. "They followed us in the ORV—to the moon? And then they picked up a hitch-hiking robot?"

Hah! That shut up the crazy little kid with his overactive imagination!

Oh, rats. There I go again. Why does Billy irritate me so much? He sure presses my buttons with his wild ideas, even when he's not even trying to get to me!

But then again, where *had* that gray dust come from?

She hadn't thought of that until just now. This Martian plain was dirty, but not dusty. And what dust there was certainly wasn't gray, it was a rust-red color. In fact, the dust on the ORV and the robot *did* look a lot like what she and Billy had seen out on the moonscape through the dome.

What happened to Mom and Dad?

Breep crept from the waving wall of grasses to sniff tentatively at the crashed Rover. It smelled very peculiar.

He got a whiff of gray dust in his snout and *sneezed*, almost backing off and retreating. But he also smelled the sweet scent of his human "mother"—and his good friend, Dave!

And sitting back against the side of the dusty vehicle was *Tommy!*

But he wasn't moving.

Breep hopped over to him nudged him with one of his three-clawed hands. No response. So the small dinosaur stomped on one of Tommy's legs with a powerful foot. No response. Then Breep *whipped* his powerful, long tail through the air to *slap* the vacantly staring android square in his face!

Breep saw that on one slack hand of the slumped figure...a single *finger* twitched.

"*Brrrreeeeepppppp!*" the dinosaur howled loudly at the prone figure, exposing his sharp-pointed teeth before lashing his tail backward to try again...

A hand shot upward to catch the hurtling tail in midair.

"Hi, Breep!" Tommy smiled at the animal. Then he dazedly looked around. "What's going on?"

The little dinosaur hopped up and down happily, his tail flopping back and forth, scampering out and back again into the clearing!

"Ok, then," Tommy grinned, jerkily rising to his feet and brushing off the clinging gray dust. "Looks like the ORV needs some work."

Sally felt much better.

After sleeping most of the day she'd awoken, eaten some of her rations, and set out again into the wilderness. Though she was now back in darkness she was determined to not stop again until reaching her goal. So she trudged on through the night—carefully winding her way amongst giant boulders, wide impact craters, and sand drifts. She didn't want to stumble and hurt herself, but was eager to make it to her "sign from heaven." She and Dave had seen too many fantastic things already to discount any timely celestial event!

And as she progressed, the landscape began to *change*. Before, it was a "typical" Martian wasteland. Now, emerging from the sandy plain, she saw isolated *spires* of glassy rock. And as she progressed further they became *clusters* of towering sharp-edged crystals! She felt like she was walking through a magical glass forest.

And just as the sun began to ascend from behind the ever-present high cliffs, she emerged from the crystalline forest into the still-smoking heaped debris thrown up from a fresh, deep impact crater. The rim, composed of yet-smoldering rock, was above her. All she had to do was climb to the top and look into the fresh crater to see what was inside.

"Ok, then," she whispered to herself, taking off her backpack and setting it carefully to the side. She unslung her rifle and made sure it was fully loaded and ready. Then she crouched, slowly ascending the slope.

Peeking over the top of the rim, she saw a football field-wide trench that was gouged out of the Martian soil. All around her was blackened ejecta. And at the deepest point of the trench—two hundred feet down below her—was...

The red Obelisk!

"Jesus Christ!" she whispered, stunned. "It's come back to its place of birth...and may be my ticket out of here!"

She almost stood up and went running down the still-smoking slope, but thought better of it. The Obelisk was half-buried in solidifying molten rock. And it was *glowing* cherry-red! Plus, it looked to be in even worse shape than when she'd seen it last at the Rock Creek camping grounds in Sulphur, Oklahoma. Now not only were the edges that should have been squared off rounded—but the entire length was *bent!*

It looked like it'd been through hell and back.

"Mom?"

Startled, thinking she'd imagined the voice, she glanced backward and saw...

—standing there with big grins on their faces: *Suzy and Billy!*

"Is it...is it really you?" she gasped.

But there wasn't any need for verbal confirmation. No, they were already on the blackened rock beside her—kissing and hugging her!

They tumbled down the slope into a laughing heap.

Now sobbing with joy, Sally sprang up, grabbed one kid in each arm, and hauled them both back up to their feet.

"I can't believe you're here!" Sally grinned, hugging them again. "What happened to you guys?"

"Wow, Mom!" Billy breathlessly began, his words tumbling out on top of each other... "We found a whole bunch of dinosaurs and then lived with a tribe of Indians and got kidnapped in a spaceship and went to the Moon and got away from a real bad lady who said she was your sister and went back in time to where we were supposed to poison this Buddhist guy but instead a bunch of bad, talking dinosaurs took us to the Cretaceous where we tried to stop a big giant Asteroid from crashing into the Earth and..."

"Hold on, hold on," Sally laughed, refusing to release her tight grip on each of their arms. "Let's back off from this crater and make a camp. Then you can tell me everything that happened to you. I'm just so glad that somehow we're back together!"

"Where's Dad?" Suzy asked, now looking up worriedly into Sally's eyes. "Is he ok?"

"I..."

"*Help! Help!*" Sally heard a plaintive cry.

Releasing her tight grip on the kids' arms, she spun around and ran back up to the rim of the crater.

There, two hundred feet below in the pit, *Dave* was trying to climb upward—while behind him lurched a MANY-LEGGED, BLACK SPIDER!

Suzy vaguely noticed that the storage panel on the side of the Obelisk had popped open.

"Billy! Take aim!" she yelled, dropping flat on the rim, whipping around her rifle...

BLAM! BLAM! BLAM!—she got off three quick shots, knocking the Spider backward.

Dave looked up and saw her. He waved at her as he kept on crawling up the side of the large crater...

But the Spider was lurching forward again, right behind him!

"Shoot out its eyespots, Billy!" Sally directed him as she cranked off three more rapid shots.

From this distance she didn't have the pinpoint accuracy to hit the large-and-small red eyespots—but Dave's *Beanfield Sniper* with its large black scope was capable of that accuracy. And she knew that Billy loved that gun and was well trained at target shooting!

"I got it," Billy glowered, squinting into the scope as he lay prone beside his mother.

BANG! BANG! BANG!—and the Spider crumpled off to the side, lying on its back with its many legs twitching up into the air.

"Come on, Dad! Climb!" Suzy yelled down to him.

He tried to stand on the slope but fell, tumbling backward—down into the pit almost back to the molten rock beside the half-buried Obelisk!

"Dave!" Sally screamed, dropping her rifle to dash down to him...

—but the Spider was closer and quicker. It was now fully recovered, scampering down upon Dave...

—as *over the rim of the crater* the Ranger leapt high into the air to *soar over Sally's head* and SMASH down upon the black spider, before bouncing over beside the red-hot Obelisk!

Dave jumped up from where he'd fallen and ran past the seemingly dazed giant Spider, scrambling up the slope into Sally's outstretched arms!

BANG! BANG! BANG!—Billy kept pumping bullets into the Spider's "face." The barrage of bullets was relentlessly driving it back across the molten lava up onto the twisted Obelisk...

—as a *furiously slashing Breep* jumped onto the Spider's head and *mashed* it back into the open storage compartment whose panel "snapped" back into place as the animal scampered away...

—and in a loud IMPLOSION the Obelisk *vanished*, taking the ORV with it...leaving in their place a *smoking hole* in the center of the crater.

"Wow," Suzy said from beside Sally, "that was exciting!"

"Dave...you're alive!" Sally marveled, helping him up the last few steps to the top of the rim of the crater.

"And ditto to you," he grinned, hugging her tightly, "and you guys too!" he added as the kids ran up and joined the group hug.

And climbing out of the crater Sally now saw *Tommy*—looking banged-up but functional—with Breep happily scampering along behind him!

And they all joined together in the *super-group-hug* to end all hugs—all laughing and crying and talking and "breeping" all at once!

Later, the sun having gone down, they sat around a blazing campfire in the crystalline forest. They'd just had a leisurely meal of stew and bottled water from their well-stocked backpacks. And, without interruption, her Mother, Dad, and Billy each told their fantastical stories.

"And what about you, Suzy?" Dave gently asked her. "I know Billy's already told us most of what happened to you guys. But you've got your own unique viewpoint, right?"

Suzy abruptly got up and walked away from the fire into the darkness, leaving them behind. She was leaning against a solid, cold crystalline "tree trunk" when she felt her mother's warm hands on her shoulders.

"What's wrong, honey?" Sally asked her.

"I did a *real* bad thing, Mom," Suzy glumly stated. "Billy thought that those velociraptors just forced us to do whatever they said. But—

I had to *agree* to it! So it was *me*. I *killed* billions of humans in the other Dimension!"

They sat silently for a moment in the night, Suzy comforted by her mother's strong arm, but trembling nonetheless.

"You don't know that for sure," Sally insisted. "After all—from what Billy told us—you didn't actually stop the Asteroid from hitting Earth. You just broke it up. The effect on the course of evolution may have been exactly the same as before when..."

"But that's what those smart velociraptors *wanted!*" Suzy sobbed. "They didn't want T-rex dinosaurs to evolve intelligence, just *them!* Either way, humans never developed on the second Earth—just stayed as little rat-like mammals! And it was all because of what *I* did!"

"Suzy, listen to me," Sally firmly stated, turning Suzy around to face her in the starlit gloom. "Even if the worse of what you're imagining is true—I've *also* done terrible things, to *multiple* timelines."

"Y-you t-too?" Suzy burbled. "Those talking raptors told me you did, but I didn't believe them."

Her Mom softly whispered in her ear. "If we ever get back to Earth I'll tell you all about my other timelines. I'm sorry I didn't tell you before. I just wanted you to live a normal life. But it's obvious that you and I will never get to have a 'regular' life. For whatever reason, we're fated to be 'disruptors' who can 'twist time'!"

Suzy took some comfort from her mother's words.

"So, we're not responsible for...?"

"Whether we like it or not," Sally broke in, "I—and now you—stand at a 'nexus of time' where things can dramatically change, depending on our actions."

"Then...we *are* responsible?"

"Ok," Sally sighed, "that's a metaphysical question higher than my 'pay grade.' Suzy, all we can do is the very best we're capable of under the prevailing circumstances. That's all we can do! Whether or not we're pawns in the 'Game of Fate' or not is beyond our ability to control or even conceive. Believe me, dear, I've had this conversation with your Father and even...well...I'll tell you more when we have time to talk at length—right now let's get back to the fire with the others, alright?"

"Ok," Suzy softly answered, wiping her eyes.

They returned to the campfire, where the others were cleaning up their utensils.

"So..." Suzy squinted as she sat back down, trying to make sense of everything: "Are we stranded here? Are we going to be here for the rest of our lives?"

Her mother sighed, sitting down beside her. Together they looked up at the too-bright stars. The flickering firelight lit up half of Sally's face in bright yellow while the other half was in darkness. It made her seem "other-worldly" to Suzy, as if her mother were part of the world and part not.

Her mother reached over and took the small pot which still had stew in it away from the fire, idly picking out a few potatoes to chew on.

"There has always been something if not controlling us, then watching us," Sally said to her daughter around her mouthful. "At first I believed that other-dimensional humans were driving me to 'save the world.' Then I thought that nonhuman smart dinosaurs were maneuvering me, even alien snakes from here on Mars! But I've been told once too often that the Creator—for whatever reason—has a special love for me...for *us!* Dave and I have already been snatched from death's grasp several times, for what ultimate purpose I don't know. So, maybe...?"

"That's what the intelligent velociraptors said about Suzy!" Billy added as he sat back down with them. "They said they needed us because we'd protect them when they broke the 'rules'—whatever the Rules were?"

"Ok, then," Sally frowned, reaching over to take Dave's hand and pull him closer to the warming fire. "But why are we on Mars? And is this in our present time or in the distant future? Either way, there should be a large tunnel leading through the cliff wall to Martian catacombs—but it's not there!" She frowned, shaking her head. "Even for us who are used to inexplicable things becoming commonplace, it just doesn't make sense."

Tommy—silent until then—tentatively raised his hand.

"Yes, Tommy?" Dave said. He now sat with his arm around the small shoulders of the android. "No need to be hesitant. You just speak up if you've got something to say. We're all family. We'd love to hear about your recent adventures!"

Tommy grinned shyly, looking around lovingly at Sally, Dave, Billy, Suzy, and the peacefully snoring Breep who was curled up on the sand beside the warm fire.

"I know what's happening to us," he sighed, looking down in dejection. "But you're not going to like it."

"Tell us!" Sally said.

She set the pot of stew on one of the uneven rocks that encircled the fire. Then she moved over and hugged the android from the side opposite to Dave's already strong embrace.

"Well, I've been here before and..." he began...

The stewpot started to slide off the rock so Suzy quickly grabbed its handle before it flopped over, setting it back in place more securely.

Then she looked up at...

—nothing!

She was alone at the fire. Billy, her Mother, her Dad, Tommy, and even the snoring Breep—were gone!

"No..." she whispered. Then, more loudly: "*No!*"

She jumped up and went running out into the darkness around the camp, *screaming* out their names: "Tommy! Dad! Mom! Billy! Where are you? Answer me if you can hear me! Breep! Come here, boy! Come to me! Come back! Come...back..." she now raggedly whispered, staggering back to sit helplessly by the dwindling fire.

I'm all alone.

In the morning Suzy went out searching for her parents, Billy, her robot brother Tommy, and Breep.

They were nowhere to be found. And there were no tracks around the camp to indicate they'd ever even been there. They were no longer in the spongy soil where the ORV had landed. So there should have been tracks in the sand if they'd all run off at once! Plus the only camping gear left was what Suzy had carried in her own backpack. Weighted down with their own packs, her runaway family should have left deep tracks! Also, both of the rifles were gone.

Even more disturbing—if that were possible—the entire smoking CRATER was gone!

Where the blasted-out rim of the crater should have been...there was now only the undisturbed crystalline forest.

But that didn't stop Suzy from trudging through ever-widening rings around her campsite, searching feverishly for any trace of her family. She hunted throughout the entire day, not even pausing to eat. But even though she almost got lost in the towering crystal "forest" she found *not one single trace* of her loved-ones.

Finally, when the returned night made it too dark to search anymore, she slumped against one of the vertical cold slabs of a crystalline "tree." Sitting with her rump on the red sand she dropped her head into her arms, tightly closing her eyes.

It was as if she were the only person on Mars...and had *always* been the only person on Mars!

But that was impossible. She still had her backpack which came from the crashed ORV, right? Maybe if she just returned to where she and Billy found it...but, no, it probably was vanished like everything else.

She hung her head and began to cry uncontrollably.

Then she remembered something.

Still snuffling, she reached into her pocket...

It was there.

She pulled out the *white pill* and held it up in front of her eyes. It seemed to say: "Eat me!" After all, it wasn't actually poison, was it? What was it supposed to do? The creepy "aunt" said it was just to take away pain and fear, right?

"All I have to do is swallow you down," she whispered to herself, "and all my troubles will go away!"

She opened her mouth wide and held the big pill up over her mouth...

"No!" she yelled, throwing it as far away as she could into the darkness.

"Nicely done," she heard a friendly, quavering voice right in front of her.

Yikes! Was it that old hag from the moon? Was that mean old witch behind all of this?

Springing up in terror...she saw standing there *a bald-headed, wide-faced oriental man!* She relaxed, seeing it wasn't the old hag. Indeed, this old man seemed particularly harmless. He was barefoot, dressed in a wrapped-around red robe that hung off one shoulder. He had a wide smile on his face, a twinkle in his eyes, dark eyebrows, high cheekbones, and was holding a *leather-bound book.*

"Who are you?" Suzy gasped, still alert to danger. She whipped out her hunting knife and held it menacingly in front of her!

But he just laughed, ignoring her threatening blade. He sat down with his back against the big, cold crystal.

Still suspicious, she slowly sheathed her sharp knife. Then she sagged down next to him.

Maybe this was all just a dream. Perhaps she was sick at home, lying in her bed, having an incredibly detailed, feverish nightmare. Or maybe she'd just gone insane—and was trapped inside her own crazy fantasies.

Well, imaginary friend or not, it was good to have someone else appear in her empty "fantasy" world.

"Oh...just call me 'Lhamo,'" he cheerfully replied. "That's a good name. In fact, I *like* that name!"

"Wait, you mean like the 14th Dalai Lama—who was born *Lhamo Dondrub?*" Suzy ventured, curious as to where this obvious fantasy-vision Monk was leading her. "In fact, you look a lot like him. Wasn't he supposed to be the reincarnation of the Buddha, who I was going to poison?"

Her brain was blown. She'd definitely gone over the edge. She was certain she'd gone totally insane. The 14th Dalai Lama was talking to her in a crystal forest on Mars, really?

"Yes! You know of him?"

"Well, I wrote a big report on him in a comparative-religion history section in my class at school," she nodded. "I got an 'A' on that project."

"Well done, Suzy!"

"Thanks, but that's not all. Like I said, a couple thousand years ago or so I almost *wiped out* the entire Buddhist religion! And then I went even further back in time and I wiped *everything* human out of existence, including all the Buddhists—at least in one Dimension...maybe! Well, I'm still not exactly sure what happened after the asteroid fragments hit the Earth, but..."

"So you're religious? Is that why you didn't take the easy way out?"

She sighed, no longer sure of anything.

"Not really," she grudgingly but truthfully admitted. "When I was just a kid in Sulphur, Oklahoma I wasn't all that interested in religion. But I faithfully went to church with my family. It seems like years ago, but I guess it's just been weeks. Anyway, in church I learned about following Jesus instead of being an evil sinner. And now, well— I think I've 'sinned' just about the worst that anyone could ever do. It hurts really bad...but I think maybe I *deserve* the pain. I need to be *punished* for my awful crime!"

"Yes, that's *very* bad karma," he nodded sympathetically. "But our lives are not ruled by our past, Suzy—rather, the past informs and enlightens us. You are right! We all commit terrible crimes. But pain and failure are not to be feared and shunned, rather appreciated for their virtues. Indeed, the cycle of life-and-rebirth is a continuing exploration—both into *intent* as well as actions! You didn't *mean* to do anything bad, did you?"

She perked up at that. Maybe the fantasy-Monk was onto something?

But then she grimaced, hanging her head back down.

"I thought I was protecting my Mom and Dad in my Dimension— but to do so I *was* willing to destroy the entire other Dimension. So I guess I *did* know what I was doing."

Her voice trailed off as she looked up to the stars. They seemed impossibly far away, lost in the vast emptiness of outer space. She felt likewise empty. She felt drained of all her emotions, just existing. Then she looked straight at the Monk with narrowed eyes, as if daring him to explain all the terrible things that'd happened to her.

His eyes also narrowed as if he were pondering her words.

"Yes, it is difficult to make complex decisions, especially when under pressure and particularly when our loved ones are threatened. But ultimately you *are* a product of your own intent and actions that..."

"Wait a minute," she suspiciously stated, stopping him. She focused on his genuinely concerned expression. She was coming to a mind-boggling realization.

"Speak your mind, Suzy."

"Are we...*dead?* And, are you supposed to be—*God?*"

He shrugged good-naturedly.

"I'm not 'supposed' to be anything...I just *am.*"

She inched away from him, suddenly fearful.

"So is this all some kind of *afterlife?* And did my family *move onward?* But, if that's true, then why did they leave me behind? Was it because...I'm not worthy—because I *failed* when you put me to the biggest test of all?"

She started weeping again, crushed by the realization that this *must* be the truth.

"Ah, my young friend Suzy, please don't be sad. I have something that may cheer you up."

"Oh?" she said, still sniffling while drying her eyes with a sleeve of her jacket.

"Here—I wrote this just for you!"

"For me?" she said, still feeling totally worthless. But she tentatively accepted his *slim, leather-bound book.* It wasn't as big as a Bible or even a New Testament. But it nevertheless had a very solid, reassuring feel to it.

"What is it?"

"I've entitled it '*The Minstrel's Lark.*' It's both serious and joyful. Should you ever want to document your recent adventures—like, say, writing a science fiction book—I think you may find it useful, perhaps even instructive."

"Is that so?" she snuffled.

"Oh, yes!" he widely grinned. "And it's lots of fun. You see, I love to sing! And the words to songs are *poetry.* Read the words of the book out loud to yourself and they will *sing* to you. You *do* like to sing, don't you, Suzy? Don't great songs make you feel happy? Especially..."

"Sure," she yawned widely, suddenly feeling very sleepy. "I really like music. Once I got a guitar, but didn't have time to take lessons. I take too many science courses in school. There's no time left after finishing my heavy home work for practicing an instrument. You see, I want to be like my Dad and Mom, who are scientists, and..."

"—one of the very *best* singing groups of all time," he continued, gently breaking into her stream of consciousness, "whose songs I love to sing, is the *Beatles!* Do you know of them?"

"Of course, they're great."

"Would you sing one of their songs with me?"

"Sure, why not?"

"Great! Then let us sing together that beautiful Beatles song...'*Let it Be*'!"

"Ok," she widely yawned again, struggling to stay awake. Yes, she sure did love those old Beatles songs, especially that particular one.

And so there on Mars, in the miles-deep Valles Marineris, Suzy joined her sweet soprano to the deep base voice of the old Buddhist Monk, singing: "*When I find myself in times of trouble, Mother Mary comes to me...speaking words of wisdom: 'Let it be!' Let it be, let it be, let it be, let it be...whisper words of wisdom...let it be!*"

On the final words she harmonized with the Monk, dropping down to alto. It was beautiful.

And, protected by the kindly Monk, with Lhamo's comforting arm laid gently over her shoulders—Suzy fell into a deep, rejuvenating sleep.

Chapter 28

DESTINY

Is "free will" but an illusion?
Thinking we make our own Fate
Are we pieces in a greater Game
Where others move us at will
And ours is but to stand upright
Thinking the next step is ours
While our decisions are mute
Whether Kings, Queens, Knights,
Or just lowly, disposable pawns
But I think not, beyond dreams...
We have greater power than that
When we exercise our "rights"
Breaking all the Cosmic Rules
Looking to leap upward
Even to the Stars
Isn't that fun?
Well, it should *be!*

The Minstrel's Lark, 28:1-3

"You ok, Suzy?"

She slowly opened her eyes, looking about in confusion.

She was lying on the ground. Her head hurt. And Billy was standing over her, looking down at her with genuine concern.

"Whu...what h-happened?" she stammered, reaching back with the flats of her hands to push herself up to a sitting position.

"You just fell off of your bike!" he said in alarm. "You smacked your head on a tree trunk! Should I go for help?"

She was woozy. She felt a growing lump on the side of her head beside one of her blond pigtails. Yep. She'd hit her head alright. But it didn't seem that bad. Her head was clearing.

"Help me to stand up," she said, reaching up a hand to Billy. He grasped it firmly, steadying her as she got her feet beneath her.

Back upright, she wobbly reached down for her bike and righted it as well.

"Why'd you fall off, Suzy? You never fell off before!"

"I...I think I...got distracted. I think I saw...something..."

"What?"

"Something...spooky..."

It was Saturday in early springtime. Hardly anyone was out vacationing in the Park near the small town of Sulphur Oklahoma. The campsites of the Rock Creek camping grounds were empty. Everything around should be peaceful—quiet, and tranquil. But to Suzy the trees looked...oddly disturbed! Their branches, just starting to get leaves, were twisted at odd angles. And the animals—particularly the birds—seemed skittish and scared. Even Rock Creek itself sounded strange, *frothing* where it should have been placidly flowing along.

"What kind of spooky thing?" Billy asked, worriedly looking around.

They were out by themselves riding through the Rock Creek campground's well-traveled roads and paths. Her Mom let her do lots of stuff by herself as long as she was careful. Since they lived only a few blocks from the main entrance to the Park, going for rides out here was something they did most every weekend. It was as if the Park was her house's own giant backyard. But her Dad was more cautious, insisting that she think of "consequences"—especially when she was looking after her pesky little brother.

But she was "impetuous"! She was the "risk-taker" who often "accidentally" left her helmet at home when she went out for a bike ride in the park. Billy just left his hanging on his bike handles because he was stupid. And where others would run away from disasters she rushed over to see what was happening.

"I think I saw something *impossible*."

And there it was again! She caught another glimpse of it hopping through the woods. It was a *person-sized, leathery lizard* that was scratching here and there at the dirt, as if it were searching for something!

"Huh?" Billy asked, "What-cha' mean, impossible?"

Taking a deep, shuddering breath she took a long look at her puzzled little brother. She saw standing there her dorky little brother. He was astride his kid-sized mountain bike. His crewcut hair was just black fuzz on his rounded head. His gray jacket was open, revealing his light green T-shirt with its Brontosaurus dinosaur stenciled on it.

But superimposed upon him she now saw a *white spacesuit*. And for a moment it seemed they were both standing on an outer-space *surfboard* looking in terror at a *mountain of spinning boulders* hurtling right at them! And...

—she suddenly remembered everything!

"Suzy?" Billy repeated, clearly concerned about her.

Shaking her head to clear it, she almost blurted-out her story.

"Nothing, it was nothing," she lied, turning her bike away from the glimpsed apparitions. "It's time for us to leave."

"But you saw something scary!" he said, turning his head around to look for himself.

"There!" she distracted him, pointing down at the ground beneath a nearby bush.

She rolled her bike over to the bush and reached down. Straightening up, she showed him...

—an old, leather-bound book!

"A book?" Billy frowned. "That's something 'impossible'? Some camper must have left that there—hey, let me see it!"

Before she could protest, Billy grabbed the dusty book from her hand. He quickly leafed through the pages.

"Ah, it's nothin' interesting," he said as he disdainfully tossed it into a nearby trash bin.

"Billy—that's *my* book! *I* found it!"

"It's just dumb *poetry*, Suzy," he shrugged. "It's not scary or impossible. Nobody reads stuff like that!"

"Well...maybe *I* want to," she admonished him, rolling over to the trashcan and retrieving the book.

Having safely tucked it away in her mountain bike's rear saddle-bag, she resolutely turned her bike around.

"Let's go home," she said, smiling brightly at him. "And...you're a smart kid, Billy. I *like* having you for my brother."

Startled, he looked at her like she'd suddenly gone crazy.

"Uh...ok?"

"Yes, it's *all* ok now," she nodded as she pushed down hard with her foot on a raised-up peddle, accelerating the bike. She sped away as he struggled to keep up behind her.

She was going to have a *long talk* with her Dad and Mom. Normally she didn't bother them with the products of her hyper-active imagination. Her folks usually just laughed at her fantastical stories and told her to go write a science fiction book. But she had a feeling they wouldn't dismiss this particular "fantasy"—instead would take immediate action!

She now distinctly recalled *everything* that her parents had told her in the other timeline as they sat around the campfire, in particular what happened to *them* after she and Billy disappeared. She knew that *terrible* things were lurking in the Park beyond just a cute extinct dinosaur. An *alien evil* threatened to destroy not just the small town of Sulphur, Oklahoma but the entire world!

And that was just in *this* Dimension. What about the *parallel* human Dimension? Was it now "set-right"—or did her previous actions *destroy* it?

She peddled faster as Billy yelled from behind, begging her to slow down!

She had to get home as quickly as possible. Her Mom and Dad would know what to do. And Suzy was certain that she would play a critical role in their plans.

After all, it was her destiny to *chase spaceships!*

But regardless of what her new future held, she was determined to have *fun!*

A generous old Monk had taught her well.

THE END
[continued in: *The Girl Who Wrangled Asteroids.*]

Thank you for reading!

Dear reader,

I hope you enjoyed **The Girl Who Chased Spaceships**. The interplay between a haughty Suzy and her "pesky" little brother was great fun to write. And delving into the Buddhist teachings for the pre-incarnation of the Dalai Lama was enlightening. The sequel to this book, **The Girl Who Wrangled Asteroids**, finds the new "girl with the turtle tattoo" all grown up and on a desperate NASA expedition into space to save the planet.

I hope you are intrigued by the sequel's disturbing question: "What do you love more than anything else?" When everything goes wrong, Dr. Susan King must choose between her humanity and something...alien.

Finally, I need to ask you for a favor. If you enjoyed this book and would like to encourage others to read it, **a review written by you** on the Amazon page for this book would be greatly helpful. It's hard to get reviews nowadays and your support will be very important to both me and other readers. If you'd like to do this, I sincerely thank you in advance for your time and effort. It can be as long or short as you wish.

Thanks again for reading my **Girl with the Turtle Tattoo** books and running alongside me and Suzy chasing spaceships.

Sincerely,

Dan Lyle

About the Author:

Daniel Basil Lyle holds a Ph.D. in Biology, is a lifelong amateur herpetologist, taught medical immunology at a University, completed a career in cell biology research, lectures on how to apply theological and psychological principles in practical ways, and has a strong interest in all aspects of cosmology and physics. From a small kid he was fascinated with dinosaurs. As such, he has always lived with exotic creatures, including harmless snakes, all housed in his own homemade habitats. Some of his tame pet pythons and anacondas ranged up to twelve feet in length. He is the author of over thirty books, many of which are religious in nature. His writings go beyond the ordinary, exposing deeper aspects of life. His books are meant to be fun, conversational, and helpful. His various works are available at LylePublishing.com and Amazon.com. The "Girl with the Turtle Tattoo" science fiction series was inspired by paintings done by his mother, movies adapting Stieg Larsson's crime novels, and various men and women sporting spectacular body-art tattoos. The story was not "plotted" in advance but flowed freely, with characters appearing on their own and taking charge of their own destinies. The author hopes that you, the reader, find his characters spontaneous, quirky, surprising, and even thought-provoking—just as did he!